"I have something for you."

Chaz pulled out a beautiful one-carat diamond set in yellow gold. "This isn't real, but you wouldn't know it without a jeweler's loupe."

In a daze, Lacey took the ring from him. The reality of it sent her thoughts back to the night Ted had promised to love her till the day he died. Her darling husband—he'd died way too soon.

Now here she was with a fake engagement ring handed to her by this remarkable PI while he tried to find out who was stalking her. She felt as though she was living some strange dream.

"Once we catch your stalker—which will happen before long—you can tell everyone the truth and they'll all understand the reason for the deception."

Lacey couldn't believe she'd agreed to this arrangement with a virtual stranger, but Chaz was the expert and everything he'd said had made a certain kind of sense. If she didn't have faith in him, then what else was there?

Dear Reader,

MY UNDERCOVER HEROES series started a few years ago. The hero in the first book, *Undercover Husband*, was Roman Lufka, who headed his own PI firm. Now, a few years later, he appears in Mills & Boon® Cherish™ and has hired three more PIs to work for him.

The first book in this new series is *The SEAL's Promise*. Chaz Roylance is a former navy SEAL who bears a heavy burden he can't shake until he's hired to track down Lacey Pomeroy's stalker. I won't go into the details, but it might interest you to know that of all the heroines I've created (one hundred and ten so far) she, more than the others, has a lot of the real *moi* in her.

Enjoy!

Rebecca Winters

THE SEAL'S PROMISE

BY
REBECCA WINTERS

First published in Great Britain 2012
by Mills & Boon, an imprint of Harlequin (UK) Limited,
Eton House, 18-24 Paradise Road, Richmond, Surrey TW9 1SR

© Rebecca Winters 2012

ISBN: 978 0 263 89439 4
ebook ISBN: 978 1 408 97114 7

23-0612

Harlequin (UK) policy is to use papers that are natural, renewable and recyclable products and made from wood grown in sustainable forests. The logging and manufacturing processes conform to the legal environmental regulations of the country of origin.

Printed and bound in Spain
by Blackprint CPI, Barcelona

Rebecca Winters, whose family of four children has now swelled to include five beautiful grandchildren, lives in Salt Lake City, Utah, in the land of the Rocky Mountains. With canyons and high alpine meadows full of wildflowers, she never runs out of places to explore. They, plus her favorite vacation spots in Europe, often end up as backgrounds for her romance novels, because writing is her passion, along with her family and church. Rebecca loves to hear from readers. If you wish to e-mail her, please visit her website at www.cleanromances.com.

This book is dedicated to Art Bell, whose nationally syndicated radio call-in program about all things inexplicable entertained me for years.

Chapter One

Since moving to Salt Lake a year ago, former Navy SEAL Chaz Roylance had developed a craving for the glazed donuts sold at SweetSpuds on Foothill Drive. They were better than any other donuts he'd ever eaten. He'd discovered that the small store wasn't that far from his work.

After buying a dozen for the guys, he headed for the Lufka P.I. firm located farther south where Foothill Drive turned into Wasatch Boulevard. Mount Olympus provided the backdrop. As Chaz pulled around the back past the shop filled with their equipment, he realized no man could ask for a more glorious setting, especially on a warm summer morning with a clear blue sky overhead.

In fact, no man worked with better guys or a more brilliant boss. Roman Lufka owned the agency and was great to work for. Chaz's P.I. job forced him to concentrate on other people's problems and blot out his own for a while. He dealt with lots of missing-persons cases, embezzlement and industrial espionage.

But lately he'd reached a point where the disease eating away at his soul was taking over again. He'd been losing sleep and didn't know the meaning of joy.

He felt it particularly strongly this morning because he'd just finished solving an insurance-fraud case—not a good place for him to be since it gave him too much thinking time.

After parking his green Forerunner in his space, he entered the office through the back door and nodded to Lisa Gordon, an ex-cop and Roman's assistant, who was making coffee in the kitchen. "I was counting on the java being ready."

She eyed his sack of donuts. "Hmm. I had hopes someone would bring me breakfast."

"Here. Take one. We make a good team, Lisa."

"That we do. Thanks." She flashed him a searching glance and put her hands on her hips. "You don't look so good. I know what's wrong with you. All work and no play makes Jack a dull boy. You need a little fun in your life. How about letting me introduce you to this very attractive brunette accountant who's a friend of my daughter."

"No, thanks, but I appreciate the offer."

She studied him with concern. "Maybe you need some professional help for what's ailing you."

"Maybe."

"I recognize the signs because I've been there."

Wrong. Even as an ex-cop, she hadn't been where he'd been. Certain work he'd had to do in the SEALs shouldn't be part of the human experience. He flashed her a jaundiced eye, then picked up a coffee before heading to Roman's office.

Lisa, the mother of two whose last child had just gone away to college, never quit when it came to Chaz. She and her husband had a tight marriage. So did Roman. Before cancer had taken Chaz's wife ten years ago, he'd been happy, too, but her death had changed his life and had prompted him to join the military, where he'd ultimately become a navy SEAL.

The work had been challenging and he'd enjoyed the camaraderie well enough. Then came his last mission in South America with Special Forces, where he'd come up against something that had torn him apart. The warlords forced their women to carry out their atrocities. Chaz's orders were to kill them, but the very thought of killing women went against everything he believed in. He couldn't do it and realized it was time to get out.

Since then, nightmares had plagued him. With his parents dead and his wife gone, there was nothing for him to go back to in Arizona, where he'd been born and raised. Desperate to find meaning in his life, he'd moved to Salt Lake. He'd taken his wife to the Huntsman Institute there for her last two months of cancer treatment.

He'd liked the city well enough, and there was an opportunity for work in a civilian setting that needed his intelligence-gathering skills. Roman's P.I. firm kept him constantly busy in an environment that gave him purpose without destroying him.

"Roman?" he called from the doorway. "You busy?"

"You're the man I wanted to see this morning. Come on in."

Chaz sat down, sharing the goodies with him.

"Thank you. Much more of this and Brittany's going to put me on a diet."

Anyone looking at Roman, who stayed in great shape, would think he was in his late thirties instead of mid-forties. He and his brother Yuri came from Russian roots and grew up in New York. They were both dark haired with fascinating personalities.

"Congratulations for winding up that insurance-fraud case so fast, comrade. Planting the camera was a master stroke. The guys cracked up when they watched the film. I did, too, when I saw the paralyzed guy get out of his bed and start walking around the minute the door was closed." He broke into laughter and consumed his donut in one swallow.

"It was a lucky hunch that paid off."

Roman eyed him frankly. "All your hunches are lucky, which proves to me it isn't luck with you. The SEALs' loss was my gain, but I've sensed something's been wrong for a while. What can I do to help?"

Chaz grimaced. "I must be transparent. Lisa's trying to find me a woman, convinced it will heal all wounds."

"Brittany changed my life, but since I know love has to happen on its own, I won't go down that path with you. Lisa cares about you. We all do. But I know there's something else. If you ever need to unload, I'm here."

"Thanks. Maybe one day," Chaz murmured. If anyone would get it, Roman would, but Chaz wasn't ready to talk about his troubles yet.

"I'm glad you came in because a dozen new cases need to be assigned. You can have your pick. But before I tell you about them, I wondered if you'd find out if the man who left this number on our answering machine is legitimate." Roman handed him a note with the name Barry Winslow on it.

"What do you mean by legitimate?"

Roman sat forward in his chair. "I mean, I don't know any details, which is a first. It's a Salt Lake area code, but the number's unlisted. If it turns out the call was some sort of prank, then come back in and we'll go over the new cases."

"I'll take care of this right now."

I CAN HARDLY WAIT TO SEE your blood on my hands, you bitch. So watch out and keep looking over your shoulder, because I'm right behind you and plan to cut out your freakin' heart first. Then I'll start on your daughter.... Both will be an in-the-body experience you won't forget.

Those horrifying words left in a message on her cell phone yesterday afternoon stabbed through Lacey Pomeroy over and over again as she walked her three-year-old to her bedroom. "Come on, Abby, honey. Time for your nap."

After Lacey put her daughter under the covers with her favorite stuffed frog, she lay down on the twin bed and cuddled her close. While she sang to Abby, she stared at the ceiling in mortal fear of what was going on in her life right now. The morning before yesterday, she'd received the first phoned death threat, but it had come on her condo's landline.

Get ready for your next paranormal experience. It'll happen when you least expect it. This one's going to burn up your brain. Literally.

Since then, the landline hadn't rung again. The calls on both phones had come from the same man. Both gruesome messages reminded her of the death threat she'd found before leaving Long Beach, California, and moving back to Salt Lake a year ago. Salt Lake had been a safe haven, the place where she'd grown up, and where her mom and sister still lived.

The death threat had happened the night of the

viewing for her husband, Ted, who'd been in the Coast Guard and had died in an accident at sea.

A big crowd had come to the mortuary in Long Beach to offer their condolences. When she went out to her car later, she found a note put under her windshield wiper. It had said that aliens were responsible for her husband's death. Now they were going to set her daughter on fire one body part at a time before they did the same thing to her.

She'd assumed the depraved monster was a listener of her paranormal radio program that was broadcast out of Los Angeles. After showing the note to her mother and sister, who'd come to Long Beach for the funeral, she'd told her boss about it. He'd assured her it was a sick prank, probably done by some messed-up teenager in her neighborhood who knew her car and had seen the obituary. He'd told her not to worry about it unless she got another one.

But Lacey hadn't waited to find out. With her husband gone, she quit her California radio call-in show. When she moved back home, Barry Winslow, a Salt Lake radio producer, contacted her to do the same show here because it was so popular. She hadn't thought about the note again until she'd gotten that first phone call.

Lacey had never needed her husband more, but Ted had been dead a year. With no father to turn to, she'd called Barry. He wasn't only the head producer for the network sponsoring her radio call-in show here, the married father of three had been like a favorite uncle to her since she'd moved back to Salt Lake.

When she'd told him she was being stalked and gave him proof, he'd taken her seriously, but told her not to try to trace the calls back to their source yet. Since they both knew the police couldn't do anything until some kind of crime had been committed, he'd told her he had an idea and would get back to her today.

Once her daughter was asleep, Lacey got off the bed and walked through the one-story condo to the kitchen. She'd left her cell phone on the counter and was still waiting to hear back from Barry. The window above the sink looked out at the other condos in the Parkridge complex where she lived in Cottonwood Heights. Hers was one of the second-story units in a three-story building that housed six condos. The stalker could be out there watching her condo this very second.

When she'd moved back from California, she'd chosen this place to be near her mother, Virginia Garvey, who taught math part-time at the University of Utah, and lived only a half mile from Lacey's condo. Lacey's sister, Ruth, had been staying with their mom for the past month after losing her job as an air cargo pilot in Idaho. With Ted gone, Lacey had needed her family.

She hoped to make enough money to sell her condo and buy a house in a nearby residential neighborhood by the time Abby was old enough to start kindergarten. In the meantime, twenty-six-year-old Ruth stayed over with her on weeknights and went to their mother's on the weekends.

While Abby slept, Ruth babysat so Lacey could do her three-hour radio show. In return, Lacey paid her well, so her sister didn't have to take a part-time job. Their situation was temporary because Ruth would be getting another job soon, but it had been working out fine. Until two days ago, when some maniac had disrupted their lives!

Lacey's family believed the horrendous threats had to have come from one of her radio show listeners who delighted in frightening her. Maybe it was the same person who'd put that note on her car in California. The possibility that this insane person had followed her here and had been watching all this time terrified her.

The bloodcurdling part for Lacey was the fact that he knew both her phone numbers. On her way home from the park with Abby yesterday, her cell phone had rung. Since she hadn't recognized the caller ID, she hadn't picked up.

When she reached her condo, she was so filled with dread it took her a long time to gather the courage to listen to the voice message. It was the same man's voice, but the death threat had been more violent and graphic. At that point she hadn't hesitated to phone Barry, who'd promised to help her.

Why hadn't he called her yet?

There was no way she would leave the condo to do her show tonight. Barry would have to get Stewart, the nighttime intern producer who also ran the phones, to play another of her taped programs from the archives. She'd told her sister to stay at their mom's tonight.

While she stood in the middle of her kitchen trapped by her thoughts and fears, there was a knock on the front door. She heard her mother's voice and rushed through the living room to open it.

"Thank goodness you're here." She hugged her hard. "I've been going out of my mind waiting for Barry to call."

"Shh," her mother said. After she closed and locked the door, she turned to Lacey. "We have to whisper." Lacey frowned. "Your condo might be bugged."

What?

Her mother led her to the hallway. Still whispering, she said, "Barry isn't going to phone you, honey. Mr. Winslow called a P.I. firm to help you."

Lacey blinked. "Are you serious?"

"Yes. The man in charge of your case is Chaz Roylance. He told Barry not to have any more phone conversations with you. Then he called me."

"You've already talked to this P.I.?"

"I just got off the phone with him. He said the fact that we haven't contacted the police works in our favor. With a high-profile person like you, the minute the police hear, the news will leak to the press and any hope for secrecy will be lost."

"That's true, but isn't it going to cost a lot of money?"

"Barry said the network will pay the expenses. To quote him, 'We're not letting the paranormal-show host with the fourth-highest ratings in the nation be hurt by some fringe lunatic.'"

Lacey's eyelids prickled. "Barry's wonderful."

"I agree. So is this P.I."

"How did he find him?"

"Barry says he's from the top P.I. firm in the Intermountain West, bar none. This Mr. Roylance has already assigned his people to keep you under twenty-four-hour surveillance."

"That fast?" She was incredulous…and grateful.

"Yes. But of course this is your decision. I'm just relating what Barry told me to tell you. If you want to call this off, just say so, honey."

"No, Mom. I know he's doing everything he can for me and I appreciate your help more than you'll ever know. Do you know what I'm supposed to do now?"

"Yes. Mr. Roylance said we're all to stick to our normal routines. You're to keep to the same schedule and go to work tonight. Ruth's planning to come over. Don't answer your phones. If you recognize the caller ID, you can phone people back when you're outside the house, but don't tell a soul what's going on."

Lacey shuddered. "You honestly trust him to know how to handle this?"

"Barry says they're an accredited firm the FBI and the police recommend if you ask them privately. He's had friends who've used them before. They have impeccable credentials. He told me he wouldn't trust anyone else to do this kind of work. Again, it's your decision, but for what it's worth, I trust him."

That was good enough for Lacey. They didn't have another solution right now. "When am I going to meet this P.I.?"

"Mr. Roylance has laid out a plan. Tomorrow night he'll come to the radio station with one of his crew. They'll be disguised as satellite-dish workers sent out by their company. While they pretend to check out the television equipment in the room, he'll talk to you while you're doing your show."

"But I don't take breaks."

"He says he's coordinated this with Barry. Tonight at work you'll announce you're going to play a tape tomorrow night from last year's Summer Solstice Conference in Milwaukee. Barry told him about it and said it would take up a half hour plus the advertisement time.

"When you get to work tomorrow night, you're to tell Stewart to start the tape after the ten o'clock news. Mr. Roylance will come into the broadcast booth then, pretending to check the place out thoroughly. You're to more or less ignore him and behave as you would around any workman.

"He said everyone who *has* or *does* business at the station is suspect, which of course includes Stewart, the night watchman and the janitor, so you shouldn't do anything to alert anyone that this night is different from any other.

"While the tape is playing, it will give him enough time to talk to you without anyone being aware. No one will have a clue what's going on. After talking to Mr. Roylance, I have no doubts he's more than capable of catching this depraved maniac."

Lacey had been listening to her mom. "I couldn't bear it if anything happened to Abby."

"I couldn't, either. Mr. Roylance has assured me they're prepared to intervene in case of trouble and he guarantees your safety. You're to try to relax and go about your business. He'll contact you through me until after he's met with you tomorrow night."

"I—I can't believe this has happened." Her voice shook.

Her mom hugged her again. "I know, but I'll always be indebted to Barry for acting this fast. Mr. Roylance wants you to stay strong and not fall apart. Remember, you're not to discuss this situation with anyone. Let the P.I. do his job. He's convinced me he'll get you through this safely."

"If you believe in him, Mom."

"I do. When you talk to him, you will, too."

Her mother sounded so sure. Lacey wanted to believe it because she was terrified.

THE CALL FROM BARRY WINSLOW had turned out to be the legitimate thing. Once Chaz had verified he was the producer for the Ionosphere Network in Salt Lake and had vetted him for everything he knew, he went back to Roman's office and shut the door. After his boss got off the phone, he looked at Chaz. "What did you find out?"

"It's the real thing. Furthermore, it's a stalking case involving a bona fide celebrity." He filled him in on the details.

Roman whistled when he learned it was Lacey Pomeroy. "A dozen people around here love her show, including Brittany."

"Obviously millions of people do or she wouldn't be ranked fourth in the national paranormal market. Her producer told me her popularity originally sprang from a novel she'd written while still in high school under her maiden name, Garvey. I'm intrigued by everything I've learned and would like to take the case."

"It's yours. Use any backup crew and equipment you need."

"Thanks, Roman. I'll keep you informed."

Whether it turned out to be a hideous prank or the work of a true psychopath didn't matter. Chaz wanted the case for reasons he hadn't fully examined yet. But he sensed that if he found the person stalking this woman and could make her feel safe again, maybe he would sleep better. To prevent a crime against her and her child might ease certain horrific memories.

Mr. Winslow had told him there'd been another death threat in the form of a note while she'd still been living in California. That incident could have been done for a different reason by a different person from the one who'd made these telephone threats. It would be up to Chaz to find out if there was a connection.

Once he'd set up the teams he used on stakeouts

and his people were in place, he called every bookstore trying to find a copy of the book on the paranormal that Lacey Garvey had written. The fiction novel had put her on the map, so to speak, and had been her entry into the world of sci-fi radio.

The bookstores and used bookstores were all sold out. In frustration, he bought the newest electronic reader on the market and downloaded the novel to read when he got home. He preferred a real book in hand, but this would have to do.

Whenever he went to work for a client, he attempted to get to know everything he could about him or her first. This book and her radio program showed where her passions lay and would inevitably be helpful to him if he hoped to get inside her stalker's mind. Tomorrow evening he'd be prepared to talk to her at the radio station.

After giving his crew instructions and coordinating who would be coming off and going on shift, he ate a quick dinner at a drive-thru and headed to his condo building at the mouth of Parley's Canyon. His sixth-floor unit was no home, but it served its purpose and was convenient being right off the freeway and close to his office.

With everything taken care of for the moment, he walked into his bedroom with his purchase. Removing his shoes and ankle holster, he set the alarm for the clock radio to go off at 9:00 p.m., the time her program started. He grabbed some licorice from the bedside table and turned on the lamp.

Finally he was ready to read and lay back on the bed, propping his head with a couple of pillows. He glanced at the title, *The Stargrazer from Algol,* a young-adult fantasy novel by new *New York Times* bestselling author Lacey Garvey, winner of the Hugo Award and the Nebula Award for the best science-fiction fantasy novel.

As he scrolled down, he discovered it had been published ten years ago and was in its seventh printing. He clicked to the back of the book where he saw a black-and-white picture of a pretty girl with long hair that could have been a high school yearbook photo. She'd been only eighteen when this book was published. That meant she'd been writing long before that.

He was impressed someone with a gift like hers had achieved that level of success so early in life.

Chaz scrolled to the dedication. *To my wonderful parents, Virginia and Bill, who've given me life and love.* On the next page was a quote by Robert A. Heinlein, the grand master of science-fiction writers of all time. He'd said something to the effect that supernatural happenings might seem as if they were in the realm of magic or fantasy, but in truth, they followed the lines of engineering and made what some people called impossible possible.

He remembered reading an assigned story in a junior high English class written by Heinlein. As Chaz recalled, it was about some college-age guy and his physicist uncle who'd flown a rocket to the moon where they'd found someone had arrived there first. It was pretty good, but he'd been too engrossed in football at the time to get fired up over anything else. In fact, he'd never gotten into science fiction.

Over the years he'd been a big reader of fiction and biographies, but to him any talk about aliens coming to Earth was absurd. So far no one had produced an alien body except in the film *E.T.* He'd never seen a crop circle, a vampire, a shape-shifter or a ghost. If he couldn't see it and feel it, he didn't believe it. Chaz needed proof.

He moved on to the preface where she'd defined terms. A stargrazer was a meteor. During a meteor shower, some swept close enough to Earth to be caught in its gravity. The meteor in her novel came from the constellation Perseus. She spent a page describing the constellation and the stars within it.

Somehow Chaz hadn't expected to be captivated by the book's preface and certainly not this fast. As he started to scroll further, his radio came on too loud, jarring him from his thoughts. It was time to listen to her show.

The tail end of the news was followed by a lead-in of an ancient-sounding instrument from Nepal or someplace, blaring a cavernously deep single note. It grew louder until he felt his body vibrating with it. Chaz didn't like the sensation. He set the reader aside and turned down the volume.

The announcer started speaking. "If you've been jolted out of your comfort zone, that means it's the twenty-first hour and you've just tuned in to the nationally syndicated *Stargrazer Paranormal Show* on your AM 500 radio dial. This is coming from the Ionosphere Network, high atop its signal tower in the Wasatch Mountains above Salt Lake City, Utah, broadcasting to two hundred and fifteen affiliates throughout the United States and Canada."

His dark brows lifted. That was a lot of radio stations. He couldn't believe how many people listened to a show like this. Barry Winslow had pulled off a coup being able to produce Lacey Pomeroy's program in Salt Lake. She obviously loved what she did or she wouldn't have gotten back into it after leaving California.

"If you're easily terrified or suffer from heart trouble, we advise that you immediately turn off your radio since we will not be held responsible."

A chuckle escaped Chaz's throat.

"The next three exploratory hours are only for the inquisitive, unafraid mind open to all the possibilities in an unending number of universes expanding as we speak. Here is your host and founder of the program, Lacey Pomeroy."

"Happy summer solstice, everybody. This is our June 20 show, the one we've all been waiting for, and you know why. On this Thursday night, the earth's axial tilt is most inclined toward the sun and is celebrated from culture to culture within our galaxy by gatherings and rituals. And *visitors*...."

Chaz blinked in surprise to hear the mellow feminine voice that came out over the airwaves. Besides having a lilt that was easy on the ear, it was sexy, but not in a way that was put on or unnatural. By her opening words, you would never know she was being terrorized.

"The boards are already lighting up from Florida to Canada. I'm going to take our first call from Max, who's been waiting the longest. He's in the Hole-in-the-Rock area of southern Utah, a very beautiful and mysterious place full of ancient lore. You're on the air, Max."

"Hi, Lacey. Yours is my favorite show. I listen to you all the time."

"Thank you. That's music to my ears. What's going on down there?"

"Plenty. I've been four-wheeling around here with my buddies in a group we call the Wolf Pack. There are eight Jeeps in the group. We've all got our headlights shining on this huge wall of petroglyphs that are three thousand years old. These aren't painted. They've been chiseled into the rock. The images are incredible. If you saw them, you would *know* the people who did this artwork are from another world."

"Describe some for our audience."

"One type of creature is represented more than the others. It's like a rounded rectangle with an oblong head. The antennae curl around the sides, but it's not like any animal you've ever seen. There are triangle shapes set at random and mysterious symbols like a corkscrew amidst dozens of suns. These people worshipped the sun, which is a source of their energy. We're thinking tonight we'll see one of their triangles land."

"It wouldn't surprise me, Max. A report just came in of a triangular-shaped UFO sighting over a park in Chongqing, China. And a few days ago Japan's first lady claimed to have flown on an alien spaceship that she said was triangular shaped and took her to Venus while she slept." Chaz shook his head, totally amused.

"I guess you couldn't get an interview with her for your show."

"I'm afraid not, but I tell you what. If you have contact tonight, call in to the station tomorrow night and we'll feature you as a guest. Now we're moving on to our next caller from Rapid City, South Dakota. You're on the air."

"Hi, Lacey. It's Mel on the Harley. Remember me?"

"The Sturgis guy?"

"Yeah. Damn, you're good. Me and the gang are hanging out in the Badlands tonight. There's a ton of meteor rocks out here. We figure we're going to see a shower of them before the night's over and who knows what else. We were wondering if any of your listeners have been out here and have seen anything else unusual. I'll hang up and listen."

"You all heard Mel. If you've had an out-of-this-world experience in the Badlands, I'll ask Stewart, who's working the phones, to fit you into the call lineup. We're moving on to Moline, Illinois. Am I speaking to Roseanne?"

"Yes. Hi! I'm so excited to be on your show. I've tried for two months to get on and now I'm so nervous I'm scared."

"Hey—we're all friends. How old are you?"

"Fifteen. I've never talked to a real-live author before. I read your Stargrazer book and loved it so much I wondered if you'd autograph it for me."

"Sure. Send it in care of the show. Off the air Stewart will give you the P.O. address."

"Thanks so much. Oh, before I hang up, I was just wondering if you're going to write another Stargrazer story. You could do one where a guy from Algol lands in the Badlands by accident. That would be so cool, especially if you made him as gorgeous as Percy, maybe his cousin? I'm the president of your fan club. I set up a Twitter account and a Facebook page dedicated to you. Our club has over twelve hundred members and we want you to write another book."

"That's very flattering, Roseanne. Maybe one day when I have more time."

"Please make it soon—we can't wait!"

Chaz had already heard enough to be curious about her novel. Twelve hundred teens waiting for another book? And that was just in one fan club. How come Lacey Garvey Pomeroy hadn't written more than one?

He was anxious to get started reading the story, but she'd come back on the air after an ad and was talking to a new caller. Chaz needed to listen to the whole program. Undoubtedly her stalker was tuned in, picking up on her every word, and might even be one of the callers.

Much to his surprise, as he listened for the next two and a half hours, jotting down notes, he didn't suffer a moment's boredom except for the ads and station breaks. She ended her show with the announcement about playing a tape from last year's Summer Solstice Conference in Milwaukee tomorrow night.

"When I open the program, I'll let you know the exact time it will come on so none of you will miss it. I've had so many calls about it, I decided tomorrow night would be the perfect time to air it again. That's all from the Ionosphere for tonight."

Because the two phoned death threats had come around the same time as the summer solstice, Chaz made a note to find out more about this conference. He wondered if the note placed on her car had also happened around June 20 of last year. There might be a connection.

Mrs. Pomeroy had followed the instructions he'd given her to the letter, and she'd done it brilliantly. Wide awake now, he turned off the radio and started reading the novel's prologue.

Apparently a time traveler from the variable planet Algol located in the Perseus constellation had flown to Earth on a stargrazer. His name was Percy, a brooding, unhappy soul who once a year rode the meteor shower, roving from one parallel universe to another. He'd been to thousands of them, but never bonded with one spot.

He had no age. He had friends, but life had made him a loner—his family had been killed aeons ago when he was a child. He was looking for something he couldn't find, but was positive he would know it if he ever came upon it.

Chaz closed his eyes for a minute, surprised by what he'd just read. It was as if the author had described Chaz's life down to certain unknown details about him. Ridiculous as it was, he felt bemused by this piece of fantasy fiction where his own life seemed to have been exposed.

He also had to admit to being fascinated and continued to read about Percy, who'd been told to bypass Earth because it could be dangerous for him, but he went anyway because it was his nature to take risks.

The author had nailed that trait in Chaz, too. He got off the bed and grabbed for the last piece of licorice on the side table. A little sugar heightened his enjoyment as he walked around the room reading the description of Percy.

Lacey Pomeroy might have been a teenager when she'd written this book, but her insights gave him the impression she'd been going on a hundred at the time. Where had a brain like hers come from? The same place as Heinlein's, Chaz supposed.

Chuckling to himself, he took a shower and got ready for bed. He needed sleep and would finish reading in the morning. But when he eventually climbed under the covers, he realized he was as hooked by Lacey Pomeroy's writing as Roseanne, the girl who'd called into the show wanting the author to pen another novel.

He reached for the reader, promising himself he would read only a little more. For a teen, Lacey had possessed an amazing imagination. Percy always arrived in another universe by a meteor depositing him over a body of water. When he landed on Earth, he found himself in Hudson Bay near the New York City docks. Luckily, his skills included underwater prowess.

Riveted by her tale, Chaz wondered if he'd find more of himself in the character she'd created and scrolled down to begin chapter one. But realizing he needed sleep, he forced himself to turn off the reader. He was supposed to be using this research to help him get a handle on Lacey Pomeroy's case, not focusing on himself.

He really was messed up. If the other P.I.'s in the office, particularly his buds Mitch and Travis, knew about his interest in a teenage sci-fi novel, they'd laugh themselves sick.

What wasn't laughable was that someone in Salt Lake or California was after this woman. Even if those phone calls had been a couple of malicious pranks with nothing more sinister intended, it still meant this person had found Lacey's unlisted number and had invaded her privacy. The culprit needed to be arrested. Let a judge slap on a harsh fine and order them into counseling to be watched.

But if they were clinically delusional, waiting to do exactly what had been put in the death threats, then they needed to be stopped yesterday.

Both phone threats and the note on her car appeared to have been tied to her work with the paranormal. But that might have been a deliberate ploy by the perpetrator to throw any police investigation off the scent. Chaz didn't know yet.

One thing he'd learned so far. What he'd heard and read tonight could spark irrational jealousy in someone who wished they'd written a novel twelve hundred teenagers were clamoring to read, but had been rejected by a slew of publishers. Or had been up for the Nebula Award and had lost out.

Certainly someone who wanted to be a famous radio or TV personality with a particular slant like Mrs. Pomeroy's and couldn't make it to first base could be consumed by envy that had escalated beyond normal bounds. Or maybe it was someone who *had* achieved great success, but it still wasn't enough.

Professional jealousy abounded in the workplace. Plenty of homicides every year attested to that. He recalled hearing about the deliberate injury to a beautiful, talented Olympic ice skater by another competitor. It had been ugly.

But this case was uglier. Or would be if the stalker followed through on his or her threats.

Doing his homework tonight had given Chaz a place to start, but as they'd announced at the beginning of her show, this was only one possibility in an unending number of expanding universes.

Chapter Two

The radio station was one of many businesses in a strip mall located in the Fort Union business area of Salt Lake. It wasn't far from the Parkridge condo complex where Lacey lived. On Friday night, after putting her precious Abby to bed with lots of stories and kisses, she thanked her sister and left. At eight-thirty it was still twilight as she backed her blue Passat out of her garage and drove the short distance to work.

She found it a strange experience knowing she was probably being watched by her stalker along with a crew of people working for the P.I. firm. Everyone in her line of vision or behind her was suspect. At the moment her life felt surreal.

Apparently Barry had okayed the work order for the satellite-dish people to come in and check the equipment for problems. That way Stewart wouldn't question letting them in.

Lacey couldn't imagine the security guard, Ben, a retired policeman and grandfather, or Stewart, the intern who was engaged to be married and in his last year of college, had anything to do with this. But she'd read enough mysteries and watched enough police shows to know anything was possible.

Hadn't she said it on her show? Anything *was* possible and she had to believe it.

She normally dressed in casual tops and jeans for comfort, but for work she always wore a dressier top and sandals to look more professional around the staff, radio hosts and guests who came in and out. For tonight she'd put on a summery print blouse in earth tones with a flutter sleeve.

Stewart's office was on the other side of the glass partition so they could always have eye contact and use hand signals when necessary. He stuck up notes, letting her know the name and location of the caller waiting on the line.

Most of the time they had fun smiling and reacting to the different callers. There were the talkers who wouldn't stop, the ones who couldn't talk once they got on the air, the cynics, the gushy ones, the ones who flirted, the ones who wanted her to endorse their Area 51 and Bermuda Triangle websites.

Sometimes a psychic called in giving her information about her future. On certain nights a ghost-watcher group called in from a cemetery to let the audience hear a child's cry. A certain Wicca liked to talk about the wheel of life. Another called from the edge of a hole in the ground that had no bottom. The calls ran the gamut and she loved it.

But the calls on her own phones had caused her to wonder. Maybe Stewart *was* her stalker. He had access to both her phone numbers and wanted to become a radio personality. No longer could she look at him the same way.

Her fear for Abby's and her family's safety dominated her every breath and thought. There was a definite risk in exposing herself to the public over the air. Say what you will, it invited this kind of evil and now her entire family was threatened.

She knew Barry was doing everything possible to help her through this because he didn't want her to quit. He was the one person she didn't suspect, not when he'd hired a P.I. at the network's expense to catch this demon. Her biggest fault was agreeing to keep the show going after she'd come back to Salt Lake.

That death threat on her windshield should have been enough of a retardant. Regardless of the growing ratings and increased salary, no career was worth this kind of horror.

Lacey had enough savings to fly her and her family to another part of the country where they could live for a month away from the spotlight with different names. If this lunatic wasn't caught by the time they returned to Salt Lake, she would ask the P.I. how to go about hiring some good bodyguards.

She turned into the broad alley behind the strip mall. It was a busy weekend night. Other cars were going in and out to movies and restaurants. She drove halfway down to park in the well-lit area at the back door of the station. Her program followed the *Smart Finance Show* with Kurt Smart. His black Audi was parked next to Stewart's white Nissan.

Stewart usually came in early to handle the business end and collect all the faxes for her show. The most interesting or relevant were earmarked for her attention. She would glance through them during the ads to see if she could use any of them. Tonight the thought of getting a fax from the stalker almost immobilized her, but she had to get out of her car and go inside.

After she'd let herself in the back door with the remote, she hurried down the hall to her office on the other side of Stewart's. She poked her head inside to let him know she'd arrived.

He glanced up with a smile. Kurt was still on the air.

"How are things going?"

"Busy. I went through your faxes. You got a ton and will never get through them tonight."

"What else is new?" she teased, forcing herself to act as if nothing was wrong. The fact that he didn't alert her to a disturbing one caused her to let out the breath she'd been holding.

But then he wouldn't have said anything if he were the culprit. Or maybe he would have....

Fear was driving her crazy.

"Barry said some guys from a dish-network crew are coming in sometime tonight to check out the equipment. Apparently it's the only time they can come and Barry wants the work done no matter what, so he says just ignore them."

"Oh. Okay. By the way, I want to play the Summer Solstice Conference tape from last year at ten."

"Right. Barry mentioned it. I have it lined up."

Unable to concentrate on anything, she picked up the receiver of the station phone to call her sister and make sure everything was all right at the condo with Abby. But then she thought better of it. Before long it was nine o'clock and time for the news before her segment started. She grabbed the faxes and left her office.

"Hey, Lacey—" Kurt was just coming out of the booth. "You're looking beautiful as usual." He always said something nice. *Everyone is suspect. Even Kurt.*

"Thanks. How did your show go tonight?"

"Callers are grumbling about the bad economy."

"It is pretty bad."

"Yup. Well, have a good one," he murmured before heading toward the back door.

She slipped inside the broadcast booth and set the faxes on the desk. After sitting down, she put on her earphones, adjusted the mic and gave Stewart the nod that she was ready. It terrified her to think that the stalker might be listening tonight, planning when he was going to kill her and her daughter.

Lacey had never had ulcers, but knew she was getting one. Whenever she thought of anything happening to Abby, the pain hit her like someone was torching her insides with a soldering gun. The antacids she'd been taking all day hadn't helped.

She waited for the long lead-in to end, then launched into the program, reminding the listeners that highlights from the Summer Solstice Conference would be aired at ten o'clock. Lacey was counting the seconds until she could talk to the P.I.

Who knew how good he was. Someone with a background in law enforcement didn't necessarily have the ability to solve a case like this. Lacey didn't know the odds when it came to stalking cases, but feared they were against her.

Barry seemed to have faith in this agency, but he was desperate to keep her on the air. Little did he know she was desperate enough to leave Salt Lake with her loved ones to keep everyone safe.

By the time ten o'clock rolled around, she was so anxious to meet the P.I., she'd developed a headache. Until now she and her mom had been running on their faith in Barry's judgment, but that might not be enough.

The advertisements ended and Stewart started the tape. That was her cue to look through the faxes and pretend she was busy. In a minute she heard the door open. Out of the periphery she saw a man enter the booth wearing a light blue uniform.

His powerful body moved around the enclosed space checking various pieces of electronic equipment, then he came near her and hunkered down while ostensibly checking the floor plugs. Not all people smelled good up close, but he did. Suddenly he lifted his head.

Although she was quite sure she'd never before seen this man, there was something about him that was strangely familiar. He had black hair that was long enough to curl at his neck and was very tall—maybe around six foot three. He was broad-shouldered, well-cut and lean, with strong, unerring hands. But there was something about his eyes.... Something that reminded her of...Percy!

Strange how in this circumstance, life imitated art instead of the other way around. The character in her novel had such eyes. A mixture of green and yellow.

Years earlier, after she'd seen a shooting star, she'd created a guy in her mind. He'd possessed unusual qualities and traits because he'd come from another universe. The meteor he was on had flown too close to Earth and had been caught in its gravitational pull.

Seeing the eyes she'd imagined years before in the flesh was a visceral experience for her.

Chaz's breath caught. The fantastic-looking woman with honey-red hair bouncing on her shoulders was staring at him with the most amazing smoky-blue eyes. In that fluttery blouse and jeans she filled out to perfection, there wasn't a man alive who wouldn't follow her down the street just to get a better look at her.

Barry Winslow had filled him in on the basics about her. Her husband had been killed while he was in the Coast Guard and she'd moved back to Salt Lake from Long Beach. She'd been a widow for a year and had a three-year-old daughter. The producer didn't know if she had a boyfriend or a lover. He'd never seen her with one or heard her talk about one.

That didn't mean a stream of men hadn't tried to get to first base with her. If one of them couldn't take rejection, he might be her stalker.

He murmured softly, "Dr. Livingston, I presume."

His first words erased her startled expression. A tiny, unexpected smile broke one corner of her mouth. He saw pure intelligence flow from those dark-fringed eyes before she said, "I heard rumors you were coming, Mr. Stanley."

Despite the deadly seriousness of the situation, he felt this palpitating connection to her. *An out-of-body experience?* That was the only way to describe it.

"One of the crew is up on the roof checking out the dish while he's videotaping the area. I'll be leaving when he comes back down. That only gives us a few minutes to talk. I know you have a lot of questions, but save them until we meet tomorrow. What's your normal schedule like in the morning?"

She kept going through the faxes on her desk, pretending to read them. "Now that it's summer, my mother usually comes over on Saturday and we take my daughter to the park. Afterward we go grocery shopping and have lunch someplace before we go back for Abby's nap."

"Do you usually go to the same store?"

"Yes."

"Then I'll call your mother and tell her my plan. Give me the name and address of the store."

When she told him, he said, "Your mother will drive tomorrow and take you to the grocery store at eleven. While she does some shopping with your daughter, you'll walk through to Produce and tell them you need to pick up a salad in the back room. I'll be there to let you out the rear door. We'll drive to my office to discuss your case. Did you keep the death threat on the voice mail of your cell phone?"

"Yes. I saved it for evidence. The death threat on my landline is still recorded, too."

"Good. Here's the plan. When we're through talking at my office tomorrow, you'll call your mother on the new phone I'm going to give you. She'll have your new number and know it's you. Once you've told her you'll meet her back at the grocery store, I'll take you there so you can enter through the produce department door. Okay?"

"Yes."

"A couple more things. When was the last time you went to your mailbox?"

"Two days ago. I've been afraid to get it."

"Where is your box located?"

"In a row of boxes between my building and the one next door."

"On your way out to your mother's car, I want you to collect the mail and put it in your purse. We'll go through it at my office. I'd also like the most recent photos of your immediate and extended family for me to make copies of and distribute to my crew. Bring a wedding album and guest book if you have them for identification purposes."

"I'll do it."

"Good. Now I've got to go."

Her eyes grew suspiciously bright. "Thank you, Mr. Roylance."

"Call me Chaz." Reading her mind, he said, "It's short for Charles. I always disliked my given name."

CHAZ LET HIMSELF OUT, NODDING to the radio intern manning the phones. The night watchman opened the main door for him. He walked over to a big van with a dish on the top and climbed in.

The van was one of the firm's many electronic-surveillance vehicles set up with state-of-the-art equipment. Adam was driving. An unmarried demolitions and electronics expert, Adam was home from the Middle East after deployment. He'd applied for a job with Roman, who was training him to become a P.I. Adam had uncanny instincts that had prompted Chaz to put him on the case.

They passed a janitorial-service truck parked a few cars away where Lon, a retired police officer who'd headed several SWAT teams in his time, was on duty for Chaz. He'd be tailing Lacey Pomeroy until six in the morning, when another member of the crew took over.

"Let's head over to Walmart." Adam nodded. "What kind of traffic did you see out here tonight?"

"A lot of vehicles, some foot."

"Good. We'll analyze the tape when I meet you at the office tomorrow."

He nodded again. "What's she like?"

Lacey Pomeroy kept on surprising him in stunning ways. Tonight it was her incredible looks *and* her sophistication. Disinclined to talk about her while he was trying to sort out all his feelings, he said, "She's handling this well."

He didn't tell Adam how she'd held herself rigid and took shallow breaths, or how her fingers tortured the top fax. He definitely didn't tell him about the voluptuous line of her mouth when she'd let go with that little unexpected smile, or her delicious fragrance that reminded him of strawberries.

Some people chattered away when they were frightened. She'd done just the opposite, displaying admirable poise under precarious circumstances. Where did hair like that come from? Red shot with gold, or gold shot with red... He'd never seen color and texture so tantalizing. He'd wanted to lift the strands to the light and play with them.

"We've arrived."

Adam's voice jerked him back to the present. "Thanks. See you tomorrow." Chaz got out of the van and walked over to his Forerunner parked in the lot full of late-night shoppers. He drove straight back to his condo. Now that he'd met the unforgettable author of *The Stargrazer from Algol,* he was more eager than ever to get into the body of the book.

After he got ready for bed, he climbed in and reached for the reader, intrigued to see how she'd started chapter one to capture the mind of a teen, her target audience.

Percy was lounging on the deck of an ocean liner observing the earthlings when he spotted a family walking his way. As they moved past him, his eyes connected with the blue gaze of one of the daughters and there was a sudden spike in his body temperature. The ferocity of it left him feeling so physically ill, he could hardly find the strength to move.

LACEY HAD GIVEN ABBY A cherry Ring Pop to lick while she pushed the shopping cart along the fruit aisle. When they reached the area near the back of the store, she whispered to her mother, "I'll call you."

Quickly, before Abby caught on, Lacey headed for the doorway leading to the area where produce was unloaded from trucks. Aware the stalker could be watching, she had to appear natural as she walked through. Two employees in back were cutting up vegetables and fruits in a room filled with crates. They nodded to her, but her gaze was drawn to the tall, striking man holding the outer door open.

Dressed in a short-sleeved black crewneck with boot-cut jeans, Chaz Roylance filled her vision. She hurried toward him. His gaze swept over her, and despite her anxiety, Lacey felt her pulse race. When she'd told her friend Brenda that no man would ever interest her again after Ted, she hadn't met Chaz Roylance. "Climb in the green Forerunner parked outside."

She did his bidding and fastened the seat belt. Within seconds he joined her and drove them past the rear of the supermarket and out to another street away from the store parking area. At the first stoplight he glanced at her. Though his eyes reflected male interest, he was a total professional. "You were right on time, Mrs. Pomeroy. That makes my plans easier to carry out."

"If you only knew how grateful I am…"

"I'm happy to help. Do you mind if I call you Lacey?"

"No."

"Just so you know, I'm wearing a mini tape recorder to pick up our conversation. Is that all right with you?"

"Yes." The man was trying to help her. How could she possibly object, especially when he was up front about it?

The light changed and they took off toward Wasatch Boulevard, where her mother had told her he worked. "I have a confession to make right off the bat."

She stared blindly out the window, wishing she weren't so physically aware of him. "What's that?"

"I've never believed in aliens or the paranormal, but if anything could make me reconsider, it would be your radio show."

Surprised, she turned to him. "You listened?"

He nodded. "To all of Thursday night's program. I've also read your book to the part where Percy sees the earthling and his temperature spikes to one hundred and twenty degrees like a hot plume of gas from Algol's something region."

Lacey smiled, secretly delighted by the admission that he'd gone to that much trouble to learn about her. "Hebulon."

His lips twitched, making him even more attractive. "That's it. I'm supposing that your traveler has to find a place to hide so the platinum streaks in his hair don't turn silver in front of the passengers. I confess I can't wait to find out."

She chuckled.

"It's no wonder your fifteen-year-old listener Rose-anne and her army of twelve hundred are waiting for another story."

An *army?* Lacey's chuckle turned into quiet laughter.

"From what I've researched, you've only had one novel published, unless you're published under a pseudonym or two."

"No. There's only the one book."

"How come? You can't tell me you don't have dozens more in your computer files. I imagine your publisher would steal them if it were possible."

"That's very flattering." She recrossed her legs. "I do have other novels, but none of them are finished."

"Why not?"

"Because I went to Stanford in California and started writing a column for the *Stanford Daily*. Between studying for classes in my geophysics major, keeping up with the deadlines and doing a weekly paranormal segment at the university's radio station, I had to put my novel writing aside."

"I can't imagine why," he teased.

She laughed.

"And after college, you went into radio instead of pursuing a career in geophysics. What happened?"

"I was torn. I loved science and writing, but it was very flattering to be given an opportunity to do a paranormal show when it was offered to me. To be honest, I didn't see how it would catch on, and after a couple of weeks I was sure it would fail. When it didn't, I only expected it to last for a season because I'm a writer first and foremost. But my old boss kept pressing me to stay another season.

"My future dream is to write science fiction for adults using the knowledge from my geophysics background. Those stories will be more advanced and interest people of all ages. As for the young-adult stories, one day I'll finish the ones I started."

He darted her a puzzled glance. "Tell me something, with all this going on in that mind of yours, how did you manage to fit in a wedding?"

"It wasn't easy with Ted being in the Coast Guard."

"Where did you two meet?"

Lacey had to remember he was firing all these questions at her because he was investigating her case, not because he was interested in her. She realized that everything she told him could be critical to finding the stalker. To hold back any information would only hurt her. But she couldn't help but wonder what it would be like to have met him naturally. Would he still have found her interesting?

"There'd been a UFO sighting over the Bay Area. I'd been working a program segment for the radio and went to Fisherman's Wharf to interview people who'd seen it and tape their responses. Ted happened to be there with some of his buddies on weekend leave from Long Beach. We started talking and one thing led to another. We got married six months later, as soon as I graduated. He's been gone a year."

She heard him exhale. "I'm sorry for your loss. You have my deepest sympathy. Ten years ago my wife's death hit me hard. She died from cervical cancer and it took me a long time to recover."

Lacey bit her lip. "I'm so sorry for you, too. Do you have children?"

"No."

The P.I. had to be in his mid-thirties by now. "I have my Abby. Without her, I don't know what I'd do." How sad for him not to have had a child. How hard. "If this stalker tries to hurt her…" She clutched her purse, unable to go on talking.

"Take heart, Lacey. I plan to catch this person before anything happens. When I do, your case will be handed over to the police and they'll make an arrest."

Since Chaz had acted so fast, plus gone to the trouble of listening to her show and reading her book, his vow convinced her he would do whatever was humanly possible to help her. No wonder her mother had felt encouraged. He did instill confidence. "I believe you," she said in a trembly voice.

He turned off the highway and pulled around the back of his office. After shutting off the engine he eyed her frankly. "In a case like this, to have trust between the two of us means everything. We're off to a good start. Let's go inside where we'll lay out a plan."

The Lufka P.I. Agency looked like any well-managed business office, with a dozen or so people on the premises. Chaz ushered her into his private office, supplying coffee for both of them. The attractive owner, Roman Lufka, came in and introduced himself. Apparently he was the one who'd listened to Barry's phone call. After he went out again, Chaz asked to see her mail.

She opened her purse. Aside from the ads and brochures, she had only three bills and what looked like a wedding invitation.

"May I open them?"

"Of course."

He did a quick check of the bills, then the larger envelope before darting her a glance. "This is an invitation to visit some time-share rentals in Park City. Free knives are being given for taking a tour."

"Just what I wanted," she said with a haunted whisper as he handed everything back to her.

"Do you know anyone at this business? Have they been a sponsor of your show?"

"No, but I'm aware they've been around for several years."

He put the mail aside. "Check your mailbox every day, but don't open anything until I'm with you. Now, let me see your cell phone."

She handed it to him and put the mail back in her purse. "There are four messages to listen to."

He put on the speakerphone and played the first one.

I can hardly wait to see your blood on my hands, you bitch. So watch out and keep looking over your shoulder, because I'm right behind you and plan to cut out your freakin' heart first. Then I'll start on your daughter…. Both will be an in-the-body experience you won't forget.

His eyes flicked to hers. "Did the message on your landline sound the same? I'm not talking words."

"I know what you mean. Yes, it was the same man's voice."

"Do you remember the essence of that message?"

"It said something about my next experience burning up my brain, literally."

He cocked his dark head. "Mr. Winslow told me about the note you found on your car windshield a year ago outside the funeral home. Try to remember any details of what it said."

Lacey shivered. "I should have saved it for evidence, but at the time I was in so much pain over Ted, I threw it away. It talked about aliens killing my husband and now they were going to burn up my daughter and me, part by part. Something like that," she murmured.

"Was the note pieced together with words from magazine cutouts? Handwritten?"

"Neither. It was typed on a piece of paper."

"What about grammar and spelling?"

She blinked. "Nothing stands out in my mind, but I think it was all in caps."

He nodded. "Let's trace the call on this phone and see where it leads."

She waited while he pressed the digits, then he was talking to someone. After a few minutes he hung up. "That call was placed from a phone booth in the E.R. waiting room of a hospital in Denver, Colorado. Anyone could have called."

Lacey couldn't prevent the shudder that attacked her body.

"I'll be interested to see where the call on your landline came from." A sober expression broke out on his rugged features. "We don't know yet if the caller is the same person who left the note under your windshield wiper, but we do know two important things. One, it's a human, not an alien entity harassing you.

"Two, whoever phoned you was using a twenty-dollar voice converter that's placed over a regular phone or a cell to distort the sound. They're so small they can be worn on a key chain. It means your stalker could be a man or a woman."

Chapter Three

Lacey's quiet gasp told Chaz a lot. "The possibility that it might be a woman never occurred to you?"

"Not really," she murmured. "I usually think of a woman harassing an ex-spouse or ex-boyfriend."

"Would it interest you to know that thirteen percent of all stalking cases are committed by women, and forty-eight percent of them stalk other women?"

"You mean they harass their ex-partners of the same gender because they're no longer together?"

"In some cases. But in others there's been no sexual intimacy. It has more to do with anger and hostility often stemming from an actual or perceived rejection by the victim."

Lacey shook her head. "I've never given any of this much thought before."

"Most people don't have to. One of the reasons you haven't is because the available evidence on women stalkers hasn't been afforded the degree of seriousness attached to male stalkers. Eighty-four percent of men stalk a female victim, so it's in the news more. Keep in mind that just because we don't hear about it as often doesn't mean women are any less intrusive or persistent in their stalking, or pose any less of a threat to their victims, physical or otherwise."

Just remembering what had happened in South America proved to Chaz that women trained by the enemy were just as capable of violence as men.

He saw her flinch. "It's all horrifying."

"I agree. But I want to assure you that most stalkers are not psychotic. In general, they suffer from depression and substance abuse, or a personality disorder. Female stalkers are significantly less likely than males to have a history of criminal or violent criminal offenses.

"What we'll do is make a list of men and women who've been close to you in the past or who are close to you now. Perhaps none of them are involved, but it's not as common for a person you've never known to harass you. That narrows the field a great deal and you should be confident that we'll find your stalker soon."

Chaz had given her a lot to think about, but he'd only scratched the surface. "First, I want to know about your daily schedule apart from your work," he said.

"Basically I take care of my daughter until I go to work Monday through Friday. We play and go to the park, shop, eat out, drop by her nana's. While she naps, I work on my material for the radio program and take care of correspondence. Sometimes on weekends we get together with my aunt's family or I meet a friend for lunch, but generally speaking it's the same schedule."

"Tell me about your immediate family."

"That would be Mom and Ruth."

"Does your mother work?"

"Yes. She's a math whiz and teaches part-time in

the math department at the University of Utah. That's where she met my dad, who was a bioengineer and worked for a company developing new software for the medical field."

He smiled. "Your smarts come from great genes."

"My parents were brilliant. When she got pregnant with me, Mom stayed at home, and didn't go back to teaching until after Ruth went into junior high. By then I'd started high school. We're two years apart.

"After I moved home from California Mom wanted to help me, so she cut down her teaching load to only two days a week. She doesn't have to work. Dad left her well enough off, but she likes to keep busy. She's also involved in her church group and spends time with her sister, my aunt Mary, and her family who live in North Salt Lake."

"Is Ruth equally gifted?"

"Mom once told me Ruth had a higher IQ than anyone in our family."

"What kind of work does she do?"

"After high school graduation she took different jobs until the one at the cell-phone store. It paid her a salary plus commission. She saved enough money there to pay for flying lessons."

"That's interesting."

"I know. It was a surprise to Mom and me, but she can be moody at times, so you never know what she'll decide to do next. Once she'd obtained her license, she worked several places and ended up flying for an air cargo company in Idaho Falls. But then the bad economy impacted everything. A month ago she was let go."

Or maybe Lacey's sister couldn't get along with

people at that job, either. But Chaz kept his thoughts to himself.

"What's Ruth doing now?"

"She's living with our mother, trying to find work. Mom's been helping her out financially. I am, too, in my own way. Since I always need a babysitter at night, I asked her if she'd like to tend Abby for me and I'd pay her until she found a new job. She took me up on the offer, for which I'm grateful."

"What about her social life?"

"Ruth's very good-looking and has always had a ton of boyfriends, but from what I can tell, those relationships are stormy. Since she's been home I've heard her on the phone with a guy named Bruce. I don't know if it's very serious. One day she'll probably get married to someone I've never heard of, then spring him on the family. It would be just like her."

"Your sister sounds like her own person," he murmured. He'd be interested to know why exactly she'd been let go from her pilot's job.

"She's that and more. I love her."

"That's nice. I never had a sibling." He studied her for a minute. "Who babysat for you before?"

"Julie Howard. I've known her for a long time. Her family lives across the street from my mother. She's college-age and attends the university. Mom heard she wanted part-time work. The hours I could offer were perfect for her."

Chaz would check out the babysitter later. "The questions I'm going to ask you now will make you uncomfortable, but if I'm to help you, I need to know the truth."

He noticed she swallowed hard. "I understand that."

"How many intimate relationships did you have be-fore your husband? I'm talking going to bed together."

Lacey squirmed in the chair. "Your warning didn't help me," she whispered. "Since a stalker is threatening me, I guess I have to answer that question." She lowered her head. "Much as I'd like to tell you it's none of your business, I can't do that, not when my life and Abby's are on the line. The truth is, I didn't have any intimate relationships before Ted."

Chaz believed her. In this day and age, that was quite a statement to make. "And since?"

Again she stirred restlessly. He could see how hard this was for her. Hell, he wouldn't like this kind of in-quisition, either.

"There's been no one."

"Tell me about the men who wanted to take you out. Were there a lot of those?"

She smoothed the hair away from her forehead. "I dated some in high school and college when I had the time. I made out with some of them, but I was never in love and the chemistry wasn't right for me to want to sleep with any of them."

Maybe not, but that couldn't be said for the men who would have had an immediate crush on her and that crush could have turned into an obsession. "Was there one guy who wouldn't give up?"

"Yes." A quick smile came and went. "It was Ted, but then I didn't want him to give up. It was one of those situations where I let him chase me until I caught him."

He chuckled. "How long were you married?"

"Two and a half years."

"May I see a picture of him?"

She opened her wallet and handed him one of Ted in his Coast Guard uniform. A nice-looking guy with dark blond hair. What a tragedy she'd lost him. He gave the picture back.

"Do you have a romantic interest in your life right now?"

"No. I couldn't imagine it."

He'd gone through that stage after losing his wife. "When did your husband die?"

"June 18. I was supposed to have flown out for the summer solstice convention in Milwaukee. I'd only planned to be gone two days. My mother was going to fly down to Long Beach to tend Abby while I was gone and stay for the rest of the week. But my whole world fell apart when the Coast Guard informed me Ted had been killed. You more than anyone would understand what that moment was like."

"I'm afraid I do."

It was possible Chaz's theory about the note and phone calls being connected to the summer solstice convention had substance. Or it could be more directly related to Ted. The note had showed up a year ago at Ted's funeral. One year later on the first anniversary of his death, she'd received two phone threats. If the stalker wanted Lacey's exclusive attention and had felt rejected by her, then he or she was glad Ted Pomeroy was out of the way, thus removing the biggest obstacle.

Then again, the culprit might be motivated by professional jealousy and would do everything possible to scare Lacey off the air permanently. Including her daughter, Abby, in the threats would rachet up the fear factor.

"Do you normally meet friends at a convention like that, or are the attendees strangers?"

"A bit of both. I belong to a core group of dedicated paranormal enthusiasts, but meet new people at each conference. They're as fascinated by the unexplainable as I am. We discuss the latest findings and compare notes. I gather information for my radio show. One of them, Gil Lawrence, who's a journalist, made certain I was sent the tape from the Milwaukee convention."

"Where does this special group come from?"

"All over the country."

"How long have you known this group?"

"About six years. After I graduated from Stanford, I attended a paranormal conference in Seattle and we became friends practically overnight because of our mutual interest."

"Are these people prominent?"

"They're a unique bunch of scientists, pilots, government workers, intellectuals, writers and journalists who've lost some credibility at their places of work because they profess to believe in paranormal activity."

He could understand that. "How do you stay in touch with them?"

"Mostly by email, but when there's some really exciting news, we phone."

"Do these people have both of your phone numbers?"

Her eyes darkened with emotion. "Yes. And my address."

"Are you a large group?"

"No. There are twelve right now. We try to meet at a conference every other month. For the most part, we've been able to keep it up."

"Are these people married? Single?"

"Both."

Chaz reached for her phone and turned on the speaker so they could listen to the other messages she hadn't erased. He let them play, then asked, "Who's Dave?"

"The man returning my call is Dave Lignel, one of the long-standing group members who's married and has a family. He's a commercial-airline pilot who at the moment is keeping me apprised on some lights in the night sky neither he nor his copilot could identify on his last flight to South America."

Just hearing the name South America filled his mind with images of what had happened there...images he fought to forget.

"That woman who informed me about the book on Sasquatch? She works in the circulation department at the main library. As you heard, the third call was from my dentist's office reminding me of my next checkup."

Chaz got up to turn on the television and play the tapes Adam and the other crew people had brought in this morning. "I want you to watch these surveillance videos filming outside your condo and the radio station. If you see something that alarms you, I need to know."

As she identified neighbors going in and out of her condo building, he took notes. "We all pretty much leave each other alone, but everyone in my building is friendly. The couple below me has two children, so we have more in common and chat now and then."

"How about the people at the radio station?"

She pointed out one of the daytime talk show hosts who'd gone inside the radio station during her program, but hadn't stayed long. "That's Sally who does the *Tiptoe Through the Tulips* garden show on Saturdays.

She's in her sixties and gives gardening classes at the water conservancy park. There could be any number of reasons why she dropped by there last night.

"The other guy just going in the station is Greg Stevens. He does the *Sports and Celebrities* midnight show. It lasts till four in the morning when the local newscaster Adrian Memmot comes on."

Chaz turned off the TV. "Okay. One more question. Do you have a website?"

"The program does. Barry manages it and Stewart deals with the emails. Some listeners send a fax. The number is on the website."

"That answers that."

He reached into the drawer and handed her a new cell phone. "I've programmed it so you reach me on one, your mother on two, your sister on three and Barry Winslow on four. For now, no others can contact you on this phone.

"Keep your other phone and answer it only if you can identify the caller. Your stalker will keep phoning you on it and your landline, leaving messages to harass you. We'll listen to them together. In time, when you don't seem to be intimidated by these calls, this person will come out of the woodwork in more creative ways to terrify you, but we'll be ready for them."

She rubbed her temples. "I don't know how to thank you for all this."

"It's my job. Before I forget, I downloaded a ringtone on your new phone from *2001: A Space Odyssey.*"

"You did?" Her eyes lighted in genuine amusement, charming him.

He picked up his own phone and called her new number. When it rang, she laughed quietly. Chaz liked her laugh. "I thought it only appropriate. Change it if you want to. It won't hurt my feelings," he teased.

"I wouldn't dream of it."

Once again he was enjoying this time with her too much and needed to concentrate on the next order of business. "Is there a paranormal conference coming up soon you were planning to attend?"

"Next Friday in Albuquerque. In runs the whole weekend. But now that this has happened, I—"

"You're going to go," he informed her without pre-amble. "I'll be attending it with you because I believe your stalker will be there. We can do this two ways. I can show up as a friend of yours who's interested in the paranormal, or I will come with you as your new fiancé. I'd prefer the latter."

Chaz watched her eyes turn a darker shade of blue, no doubt from shock. *"Fiancé?"*

"I need to get into your world as fast as possible, Lacey. It's my opinion this stalker has harbored a deep-seated jealousy of you, either personally, because of your happy marriage and child, or professionally. Maybe both. By being your fiancé rather than just a friend with a similar interest, I would have the right to keep a closer eye on you as well as a legitimate, imme-diate entry into your home and life.

"If your stalker is a woman, she'll be infuriated that you've found a new love interest. If your stalker is a man, he'll hate the fact that you have a fiancé and are in love again. In either case the engagement will frus-trate his or her plans."

Her hand tightened around her purse. "I suppose you're right. But if the stalker has been watching me every minute, won't he or she know our engagement's a lie?"

"Yes, and it will anger him enough that he'll make a costly mistake. But if this person hasn't been able to spy on you all the time, then he'll have to believe it. I'm planning on the unexpected engagement to infuriate him and he'll eventually show his hand. That's what I'll be waiting for. Either way, we can't lose."

She stared at him as if she'd never seen him before. "How would we explain how we got together?"

At least Lacey hadn't said no yet. He was convinced an engagement would bring things to a head sooner. When Roman Lufka had taken on a stalking case years ago, he'd gone undercover as Brittany's husband. The action had resulted in a quick capture of the culprit. It had also resulted in a real marriage taking place.

Chaz had decided to take a leaf out of his boss's book. Not quite as drastic as pretending to be Lacey's husband, but it would have the same effect on the stalker.

"That part's easy. You'll introduce me as Chaz Roylance, a guy who grew up in Long Beach and played football with your husband in high school. We were good friends, but lost track when he went into the Coast Guard. I saw the obituary in the paper and met you at the viewing. Before you moved back to Salt Lake, I came to see you several times. After that I flew up for visits.

"We've spent a lot of private time together so I could get to know you and Abby better. One thing has led to another, but we haven't told people how we feel. I finally quit my landscaping business in Long Beach and moved here. While I've been staying with you, we've gotten engaged, but we haven't made definite wedding plans yet because your daughter has to get used to the idea first."

Her head flew back, causing that wave of red-gold hair to settle on her shoulders. "So…you're planning to stay at my condo?" Maybe it wasn't panic, but he saw some emotion resembling it in her expression.

"Starting tonight," he informed her. "We'll let people know I'm looking for a home to buy for us while I get my landscaping business started here. I don't think any of your friends will recognize me, since I've only lived here a year and I've kept a low profile." He could read her mind though she wasn't saying anything. "I've already cased your place from the outside and will throw down an air mattress and sleeping bag on your back deck."

She bit her lip. "I wouldn't let you stay out there."

"Most of my time in the SEALs I slept outside and liked it. You and your family will be able to carry on with your life and hardly know I'm there. But if you'd prefer not to go with an engagement, then tell me now and I'll work out a different plan for us. The decision is up to you."

He heard her suck in her breath. "I have to admit it would be a huge relief to know you're on the premises at night."

"I'll feel better about it, too. Is that a yes?" he prodded.

"Yes," she whispered after a sustained silence.

"Do you have those family photos for me?"

"Oh, yes. I wrote names and relationships on the backs." She pulled a manila envelope out of her bag.

"I'll scan them so they can be emailed to the crew.

Be assured I'll return them tomorrow. What I'm going to do now is run you back to the supermarket. After you're home, I want you to make out that list of people I was talking about. Put down everyone you can think of, along with the core group. Tell me as much about them as you can, including phone numbers, email and home addresses. If you have pictures, attach them."

"I have a picture of the core group from the convention two months ago."

"That's even better." He got to his feet. "What time will you put your daughter to bed this evening?"

"Seven, but it usually takes twenty minutes to settle her."

"In that case I'll be there at seven-thirty with Chinese takeout, unless you prefer something else."

She looked surprised. "No. I love it."

Good. "While we eat, we'll put in a session. Tomorrow morning you can introduce me to Abby. The faster we work together, the faster we'll catch this perpetrator. Go ahead and let your mother know you'll be picking up that salad in a few minutes."

As Lacey glanced at Chaz, who'd driven her to the rear of the supermarket's loading dock, she saw that a sober expression had entered his eyes, muting the vibrant green-and-yellow color to a nondescript hazel.

"See you tonight." His deep voice resonated inside her. "Before I forget, I have something for you." He reached into his back pocket and pulled out a beautiful one-carat diamond with a smaller diamond on either side set in yellow gold. "This isn't real, but you wouldn't know it without a jeweler's loupe."

In a daze, Lacey took the ring from him. The reality

of it sent her thoughts back to the night Ted had slipped the ring he'd bought for her on her finger, promising to love her till the day he died. Her darling husband... He'd died way too soon.

Now here she was with a fake engagement ring handed to her by this remarkable P.I. while he tried to find out who was stalking her. She felt as if she was living some strange dream.

"Once we catch your stalker—which I suspect will happen before long—you can tell everyone the truth and they'll all understand the reason for the deception. Let your mother know that while we're in New Mexico, she'll have twenty-four-hour surveillance outside her house."

"Thank you," she whispered. Grasping the ring in her palm, Lacey jumped out of the car, feeling his gaze on her back as she pushed open the metal door. Once inside the store, she stared at the ring burning its shape into her skin.

She couldn't believe she'd agreed to this arrangement with a virtual stranger, but Chaz was the expert and everything he'd said had made a certain kind of sense. In truth she wouldn't dare consider going to Albuquerque if he weren't going to be right there at her side. He believed her stalker would be there and thought this was the best way to handle the situation. If she didn't have faith in him, then what else was there?

He's putting his own life in danger to protect you, and believes this is the best way, Lacey.

Without any more hesitation, she put the ring on her left ring finger. It fit! Naturally it did. Chaz Roylance knew exactly what he was doing at all times. She'd never met anyone who possessed such innate confidence. He made her feel safe in a way no one else ever had before. Almost as if she was cherished and—

"Can I help you with something?" an employee spoke up, breaking in on her train of thought.

"Oh…yes…I came back here for a fruit salad."

"We've put some on the cart over there. Take your pick."

"Thank you."

Lacey chose one and headed for the checkout counter at the front of the store, but she felt weak in the legs.

For the first time since the phone threat on her landline, the sensation had little to do with fear of her stalker. Her new, temporary fiancé possessed a masculine appeal strong enough to have thrown her senses into chaos from the first moment. As she walked out to her car, she had to admit that the chemistry missing when she'd been around other men was so thick in his presence she was drowning in it.

"You're back, Mommy!"

"Of course I'm back, honey."

"How did it go?" her mom asked after Lacey had slipped in next to Abby and kissed her.

"*This* is how it went." She sat forward and put her left hand over her mother's shoulder so she could see the ring. "Chaz is pretending to be my fiancé from California who's staying with me and Abby. He says he'll sleep out on the back deck. It's for our protection, and also to enrage the stalker. Chaz believes he'll trap him sooner this way."

"That makes a lot of sense."

"The diamonds aren't real."

"They look authentic to me, which is the only thing that matters. In my opinion it's a brilliant plan, honey.

Now you won't be alone while this menace lays his trap. Nothing could make me happier," her mother said before driving them to Lacey's condo.

"Chaz is going to attend the Albuquerque paranormal conference with me so he can meet everyone."

"In that case I'll tend Abby. Before all this happened, I was already planning to."

"I know. Thank you so much, Mom. I don't know what I'd do without you. Chaz will assign someone to guard you and Abby and Ruth while we're gone." She had to take another quick breath. "If you talk to Ruth before I do, tell her we'll be having a visitor at night at the condo for a while. He wants us to go about our business as if he weren't there."

"Though she'll pretend otherwise, you know this is a frightening experience for Ruth."

"I know. I also realize this is frightening for you, too, Mom. I'm so sorry."

"Honey, this isn't your fault."

"If I didn't have a radio show, it wouldn't have happened."

"You don't know that. Chaz told me these kinds of cases happen for all sorts of reasons. Do you believe he can catch this person?"

"Yes. He's…incredible."

"I agree, so let's stop talking about being sorry."

"Okay."

Lacey got out of the Buick and unfastened Abby from the car seat. After waving her mother off, she hurried toward the stairs, juggling her daughter and the sack containing the salad. She still couldn't comprehend how much her life had changed since that first phone threat the other morning.

Luckily Abby's needs didn't leave her much time to ponder what was happening. They played games, then came her dinner and bath. Her daughter noticed the engagement ring and tried it on several times. Anything that sparkled caught her eye. Lacey explained that a friend named Chaz had given it to her. Once Abby was in her jammies, they went through her bedtime ritual until she fell asleep.

Lacey tiptoed out of the bedroom and hurried into the bathroom to freshen her lipstick and brush her hair. Chaz would be here any second. It surprised her how she was counting the minutes. She'd set up her laptop on the dining room table. Her family room was a combination eating area and kitchen along with an entertainment center and TV. Lacey liked the open arrangement.

Waiting for Chaz to arrive, she continued to compile a list of names, but it was by no means complete. When her cell phone rang with its new music, she jumped and pulled it out of her pocket. It was Chaz. Her pulse sped up. "Hello?"

"Hi. I'm outside the door, but didn't want to ring the bell and chance waking up your daughter."

Lacey appreciated his thoughtfulness. "I'll be right there." She clicked off and rushed to the small foyer to open the door. Warm air, still in the low eighties, filled the condo with its scent of honeysuckle. It was that *summer* smell she loved so much.

Chaz handed her their sack of food before he stepped inside wearing a backpack. He'd brought a bedroll and an inflatable air mattress. After locking the door behind him, she told him to put everything on the living room couch.

He'd showered and changed clothes. Tonight he had on a silky dark chocolate-colored shirt and tan chinos. She averted her eyes to keep from staring. "Come into the family room. I thought that would be the best place to work. Are you hungry?"

"Starving." He followed her into the other room where she put the sack of Chinese takeout on the table.

"So am I. I'll dish everything up right now."

He darted her a glance. "While you do that, I'll take a look around," he said quietly. "If by any chance your stalker broke into your condo to plant cameras or listening devices, I'll find them."

Lacey remembered her mother telling her to whisper because their voices might be picked up.

"Go ahead. Abby's a sound sleeper, but even if you disturb her, I don't mind. The thought of being spied on is terrifying."

"I'll be careful not to waken her."

By the time he'd come back to the family room and inspected it as well, she had everything ready, including the fruit salad and coffee.

"The place is clean in more ways than one."

"That's a huge relief…in more ways than one," she added. He chuckled and sat down opposite her. "Thank you for the food, Chaz. It's smells delicious."

"My pleasure. Your little girl looks like an angel sleeping in there." His gaze roved over her hair before he started eating. "It's not hard to tell you're her mommy."

"Nope. We stand out." She bit into an egg roll. "My daughter will have to learn to live with the curly red hair the way I did. Ted wanted to name her Anne, with an *e*."

"Of Green Gables, I presume."

They both laughed.

"You have a lovely condo. I like the Swedish-modern motif."

"Thanks. I plan to buy a real home in a few years, but this suits my needs right now."

"I know what you mean. I'm in a condo, too."

"Did you move here recently?"

"About a year ago."

"Where are you from?" Now that they were pretending to be engaged, she realized she needed some background on him. The truth was, she had a great curiosity about him. It came as a shock considering she'd thought Ted's death had permanently taken away her interest in other men. But there was something about Chaz....

"I was born and raised in Tucson, Arizona. After my wife died, I became a navy SEAL. After close to a decade I got out and joined Roman's P.I. firm. Only a few people know I was a SEAL. That's for your ears only. Not because it's a secret, but because I'm a private person and prefer not to talk about it."

So was she. "Understood." It explained so much about him. She opened a fortune cookie. Good luck was coming her way. With Chaz helping her, she could believe it was true. "Are SEALs allowed to have longer hair?" He was so attractive, the question just popped out, causing her to blush.

He smiled at her over the rim of his coffee cup. "No. After I left the service I let it grow again."

The SEALs had an extraordinary reputation for being the most highly skilled and trained amphibious units in the world. She'd talked to several who'd called in to her show before and knew they were deployed for hostage rescues and counterterrorism.

Until now, Lacey had assumed Chaz had come from a background in law enforcement. It made her shiver just to imagine the situations he would have been in as a SEAL.

"Why did you come to Salt Lake?"

"Before my wife passed away, I brought her to the Huntsman Cancer Institute, hoping for a cure. It didn't happen, but Salt Lake has mountains and deserts and four distinct seasons, which I like, so I gravitated back here. However, I'm finding that condo living is getting old. No place to put all the things I have in storage. No yard."

"Tell me about it. I've got boxes and boxes of books and DVDs of old sci-fi TV shows stored, too." As they talked, she realized that if she didn't keep her wits about her, she might forget why he was here.

"Forgive me for causing you any undue stress, but do you have a guest book signed by people who came to your husband's viewing and funeral?"

The mention brought back painful memories, but she had to admit they hadn't been surfacing quite as often these days as they had in the first few months after Ted's death. She realized Chaz needed everything she could provide to do a thorough investigation on her case. "Yes. I'll get it."

"Is it in storage?" he asked quietly.

She bit her lip. "No. Everything's still on a shelf in my closet with a few of the programs from the funeral."

"I'd like to look at one of those, too."

"Of course. I'll get everything for you before I go to bed. By the way, please feel free to use the guest bedroom. I'll show you. Ruth doesn't stay here on weekends. The rest of the time you can sleep on the Hide-A-Bed couch in the family room."

He smiled. "That's very considerate of you. Tell you what, if there's a summer storm that threatens to drench me, I'll take you up on your offer. Otherwise, I like sleeping outside. I can hear things better."

Like her stalker creeping around...

After they finished eating, she got up to clear the table. He helped her, but she wished he wouldn't because he stood too close to her at the sink and she was afraid he could hear her heart thudding like a jackhammer. In a few minutes she sat down again and pulled the laptop toward her.

"I've been making up that list of people you asked for."

He poured himself another cup of coffee. "Let me hear what you have on your core group."

She handed him the big photograph. "I listed their names in order from right to left."

He studied it as she read him the information. After listening, he said, "You travel in some impressive circles. I've heard of several of these people. It appears they all have substantial credentials and in some cases have put in years at their various professions."

"They're exceptional. That's why it's so hard to imagine any of them having a dark side."

Chaz put the photo down. "Unfortunately all human beings have that potential. Go ahead and tell me about the rest of the people on your list."

Lacey read the sketches. None of them sounded or seemed capable of doing harm to anyone, let alone to her. She couldn't fathom it, but the fact remained some-one was out to kill her.

"So far you've talked about colleagues and college personnel, the people at your former radio station, friends you and your husband did things with socially, church friends, extended family on both sides. You've made a good beginning. Now I need the names of your neighbors here in the complex, your landlord."

"Of course. I forgot all about that."

"Don't worry. It's my job to help you remember. What about childhood friends?"

She blinked. "You mean like an old girlfriend?"

Chaz nodded. "And guy friends. Some you might have played Kick the Can with." He lounged against the counter drinking the hot liquid.

"No guy friends like that. Just Jenny and Brenda, who were my two closest friends from grade school, and still are my very best friends. I forgot to put their names down. They come to as many paranormal con-ferences as they can. The three of us were science-fiction nuts from the beginning. We formed a club in high school our sophomore year called the Bengal Al-golans."

A heart-stopping smile started at one corner of his mouth. "How many belonged to *your* club?"

She laughed because he knew too much about her already. "Eight on a good month. We'd read science-fiction stories out loud and watch science-fiction mov-ies. After I got my driver's license, we would head out to Great Salt Lake with my telescope."

His dark brows lifted. "A good one?"

"Very good. Expensive. My parents gave it to me on

my fourteenth birthday because they knew how much I loved astronomy."

"I read your dedication to them in your book. Your sentiments were understandable."

Lacey nodded. "Daddy died of a lung clot soon after that." Her eyelids prickled. "Anyway, when the club went to the lake, we'd roast hot dogs and look for meteors coming close to Earth."

"For Percy?" he prodded.

Lacey loved that he knew so much about her novel, but she realized he'd read it as part of his investigation, no other reason.

"The birth of my restless Algolan happened the first night we were out there and I saw a shooting star spike through the heavens like a javelin. As I watched, I thought, what if that star was really a meteor that someone from outer space was riding to reach Earth?

"At first I wrote Percy landing in Great Salt Lake, but I soon discovered the lake was too small to give him enough scope for all his underwater powers. Worse, the heavy salt water clogged up the holes behind his ears, interfering with his transmissions to and from Algol."

Something flickered in the recesses of Chaz's eyes. "Your mind continues to fascinate me. So do your teenage exploits. While some teens are out at night getting into earthly trouble, you and your friends were out daring aliens to come and visit. Put your friends' names on the list with phones and addresses."

"Except for Jenny and Brenda, I haven't seen those other kids from the club since we all graduated from high school."

"I still want a full list," he insisted.

Her throat tightened. "But surely you don't think

any of them would—" She stopped midsentence. Now that she knew he'd been a SEAL for the past ten years, she realized he would be thorough to the extreme, considering every possibility in order to save her life. She should be thankful for that. She *was* thankful.

Taking a quick second breath, she typed in all the names and added the information he'd asked for. "I'll print the list for you now."

"While you do that, I'll leave to get another key made for your front door. When I come back later on tonight, I'll be able to slip into the condo without disturbing you."

"Oh—" She'd forgotten about giving him a key. Of course he'd need one.

Her purse was on the counter. She jumped up from the table and walked over to get it. After finding the keys, she took the one in question off the ring. "I'm sure you're anxious to get going." Lacey didn't want him to think she was hoping he'd stay longer, but when she handed the key to him, he looked at her so strangely. "What is it, Chaz? Have you thought of something else?"

"No. This will do for now," he said, but he sounded far away. When they reached the front door, he turned to her. "What's your schedule like tomorrow?"

"I was planning to take Abby to Mother's and stay for lunch."

He nodded. "I'll be out of your condo early in the morning, so if you're not up when I come back tonight, we'll touch base tomorrow and get together." After a slight pause he added, "I need to get acquainted with Abby and we have more to discuss. For your information, I listened to the message on your landline in the bedroom earlier."

"I didn't realize." The mention of it made her feel ill.

"I traced the call. It came from a public phone at a casino in Reno, Nevada. Think about anyone you know who might have visited there recently. Your stalker gets around. Good night."

"Good night."

Lacey locked the door behind him before sagging against it. She couldn't think who would have been in Reno or anywhere near there. The deeper timbre of his voice had sent a little shiver down her spine. In a minute she pulled herself together and retrieved her laptop.

Being as quiet as possible, she hurried through the condo to her bedroom. While she printed the file she'd been creating, she went to her closet for the funeral guest book and program he'd requested.

Her high school and college yearbooks were on the same shelf, along with some of her old elementary school yearbooks and scrapbooks. She decided to get everything down for him. She'd put all the items on the dining room table for him to study.

There was no point in waiting up for him. It was none of her business where he was headed after he made the key, or for how long he'd be gone. He could come and go without worry since he had a crew who kept her and the condo under constant surveillance, but she'd sensed he was eager to get going.

He probably had a date. It was the weekend, after all. *And he was gorgeous.* Few women would be immune to him.

Chapter Four

Chaz left Lacey's condo and walked out to the guest parking area, nodding to Adam who was on duty in an unmarked van in guest parking. On a purely selfish level, Chaz hadn't been ready to leave her. But the fact that she'd jumped up so fast to make him a hard copy of her list before she went to bed had prompted him to say good-night. Lacey was tired, of course. Besides being a busy mother and doing a radio show, he knew she had to be emotionally exhausted from fear.

By the time he'd driven off, he had to admit that the strong attraction he felt for her when they were in the same room had him tied in knots. What if the attraction was only on his part?

Her husband hadn't been gone that long. The questions he'd asked her, the mention of the funeral guest book had disturbed her. As she'd told him, she couldn't imagine being with another man. From a professional standpoint, her disinterest in men worked in his favor, but this was one time when he wished the reverse were true.

Since joining Roman's firm, Chaz had been with other women, but he'd never gotten personally involved with a client. It went against the rules. But this case seemed to have been different from the outset. He'd taken it on for reasons tied to that black period in the SEALs, and now he was pretending to be her fiancé.

After spending time with Lacey Pomeroy, more than ever he wanted to catch the person tormenting her. It was fast becoming his raison d'être. But he needed to be careful that *she* wasn't becoming someone of importance to him on a personal level. If he let that happen, then he could lose his edge. Physical attraction was one thing. Emotional involvement was another. Neither had any place in his life while he was trying to catch her stalker.

But after Chaz had gone back to the office and had let himself into the shop to make another front-door key on their machine, he liked the idea that he would be returning to her condo for the night. The thought of his own sterile living quarters left him numb.

An hour later, all was quiet when Chaz used the new key to enter Lacey's place. Even if she wasn't asleep, she'd gone to bed.

He went out onto the deck to inflate his mattress, then threw his sleeping bag and pillow on top of it. Knowing he wasn't tired enough to sleep yet, he went back to the family room where she'd put the printouts and funeral guest book on the table. It pleased him to see the pile of yearbooks and photo albums with them.

On top of the big ones—including a few of her husband's, who'd apparently attended the University of Southern California—there were some brochurelike yearbooks with Lacey's name written on the covers. These would contain valuable information.

Though he could feel his work calling to him, Chaz found himself reaching for the reader he'd left on the table. He couldn't kid himself about certain feelings Lacey had aroused in him on several levels. Those feelings had grabbed hold and weren't about to go away. With a sense of excitement, he scrolled to chapter two of the Stargrazer book, eager to read more.

He soon discovered this was where the female earthling named Olivia came into the story. She was on her way to boarding school in Europe and was in her cabin aboard ship, typing an email on her laptop because she'd just undergone a bizarre incident.

Brenda—at first I thought it was a trick of light, but now I'm positive I saw an angel out on deck!

Chaz rubbed his bottom lip with his thumb. Brenda was the name of one of Lacey's oldest friends. It had crept into her book. What could be more natural? Much as he wanted to go on reading, he was curious to know more about her friend.

He turned off the reader and reached for the list of names and information she'd given him.

Brenda Halverson Nichols. Twenty-eight. Sandy, Utah, address. Parents' home in Cottonwood Heights. Graduate of Bengal High School. Married to attorney Robert. Graduated from University of Utah with master's in theater arts. Part-time actress in various theaters around Salt Lake Valley. Sci-fi lover.

Sandy and Cottonwood Heights were next door to each other in terms of neighborhoods. Chaz's gaze lit on her other friend's name.

Jennifer Bradford West. Twenty-eight. Los Angeles, California, address. Parents' home in Cottonwood Heights. Graduate of Bengal High School. Divorced.

Ph.D. from the University of Southern California, Los Angeles. Professor of English literature at UCLA. Sci-fi lover.

As he'd asked, Lacey had also written down the names of the other six students who'd belonged to the Bengal Algolans Club.

Curious to put names with faces, he opened one of the elementary school yearbooks first. It contained a series of schoolroom pictures taken with the individual teachers. Chaz found Lacey Garvey's name in the third-grade photograph.

She sat in the front row, a cute little redhead with curly locks, reminding him of her daughter. In the second row he spotted Jennifer Bradford. Her blond hair had been put in French braids. At the other end of the row sat a taller brunette with short pixielike hair named Brenda Halverson.

Going from that yearbook, he searched for Lacey's Bengal High School yearbook when she would have been a sophomore. After turning to the section listing the school clubs, he found a half page devoted to the Bengal Algolans Club showing Lacey Garvey as president, looking through her telescope. It resembled the picture of her at the back of her published novel where she had long hair.

Also in the picture were Jennifer, Brenda and six other students, four females and two males. He checked the names against the list she'd given him. Everything lined up exactly as she'd presented it.

The index at the back of the yearbook listed all the names and the pages where the students' pictures could be found. He found four more listings for Lacey: one as a member of the sophomore class, one as a member of the literary club, another in the science club and the last as a reporter for the school newspaper. She'd been a busy girl and obviously an outstanding one.

Brenda had more pictures besides being in the Algolan club. She was an officer in the drama club, a member of the debate club and she belonged to the literary club.

His search for Jennifer turned up three listings of photos besides the yearbook picture. She'd been an officer in the literary club, a member of the Algolan club and sang in the girls' choir.

He put that yearbook aside and reached for Lacey's senior yearbook. The index listed seven pages by her name. Besides being an officer in her favorite clubs, she'd been the top physics student in the state of Utah and had received the Sterling Scholar award. A four-point student, she'd also been the senior-class valedictorian. Last but not least, she'd received a full academic scholarship to Stanford University.

Chaz stared into space. Someone out there in the cosmos hated the fact that Lacey Pomeroy was the girl who had everything.

Maybe it was a man deeply twisted by insecurity who knew she would never give him a moment's notice. Maybe it was a scarred woman begging for the attention Lacey constantly received without even thinking about it.

Out of curiosity he looked up her sister's picture. She would have been a sophomore when Lacey was a senior. All the Garvey women were attractive. Ruth looked the most like their mother. She had been in the ski club and the hiking club.

Lacey resembled her redheaded father. Chaz noticed from the family photographs that Mr. Garvey's deceased brother had been redheaded, too.

He shut that yearbook before turning to the guest book from her husband's funeral. After cross-checking the names against the ones on her list of friends and associates, he made a startling discovery. It appeared that at least ninety percent of the people on her list had either attended the viewing or the funeral itself.

Considering the distances most of them had to travel to Long Beach, the loyalty and devotion to her and her husband was phenomenal. Except of course for the one person who put that death threat on her windshield and might—or might not—have signed the guest book.

He made more notes to himself. Finally he put everything to do with the case in his backpack and carried it out to the deck where he could smell honeysuckle. The scent took him to an earlier period in his life when he had few worries and hormones filled him with longings. This was one of those incredible summer nights.

No one was about outside. Ten minutes later his mind was still percolating with ideas. On a personal level, it was a good thing he didn't have to wait any longer than the rest of the night to see Lacey again. Professionally, he had a dozen new questions to ask her.

When morning came he left the condo early, waving to Tom, who'd taken over for Adam. Chaz drove to his own place to shower and eat breakfast. At 9:00 a.m. he phoned Lacey. Upon answering, she sounded slightly breathless. "Chaz?"

"Good morning."

"You sound wide awake. When did you leave the condo?"

"At six-thirty. I left your door key on the kitchen counter."

"I saw it. Thank you."

"I would have put all your yearbooks away, but didn't know where you keep them."

"No problem. I've already reshelved them in the closet."

"They were a great help. I know you're going over to your mother's with Abby, but I need a question answered. Do you have a minute or are you too busy with her to talk?"

"I can do both. She's playing with her buckets."

"How does one do that?"

"They're different sizes. You fit them into each other. She's still having problems with the medium-size ones, a little matter of visual perception." So spoke the physicist. "But it keeps her busy for five minutes at a time."

He chuckled. "Tell me something. Why did you pick Brenda to be in your book? I've just gotten to the part where Olivia tells her friend she's seen an angel. At the time you were writing your novel, why didn't you choose a name from among your other friends? For instance the other girls in the Algolan club?"

"The Brenda in my novel wasn't named for my friend. That was just a coincidence. It was named for my favorite female Hollywood actress at the time, Brenda Joyce. That wasn't her real name, but the point is, she played opposite Johnny Weissmuller and Lex Barker in the first Tarzan movies.

"I loved Edgar Rice Burroughs's books and watched the films. A lot of people don't know that before he created Tarzan, he wrote all kinds of science fiction with a romantic element I devoured. There was one series called Under the Moons of Mars. It's about a guy named John Carter who lies dying in a cave in Arizona—your home state, as I recall—and he finds his spirit staring down at his body.

"He looks up at the planet Mars and he suddenly finds himself on the Red Planet where he's thrust in the middle of different tribes fighting each other while the air on their planet is running out. Those Barsoom books were the best series! I would always picture Brenda Joyce as one of the Red Planet maidens. She had beautiful blond hair. I hated my hair and dreamed about looking just like her."

Chaz had news for her. Lacey had enough beauty with her face and flame-colored tresses to fill a thousand men's dreams. The excitement in her voice infected him. "Does Brenda know the story behind your choice of the name Brenda?"

"I don't know if we ever talked about it. She and Jen read a lot of the stuff I read and they both knew how much I loved Brenda Joyce."

He sipped his coffee. "Thanks for putting out those yearbooks. They helped me fit names and faces together. I noticed from your sophomore yearbook that you and your friends belonged to the literary club. What went on there exactly?"

"A group of about twenty sophomores, juniors and seniors got together twice a month after school to write short stories and poetry. The head of the English department coached us and then chose the best writings to feature in a magazine put out for the student body at the end of the year."

"How many of your stories made it?"

"Two of them."

"Science fiction, of course."

"Of course." Her laughter brought a smile to his face. "One was about a family that lived in a black hole."

Unbelievable. "And the other?"

"It was a story about Galileo. While he was looking through the lens on the long telescope he built, he suddenly found himself trillions of light-years away. He had all sorts of adventures, but when he returned to Earth, no one believed him."

"I want to read both stories."

"They're in one of those famous boxes in storage."

"We'll have to dig them out. What about your friends' stories?"

"Jenny had several accepted. Brenda wrote a series of poems, but the teacher didn't put them in, which was a shame."

After swallowing the last of his brew he said, "Did you ever read parts of the Stargrazer to the students in the literary club while you were writing your novel?"

"Heavens, no!"

Her reaction surprised him. "Not even to your two best friends?"

"Never. I was too scared."

"Scared?"

"Yes! I was afraid they'd laugh. That novel was a secret. One day I asked the school librarian if there was a book that listed a lot of publishers. She found me one called *Writers' Market*. In there I discovered various publishing houses dealing with all genres of fiction and nonfiction.

"I studied it for days and days and finally sent my story to some different editors of young-adult fantasy fiction who didn't require an agent. When I got a letter back from one of them telling me they were interested, I showed the letter to my mom."

"That's the first she'd heard?" Chaz was incredulous.

"Well, my parents knew I loved to write, but I didn't tell them about that particular story. By then Dad had passed away."

"He would have been very proud of you."

"Thanks. I loved him so much."

"When your book came out, did you give your girl-friends a copy?"

"No. By that time I'd left for Stanford. How would it have looked if I'd said, 'Hey, everyone, see what I wrote while I was in high school!'"

"But what about other people?"

"Not everyone likes science fiction. Did you?"

"Maybe not then."

She chuckled. "It's okay that you didn't like it, then or now."

"I'm crazy about the Stargrazer," he declared and meant it.

"I'm glad, but the truth is, I would never force my writing on anyone."

Lacey didn't have an ego. "So Jenny and Brenda probably went out to buy a copy. What did they say when they read it?"

"By that time Jenny was at UCLA."

"Was she given a scholarship like you?"

"No. She phoned to congratulate me and told me she was blabbing it up to everyone in the English department down there. She was very sweet. As for Brenda, when I was in Salt Lake for Christmas break, she came over to my mom's house with a box of books and asked me to autograph them so she could give them out to her family and friends. She said she was madly in love with Percy."

"She and Roseanne," he teased. "I'm sure that was all very gratifying to hear."

"Coming from my closest friends, you can't imagine."

"When Brenda read your book for the first time, do you think she might have thought you named Brenda after her, rather than the actress?"

"Maybe. I simply don't know."

Chaz pondered her comment. Whatever Brenda thought, she hadn't been the one to write a novel that got published. And if she knew Lacey had put in the name Brenda in honor of Brenda Joyce, she might have taken it as a slight.

Acid on the wound because Brenda hadn't been published in the school magazine? Another failure in her eyes because she hadn't written the bestselling novel created by her best friend? One who'd kept it a secret until it came out and became a sensation?

His thoughts switched to Jennifer. Her name hadn't been mentioned in the book. Did it bother her that Brenda's name had slipped in? Jenny was an English professor. If she'd always wanted to teach English at the college level, then it meant she had to publish to build tenure.

It might have been a blow to learn that Lacey had gotten published while she was still in high school and had never told anyone. A big enough blow for seeds of envy to burst out of control?

While his mind kept coming up with more thoughts

and questions, she said, "Do you mind if I ask why you want to know?"

"It's not a case of minding, Lacey. Right now my thoughts are darting to and fro about the people on your list and I'm thinking out loud. When was the last time you saw Jenny?"

"At a paranormal conference in Houston in April. Mother watched Abby."

"What about Brenda?"

"She went, too. We flew down together."

"Does she have children?"

"Not yet, but they're trying."

Chaz paced the floor. "Have you seen Jenny since then?"

"No. We've had too many deadlines and she lives in Los Angeles."

"How about Brenda? How often do you see her?"

"Every two weeks or so. Sometimes not that often if she's doing a play. She came over last Saturday and we watched some DVDs of *Otherworld*. I'd ordered them off the internet."

"I haven't heard of that show."

"It was a sci-fi series made for TV years ago, but only played for one season. We loved it."

"You'll have to put it on for me to watch."

"Anytime."

"I'm going to take you up on that. Now go enjoy your daughter and call me later after you're home from your mother's. Then I'll come over."

"We'll be back by four. Mom has plans with her church group for the rest of the evening."

"In that case I'll be there then. I'm anxious to meet Abby and get to know her while we talk about the case."

"I'll be here and supply the leftovers from dinner. Mother's lamb roast is to die for."

"You shouldn't have told me," he murmured. "I'll be salivating all day."

He hung up, wondering how he was going to make it until he could be with her later. At the same time he was trying to wrap his mind around the idea of professional envy being a motive for the death threats. It was a thought he'd entertained from the first moment he'd heard Lacey had her own radio show.

Brenda Halverson Nichols lived right here in Salt Lake. She and Lacey had been joined at the hip from childhood. She'd signed the guest book at the funeral. Brenda was supposed to be one of Lacey's best friends, yet Lacey hadn't said anything to her or Jenny about her novel until after she'd gotten published. Not only published, but honored with prestigious awards that led to a sci-fi radio show.

Were either of her friends the type who believed a real friend shared *everything?* What was the old adage about jealousy? It's a tiger that tears not only its prey, but also its own raging heart.

If Brenda were an actress at the very top of her game, why wasn't she onstage in New York instead of having to settle for less by doing part-time theater here in Salt Lake? Over the past six years of attending various sci-fi conventions with Lacey, who'd become so prominent, had Brenda developed a raging heart from coming in second best on all fronts?

Was there enough anger to welcome Ted's death and

go gleefully after Lacey, whose life no longer looked so rosy without her husband? How would she react when she heard Lacey was engaged? For the moment, Brenda Nichols was emerging at the top of his list of possible suspects.

Jennifer came a close second. She'd been at the funeral. Though she'd distinguished herself, she didn't have Lacey's celebrity status. A professor at UCLA was impressive, yet she wasn't the girl who'd won a four-year academic scholarship to Stanford. Her marriage had ended in divorce.

Three friends from childhood, yet only one shining star nationally acclaimed in radio and fiction writing. Interesting that of the three of them, Lacey was the only one with a child. A sweet little daughter any would-be mother would yearn to call her own.

But these were early days and he knew this was only the tip of the iceberg.

After reaching his office, questions continued to bombard Chaz while he dug up more information on her core group of friends he'd be meeting next weekend. The knowledge that he'd be spending the weekend with her brightened his mood despite the seriousness of the case.

Chapter Five

Despite the ever-present menace, Lacey returned to her condo at ten to four, more excited than she should have been because Chaz would be arriving shortly. She moved Abby's small white table and chair from her bedroom into the family room, where she could draw on her pad with her colored markers. That way she could see her mommy working at the dining room table.

Her little girl loved to dance and wear frilly skirts. As soon as they walked in the door, Abby ran to her room to play dress-up. She added her butterfly wings and a garland, which she plopped at a tilted angle on top of her curly red hair. When she smiled at Lacey with Ted's light blue eyes, she melted Lacey's heart.

Earlier Lacey's mother had helped paint Abby's finger- and toenails a scarlet pink. Abby had covered both arms with red ink valentine tattoos from her little set of stamps. Her play lipstick went beyond the lines of her rosebud mouth. That was the sight to greet Chaz when Lacey let him in the condo. He carried his backpack and wore jeans and a blue T-shirt revealing a well-defined chest.

Her daughter got up, carrying her magic wand, and walked over to them. Lacey looked down at her.

"Honey? This is my friend Chaz. He was the one who gave me this ring. Can you say hello to him?"

"Hello," she said in a small voice.

While Lacey shut and locked the front door, Chaz got down on his haunches. The smile in his eyes matched the one on his striking features. "Hi. What's your name, sweetheart?"

"Abby."

"Are you a princess?"

"Yes. I'm Princess Butterfly Abby. I can fly." With that, she ran around in her bare feet, flinging her arms.

Chaz's deep-throated laughter filled the condo. Lacey loved his laugh. Abby loved the attention. She circled the room several times, then stopped in front of him. "Abracadabra," she said, pointing her wand at him. "You're a frog!"

"Don't feel slighted," Lacey whispered to him. In a louder voice she said, "Abby? Go get Mr. Frog and show Chaz."

"Okay. Don't leave, Mommy."

"I won't."

Still staying in character, she flew down the hall. Chaz's gaze swerved to Lacey's. His eyes were dancing. "I've never seen such a cute little girl in my life."

Lacey almost said she'd never seen such a gorgeous man in her life, but Abby saved her from making a complete fool of herself by running back into the living room. She stood in front of Chaz, hugging her frog tightly.

"He's your favorite animal, isn't he, honey?" Lacey said.

Abby nodded.

"What does Mr. Frog say?" he asked her.

She made the best frog sounds she could with all the intensity she possessed. Lacey had been working on it with her. Again Chaz laughed and clapped his hands as if she'd given a marvelous performance. "You sound just like a frog. Come on over to the couch. I have a present for you."

That word caught her attention in a hurry. "What is it?" She followed him.

He sat down and pulled a doll out of his backpack. The minute Lacey saw it, she let out a little cry of delight. "A nesting doll—"

Chaz flicked her a glance. "My boss's wife says she raised their daughter on one of these. When you told me about the buckets, I thought Abby might like this. Roman comes from Russian descent and sent me to a shop where they're imported."

He undid the top of the doll and another doll just like it was inside. Abby stood there fascinated while he kept finding another smaller doll. When he'd finished, there were seven dolls lined up on the cushion.

"Those are going to keep you busy for a long time, honey. Can you say thank-you to Chaz?"

"Thank you, Chaz." But already she was trying to figure out how to fit all the parts together. "Look, Mommy, a teeny baby." *Teeny* was one of her favorite new words.

"Yes. Isn't she sweet? She looks just like her mommy. Come on. Let's put these on your table," Lacey suggested.

Chaz helped pick up the fourteen parts. Pretty soon Abby was working away at her new project, the frog and drawing pad forgotten. He assisted her to find the right bases for the right tops. Watching them interact caught at Lacey's heart. Abby thanked him every time he put another one together. Like Chaz, Lacey's daughter had a brand of charm that got to you.

As she stood by and watched, she sensed Abby wasn't the only one having fun. "I've warmed up your dinner, Chaz. Come into the other room whenever you're ready." As promised, she'd brought home the leftover lamb roast and everything that went with it.

The three of them spent a pleasant evening together. By the time Abby got out of the bath and put on clean jammies, she wanted Chaz to read her a story about the buzzing bee. It was one of her favorites from her birthday in May.

The week before, she'd gotten stung by a bee on her leg and needed to show Chaz and talk about it. When he turned to the last page, it made a big buzzing sound and surprised him. His exaggerated cry for Abby's benefit caused her to go into gales of laughter. She couldn't stop. He opened and closed the last page half a dozen times, delighting Lacey, too.

"Okay. It's time for bed. Say good-night to Chaz."

"G-good night, Chaz." She was still giggling.

"Good night, sweetheart. Here's Mr. Frog." He put the toy in her arms.

"Thanks." She waved bye-bye and grabbed the tiniest nesting doll before going with Lacey.

CHAZ HADN'T BEEN KIDDING when he'd told Lacey how cute her daughter was. In reality, *cute* wasn't the right description. She was adorable. Smart. Creative. Even at three years of age, she had an amazing sense of humor. With those red-gold curls bouncing just like her mother's against the pink candy-stripe pajamas, she came close to looking and acting like an enchanting angel.

When he thought of the death threats against the two of them, the blood in his veins turned to ice.

"Chaz? Is anything wrong? You have a fierce look on your face."

He jerked his head around, unaware Lacey had come back to the family room. "I want to catch the person who's threatening yours and Abby's happiness." Chaz eyed her solemnly. "She's a precious little girl."

Lacey sat down opposite him. "You made a big impression on her. Did you notice she took the baby doll to bed with her?"

He would have told her yes if her old cell phone hadn't rung. She'd left both cells on the table. "Do you recognize the caller ID?"

"No," she said, sounding frightened.

"Answer it and we'll see what happens. Be sure to put it on speakerphone."

She picked it up and clicked on. "Hello?"

"Lacey?"

"Oh, hi, Ken. I didn't realize it was you calling."

Remembering there was a Kenneth on her coregroup list, Chaz reached for the printout and read the information on him again.

"The juice went out on my cell, so I'm using the phone in the front office. I'm glad I caught you. How are you?"

"I'm good. And you?"

"Couldn't be better. Are you flying to Albuquerque this coming weekend?"

"Absolutely." Chaz watched her, noticing how hard she was trying to sound upbeat.

"That's what I wanted to hear. I was hoping you and I could go out to dinner after the seminar on Saturday night. There's this Mexican restaurant with the greatest mariachi band you ever heard."

Chaz checked his picture in the group photograph. Ken Simpson was the biochemist from Indiana and looked to be in his early forties. Was this the first time he'd asked her out?

"Ken, much as I'm flattered by the invitation, I'm afraid I can't. You see…" She lifted her eyes to Chaz. "I just got engaged."

Lacey was a remarkably quick study. Naturally she would be, with her intelligence. *And* her life on the line.

The silence coming from the other end needed no translation. Then, "You're teasing me. Right?"

"No. Why would I do that? His name is Chaz Roylance. He'll be coming with me."

"I guess I don't understand. I wanted to take you to dinner at the last conference, but when I spoke to Brenda about you, she said you needed more time because of Ted."

Lacey flinched visibly. "I didn't know you'd had a conversation with her. I'm sorry about this, Ken."

"So am I," he said with a tinge of bitterness. "I had no idea you were seeing anyone else. I guess Brenda was covering for you."

"She doesn't know about Chaz yet. You're the first person I've told besides my own family," she answered honestly.

"Is he from Salt Lake?"

"No. California."

"Someone you and Ted knew?"

The guy was starting to lose his cool. Chaz shook

his head. "Don't tell him anything else," he mouthed the words. He wanted to see just how anxious the other man would get if she refused to tell him everything.

Lacey's eyes went a smokier blue. "Ken? I have to put my daughter to bed now, but I'll look forward to seeing you at the conference."

"It's debatable whether I'll attend."

"Please don't say that. We've been friends for years. The group wouldn't be the same without you."

"Don't patronize me, Lacey. Surely you realized I was interested in you."

"As a colleague." She gripped the phone tighter. "You've always been an integral part of the group. That's why I'm hoping you'll be at the conference. I really do have to hang up now. Good night." White-faced, she rang off and jumped up from the table. She stared at Chaz in anguish.

"You handled him perfectly."

"Then it was an accident. I've never once suspected Ken wanted to take me out. I don't understand why Brenda didn't tell me."

Chaz had his own theory about that. "If there were no stalker, would you have said yes to him, if only as a friend? He's nice looking."

She shook her head so fast Chaz sensed she was telling the truth. "When he asked me to dinner just now, I was thankful to be able to tell him I was involved with someone else. I don't want a personal relationship in my life. After Ted…" Lacey stopped talking, reminding Chaz once again that deep inside she was still mourning her husband's death.

"You wrote down here that Ken's divorced. Do you know for how long?"

"I think about two years."

"Do you know the reason for it?"

"He told the group that he and his wife had irreconcilable differences. Just now he came off sounding so angry. It wasn't at all like him."

Chaz raked a hand through his hair. "Speaking from a male point of view, I would imagine he's been attracted to you for a long time and thought he finally had a chance. After what Brenda told him, finding out you're suddenly engaged would disappoint any man anxious to start a relationship with an extraordinary woman such as yourself."

She grimaced. "Extraordinarily weird, maybe. I know that's what a lot of people think about me. I never dreamed my interest in the paranormal would put me or my daughter in this kind of danger." She clutched the back of the nearest chair. "After that conversation with Ken, I guess it's possible he's been the one making those death threats."

"Possible, but not probable. I see he signed the funeral guest book. He wants to date you, not terrify you. Since this was the first time he asked you out, he didn't know you would reject him. I doubt very much he put that note under your windshield wiper, which means he didn't make the threatening calls. Remember, they're all of a piece."

Lacey's eyes flashed blue fire. "No matter the answer, you're a genius to have suggested this mock engagement. I would never have seen this side of him otherwise. What I find strange is that Brenda never told me he'd talked to her. She's had plenty of time to tell me. The last conference was in April. I'm beginning to wonder if I know anyone as well as I thought I did."

Chaz was glad to see the blinders were coming off. The more she started thinking outside the box, the more useful she would be in helping him solve her case. "You could ask her the next time you talk to her."

"I intend to."

"While we're on the subject of Brenda, I need to make a reservation to fly to New Mexico with you two."

"I'll take care of it now. You'll need a hotel room, too."

She sat back down in front of her laptop. He reached into his wallet for his credit card and handed it to her. In a few minutes she said, "It's done, but I don't think the three of us will be able to sit together."

Chaz put the card away. "I suppose I can sacrifice long enough to sit alone for the flight there. But I insist on being seated next to my fiancée for the return trip."

She blushed, bringing the color she'd lost during the conversation with Ken back to her lovely face. Her reaction secretly thrilled him because it might mean she wasn't completely disinterested.

In a lightning move she got up from the table. "Thank you for the gift for Abby," she said. The quick change in subject told him she was oddly rattled. "It went beyond your job as a P.I."

"I like doing things for little girls with bouncing curls."

Lacey averted her eyes. "You made a friend tonight."

"Your mother made a friend of me. I'll thank her later, but in the meantime please tell her how much I loved the roast. I'll eat her leftovers anytime."

She smiled. "I'll let her know. If you'll excuse me, I'm going to bed."

Chaz realized Lacey Pomeroy had a lot to think about. So did he. "I'll be heading for the deck myself in a few minutes. Get a good sleep. Remember, you're safe."

"Who keeps *you* safe?" came the question before she disappeared too fast for him to answer.

Funny, no one had ever asked him that before. It was as unexpected as she was. Unexpected, and growing on him in ways he couldn't stop even if he wanted to.

His thoughts darted to Ken, the first of her core group to be knocked sideways by the news of her recent engagement. Pleased that his plan had already produced a reaction, Chaz decided to celebrate. What better way than to reach for the reader on the table and continue reading her novel. All day he'd been waiting to get to it.

At first he thought he'd read only another chapter before calling it a night, but forty-five minutes later he was still immersed in her tale. He stopped a chapter before the end of the book. This story was more than a good read. Young-adult readers would find it sensational.

He could have finished it, but forced himself to save the last chapter for tomorrow night. When it was over, there wouldn't be anything else of hers to read. Except that wasn't true. Besides her school-magazine stories, she said she'd written other novels, but hadn't finished them. They were probably in storage. He planned to help her dig them out.

More than ever he understood why Roseanne had begged her to do another story. She'd wanted Lacey to write a sequel. Chaz would read it with equal enjoyment. There wasn't anything about Lacey he didn't enjoy. Like her radio show, there ought to be a warning for simply being around her—If you have a tendency to suffer from heart failure, we advise that you proceed with care since we will not be held responsible.

He got up from the table feeling both drained and exhilarated in a way he couldn't describe. After using the guest bathroom to brush his teeth, he made certain everything was locked up before shutting off the lights.

A man could get used to evenings like this. After he got ready for bed, he lay down on top of the sleeping bag wearing the bottoms of his sweats. It was too warm to cover himself. The fragrant night air called to him. The only way this scenario could be improved was if someone were to join him. A someone who'd created a fantasy world he longed to live in with her while they made love for hour upon hour.

CHAZ LEFT THE CONDO AT quarter to seven the next morning. It was already warm. He'd listened to the weather forecast and found out the temperature would climb to the nineties before thunderstorms moved in later in the day.

He could see clouds starting to gather over the mountains. Maybe he'd be sleeping on the couch tonight. Driving out to the main street, he phoned Tom, who was doing surveillance in the van. "What have you got for me?"

"It's been quiet."

"Things will have to pop before long."

"Agreed. I'll bring the tape in when I'm off duty at three."

"Thanks, Tom."

After stopping by his place for a shower and change

of clothes, he caught up with his friends at the Cowboy Grub for breakfast. It wasn't far from the office. They often met there to kick back and talk shop.

This was one time he wanted some input, but he was late. When they saw him walking toward their table, Travis, a former Texas Ranger, motioned the waitress over for more coffee. "Roman told us you're working a stalking case."

"It's a beaut!" Chaz sat down.

Mitch, who'd been a federal marshal in Florida before moving to Salt Lake, pushed a plate of bacon and scrambled eggs toward Chaz. "He said your client is that radio sensation who does the UFO stuff. What's she like in person? A little wacko?"

"I know what you're thinking. It's the same thing I thought before I met her."

"*Before* being the operative word?" Mitch drawled. Both men smiled, waiting to hear what was coming.

"If you want to know the truth, Lacey Pomeroy is the personification of any man's fantasy." Her little three-year-old would grow up to be just as beautiful and charming.

"That's the trouble with the best-looking women," Travis grumbled. "There's always a catch. Does she really think the government has a couple of ETs hidden under lock and key at Area 51?"

Chaz couldn't help but chuckle. "No, but if it were true, I assume she'd want to be the first person to break the news to her listening audience. How's your latest case going?"

Mitch made a face. "I'd rather think about your new assignment than the mail-fraud business I'm working on."

Travis finished off his coffee. "I feel left out. Roman's going to assign me to a new one when I get to the office. Use us while you can, Mitch."

For the next while Mitch brought them up to speed. Then the topic switched to Chaz. "Any new leads yet?"

"Just theories. I'll find out more when I go to this UFO conference with her this weekend."

Both men grinned. "We might as well let you know Roman told us your news."

"What do you mean?"

"That you're engaged."

"Come on, guys. You do what you have to do."

Mitch burst into laughter. "You sly dog."

"She must be something." Travis's eyes danced. "I'm afraid everyone in the office has seen her picture on the radio station's Ionosphere website and is betting that she'll end up your wife. You could have saved yourself the trouble by marrying her instead."

"You're right," Chaz admitted, "but she's still in love with her dead husband's memory. That would have been pushing it."

"What are your theories so far?"

He eyed them more soberly. "She's a celebrity who's written a *New York Times* bestseller, and she has the fourth leading paranormal radio talk show in the country. Lacey has two best friends who date back to elementary school and go to those UFO conferences, too. With a track record like she has, envy and jealousy for her success could give them opportunity and strong motives to see her harmed."

"That's true." Mitch pursed his lips. "Over that many years in a friendship, you pick up a lot of baggage along the way, good and bad. Some you can't slough off."

"My thoughts exactly," Travis echoed.

"But it's early in my investigation. There's this guy named Ken she's known for six years who had a meltdown on the phone when she told him she was engaged. But I didn't sense built-up rage behind his reaction."

"Maybe not at her." Travis winked. "But if he shows up at that conference, watch your back."

The three of them chuckled while Chaz finished off his eggs and bacon with a Danish.

"What's the gender ratio in this group?" Travis asked.

"Seven men, five women." Chaz had their profiles memorized down to their ages. "All are successful and in some cases prominent. Some are married, others divorced or single. Some have children."

"You've got your work cut out for you, but with the list you've compiled so far, I'd still wager the culprit's someone who has known her through thick and thin," Mitch reaffirmed. Then his phone rang, and he answered it.

After he clicked off, he stood up. "I've got to run. Stay in touch, guys." He shot Chaz a wicked glance. "Don't get any permanent ideas about that engagement business. You'd break up our triumvirate. We can't let that happen." He threw some bills on the table and took off.

Trust Mitch to zero in on Chaz's private thoughts about Lacey. He wasn't known around the office as the bloodhound for nothing.

Travis checked his watch. "I'm going to be late for a meeting with Roman I can't miss." He pushed himself away from the table and got to his feet. "I'll buy tickets if you want to catch the soccer game at Rio Tinto on Thursday. Six o'clock. Real Salt Lake is playing Dallas."

That was why Travis was excited. Once a Texan, always a Texan.

"Count me in for three."

His eyes lit up. "Yeah?"

Chaz grinned. "Yeah. May the best team win. Thanks, Travis. Put your money away. I'll take care of breakfast. I owe you for last time."

Chaz watched his friend walk off, but his mind was focused on the very real possibility that one of Lacey's childhood friends wanted to injure her. Perhaps not physically. Mental torture could cause horrendous fear and grief.

Why not use fear to force her to give up her radio show so she would disappear from the public eye for good? What better way to pay Lacey out for imagined sins.

The latest statistics proved that less than half the female stalking victims were directly threatened by their stalkers. Instead they were bombarded with threatening phone calls and letters.

He knew for a fact that more often than not female stalkers targeted professional contacts they hated or envied and were less likely to harass strangers than men. Female stalkers were also more likely to pursue victims they knew, who were of the same gender.

Chaz had already ruled out a lot of people on her list who didn't fit the profile, but Lacey's best friends *did*. The harassment had started at Ted Pomeroy's funeral when she would be her most vulnerable. It seemed his death had triggered the beginning of long-awaited plans of torture.

"More coffee?"

"No, thank you."

He paid the waitress, then left the restaurant. Once he reached the office, he had more research to do and planned to pore over the latest surveillance tapes before going back to Lacey's home. His pulse picked up speed just thinking about seeing her and Abby.

"MOMMY! THAT'S CHAZ!"

As Lacey was removing her daughter from the car seat, he walked up to them dressed in tan chinos and a white polo.

It certainly was.

The moment she saw him, she felt that weakness in her legs again. They both must have pulled into their parking spaces at the same time. "Hi!"

The green flecks in his irises seemed to be more intense all of a sudden. "I'd say this was perfect timing." His gaze looked alive before it swerved to Abby. Lacey had just put her down so she could walk. The three of them headed for the stairs of the condo. Chaz gave her his full attention. "How's the butterfly princess?"

"I went to the libary."

The way his lips twitched at her daughter's mispronunciation caused Lacey's heart to kick. "Did you find a book you liked?"

She nodded. *"Pooh Bear and the BEES."*

He shared a smiling glance with Lacey, recognizing her daughter wasn't over the bee incident yet. "Did you bring it home?"

"Yes."

"Will you read it to me?" Chaz asked.

"No. Peach."

"Who's Peach?"

Lacey opened the door to her condo and they went inside. "Today my daughter is Peach, her favorite starfish from the movie *Finding Nemo*. She'll look at the pictures and tell you her own version of the story."

His eyes held a gleam. "We know where she gets her creativity from."

"But we don't know if she'll have an interest in UFOs. When she grows up, it will be just my luck if she writes a book denouncing me as a fraud."

She loved his rich male laughter. Abby didn't know the reason for it, but she laughed, too.

"Come on, honey. I'll warm up your mac and cheese. Would you like some, too, Chaz?"

"No, thank you. I had a late breakfast with some colleagues."

"I see. Then how about coffee? Lemonade?"

"In this heat, lemonade sounds good."

Abby climbed onto one of the dining room chairs with her Pooh book. She didn't like sitting in her high chair anymore, so Lacey had given it to the couple living in the unit below hers. They had a two-year-old and a new baby. Abby's high chair had been a welcome gift.

Chaz took a seat next to Abby. While he listened to her quaint version of the story complete with sound effects, Lacey served up lunch with some fruit, milk and lemonade. He dared Abby to eat her apple slices. She did, then he ate one, and they entertained each other eating up all the fruit with Abby laughing hilariously. For a man who'd never had children, Chaz was a natural with her.

In the midst of the laughter, the doorbell rang. Chaz shot her a glance. "Are you expecting anyone?"

"No."

"Go ahead and get it."

Lacey wiped her mouth on a napkin and got up from the table. When she opened the door, there was her striking friend whose black hair had been cut in a Cleopatra style for the play she'd been in at Pioneer Memorial Theater.

"Brenda—" Her voice caught. They'd known each other since third grade, but the terrorizing phone calls had turned her life inside out and she couldn't act natural with her friend.

"I know you weren't expecting me, but I had to come. Is it true you're engaged?"

"Guilty as charged." In the background she could almost hear Chaz telling her not to let on anything was wrong. "Come on in."

Once inside, her friend's brown eyes caught sight of the engagement ring. "You really are engaged!" She grabbed hold of Lacey's hand and studied it for a moment. "It's beautiful! Ken called me this morning and told me. I simply couldn't believe it!" She gave Lacey a warmhearted hug. "I'm so happy for you, I can't stand it. When did all this happen?"

Lacey would have answered, but Chaz came into the living room with Abby, who ran straight for Brenda. They gave each other a big hug before the little girl suddenly darted out of sight.

"Brenda Nichols, I'd like you to meet Chaz Roylance. I've told him our friendship goes back to childhood. He knows about you and your marvelous acting career."

"I'm pleased to meet you, Brenda." He shook her hand.

"She's just finished doing Shaw's *Caesar and Cleopatra*," Lacey explained.

"I'm impressed."

Brenda's gaze had been fastened on Chaz. There was a lot to take in. All of him was beyond attractive. After a minute she turned to Lacey. "Poor Ken. He never stood a chance anyway, and now…this." Her arms flew toward Chaz in a dramatic gesture.

That was the icebreaker for Lacey, who laughed out loud. "Poor Ken is right. How come you didn't tell me he wanted to go out with me?"

"Lacey…" She made a funny face. "How can you ask me that? Every time I bring up the subject of a man who'd like to meet you, you ask me to leave it alone and don't want to hear it. I knew you'd never had an interest in Ken, so I decided to stay quiet."

"Sorry I've been so difficult."

"I understand. Months ago I tried to put him off the idea of approaching you. But I didn't know about *this* man. Ken really took the news hard. If he comes to the conference this weekend, he'll probably wish he hadn't." She flashed Chaz a broad smile he reciprocated.

"Look!" Abby ran up to Brenda. She was hugging Chaz's present.

"Well, well. Diamonds and nesting dolls. I can see there's been a lot of excitement going on in *this* house."

Abby couldn't get the top open. She handed it to Chaz to help her. He undid it and soon she'd pulled all the dolls apart and had put everything on the couch.

"Here's the teeny baby." She handed it to Brenda to look at.

"Oh. She *is* teeny."

"Come on, honey." Lacey gathered her daughter. "It's time for your nap. Tell everyone you'll see them later."

"Okay. Bye, Chaz. Bye, Brenda." She took the baby with her.

Lacey sent Chaz a private glance. "I won't be long."

"Take your time. I want to get to know the friend who went out to the Great Salt Lake with you looking for meteors through a telescope."

Brenda's wide mouth broke into a grin. "I'm afraid my curiosity over you is even greater than yours about me. *I* want to hear the details of how you two met and how long this has been going on behind my back. This is an even bigger secret than her famous novel she never told anyone about!"

With her heart pounding until she felt sick, Lacey left to put her daughter down. When she returned to the living room ten minutes later, she found the two of them standing at the front door. He was telling her about his intention to start up a landscaping business.

Chaz saw her. "Brenda has to leave." To her shock, Chaz motioned her over and put his arm around her shoulders, drawing her close. Her breath caught in reaction to the first physical demonstration of affection from him. Heat stormed her face. Not only because he'd caught her by surprise, but because she liked being in his arms and wished it weren't an act.

"Brenda has agreed to let me sit with you during the

flight down. That's a real friend for you." He kissed her hot cheek.

Brenda put a hand on Lacey's arm. "I told him I wouldn't tell anyone else about your engagement. You can surprise everyone at the conference yourself. It'll be bigger news than a new UFO sighting." That drew a chuckle from Chaz.

"Unless Ken has already said something," Lacey murmured.

"I doubt it. He was pretty broken up."

"I didn't mean to hurt him."

"Of course not, but he obviously thought you knew how he felt. Maybe he's obtuse and that's what went wrong in his marriage. Anyway I told him you've always operated on a different wavelength so he shouldn't take it personally. But enough of that. I've got to run. I'll see you both on Friday morning at the airport. Congratulations again."

When she'd let Brenda out and closed the door, she found Chaz staring intently at her. "Was the Brenda I just met the Brenda you've always known?"

"Yes. If she's my stalker, she's the greatest actress alive, but then acting is her profession."

"You did a superb job yourself. If she's the culprit, then she left disappointed because you gave nothing of your terror away."

"I don't know how long I can keep this up."

His black brows furrowed. "Why? What is it?"

"Oh, just something she said. I would never have picked up on it if there were no stalker in my life. I've become paranoid."

"Like what?"

"She said I operated on a different wavelength.

We've been close for so many years, her comment came as a surprise because I don't know how she meant it. But I *do* know one thing no matter what. I love Brenda. She couldn't be the stalker, Chaz."

"Is it like her to just drop in on you?"

"When we were teenagers, yes, but since our marriages, she's always phoned me first and I, her."

"Ken's call caused her to do something out of the ordinary. In time we'll see if your friend has claws."

"I don't believe it." But a shudder racked her body anyway.

"Have you brought in the mail yet?"

She shook her head. "I'll get it now. Then I need to do some work before tonight's radio program."

"Is there anything I can do to help?"

A wry smile broke out on her face. "Not unless you want to read the book on Sasquatch I brought home from the library. The author is going to phone in tonight and be a guest. I need to read through it again. Especially the parts where he believes Sasquatch is one of the beings from another planet brought here as an experiment to see how they adapt."

"I'm looking forward to listening to the program."

His words said one thing, but the way he was looking at her was saying something else. Her bones had turned to water. Lacey could still feel the weight of his strong arm around her shoulders. He'd played the part of her fiancé just right. So right, she could almost believe they were really engaged. She hated that she felt so breathless.

"I'll be back in a minute."

She grabbed the keys from her purse and hurried outside to the mailbox. The usual stack of stuff was in there. Lots of brochures from scientific institutes and publishers of UFO fiction, a new catalogue of DVDs from Sinister Cinema where she'd ordered her Buck Rogers series. In the back was a package of vintage time-travel books.

When she returned, Chaz took the bundle from her and went into the family room to sort it out on the table. He went through the mail methodically. "The post office must know you well."

Lacey sat across from him. "I'm afraid so. I've been collecting paranormal material for a long time. One day years from now, I'm going to open my own sci-fi shop where people can browse and listen to old recordings, watch old videos and find books that have been out of print for years."

"It'll be a huge hit with all your fans."

"Right now it's just a dream. I've been looking into ways of preserving everything, but unfortunately today's methods are already obsolete. It's almost impossible to know where to start."

"But you'll try," he teased. "Here's a letter to you from the Albuquerque UFO Seminar Committee."

"Oh, good. After I got their first mailing a month ago, it occurred to me they didn't have Ed Margolitz on the docket to speak. I emailed them to find out why." She opened the creased envelope. "I hope this says he's going to be there."

"Will you shoot me if I ask you who he is?"

She laughed. "No. He's renowned for being the foremost authority on government conspiracies concerning UFOs." But when she unfolded the letter, there was nothing on the paper but two sentences typed in caps.

YOU'RE GOING TO BURN UP WHEN YOU
REACH ALBUQUERQUE. THAT'S NOTHING
COMPARED TO WHAT WILL HAPPEN TO
YOUR FREAKIN' DAUGHTER.

Chapter Six

When Chaz saw the blood drain from her face, he sprang from the chair and came around to read the letter himself. His torso brushed against her hair, sending a shock wave through his body.

"Don't touch the letter or the envelope, Lacey. Do you have any plastic bags? You know the kind."

She nodded and got up to find him some.

"I need tweezers if you have any."

"There's a pair in my bathroom." She returned with them seconds later.

He used them to carefully fold the paper over and place it in one bag. In the other, he slid the envelope. It had been postmarked last Friday from Albuquerque. "You told me the note you found on the windshield a year ago was done on white paper in caps." The author had used the word *freakin'* in other threats, as well. "This establishes a positive link between both time frames." His hunch had been right.

"Then it means I've been watched for a year now." Her voice shook.

"One way or another." Chaz clenched his teeth. "It's going to end soon." He needed to find the person responsible for causing so much chaos and pain in Lacey's life.

"Who's your contact on this committee? I'll need an address and phone number, too."

She looked up the information on her laptop and wrote it on a piece of paper. "How could he or she be in so many places?" she asked.

"Give me time and we'll get the culprit."

She nodded and handed him the paper.

"Thank you. When is your mail usually delivered?"

"Around one."

If Brenda was the stalker, then her unexpected visit might have been timed to see the state Lacey was in after opening her mail. Using Ken's phone call as the reason for dropping by would be a clever move on her part.

He wanted to take a look at today's surveillance tape. It would show the mailman filling the boxes. How soon after he'd left had Brenda arrived at the condo? Had she been out in her car waiting?

"I'm going to drop these off at the crime lab." Maybe there were no fingerprints for them to lift, but it was worth a try.

"What are you thinking, Chaz?"

"I'll tell you later." He squeezed her hand before he realized she might see the gesture as stepping over the line. He'd done it automatically. "Hang in there. You're doing brilliantly."

When he'd left the condo and reached his car, he phoned Tom. "How soon will your relief be here?"

"Half an hour."

"Come straight to the office. I need to analyze today's tape ASAP."

After going to the forensics lab downtown, he headed for work. On his way back to the office, his phone rang. He saw the caller ID and picked up. "Lacey?"

"I—I was just checking my email and there was another death threat."

"Read it to me."

"'Beware, you freakin' bitch.'" Her voice trembled. "'Life has been too easy for you, but aliens are going to take care of you and there's nothing your fiancé can do about it.'"

Though he knew it had terrified her, this couldn't be better news. "I had a hunch the engagement was going to be the catalyst to make things come to a head sooner."

"But only a few people know about it."

"Ken's had time to spread the word."

"Oh, Chaz—I'm scared."

"I know, but this is simply more of the same thing. We're getting closer. Don't forget. You've got protection right outside your door. Do you want me to phone your mother and ask her to come over?"

"No. Now that I've talked to you, I'm okay. Thanks."

"Call me anytime, Lacey, and I mean *anytime*."

"I will. Talk to you later."

He clicked off and parked behind the office. After hurrying inside, he found Roman testing out a new monitoring device his brother's spy-technology company had invented. Chaz knocked on the open door. His boss looked up. "Come on in. How's the stalking case coming?"

"Things have started to heat up since the word got out we're engaged. Lacey received a new death threat by email a little while ago." The stalker was clearly someone from her core group to have heard the news so quickly. "I need your help."

"Name it."

"It will require the authority to look through the records of the Albuquerque UFO Seminar Committee. The records are probably located in someone's home. This is Lacey's contact." He put the paper she'd given him on Roman's desk.

For the next few minutes he went over the details of the case. "The stalker got hold of their official envelope, or had one made up to look exactly like it. I want to go through their phone bills, email and check dates and times of their mailings.

"I need to know if they have a lot of envelopes on hand they use from year to year. Do they print their own or use a printing service? Who has access to the supplies, one person or several? In the meantime the crime lab will call and tell me what they find out about the note. I'm hoping for a fingerprint, anything they can find."

"I'll talk to Chief Mahoney and see what strings he can pull for us with the Albuquerque Police Department."

"Thanks, Roman."

Chaz went back to his office to watch the tape Tom had brought in. It had filmed the mailman pulling up in his minivan at ten to one. Brenda got there at quarter after two. She wouldn't have known when Lacey went out for the mail, but she could have been on a fishing expedition all the same.

Before Chaz knew it, the day was gone. Hungry for dinner, he picked up some pizza with salad and drinks to go before heading to Lacey's condo. He bought some cinnamon bread sticks, too. Abby might like those.

Adam had parked his surveillance van in the guest area. His presence gave Chaz peace of mind and was helping Lacey get through this without falling apart.

Chaz pulled into the stall he used. After grabbing his backpack, he hurried up the stairs with the food, eager to be with her and Abby. Hopefully he'd get some time alone with Lacey after the program. The predicted storm front had moved in. Gusting winds were so strong that when he unlocked the door, it blew open to reveal a woman standing in the living room.

As he stepped inside and shut it, he didn't know who looked more surprised, he or Lacey's sister. He knew her from the yearbook and photographs placed around the living room, plus the photo Lacey had given him to scan.

"Sorry if I startled you, Ruth. I'm Chaz Roylance. Nice to meet you." He shook her hand.

Beneath shoulder-length strawberry-blond hair, her sky-blue eyes swept over him. "You look like one of the studs I saw on a P.I. show last month."

That was direct. "Hopefully it won't be too long before I catch Lacey's stalker."

"It's probably a guy she never noticed and the rejection crushed him. Lacey has a tendency to do that. Just cut the dude's heart out."

Chaz was glad Lacey had told him about her sister's unique personality. "Then again it could be a woman who'd been in love with Ted and couldn't take it when he married Lacey."

She put her hands on her hips. "Then she told you about Shelley."

Shelley? "No. I was only throwing out another possible scenario."

"You must be psychic."

"Why do you say that?"

"Because this one was obsessed with Ted and continued to be up to the time he died."

Chaz weighed her comment before he said, "I'll ask her about it. Excuse me while I put this food on the dining room table."

Ruth followed him into the family room. Unlike Lacey, she was blunt and very much aware of herself. He'd met attractive women with an attitude who liked to challenge a man on a first meeting. She was one of them, standing there in a light green tank top and jeans.

He judged her to be a couple of inches taller than Lacey, who stood five foot five. Of the two, Lacey was the more curvaceous. Ruth was good-looking, but compared to her sister… In truth he couldn't think of another woman who came close to possessing Lacey's stunning attributes.

"Do you like your job?"

What a question. He lowered his backpack to the floor. "I do. Every case is different."

"I'd be curious to know what the odds are of you catching this pathetic person."

"A hundred percent."

She smiled. "Wow. A man totally sure of himself. Most guys like to *pretend* they are."

"So do most women. Where your sister's and Abby's lives are concerned, I'm deadly earnest about my job."

To his surprise she gave a little mock shiver. "You've convinced me." She was flirting with him. There was no law against it. Ruth was single. Lacey would have told her he was a widower.

But Ruth had several strikes against her. Besides the fact that she was Lacey's sister, she didn't appeal to him. Since he'd see her coming and going, he needed to strike the right balance with her while he was doing his investigation in order not to offend her.

"Is your sister putting Abby down?"

"Not yet. She's getting ready to go to work."

"Then I'm not too late. I brought treats for them."

"Abby's watching *Dora*."

"Is that a film?"

"It's a children's program," Lacey answered, having just come in from the living room. "I thought I heard a voice, but Abby picked up on it first. She said, 'Mommy, that's Chaz!'"

He liked hearing that.

Lacey's little girl was right behind her, hugging her toy frog. When she saw Chaz, she made a happy sound and ran over to him in her pink princess jammies. Without conscious thought, he swept her up in his arms. She smelled sweet like her mother. "Where are your butterfly wings?"

"I can't find them."

He chuckled. "Would you like a surprise?"

Lacey's gaze met his head-on. "You're spoiling her."

"Am I bad?" He grinned.

She smiled back. "Yes, you are."

"Has she had dinner?"

"Luckily, yes."

"What's my surprise?" Abby wanted to know.

He put her down and opened the box of warm cinnamon bread sticks. "Go ahead and try one."

She reached carefully for one, looked at it for a minute, then took an experimental bite. "Mmm." Her eyes lit up. She took another bite and finished the bread stick off in no time. "Thanks."

He eyed Lacey, who'd put on a silky peach blouse with a beige wraparound skirt. With her coloring and figure, she looked sensational.

"There's food for all of us, Lacey."

"I didn't realize you'd be bringing dinner home. That's very thoughtful. I hate not being able to join you, but I had to eat early because I need to get down to the station and set things up for tonight's guest. Come on, Abby. Now that you've had your treat and seen Chaz, it's time for bed. Let's brush your teeth."

"Come on, Chaz." Abby pulled on his leg.

"No, honey," Lacey said. "He has to eat his dinner. Say good-night."

"Okay. Good night, Chaz. Good night, Auntie Ruth."

"Get a good sleep."

When they disappeared, Chaz turned to her. "Have you eaten, too?"

"No. I barely got here before you blew in."

He remembered unlocking the door before the wind blew it wide open. "So I did," he said with a chuckle, still aware of the weather getting nastier out there. He didn't like the idea of Lacey driving to work in it. "Please join me, then. I don't want this food to go to waste. It's never as good the next day."

"You're right. Thanks. This beats peanut butter and jelly." She sat down opposite him and they began to eat. "Lacey told me about the latest threats. She's asking for it by doing the talk show here. I think she's a fool."

He detected impatience in her tone. "People have to work."

"She doesn't have to do this kind. It's put Mom out. You would have thought she'd have given it up after she got the first threat down in Long Beach. But she loves the limelight too much to worry about Abby, who dreads it every time she leaves for work. Dad would turn over in his grave."

"Your father wouldn't approve of her radio show?"

"Hardly," she muttered. "He was the most private man I ever knew. I wish he were still alive. Life would be very different if he hadn't died."

"In what way?"

She darted him a chilly glance. "Lots of ways that are none of your business, even if you are a P.I." Then she smiled. "You've got enough on your plate dealing with Lacey's problem. She's been a mess without Dad."

Not Ted?

Ruth puzzled him. Her mind really wasn't on Lacey's stalker. In fact, he felt a disconnect here that wasn't normal. Finding the culprit was uppermost in the minds of most family members of the victim, but Ruth was focused on herself. In less than a minute her mood had changed from being accusatory to angry to introspective and defensive. It all seemed to be tied up in thoughts about her and her father. He could hardly keep up.

"Even so I find your sister to be a strong woman."

"That's because *you've* been hired." Her eyes lingered on him.

"No, she has inner resources and a little charmer who needs her. That helps her cope. You and your mother have the same kind of strength, otherwise you wouldn't carry on as you do in the face of this stalker. I admire you for coming over here to tend Abby."

"Lacey said you've put her under constant protective surveillance. Knowing that, it isn't hard for me to stay here. The stalker isn't after me and I need the money."

The coldness of her comment didn't sit well with him. "It's still a frightening proposition and takes courage, even if you *are* a gutsy pilot."

Her brows went up as if she was surprised he knew about her job. "An unemployed one at the moment."

"I hope that changes for you soon. In the meantime I know Lacey's grateful you're able to be here for Abby."

As he finished off another piece of pizza, Lacey came back into the family room. "Abby's asleep. Goodbye, you two. I'll be home at twelve-thirty."

Chaz got up from the table. "There's going to be a downpour pretty soon. Since Ruth is here, I'll drive you to the station and watch you in action."

"You don't need to do that."

He put his hands on his hips. "It's part of what I do." If she knew the strength of his feelings, she'd probably run a mile.

Her eyes rounded. "All right, then." She looked at her sister. "Thanks for watching Abby. I couldn't do this without you."

Ruth didn't say anything. After what she'd shared with Chaz, he deduced that tending Abby helped pay a few bills but wasn't a labor of love on her part.

Chaz brought his bedding into the kitchen from the deck and locked the sliding door. After picking up his backpack, he headed for the front door. Lacey followed. They hurried down to his car where he helped her inside. Once he'd stowed his pack in the trunk, he got in behind the wheel.

The second he started the engine, the rain descended in a torrent accompanied by lightning and thunder. Lacey's eyes flicked to his. "We made it to the car just in time. I'm glad you're driving me tonight," she whispered.

He struggled to catch his breath. "So am I. This hasn't been an easy day for you and now this storm. It'll be fun to sit in on your show."

"I'm afraid you'll die of boredom."

"Want to bet? Do you have that library book with you?"

"It's in my bag, but thanks for reminding me. I've tucked notes all the way through to help me remember the questions I need to ask my guest."

"I have no doubt you could wing it if you had to. When we arrive at the station, go ahead and introduce me as your fiancé." Being her fiancé sounded right to him and was sounding more right all the time. The line he wasn't supposed to cross had disappeared.

"It'll be a huge surprise to everyone there."

"I think it surprised your sister." He was still trying to sort out his impression of Ruth, who'd come off sounding narcissistic.

"Except that she knows the reason for it and she likes you."

His hands tightened on the steering wheel. Had Lacey said that to remind him their engagement was only temporary? The heat of frustration permeated his body. If she was going to start playing Cupid, he had news for her. "What makes you say that?"

"She would have gone to her room otherwise."

"It was the food. She was hungry."

No. It was much more than that. Ruth was interested.

Lacey had seen the deflated look on her face when Chaz insisted on driving Lacey to the station. With the slightest encouragement from him, her sister would go in pursuit. Ruth had probably never met a man who was larger than life before.

If Lacey was being honest with herself, neither had she.... When she'd awakened this morning, her first thought had been of Chaz. She had to face the fact that he'd become very important to her and she wanted him to feel the same way. Abby was already crazy about him.

"Have you ever been to a soccer game, Lacey?"

The subject was totally unexpected. She darted him a curious glance. "No."

"Would you like to see one?"

"Probably about as much as you wanted to read a young-adult fantasy. Both activities have to be acquired tastes, but since it's *you* inviting me…"

An unmistakable gleam of satisfaction entered his eyes, thrilling her. "We need a break from the stress. I have another ticket for Abby. Might as well get her started early."

A real family activity. She hadn't done anything like it for over a year and had trouble hiding her excitement. "I take it you love soccer."

"I'll always love American football, but I've been around the world with the SEALs, and soccer's the only game in town. It's on Thursday at Rio Tinto Stadium. Starts at six. Real Salt Lake is playing Dallas. If Abby gets too restless, we'll leave early. We can still get you to the radio station on time for your program."

"Abby and I would love to go. That part of my education has been neglected too long. Thank you."

Though some maniac was after her, Chaz had burst into her life with all the power and speed of a stargrazer. He'd brought an energy foreign to her. She couldn't get enough of it. *Of him.* She wanted to go with him, be with him.

When she'd seen the way Ruth had looked at him back at the condo, she'd almost warned her sister that Chaz was off-limits. It was a primitive emotion, one that really surprised Lacey because she'd never known such a possessive feeling before. She'd never been a jealous person, but the thought of him being with anyone else…

"We've arrived." His deep voice broke her train of thought. "While there's a lull in the storm, let's make a dash for it."

"I'm afraid we don't have a choice, anyway. My guest for the show is waiting for a phone call."

He came around to her side and helped her out of his Forerunner. Together they ran for the door. It hadn't been much of a lull. Once inside the building, they shook off the rain and smiled at each other.

Chaz was so handsome. "There you are, looking like the underwater SEAL you used to be, while I…well, let's just say this is why I don't do a TV show."

His hazel eyes reflected pleasure as they roamed over her hair and features. "You're beautiful wet or dry."

The huskiness in his tone sent scorching heat to her face. She murmured a thank-you and headed down the hall, her pulse racing. She needed to let Stewart know she was there.

Kurt was in the broadcast room doing his show. All seemed well until she saw her normally happy intern. When she appeared in his doorway, she caught sight of him standing at his desk looking anxious and unnerved. He was on the phone with Barry because she heard him say the producer's name. When he saw her, he dangled a fax in front of her.

It proved one thing. Stewart wasn't her stalker. There was no way he could fake a demeanor like that or his loss of color.

Before she could blink, Chaz stepped forward and took the fax from him. Knowing she'd just received another threat, she would probably have suffered an anxiety attack if Chaz hadn't brought her to the station. He was always so calm.

Instead of showing it to her, he said, "Go ahead and make that long-distance call in your office. I'll join you in a minute."

Thankful for Chaz, she went through to her office. During the conversation with her guest, she had to concentrate, but it was hard to do when she could see into Stewart's office. The two men talked the whole time she was on the phone.

Once she got off, she made her way to the broadcast booth Kurt had just vacated. Soon she was on the air. The Sasquatch topic had the lines jammed with callers. For the next three hours, Lacey was forced into the paranormal world she loved.

Chaz stayed in Stewart's office. Every once in a while he caught her eye. The warmth in his expression was the only thing that kept her going. Somehow she made it through the program. When she was off the air, he came to the door of the booth to hustle her out of the building.

They swept past the night watchman, trying to avoid the puddles left by the cloudburst. It had passed over, but you could still hear rumblings to the south. He helped her into his car.

On the drive home he glanced over at her. "That was a great show. You're a real star, Lacey. I don't mean in the celebrity sense, though you are that. I'm talking about the professional way you handle yourself in the face of terror."

"You know very well it's a facade." She rubbed her arms. "What did the fax say?"

"The same kind of threat. Barry told Stewart he'd handle it and asked him not to discuss the incident with anyone. I told him that as your fiancé, I won't let anything happen to you. It's clear he was genuinely horrified by the fax."

"How cruel for this to affect his work, too."

"If anything, he's worried for you. While you were doing your show, I traced the fax back to the Cowboy Mart in Evanston, Wyoming. They provide a customer fax service. Because of privacy issues, they couldn't tell me who sent it. Even if I'd had access, it wouldn't be the real name of your stalker."

Lacey shifted several times. "When did it come through to the station?"

"Three o'clock this afternoon."

She groaned. "How can the threats come from so many places almost at the same time?"

"This person is probably getting help."

"Two people?" she cried in panic.

"It's only a possibility. Let me worry about it."

"Every time a new threat comes, it wears me down a little more."

"That's the stalker's purpose, but you're not going to cave. Stewart told me the station has never had more callers for your show. He has nothing but praise for you and sent his congratulations on our engagement."

Her hand shook slightly before smoothing some hair away from her temple. "About the engagement—"

"It's working like a charm," he broke in. "Your stalker is losing control of the situation and it's showing."

Lacey's racing heart was proof that her feelings for him were also getting out of control.

The flash from the fake diamonds in the ring reminded her of the dangerous game she and Chaz were playing.

When he caught the person or persons menacing her—and he would, she had no doubt of that—she'd have to give the ring back. Then he'd be out of her life and on to a new case that had nothing to do with her.

Better get used to the idea, Lacey. Better not get too comfortable. Better focus.

Chapter Seven

Chaz felt disappointment when he walked into the condo with Lacey and saw that Ruth was still up watching TV in the family room. He'd hoped for a few more minutes of privacy with Lacey before they said goodnight.

"Hi," Ruth called out from the couch.

"Hi," Lacey said in a quieter voice. Chaz wondered if she was also disappointed Ruth was still up. "How did it go tonight?"

"Abby never wakes up. You had a call from Jenny. When I saw her caller ID, I picked up and caught her so she wouldn't have to leave a message."

"Did she say what she wanted?"

Chaz listened to them talk as he put his backpack next to his bedding, which was resting against the sliding door to the deck.

"She was ticked off that she had to hear about your engagement from someone else. You're supposed to phone her in the morning."

"I'll call her." Lacey's gaze swerved to Chaz, who by now had gone to the sink for a glass of water. "I guess Ken was more upset than I thought."

"Or maybe Brenda couldn't hold back from telling the news to her other best friend," he murmured.

Ruth turned off the TV and came into the kitchen. "Ken? Isn't he the rocket scientist?"

"No. That's Derrick. Ken's the biochemist."

"Why would he be upset?"

"He called the other night to ask me to dinner after the seminar on Saturday. I told him I couldn't because I just got engaged."

Ruth eyed her speculatively. "Maybe he's the one who's been harassing you." Her gaze flicked to Chaz. "What do *you* think?"

"The man is on my list of suspects."

She lounged against the counter in a pose meant to be provocative. "Is it a long one?"

"Until I find your sister's stalker, everyone is on it."

"I guess that includes *moi*."

"Don't ever say that!" Lacey rushed over to hug her. "Not even in jest. Thanks for tending Abby. I don't know what I'd do without you and Mom."

"Or your fiancé?" Ruth smiled at him over Lacey's shoulder.

Her younger sister had what he would politely describe as a cheeky attitude. It was in her makeup to push an issue or a man to the edge. The woman didn't recognize boundaries. Maybe he was wrong, but he suspected she'd stayed up late in the hope of talking to him once Lacey had said good-night.

"Abby will be up early. I don't know about you, Ruth, but I'm exhausted and am going to bed." Lacey turned to Chaz. "I'm afraid the deck might be too wet for you tonight. The family room is all yours."

"Thanks. Good night, you two." He purposely included Ruth in his glance. "I'll lock up and turn off lights."

Glad to see Ruth leave with Lacey, Chaz checked the deck. The rain had lowered the temperature to the seventies. Perfect for sleeping and the boards were dry enough. He preferred staying outside.

Perhaps it wasn't fair of him, but he wouldn't put it past Ruth to saunter into the family room early in the morning on some pretext of getting a bite to eat or a drink. Chaz didn't want to be caught lying there and be forced to talk to her. And he certainly didn't want Lacey to get the wrong idea if she saw them together.

He felt sure Ruth wouldn't have any qualms about opening the door to the deck tomorrow just to say good morning if it were just the two of them, but she might think twice about it with Lacey in the house. How ironic that he was staying here to protect Lacey, yet he found *himself* needing to be cautious when it came to Ruth.

Chaz had been around women like her before. Lacey hadn't needed to tell him her sister liked men.

Checking to be sure the front door was locked, he turned out the lights and got ready for bed. Once *inside* his sleeping bag for a change, his thoughts remained on Lacey and her sister. What was it he'd studied about the sibling bond? It was life's longest relationship, outlasting parents, spouses, even best friends.

He hadn't grown up with siblings, but knew they weren't minor players on the stage of life. They went through distinctive emotional periods. Besides rivalry, they experienced longing, hero worship, shame, envy, jealousy, tenderness and feelings of obligation.

One comment from a prominent psychologist claimed

that a sibling could be your sweetest companion or your worst enemy.

Your worst enemy.

Ruth's own comment about being on the suspect list—a comment that had upset Lacey—was troubling him. When he thought about it, except for Mrs. Garvey, Lacey's longest relationship had been with her sister. Longer than her association with Brenda and Jenny.

Curious to know more about her, he phoned Lon, one of his backup crew.

"Chaz? What's up?"

"Sorry to wake you. Can you be at Lacey's place by six in the morning?"

"Sure."

"Tom will be on duty to watch her and Abby. I need you to keep an eye on her sister, Ruth. You have a picture of her. Strawberry-blond shoulder-length hair, five foot seven. She drives a red 2009 Mazda with Idaho plates. Check on her registration and do a police background check. If she leaves the condo in the morning, go wherever she goes and check in with me."

"Will do."

"Thanks, Lon."

Chaz had no idea how Ruth spent her time when she'd exhausted her job search for the day, but to do a thorough investigation, he had to find out. According to Lacey, her sister was out of work and looking for employment with an air cargo company. For the time being, Lacey didn't need to know he was having Ruth followed.

Lacey… If all went well tomorrow, he had plans for her and Abby.

The next morning he left Lacey's earlier than usual.

To his surprise, Lon rang him at eight while Chaz was leaving his own condo to drive to the office. He picked up. "Have you got something for me already?"

"Ms. Garvey is the owner of the Mazda. She's clean. No arrests, no warrants out on her. She left the condo at ten after six and stopped at a drive-thru for breakfast. I followed her to the small airport at Salt Lake International. She parked her car and walked over to one of the hangars to talk to a guy who looked to be in his late twenties. From there they got into a Cessna Skylane and took off, with him at the controls.

"I phoned Roman. He used his airport sources and learned they were headed for St. George, Utah. The pilot's name is Bruce Larson. His home base is Idaho Falls, Idaho."

Lacey had said she'd heard her sister talking to a Bruce on the phone. Obviously they'd met in Idaho. "You're the best, Lon."

"What do you want me to do now?"

"Nothing more at the moment. What's your schedule like tomorrow? Is one of the other guys using you?"

"No. I'm free."

"Unless you hear from me, plan to do the same thing in the morning, same time."

"Will do."

Chaz hung up, wondering what the pilot was doing at Salt Lake International. It cost money to fly all those places unless he was doing a cargo run. Were they lovers? Had Ruth gone along for the ride while she was waiting for a job offer to come through?

When he let himself into the office, Roman was in the back room drinking coffee. He flashed Chaz a smile. "You've been busy and keeping everyone else busy, too."

"Tell your wife I'm sorry I had to wake you so early with that phone call."

"Comrade," Roman said with his Russian accent, "that is the name of this *beezness*. She understands. Doing *beezness* for her was how we met."

Chaz couldn't help but chuckle. "Things are starting to happen."

Roman pointed at him. "That's because of you. Grab a cup of java and come into my office. I've got news from the crime lab about the envelope and note you took in for analysis. They sent a fax."

A few minutes later Chaz lifted his head from the paper. "Latent fingerprints weren't distinct, but they found two hairs in the envelope, one four inches long, the other seven."

Roman nodded. "Read on."

"'Test reveals the hairs are human, Caucasian, blond with traces of red pigment containing pheomelanin. The hairs have been treated. Blond hair can have almost any proportion of pheomelanin and eumelanin, but both only in small amounts. More pheomelanin creates a more golden-blond color, and more eumelanin creates an ash blond.'"

Chaz let out a whistle. "Whether male or female, whoever put the death threat in that envelope could be the stalker. The problem is, I don't know if the hairs were already inside it when the stalker got hold of it. What about the Albuquerque police, have they come up with anything?"

"Chief Mahoney said he'd get back to me when he's had word. If he hasn't called by this afternoon, I'll give him a ring. Obviously the information from the UFO committee is critical."

Chaz paced in front of Roman's desk, drinking his coffee. "Whoever put the note in the envelope probably used gloves, but they didn't notice that two hairs were either already in the envelope or fell into it as they worked."

"Every criminal makes a mistake somewhere," Roman muttered. "This may be the evidence you need to crack the case."

Adrenaline surged through Chaz's body. "Depending on what we learn from the Albuquerque police, the hair color could narrow the field by a huge margin." When he flew with Lacey to Albuquerque, he'd get a firsthand, up-close look at every blond man or woman in her group, including any on the UFO planning committee.

"I've got to go. Talk to you later, Roman."

On the way out to his car, he bumped into Travis. His friend pulled some tickets out of his pocket. "I got us good seats."

"Excellent." Chaz drew a few bills from his wallet to pay for them. "Who's coming?"

"Roman, Rand and Eric with their families, Mitch and I, Lisa and Jim. And you with your…" His eyes danced.

"The jury's out at the moment." Chaz couldn't solve this case fast enough. He wanted to be with her in a nonprofessional way. "Thanks for getting these. Why don't you surprise everyone and bring a date."

Travis paused in the doorway. "Your surprise is going to be enough for one night." He still hadn't gotten

over the loss of his wife, who'd been murdered in a revenge killing. Who could? "See you later."

THE SCREAMS COMING FROM the other part of the condo
had Lacey racing from the kitchen to reach her daughter. Abby came flying down the hall in hysterics.

"Honey—" She crushed her in her arms. "What's
wrong? Tell Mommy."

Her little girl actually shook and thrashed about, still
screaming so hard she couldn't talk.

"Abby, sweetheart—"

The next thing she knew Chaz's hard-muscled body
filled the hallway. She hadn't heard him come in.
"What's happened?"

At the sound of his deep voice, Abby turned her
tear-drenched, splotchy red face to him. "A big bee!"
She reached for him and buried her body against his
broad chest. He wrapped his strong arms around her
and rocked her while she sobbed.

When Lacey had recovered from her fright, plus
from the fact that her daughter had automatically
sought Chaz's protection, she said, "Where did you
see it?"

"I-in the w-window!" She half hiccuped the words,
pointing to her bedroom before she hid her face in
Chaz's neck once more.

"Mommy will get it."

"No!" Abby screamed again.

"Honey, I'm not scared of the bee. You stay with
Chaz."

Her daughter's cries followed Lacey into the bedroom. When she reached the locked window where
Abby had been arranging her nesting dolls along the

sill, she saw a wasp outside, climbing on the other side of the glass.

Though Lacey knew it couldn't hurt her, it was black, and the sight of it was a surprise to her, too. She could just imagine how terrifying it looked to Abby, who still wasn't over the fright from her bee sting.

She hurried back out of the room. Her eyes fused with Chaz's searching gaze before she reached for Abby. "That bee can't hurt you." She covered Abby's face and hair in kisses. "He's outside."

"No. He isn't!" she insisted.

"Yes. Chaz will go in the room first and show you. That mean old bee can't come in."

Abby practically strangled her as they followed him into the bedroom. "Chaz—" she spoke softly "—if we don't help her through this, she won't go to sleep in here. That would be another nightmare I don't want to live through."

"Message understood," he whispered back. "Yup. I can see him, Abby. He's outside the window, just like your mommy said. He can't come in, sweetheart. Do you know what I'm going to do?"

She was still trembling. "What?"

"I'm going outside to kill it. Do you want to watch?"

Abby clung tighter to Lacey. "Yes."

"Okay. Stay right where you are." His eyes flicked to Lacey's. "There's a ladder in the surveillance truck. See you in a minute."

They stayed right where they were. Abby kept her head burrowed against Lacey's chest. Before long, she saw Chaz at the window, former navy SEAL performing the kind of surgical maneuver his training had taught him. For a uniform, he wore a dark blue sport shirt and gray chinos. He had an incredible physique and was an eyeful in whatever he wore.

"Look at the window, Abby. There's Chaz. He's waving to you to come over."

"Where's the bee?" She probably didn't realize her right hand was pinching Lacey's arm.

"It's dead. He wants to show you. Shall we go see it?"

Slowly Abby nodded. Lacey took a few steps closer. Chaz's smiling face transformed him into the most attractive man she'd ever seen in her life.

"Hi, sweetheart." He held up a rag with the wasp lying on it. "See?" He picked it up and put it in his hand. "He's dead!"

Abby finally believed it and the tension went out of her body. "He won't come back?"

"Never!" Chaz promised her. "Shall we flush him down the toilet?"

"The toilet." She laughed hilariously.

"That's where we put all bad bees," he told her. "Do you want to watch?

"Yes."

"Okay. Just a minute."

The hero of the hour returned before Lacey could blink. He went into the guest bathroom. Lacey stood by the door with Abby. "One, two, three." He let the wasp fall into the water, then he flushed it away before smiling at her. "He's all gone."

"Let me see." Abby got down and hugged his leg while she looked. "He's gone, Mommy," she said in her bright little voice.

Even though it was just a bee, the incident had caught Lacey with emotions that were already raw.

"Yes," she said in a tear-filled voice. "The mean old bee is gone." Her wet eyes lifted to their hero.

"Oh, Chaz..." Without conscious thought she took a step to hug him. She needed his solid warmth to work through the moment. "What would I have done if you hadn't been here?"

With his arms enveloping her, he crushed her against him. "You would have handled it like you've been doing since she was born, but I'm glad I was here. I've never been a parent, but when I heard her screaming, it terrified me and gave me a taste of what it would be like."

He kissed her hair and temple. "She's a priceless little thing. Though we haven't known each other very long, I love your daughter."

His admission tugged at her heart. "I love her, too. That's why I'm so grateful." Suddenly Lacey realized where they were and what she was doing. He'd done a lot more than help Abby through an emotional moment. He was saving Lacey's sanity. Embarrassed to have let her feelings explode on him like this, she eased out of his arms.

"Come on, honey." She reached for Abby's hand and walked her into the living room.

Chaz trailed them. "I have an idea. What do you say we go get lunch, and then play at the park. The temperature is up in the low eighties. Not a cloud in the sky. After last night's storm, it's perfect weather."

Lacey looked down at her daughter. "Do you want to go to the park with Chaz?"

"Yes." She clapped her hands.

He leaned over her. "Do you have a ball?"

Her nod caused her curls to bounce. "I'll get it." She ran out of the room.

They both watched her disappear. "Thanks to you, she's not afraid to go to her bedroom," Lacey said.

Chaz studied her upturned face. "To make certain this doesn't happen again soon, your landlord needs to be called. I saw some wasp nests beneath the eaves. They should be knocked down and sprayed."

"You're a lifesaver in more ways than one. I'll call his number right now and leave a message."

Abby came back as Lacey was hanging up the phone. She had her big-girl bag stuffed with some of her toys.

In a few minutes Lacey had collected a blanket and they left for the drive-thru where they could park beneath a covered area to eat. They agreed that if they didn't eat food at the park, maybe the bees would stay away.

Lacey drove her car because it had the car seat in the back. This was the first time she'd taken Chaz anywhere. So far he'd done everything for her. She loved the idea of being able to reciprocate.

After they'd eaten, she headed for the neighborhood park dotted with plenty of trees. They found shade on the grass next to the playground and set out a blanket. Lacey had brought some bottled water from the fridge.

Chaz watched as she put sunscreen on her and Abby. "Considering your gorgeous coloring, that's a good idea. The sun's hot out here."

She kissed Abby to hide her reaction to his choice of words. "We redheads have to be careful."

Her daughter found the ball in her bag and rolled it to Chaz. He rolled it back and a game was on. She would try to catch it before it whizzed past her. Abby was in heaven. So was Lacey. They took turns playing catch.

For a little while she could pretend nothing was wrong in her world.

Next, Abby wanted to swing. She pointed to the swing set. "Come on." With those fast legs of hers, she darted toward them. But the seats were too big and she had trouble getting in.

Chaz reached one and invited Lacey to sit on it. "I'll swing you both." He put Abby in her arms. "Ready?"

"Yes!" Abby squealed in delight.

He started out with care to make sure she was handling it, then he pushed a little harder. At one point the swing went high enough both Abby and Lacey cried out in excitement. Lacey could hear Chaz laughing behind them. When the swing went back to him that time, he caught them in his arms. "Got ya."

Abby giggled, waiting for him to let them go again. Lacey's heart was pounding out of control because Chaz's cheek was against hers. Being cocooned in his arms, her back was pressed into his chest where his heart beat just as hard as her own. It made her so aware of his masculinity, she felt desire, hot and unmistakable, curl through her body. She almost lost her breath. If he hadn't been holding on to them, she would have fallen.

He must have realized what was happening to her because he let them go gently, otherwise they would have gone flying. When the swing came to a stop, Abby wanted to go again, but Lacey needed to recover from being in Chaz's arms and stepped to the ground. She set Abby on her feet, as well.

Avoiding his eyes she said, "I'm thirsty. Shall we go get a drink?"

"Chaz, swing me!"

"Say please, Abby. Maybe he's thirsty, too."

"Please."

Without a word, he sat in the swing and put Abby on his lap. While he entertained her daughter, Lacey walked back to the blanket and sank down, still trembling from the experience. Not since Ted had she felt this alive.

She'd wanted Chaz to kiss her. Her face went hot because she knew he knew it. That's why he'd been so quiet.

It hadn't been a full week, yet already she couldn't imagine her life without him. Though a stalker was after her and her fear was very real, Chaz had taken away her terror. In its place something else was growing. She didn't dare put a name to it because once she did, she'd want it too much.

Just as she was thinking the sun was too hot, Chaz and Abby walked back to the blanket. "Here's your water, honey." She undid the cap.

Abby plopped down by her toy bag and reached for the water. Chaz lay down on his side and propped his head in order to drink his. What a beautiful man.... He was close enough Lacey could feel his warmth and breathe in the scent of the soap he'd used.

She felt his gaze travel over her body. She'd dressed in a simple cream top and jeans, but he clearly liked what he saw. "Did you get a chance to talk to your friend Jenny this morning?"

Though his eyes were on her, his mind was on her case. He could do two things at once. She had an almost impossible time focusing on anything but him. "I caught her before she left for the university."

"How did she find out about the engagement?"

"When she phoned Mom in an effort to find me, Mom told her."

"Was she happy for you?"

"Cautiously pleased. Her divorce has jaded her somewhat. She warned me it was awfully soon to jump into marriage again. Why be in a hurry for something that might not work out a second time?"

Chaz frowned. "She really was hurt."

"That's because her ex-husband had an affair on her."

"Did you see it coming?"

Lacey smoothed some hair out of her eyes. "No. I really liked Mark. They seemed to be crazy about each other. His infidelity came as a shock to everyone."

"I'm sorry for her."

"Me, too."

"Is she coming to Albuquerque?"

"Yes. I didn't realize her dad's going through chemo for prostate cancer. She's going to fly back here after the conference and stay with her parents for a couple of weeks. She wants to get together. That's why she called."

"Then I'll have an opportunity to meet her."

Lacey winced. "Jenny isn't the one, Chaz. I just know she isn't."

She jumped to her feet, hating the direction of their conversation. Here she'd had one of the most wonderful days she'd ever known, but the specter of the stalker tainted everything. "Come on, honey. It's time to go home for your nap. It's going to be a late one today."

While Chaz helped Abby put her toys back in the bag, Lacey threw the empty bottles in the recycle bin and folded up the blanket. When they got home, Abby had no qualms about going to her bedroom, but she wanted Chaz to stay with her until she fell asleep with her frog.

Lacey went into the family room and sat down in front of her laptop to plan out tonight's radio program. Before long Chaz joined her, wearing a sober expression. "I'm sorry to have upset you at the park."

Guilt swamped her. "Surely you know it wasn't you," she blurted. "How could I blame you for anything? We had a marvelous time today and it's obvious my daughter sees you as her champion. From the moment Barry hired you, you've saved me from going over the edge. I'd be an ungrateful wretch if I didn't tell you how thankful I am." *How crazy I am about you.*

"I think you've said it a dozen times already." He picked up the reader from the table. "I promised Abby I'd be here when she wakes up. She wants me to inspect the window for bees."

Lacey shook her head. "I'm sorry. The poor little thing really is terrified of insects. I hope it's a passing phase."

"I'm sure it is. While she's asleep, I'm headed for the deck where I can stretch out and finish your book. It's part of my investigation. I've been saving the last chapter to read when I could relax. If you want, why don't you bring your laptop and join me."

What?

"When you're through working, I'd like to talk to you some more about your case. We'll leave the door open so we can hear Abby if she needs you."

Her heart literally jumped. He wanted to be with her. And heaven help her, she wanted to be with him.

"Is there enough room on your sleeping bag for both of us to sprawl?"

His eyes gleamed mysteriously. "Let's find out."

It was crazy, unwise, but after lazing next to him at the park, she wasn't thinking straight and had no will to resist. In another minute he'd pulled the screen door across to keep the bugs from getting in. They lay down on their backs, side by side, to read and work.

The fragrance of honeysuckle was stronger than ever. Just knowing he was this close, there was no way she could concentrate on tonight's show. Helplessly she let the laptop slide off her and closed her eyes, never wanting to move from this spot.

Once in a while she stole a covert glance at Chaz. He was a remarkable, fantastic man whom she trusted implicitly. In another minute he put the reader aside and raised up on one elbow to look down at her. "Well done. You're an amazing writer, Lacey Pomeroy."

In a lightning move his dark head descended. When his mouth covered hers, it was no tentative kiss on his part. Unable to hold back, she opened her mouth to him. She'd been wanting this for days now. That moment on the swing had set her on fire. They came together in an explosion of need, something she'd been secretly dreaming about.

He rolled her toward him, thrusting one hand into her hair. His lips made a foray over her features, kissing every centimeter before claiming her mouth once more. Their legs got tangled. She wanted this to go on and on and never stop. To be alive again—he was making her feel immortal.

"Lacey?"

Through the mist of euphoria she heard her sister's voice.

Oh, no...

Embarrassed to be caught like this, she extricated herself from Chaz's arms. Hot faced, she got clumsily to her feet. Chaz stood up behind her. When she looked around, there was Ruth on the other side of the screen. Normally she didn't come to the condo until time for Lacey to leave for the radio station.

Her blue eyes could take on different shades, depending on her emotions. Right now they looked like cobalt as she took in the sight of them. Lacey had no idea how long she might have been standing there.

She was sorry her sister had seen them like this. Ruth might have a boyfriend at the moment, but Lacey knew her sister had been attracted to Chaz the second they'd been introduced.

"Abby's awake. She won't let me go into the bedroom. She wants Chaz."

He squeezed Lacey's arm. "I'll go to her," he whispered.

After picking up the reader and laptop, he stepped past her and opened the screen. "Thanks for the heads-up, Ruth. Abby had another scare today, with a wasp this time. I promised I'd inspect the window before she got up from her nap."

On his way through to the bedroom, he put the reader and laptop on the dining table. Lacey followed him. Her little redheaded cherub was waiting for him on the side of her bed, dangling her feet.

"Here I am, sweetheart. I'll check the window for you." She watched his every move. He raised the blinds. "No bees. See?"

She looked back at Lacey and ran to her. "It's in the toilet, Mommy."

"That's right. Say thank-you to Chaz."

"Thank you, Chaz." She darted to him. When he picked her up, she hugged him with all her might.

"You're welcome."

The three of them gravitated to the family room. Ruth was fixing herself something to eat. "There's no bees, Auntie Ruth."

But Lacey's sister wasn't listening. She was in one of her ugly moods, as their mom called them.

Chaz slipped past them and went out to the deck for his backpack. He glanced at Lacey as he came through again. "I need to get to the office. Good luck with tonight's program. See you later."

Just like that he'd vanished out the front door. After what had happened on the deck, Lacey felt a loss and knew she was in real trouble.

Ruth eyed her. "How come you were out there instead of your bedroom?"

"You know I would never go to bed with any man unless I were married to him. Having said that, I admit I'm very attracted to Chaz. I didn't know it was possible after Ted."

"It was so intense out there, the stalker could have snatched Abby and you wouldn't have known."

Lacey sucked in her breath. Her sister never minced words. She was used to that, but this time she'd gone too far. "That was cruel, Ruth. Especially when you know Chaz has men guarding the condo day and night."

"While he enjoys your phony engagement."

She'd never known Ruth to be this openly hostile

to her before. "He had his reasons for the engagement. They made sense to me and Mom."

Ruth ate one of Abby's apple slices. "Is he for real?"

"He's a real P.I. if that's what you mean. I've been to his office and met his boss."

"Have you stopped to consider he might pull this fiancé business on his other female clients? You know. To get a little on the side?"

Lacey frowned. "Where's all this coming from?"

"I watch a lot of *Law and Order*. Anyone can decide to be a P.I. and hang out a shingle. It doesn't mean he has any real experience. Seeing him making out with you on a summer afternoon instead of doing his job leads me to think you're being conned."

"Chaz was a navy SEAL for ten years before he became a P.I." Lacey hoped he would forgive her for telling Ruth, but her sister was behaving like an attack dog.

Ruth's eyebrows lifted. "I'll admit he's the personification of what most women imagine a SEAL would look like, but do you have proof?"

"His word," Lacey declared crisply.

Ruth shook her head. "Sometimes you're pathetically naive."

Lacey had taken enough. "I don't vet you about your boyfriends. The point is, I believe in Chaz, and until he gives me a reason not to trust him, I'll go along with his plan. He's been wonderful with Abby."

"If it gets him what he wants…" she said.

Ruth was enjoying baiting her. Lacey could feel it. Something was definitely wrong. "How did the job search go today?"

"What do you think? Every merchandising company

in Salt Lake uses big carriers and none of them are hiring right now."

That could be one explanation why Ruth was needling her mercilessly, but Lacey feared Ruth's jealousy over Chaz was at the bottom of this.

"Would you consider going back to your old job at the cell-phone company?"

"You didn't really ask me that question, did you?"

"I know it can't compare to being a pilot, but until things pick up, it would be better than nothing. Right?"

"Wrong. Let's put the shoe on the other foot. What if you couldn't get a radio show anywhere. Do you think you could sell phones for even one day without going berserk?"

Lacey wished she hadn't said anything. Wanting to smooth things over she said, "Do you have dinner plans?"

"No."

That emphatic answer didn't sound good coming from her sister. "I have an idea. Why don't I call Mom and the four of us can go for a pasta dinner. I'm sick of worrying about the stalker." She also needed something to get Chaz off her mind for a little while. "If we leave soon, I'll be back in plenty of time to get to the station for my program."

"Why not."

Chapter Eight

Chaz drove away from Lacey's home deep in thought. To his chagrin he didn't realize he was breaking the speed limit until a policeman pulled him over and gave him a ticket. He hadn't had one of those since he was a teen.

After he reached the office, he sat in his vehicle for a minute replaying the day's events. Ruth's return to the condo was unfortunate timing. He'd assumed she wouldn't be back from St. George until much later.

But on second thought, it was probably a good thing she'd shown up when she did. Hopefully what she'd seen, with Lacey locked in his embrace, would dampen any interest she might have in him.

As for Chaz, he was so on fire for Lacey, he could easily have lost his head out there on the deck. The chemistry between them had been building from the moment he'd looked into her eyes at the radio station. Since then, something magical had been happening to both of them. She couldn't have responded to him the way she did without desire driving her.

When he'd hugged Abby after being in her mother's arms, he knew it was imperative he catch her stalker before things went any further. He'd said that before, but now he really meant it.

"That's quite a conversation you're having with yourself."

Chaz jerked his head around to see his friend. "Mitch." He levered himself from the seat of the Forerunner.

"How's it going?"

Chaz pulled the speeding ticket out of his pocket and showed it to him.

Mitch chuckled. "I got one just like it in the same spot three weeks ago. They must be making a ton of money."

"That's what I thought," Chaz grumbled.

"Maybe I should have asked you how the engagement is going."

Chaz squinted at him. "For anyone else, that information is classified. But since it's you, I have to admit it's a double-edged sword."

"I believe it. Even so, is it producing results?"

Chaz rubbed the back of his neck. "Yes."

"Come into my office and let's talk."

They walked into the back room and headed down the hallway. Roman saw them and asked them to join him in his office for a minute.

"Mitch? Just wanted you to know I got the judge to issue that warrant for you to search the insurance office in the morning. You can pick it up at nine at the courthouse."

"Hallelujah."

Roman's dark eyes swerved to Chaz. "Chief Mahoney came through for you, too." Roman handed him a piece of paper with a name and number on it. "This woman is on the Albuquerque UFO committee. You call her after eight her time tonight and she'll try to answer your questions. If there's nothing else, I'm on my way home."

They thanked him before sequestering themselves in Mitch's office. Chaz sat down opposite the desk and stretched his legs. "Tell me something honestly," he said. "Have you ever gotten involved with a woman who was a client?"

"Not doing P.I. work, but there was a time in my marshal days when I got called in on a witness protection case. There was this woman who worked for the government. She knew classified information that could get her killed. I got too close to her. Luckily I didn't blow the operation, but I lost my concentration. Needless to say it never happened again."

"That's my problem. I can't promise that it won't happen again. I blew it today," Chaz confessed. He told Mitch what had happened without going into detail.

Mitch cocked his head. "Then don't go over there until you know she's home from the radio station and in bed. With her sister sleeping there, your problem's solved."

"You're right. I've got work to do and won't go near her until Thursday. I'm taking her and Abby to the soccer game."

Mitch's mouth curved in a half smile. "Travis told me. We're all anxious to meet this celebrity. We've decided we're going to listen to her show tonight."

"You'll be surprised how entertaining it is." Chaz got to his feet. "You going to be here long?"

"Afraid so. I'm backlogged with paperwork I need to clean up."

"Tell me about it. I'm going home and making the phone call that might tell me I'm getting close to her stalker."

"Good luck. Watch your back."

"Always."

Chaz left for home, intending to take his friend's advice. But he felt as if he'd just gone on a diet and was already experiencing deprivation. Worse, he'd finished Lacey's novel and was out of reading material. He could stop at a bookstore and pick up a new police procedural, but there'd be no thrill.

Lacey's story had enchanted him and he wanted more of the same. Since he couldn't be with her right now, maybe he'd download another YA sci-fi book. Although he doubted he'd enjoy it nearly as much.

When he got home, he fixed himself a couple of turkey sandwiches and downed them with a quart of milk. With a new pack of licorice in hand, he went into his study to make the call. He needed answers and hoped he was going to get them.

"Mrs. Bateman? This is Chaz Roylance. I'm investigating on a case and need some information."

"Oh, yes, I've been expecting your call. What can I do to help you?"

He tightened his grip on the phone. "Could you tell me how it would be possible for someone who's not on the UFO committee to be in possession of one of your official envelopes?"

"Well, I'm sure the printing company we use has some, but we keep the rest of them stored in boxes at my house. I have done so for the past five years."

Good. That's what he'd hoped for. "So when you

send out flyers, are you the one who stuffs them into the envelopes?"

"Elaine Stafford, who's on the committee, usually helps me."

"The next question I want to ask you may sound strange, but it's vital I get a correct answer from you."

"What is it?"

"What color is your hair?"

She chuckled. "That's strange, all right. I'm a brunette."

"Do you dye it?"

"No."

"So when you stuffed the envelopes for the coming seminar, you were a brunette."

"Yes."

"What about Elaine?"

"She has brownish hair."

"Her natural color, do you think?"

"Yes. She's only twenty-seven. I doubt she dyes it."

Chaz's pulse picked up speed. "Thank you. Now, excluding anyone from the printer's shop, could you explain how someone other than you or Elaine could get hold of an envelope for their own purposes?"

"Oh, I see what you're driving at. Of course. We have a mailing list we add to each year as people attend the seminar. Whenever there's a new event coming up, we send them a flyer and also enclose an envelope and flyer in the hope they'll spread the word. That's how we're building our program."

"So you have to fold the additional envelope and flyer to fit inside."

"Yes."

That's why the one sent to Lacey had looked creased.

"How long ago did you send a flyer announcing this weekend's seminar?"

"Five weeks ago. That gives everyone a chance to arrange flight schedules and hotel accommodations."

Five weeks. "Where did you go to mail them?"

"I always take the big committee mailings to the airport post office."

Chaz reached for another piece of licorice. "I'm sitting in front of my computer. Could you email me the complete list of people you sent flyers to for this weekend's seminar?"

"Yes. I'll do it right now, but I'll need to go into the other room to my computer."

"I'll wait. I may have more questions."

"Just a minute."

To his relief he didn't have to wait long. "I'm sending it now."

"I got it."

"This must be very important."

"It is. Believe me. Please stay on the line with me."

"Of course."

Two hundred and twenty-four names were on the list. Amazing to see that many people would attend a UFO conference. He zeroed in on the familiar ones from Lacey's list of people. Her name was there, naturally.

Then he went through the whole list alphabetically. He came to the *G*s and was surprised when he saw Ruth's name. Chaz hadn't known she went to those seminars. Lacey'd never mentioned that her sister was also interested in UFOs. He would have to ask her about that.

"Mrs. Bateman? There's a name here I'm curious

about. Ruth Garvey. Can you tell me when she first started showing up on your mailing list?"

"I'll check the lists for the past five years. It's all I have."

Again he had to wait. In a few minutes she came back on. "She's on last year's list only."

Adrenaline shot through him. That meant she'd attended last year's seminar, or at least registered for it. He would verify that information with Lacey. "What was her mailing address?"

"Idaho Falls, Idaho."

"I need her street address and telephone number."

The woman complied.

"Thank you, Mrs. Bateman. You've been more helpful than you could possibly know."

"Since it's official police business, I was glad to do it. Goodbye."

The second he hung up Chaz called Lon. "I still need you to follow Ruth Garvey in the morning. If she leaves her car at the airport again, wait for Jim to show up. He'll relieve you so he can watch her car until she gets back to the airport. I also need something else from you."

"Shoot."

"There's a phone number I'd like you to check out in the morning. When you learn anything, call me. If I don't answer, just leave a message on my voice mail." Chaz gave him the information and the reason for it.

"I'll get on it first thing."

"I can always count on you. Thanks, Lon. Keep me posted."

Thoughts bombarded Chaz's mind, chilling him so badly he didn't want to put them into words. Not yet…

Tomorrow he had a plane to catch to Idaho Falls. He drew out his wallet and removed all his ID. In its place he supplied fake credentials for himself, then made a round-trip reservation online for early in the morning.

With that matter taken care of, he had a long night to face. The next best thing to being with Lacey was listening to her.

He turned on the radio. Her program had already started. Chaz sat through the next three hours thinking hard about her case, making more notes, checking and rechecking facts. When she went off the air, he headed for her condo, hoping to heaven that what he was thinking wasn't true. He planned to fly to Idaho in the morning to help *prove* that it wasn't true.

From the start, his instincts had told him Lacey was being menaced by a woman. The patterns pointed to it for many reasons. But it had never occurred to him it might be her own flesh and blood. One, furthermore, who had total access to Abby.

When he'd left the SEALs, he'd promised himself and the Almighty that he would never deal with a female enemy again.

Once more, the past's debilitating, haunting blackness began to seep through him, robbing him of the joy of listening to the woman whose kiss had shaken him to the core today.

LACEY HAD LISTENED ALL Wednesday morning in case Chaz phoned to check in with her. She was a complete wreck, having tossed and turned through the night, angry with herself for going out on the deck with him in the first place. He'd seen through her as though she were a plate-glass window. She'd left herself wide-open and had made a perfect fool of herself.

Not even with Ted had she behaved that way before—not in the beginning, anyway. The excuse that she was being stalked didn't wash. She'd loved it that Chaz had bought her book and was enjoying it. Somehow she'd felt closer to him because of it and he knew it. Her attraction to him had stood out a mile.

Ruth had been right about a lot of things. Lacey would never have agreed to a mock engagement if she hadn't already been spellbound by Chaz's compelling aura. Her sister had voiced the possibility that Chaz was in the habit of getting close to his female clients. Ruth was probably right. How embarrassing was it that when he'd first questioned her, she'd told him no man had interested her since Ted. She couldn't imagine being with another man.

What a joke!

By now he likely believed she wasn't the innocent she purported to be and had been lying about being unaware of Ken's interest, too.

She couldn't take back those minutes when she'd kissed Chaz with a hunger that had shocked her. To think Ruth had witnessed their embrace made it all the more humiliating. The only thing Lacey could do was never let it happen again.

Miserable and at loose ends, she called her mom, who told her to bring Abby over. They'd all have lunch and spend the rest of the day together. Abby loved seeing her nana. It was a good thing, since Lacey was going crazy with her own thoughts. To sit around waiting for Chaz to call was childish and ridiculous. He was a P.I., for heaven's sake, doing his best to help capture this monster.

On her way to the car, she stopped at the mailbox and put the small pile of delivered mail in her bag. Chaz had told her not to open it until he was with her. If he was there when she got home from the radio station tonight, she'd leave it on the table for him to do the honors and hurry to bed.

She didn't think she could handle finding another death threat. There was something so hideous about the thought of a person actually composing words to terrorize her.

So far no one seemed to have been following her, let alone attempting to attack her. Chaz's presence had no doubt prevented her stalker from doing anything more than making harassing phone calls and sending threats. But Chaz couldn't go on doing this forever.

Lacey believed in Chaz, but the longer this went on, the harder it would be to hide the way she felt about him. She'd been in his arms and tasted his mouth. No way could she forget what that had been like.

NOTHING IN THIS BUSINESS worked without precision timing and cooperation. After Chaz returned from Idaho Falls, he checked with Adam, who told him Lacey had just left the condo with her daughter. As for Jim, he was still at the airport watching Ruth's car.

Hearing that news, Chaz phoned Roman, who arranged for Simon Evans, the same forensics expert who'd discovered the hair samples in the envelope, to meet him at Lacey's place ASAP.

"Thanks for getting here so fast. We only have a short window of time in case Mrs. Pomeroy decides to return." He walked the other man through to the guest bedroom where Ruth slept. He hoped the sheets and pillowcase she'd slept on hadn't been washed yet.

"If you'll check this room and the guest bathroom across the hall for samples of DNA, those are the only areas I need covered."

It didn't take Simon long to do his business. Chaz walked him out to his car. "I appreciate you doing this."

"Happy to oblige, but I probably won't have results before Monday. You have no idea of my backlog."

"No problem. I'm indebted to you."

Once the man drove off, Chaz left for his own home. By Monday he and Lacey would be back from Albuquerque. If Simon's work produced a match to the hair in the envelope, then the case was solved and Ruth was the stalker. And then another nightmare would begin for Lacey and her family. The pain they'd go through knowing it was their daughter and sister would be horrendous.

He could be wrong about Ruth, though he didn't think so. His trip to Idaho had provided more of the kind of information he'd been looking for.

After arranging for a rental car that morning, he'd driven to the few air cargo companies listed. None of his questions produced results. His last stop was at Landis Air Cargo. He approached the fortyish-looking guy at the counter.

"Hi. I'm Don Archer and I've just moved here from Portland. A while back I happened to meet a pilot of your company and she told me you could do a good job for me handling my computer-merchandise business."

"That's nice to hear. Who was it?"

"I only remember her first name. Ruth something."

The other man shook his head. "No one by that name has ever worked here. One of our pilots, Bruce Larson, lives with a woman named Ruth."

"Is she a brunette?"

"No. Blonde."

"Then she's not the one. I've come to the wrong place, but it doesn't matter. As long as I'm here, do you provide service to Albuquerque? That's one of my new markets."

He nodded. "It's one of our oldest routes. Take a look on the wall chart. We fly a lot of places."

Chaz gave it a quick glance. Their reach included Colorado, Wyoming, Nevada, Utah, Oregon and of course Idaho. Except for Oregon, those were the places where the phone calls and death threats had originated.

He could hear Lacey's question. *How can this stalker be in so many places almost at the same time?*

"That's all I wanted to know. Thanks. I'll be back."

Leaving the air cargo company, Chaz drove his rental car to the address Mrs. Bateman had given him. It was an apartment in an eightplex. No one answered the door. He checked the mailboxes. B. Larson was one of the tenants. In case Larson was an accomplice to the stalking, Chaz didn't ask questions of any of the tenants coming and going from the building—it might get back to Mr. Larson.

New information revealed Ruth hadn't worked as a pilot in Idaho Falls. Besides living with a pilot, what had she been doing? Why had she come home to Salt Lake this past month? Her family knew nothing about her or her activities. Chaz's mind flooded with more questions demanding answers.

He got back into the rental car and phoned Lon,

whose input revealed that there was no phone listing for Ruth in Idaho. The number Mrs. Bateman had
given him off the application Ruth had filled out for the
UFO convention belonged to someone else. The phone
company claimed it had never been assigned to Ruth
Garvey. Not only that, it didn't match the cell-phone
number Mrs. Garvey had given Chaz for Ruth when
they'd met the first time.

Armed with the knowledge that it *could* have been
Ruth, with the help of her boyfriend, who'd sent Lacey
that envelope from Albuquerque last Friday, he'd flown
home, anxious to get the DNA samples gathered from
Ruth's bedroom while Lacey's condo was empty.

He drove back to his office and looked at the photograph Lacey had given him of her core group. Three
of the women and two of the men had various kinds of
blond hair. One of the men wore his to the shoulders.
It could have shed a seven-inch-long strand. But it was
difficult to tell the actual color from a picture. He had
yet to meet Jennifer, who was also a blonde.

Chaz pulled a cola from the office fridge and took
a gulp. If Ruth's DNA didn't match the hair samples in
the envelope, then he was back at square one. After he
went to Albuquerque, his list might grow depending on
the number of blonds on the UFO committee. In that
case Roman would have to arrange for interstate cooperation to get a judge to order samples of DNA taken
from each of them.

As he finished off his drink and tossed it into the
wastebasket, the thought came to him that maybe it was
Bruce Larson's hair that had gotten into the envelope.

Neither Lacey nor her mother had ever met Bruce,
so no one knew what he looked like. But *Lon* knew. He

said he'd seen Ruth talking to a guy before the plane took off at the small airport.

Chaz got him on his cell phone. "A question for you, Lon."

"Shoot."

"This guy who's been flying Ruth around. What color hair does he have?"

"He's a blond. Shaggy."

"Thanks for the info."

Chaz headed for Lacey's condo thinking about several new possibilities. If Ruth had gotten Bruce involved, then they could be coconspirators. More than ever, he needed to know the results of that DNA report. If one of the hairs was Ruth's, then Chaz needed a DNA sample from Bruce Larson. He would call Roman and see what could be arranged to get a sample from the pilot while Chaz flew to Albuquerque with Lacey.

To ease his fears, he phoned Lacey and told her Tom would be staying inside the condo with Ruth and Abby until the radio program was over. "It's a precaution I feel is necessary now that we're getting so close to exposing the culprit." She didn't fight him.

Chapter Nine

Lacey stayed at her mother's until time to go home and put Abby down for the night. Her daughter talked about Chaz quite incessantly. It was only natural. She'd been only two when Ted was killed, and there'd been no other men in their lives until Chaz. He'd brought gifts and rescued her from a wasp. He'd played ball with her at the park and put her on the swing with him. What more could a little girl want from the most exciting man in existence?

Tom, one of Chaz's crew, arrived while Lacey was getting ready for her radio program. He said he would work at the kitchen table. Then Ruth let herself in with more bad news about the job situation. But after being introduced to Tom, who wasn't bad looking, she didn't seem to mind that she had company.

Lacey peeked in on Abby one more time before leaving for her car. Her heart leaped when she saw Chaz's Forerunner pull into the guest space. When he got out, she noticed he was wearing a tan jacket over an open-necked shirt and khakis. The sight of him made her stomach flip.

He smiled at her through veiled eyes. "Perfect timing,

I'd say. Is Tom upstairs?" She nodded. "Good. Come get into my car. I'll drive you to the radio station."

Chaz walked to the passenger door of his car and opened it. She climbed inside. "I got here as soon as I could. I need to ask you a few questions. No better time than now. Once your broadcast is over, we'll both be too tired to concentrate on your case."

But hopefully not too tired to concentrate on each other.

She wasn't sure what to think, but she was aware this was a different Chaz than she'd seen before. He'd been the total professional when she'd first met him, but tonight he was…masterful. There was no other way to describe him. Something had changed.

Maybe he was letting her know that what had happened on the deck was an accident and there'd be no repeats. Then again his demeanor could have more to do with the investigation.

"So you honestly believe you're getting closer to finding the stalker?" As they drove off, she gave him a sideward glance. What she saw sent a shiver through her body. In the semidark, his black brows and hardened jaw gave him a slightly forbidding cast.

"I *know* I am," his voice grated. The authority in his tone left her in no doubt he was speaking the truth.

"Can you tell me anything?" she asked softly.

"Not yet. I'm curious about something. Have I got this straight that the summer solstice seminar in Milwaukee and the UFO seminar in Albuquerque are held a week apart?"

"Yes, but that's not unusual. There are dozens of paranormal conventions going on all over the country at any given time. Those two just happen to be close together. Normally I would never schedule them back-to-back, but they're two of the most important ones for me."

"Has your mother ever gone to any of these seminars with you?"

"Only one in Salt Lake this year, just to see what goes on. It didn't make her want to become a regular."

Lacey thought he might smile. Instead he said, "What about Ruth?"

"She went to the one in Albuquerque a year ago to help me out. It was right after the funeral. I was supposed to be on the program. She read the speech I'd prepared weeks earlier. Unfortunately she had to take time off work. I paid for her flight down and back. Why do you ask?"

"Only that Ruth could provide some eyes and ears. She was there and undoubtedly met the people on the committee. Maybe she saw something she didn't know was important. I'll ask her later."

They pulled into the back of the radio station and he shut off the engine. "One last question. Why did Ruth tell me about Shelley instead of you?"

Lacey blinked in surprise. "Are you talking about Shelley Marlow?"

"If that's her last name."

"She was Ted's girlfriend before he met me."

"Your sister seems to think she might be someone to add to the list."

"That was a long time ago. I'd forgotten about her."

"How long did he date her?"

"A month. She had a hard time getting over Ted."

"How hard?" he persisted.

Chaz and her sister had covered a lot of ground in

the short time they'd spoken. But then he was a P.I. in the middle of a stalking case, gathering information as fast as he could. With his rare brand of heady male charisma, Ruth was more than a little interested in him.

"She called him a lot before we were married."

"In other words, she was intrusive."

"Yes. She'd stay on the phone and sob."

"After only knowing him a month?"

Lacey nodded. "Ted said he'd already decided to stop seeing her before he met me."

"How did they meet?"

"She was a college student from Long Beach. They met at a party at Rob Sharp's house. He was in the Coast Guard, too, and best man at our wedding. I put him on the list I made up for you."

"I remember," Chaz murmured. "Did Shelley come to your wedding?"

"No. Ted wouldn't have invited her. After our honeymoon she started up the calling again. He warned her to leave him alone, so she wrote to him instead. He didn't answer her letters. She wrote three, then they stopped. I haven't thought about her since."

Chaz's black brows furrowed. "Ruth said she came to the funeral."

Incredulous, Lacey stared at him. "That's impossible. For one thing, Ruth wouldn't have known who she was. Neither would I. I never saw a picture of her. If Ruth found out somehow that Shelley was there, why didn't she tell me?"

"Is it possible she could have forgotten at the time?"

"Maybe."

"We'll talk to her about it later." He pulled the keys

out of the ignition. "Sorry for putting you through the interrogation, but it's part of the process."

"I realize that."

His compelling mouth broke into the first smile tonight. "I'll have you know I'm looking forward to taking you and Abby to the soccer game tomorrow. A whole crowd from my work will be there with their families. Sydney has a little four-year-old girl named Cindy, her second child. She and Abby will probably get along famously."

Lacey took a deep breath. "A ball game sounds like exactly what I need to get my mind off everything."

"That makes two of us. Don't be concerned if the guys play it up about our pseudo engagement. They're hard-core teases."

She laughed, but inside she moaned because she didn't want to think about the day she would have to give the ring back. She was getting used to wearing it. Lately she'd been wishing that what she had with Chaz was real.

His gaze studied her mouth, fanning the flame burning inside her. "You need to laugh more often."

Averting her eyes, she reached for the door handle and got out. "I need to hurry inside or my broadcast will start without me."

"I have a phone call to make, then I'm going to listen to your program in the surveillance van parked over there while Adam and I look at tapes. If you want to give my friends a thrill, say hi to Travis and Mitch while you're on the air. They'll be listening tonight."

"You're serious?" The thought of it tickled her.

"You'll find out tomorrow at the soccer game. See you after you're through with your show. When we get back to the condo, let's watch your DVD of *Other-world*."

Her limbs felt as if they'd just turned to mush. "It's a fun old TV show, but you'll probably think it's corny."

"That's exactly the kind of thing I feel like watching tonight."

Me, too. With you. Alone.

She hurried away.

WHEN THE BLAZE OF RED GOLD disappeared inside the building, Chaz accessed the file on his computer from his iPhone and called Rob Sharp's number. It was only quarter to eight in California, not too late to be phoning him if he was around.

His wife answered. When he identified himself as a friend of Lacey Pomeroy's and asked if he could speak to her husband, she told him to hold on. In a minute he came to the phone.

"Hi! This is Rob. You say you're Lacey's friend?"

"Yes." After telling him he was a P.I. and explaining he was trying to catch Lacey's stalker, the other guy sobered. "If I thought you were her stalker, I wouldn't be having this conversation with you. You have brown hair. I've already identified the stalker as a blond."

After a long pause Rob said, "She's really being stalked?"

"She and Abby. I need some vital information and hope you can supply it."

"I'll tell you whatever I can. Lacey's the best."

"I agree. Do you remember Shelley Marlow, the girl Ted was dating before he met Lacey?"

"Sure. She went to my high school."

"What was she like?"

"She was a nice girl, but I should never have lined them up because I didn't know she was so fragile. He took her out a few times and realized it was a mistake. Unfortunately she didn't understand the word *no* and refused to give up on him. He finally had to put her straight."

"That's what Lacey said. Tell me something. I know you were at Ted's funeral. Did you see her there?"

"She couldn't have been there."

"Why? Someone else said they saw her."

"That would have been impossible. Shelley died about two years ago. In the paper it said natural causes, but I think she was on drugs and overdosed."

The air froze in Chaz's lungs. Either Ruth had made an honest mistake, or she'd told another lie. This one couldn't be swept under the rug.

"That's all I needed to hear. You've been more helpful than you know. Do me a favor and don't tell Lacey I called. When I've caught her stalker, I'll tell her to phone you herself with the good news."

Chaz clicked off and joined Adam in the van. To his surprise, the other guy already had Lacey's show on. Listening to it wasn't one of his duties. The announcer was just giving the intro. "And now here's the founder and host of the Stargrazer program, Lacey Pomeroy."

"Hello, everyone out there. It's a beautiful evening and there's no other place I'd rather be than right here, anxious to talk to all you callers. Stewart tells me the phone calls are lined up. I promise to keep things moving, but before I get started, I'd like to welcome two new listeners who've just discovered the show.

"Mitch and Travis, if you've got your radios on, welcome to my paranormal world. I can promise you thrills and chills." Chaz grinned. The guys would love this. "If you decide to call in, I'm sure Stewart will fit you into the lineup. And now let's take our first caller. It's Glen from Fayetteville, Arkansas."

Chaz glanced at Adam. "I didn't know you liked her program."

He smiled. "I've been enjoying it since you put me on the case. How would you like to introduce me to her after you've caught the creep harassing her?"

Gritting his teeth, Chaz said, "I'll ask her if she's agreeable."

"I'll owe you big-time. She's a knockout and has more going on upstairs than any woman I've ever known. Did you hear her the other night poking holes through some guy's theory because his physics were all wrong? She mops the floor with any pseudointellectual who tries to take her on. I like a woman with her kind of brains, you know?"

"As a matter of fact, I *do* know. If you really want to get inside the creative part of her head, read her young-adult fantasy. I've got a copy of it you can borrow, but it's at the condo. I'll give it to you tomorrow."

"Thanks. She's sure got a cute little girl. Looks just like her. Her curls bob when she does that circle thing." It was her butterfly walk, but Chaz kept that to himself. "Can you believe hair grows that color? It's so beautiful it's unreal."

Chaz liked Adam a lot, but he'd heard about as much of this kind of chat as he could handle. He'd played with that hair, kissed it while he was devouring her ardent mouth. She'd been hungry for him, too. If it hadn't been for Ruth… He sucked in his breath. "I agree."

"Her sister's nice looking, too. Runs in the family obviously, but I have my eye on Mrs. Pomeroy."

"Understood." Once you'd seen her, she ruined you for other women. "Let's see what you got on tape today." While Chaz listened, he turned on the screen.

Various people were leaving the condo building to go to work. Soon Ruth appeared in designer jeans and a tank top. She talked on her cell phone all the way to her Mazda and was still talking as she drove off.

He fast-forwarded the tape and suddenly there was Lacey in white denims and a summery plaid blouse walking out to her car with Abby. She stopped at the mailbox and put whatever was in there in her purse. He noticed with satisfaction that Abby, dressed in a pink top and shorts, was hugging the big nesting doll under her arm.

If he were alone, he would have played the tape of her again. Once he'd seen everything on it, he turned off the screen and found a seat to listen to the last of the broadcast. The calls just kept coming.

"Stewart tells me he's got Travis on the line."

Hearing her mention his friend's name, Chaz sat forward. Adam rolled his eyes at him. "Is that *our* Travis?"

"The one and only."

"So, Travis, where do you hail from?"

"West Texas."

"I guess I don't have to tell you that up in those Davis Mountains is one of the best places in the U.S. to look at the stars. Folks? It's so dark up there, with your naked eye you can see falling stars zipping through space."

"Yup. I've spent many a night out there watching for them."

"You're one of *us,* Travis, you just didn't know it until now. I have an astronomer friend who runs the observatory up there."

"You know about that?"

She'd surprised Travis. Chaz was loving this.

"I spent a semester there while I was in school."

"Doing what?

"Geophysics. We were studying one of Jupiter's moons, looking for water." Even Chaz hadn't known of the exact project she'd been working on. "While there I got the idea for a new sci-fi novel, but that's another story for another day. Thanks for calling in. Don't be a stranger, now, y'all hear?" she teased with a fetching, authentic-sounding Texas drawl.

Lacey...

"The next person on the line is Scott from Fairbanks, Alaska. He told my producer something strange is going on up there. Lights are everywhere in the sky, but they're not the aurora borealis because it isn't visible this time of year. Tell us what's happening, Scott. We want to know exactly what you're seeing."

"You're a freakin' bitch who'd believe anything." The sound of the male-enhanced voice drove Chaz to his feet. He recognized the distortion technology being employed by the caller. *"Well, believe this, bit—"*

Stewart must have pressed the cut-off button, but Lacey would have heard enough to be traumatized.

"Too bad there's an occasional caller who uses this show to vent his frustrations," she spoke again, her delivery calm and seamless. She was incredible. "But America's a free country. That's what makes it the greatest place to live on Earth, right? Our next caller is Shay from New Orleans."

Chaz couldn't get out of the van and into the station fast enough. The look of relief when Lacey saw him enter Stewart's booth told him he'd done the right thing. For the rest of the show she would eye him from time to time, needing that support. He wanted her to need him. He wanted her to need him so badly she wouldn't want to lose him when this was all over.

After her show ended, he ushered her through the radio station to the door. The night watchman had heard about their engagement and congratulated them before Chaz helped her into his Forerunner.

"You were magnificent, Lacey." He hugged her to him for a moment before letting her go. He couldn't help himself. "When the call came in, Adam and I were listening to your show in the van. As soon as I reached Stewart's booth, I tried to locate the caller, but it must have come from one of those prepaid cellular phones, because I couldn't trace it."

She eyed him earnestly. "It's because of you that it didn't bother me that much. I hate it that someone's out there determined to kill me, but the shock value is beginning to wear off."

"You're beating this person at their own sick game. I can't tell you how proud I am of the way you handled it. Stewart's in awe of you."

"Good old Stewart. He cut off that stalker so fast, the maniac probably didn't know what hit him."

Chaz chuckled. "I don't think Travis knew what hit him, either. You're an exciting woman. Even Adam, one of my support crew, is captivated by your show." *And you.* "You can add another couple of fans to your millions."

"Hardly millions, but a comment like that makes Barry's day."

How different she was from Ruth. The one craved attention, the other eschewed it. So went the history of siblings.

They drove back to Lacey's condo. The second Tom saw them at the door, he nodded to Chaz and went out to the van.

When they walked in, Ruth was still up, talking on her iPhone in the living room. Lacey asked him if he wanted a soda. He nodded and followed her into the kitchen. Ruth soon caught up to them.

Lacey turned to her. "How did things go?"

"Quiet on both counts." Lacey took that to mean Ruth kept to herself.

"I know. She's so good. Do you want a soda, too?"

"No, thanks. I'm going to bed."

"Before you do, I wanted to ask you something."

"Shoot."

"Chaz said you told him Shelley Marlow came to the funeral."

"Yeah. She introduced herself."

"Why didn't you say anything to me at the time?"

"I told Mom while we were in the hearse, but she decided you didn't need to know. You were grieving so much over Ted, she didn't want to burden you during the funeral. I agreed with her. But now that you're being stalked, I thought Chaz should know. She was sick."

Lacey nodded. "Maybe she has been the one all along. I got another threat tonight during my broadcast."

Ruth flicked Chaz a glance. "Any luck tracing it?"

"None, but I'm not worried. I have other leads and

it won't be much longer now. Do you want to stay up and watch *Otherworld* with us?"

"Sorry, but all that sci-fi crap really is the dregs."

Ruth's vitriol was spilling out, but she didn't care. Had Lacey always had to put up with the nasty side of her sister, or was this behavior worse than usual? "After tonight's program, I'm in the mood for more of it."

"I'll make popcorn," Lacey piped up.

"Good night." Ruth wheeled away.

Within a few minutes all was quiet. Lacey made good on her offer. Soon she sat next to Chaz on the couch in the family room while they watched the first episode and ate popcorn. Since the death of his wife, this was the kind of night he'd forgotten existed.

"In case you get hooked, I thought you'd better see the beginning. It starts in Egypt at the Great Pyramid. The reason I like the show so much is that they're a really cute and resourceful family who adapt fast after they're transported to this different world. I would've loved to have been a writer for this show. Now I promise I'll stop talking."

Low laughter rolled out of Chaz. When there was no more popcorn, he put his arm around Lacey. She rested her head against him and they settled down to watch the show. Corny or not, he liked it.

Lacey was right. A good cast had been chosen to portray the family of four. It was the kind of family he'd pictured having one day. With Lacey's warm curvy body nestled against him, he could imagine she was his wife, and he was feeling better than good. Her subtle fragrance teased his senses. She would have been beautiful while she carried Abby.

How would it be to make her pregnant, knowing the little boy or girl inside was part of him and her?

"Do you want to see the second episode?" Lacey had asked the question, but he was slow on the uptake, not having realized the first one had ended.

"I'm crazy about the idea."

"Sure you are." She half laughed.

"I like the show, but sitting next to you any longer isn't a good idea. It makes me want to take up where we left off out on the deck." He planted a thorough kiss on her mouth. For a few minutes they forgot everything else and gave in to their passion. But things were heating up so fast that they'd need to move to the bedroom. To his chagrin, they weren't alone in the condo.

He found the strength to tear his lips from hers. "Much as I'd love to go on kissing you till morning, until I've caught your stalker, I promised myself to try to keep my wits about me. Otherwise you're going to think I had ulterior motives for becoming your temporary fiancé."

Lacey shut off the TV and DVD player with the remote and got up from the couch. "I promised myself the same thing," she said and hurried into the kitchen with the empty bowl. That kiss had gotten away from both of them.

He eyed her from a distance. "I'm going to brush my teeth, so I'll say good-night now. Thanks for a perfect ending to the day. Be ready at four tomorrow. I'll come by for you and Abby. We'll eat dinner out before the soccer game. "

"That's sounds exciting. Good night."

When Chaz bedded down for the night outside, he thought he might not fall asleep for a while, but to his surprise he must have passed out. The next thing he knew, he heard someone knocking. Opening his eyes, he saw Abby on the other side of the glass door. She was still in her jammies.

He sat up and slid it open. It was twenty to seven in the morning. He'd slept later than usual. "Well, hi, sweetheart. Are you awake?"

"Yes."

She was crying softly. "What's wrong?"

"My teeny baby's gone."

"Did you look inside your big-girl bag?" That was what Lacey called the bag she was holding on to.

"Yes. It's not here."

"Do you want me to look again?"

"Yes." She came closer and plopped it next to him.

He opened the bag and took the items out one by one. The nesting dolls weren't in there because he knew she kept them on her windowsill. She had a conglomeration of treasures, even a GoPhone. It was a cheap kind of cellular phone. When prepaid with cash, the call couldn't be traced. It looked new. "Is this your mommy's?"

"No."

"Then who does it belong to?"

"I don't know. I found it."

"Where?"

"In Auntie Ruth's closet."

"I see."

He'd seen Ruth talking on the phone last night, but she'd used an iPhone like Lacey's. Chaz closed his eyes tightly for a moment. Everything confirmed what he suspected. Then he turned the bag upside down and shook it.

"Your teeny baby isn't in here, but we'll find it. I bet you left it at your nana's house, or it's in your mommy's car. Go into your mommy's room and tell her I need her car keys to find it."

"Okay. Don't go away."

"I won't."

The second she ran off, he pulled out his iPhone and took a picture to prove that the GoPhone was in with the toys. Then he put everything back except the phones. After getting dressed, he slipped both phones into his backpack.

As he was locking the deck door behind him, a tousle-headed, red-haired Lacey appeared barefoot in the kitchen wearing jeans and a pink T-shirt. Some people didn't look good when they'd just been awakened from sleep. With that combination of her red hair and pink T-shirt, she'd never looked more delectable.

Her blue eyes were still foggy with sleep. "Good morning. What happened?" She smoothed some curls away from her cheek.

"Abby came out to the deck crying because she couldn't find her teeny nesting doll in the toy bag." He handed the bag to Lacey. "We went through it, but it wasn't there. I told her I'd go out to your car and search for it."

"Oh, honey, it's here on the counter next to the toaster." Lacey retrieved the doll and handed it to her. Abby made a crooning sound and walked around with it and her blanket pressed against her cheek.

He smiled. "Crisis averted."

"Yes," she said with a half laugh. "I'm sorry she wakened you."

"Since I've never had a child, I loved it that she came to me for help."

"You're her hero."

He felt the warmth of her gaze clear through him.

"I couldn't handle seeing her in tears."

"I know what you mean. Since you're still here and we're all up, would you like to stay and eat breakfast with us?"

"I wish I could, but I've got a full day ahead of me." While she followed him with her eyes, he picked up the reader from the dining room table and put it in his pack. "I'm taking this to the office. Adam wants to read your novel."

"You're kidding!"

"No. After doing surveillance, he's developed quite a crush on you."

It was fun watching color come through her fabulous skin. "I'll see you at four," he said, heading for the front door.

Abby chased after him and caught his leg. "Don't go."

It astonished him how powerfully she tugged on his heart. He hunkered down. "I have to go to work, but I'll see you later. We're going to go to a soccer game."

"What's soccer?"

He flicked Lacey a glance. "Your mommy will explain."

"Okay. Bye, Chaz." She threw her arms around his neck and gave him a kiss on the cheek. His first from her. He thought of it as his angel peck.

Once outside, he saw there was no sign of Ruth's red Mazda in the parking area. She always left early and this morning was no exception. Abby must have heard her on her way out and woken up.

After he got into his car, he reached into the backpack for the GoPhone and undid the back of it. The SIM card was missing, but the International Mobile Equipment Identity number was there on the inside plate. He'd take the phone to Roman and show him the picture evidence he'd shot with his iPhone. If a forensics expert from the police department had been with him, the other man would have taken a picture. As it was, he followed procedure. Roman could arrange for a subpoena to trace it to the account holder.

Since seeing the phone, he felt as if he'd been punched in the gut. In Abby's innocence, she'd provided a piece of evidence that might prove her aunt's guilt. Chaz was saying *might* right now because so far, there could be a plausible explanation for Ruth's behavior that had nothing to do with the case.

Ruth was a liar, but it didn't necessarily follow she was the stalker. Still…

En route to the office he phoned Mitch. "Forgive me for calling you this early, but I've got to talk or I'm not going to make it." Roman wouldn't be at the office yet.

"I've never heard you sound like this before. Hold on and let me grab the coffee I was making. Then I'm all yours."

The seconds passed like hours.

"I'm back. Now, tell me what's wrong."

"You might as well ask what *isn't* wrong."

"Lacey doesn't feel the same way you do? I don't believe it."

"No. I'd stake my life on the fact that her attraction to me is just as powerful. It's getting harder to keep my distance. That's the problem. I'm going down a path I don't think I can handle any longer."

"What do you mean?"

"Ever since I met her, I intended that when the case was over, I'd explore what's going on between us. But the closer I'm getting to the truth, the more terrified I am that I'm going to lose Lacey."

"You're not making sense. Once you find the person who's harassing her, I don't see you having a problem."

"It's not that simple, Mitch. When I tell you what happened to me near the end of my time in the SEALs, you'll better understand why this is tearing my guts out."

For the next little while Chaz unloaded on him. It was the first time he'd told anyone about the most horrific period of his life. "After I got out, I promised myself I'd never put myself in that position again. It's why I didn't go into law enforcement. Roman's firm offered me challenges where I could use my skills in ways that wouldn't put me in any more untenable positions. Or so I thought.

"When the call from Barry Winslow came in to the office, I asked Roman if I could be the one to take on this stalker. Wouldn't you know I made the classic mistake of assuming it was a man? I wanted to protect Lacey and her daughter. After what I'd come up against in the SEALs, I saw this as my opportunity to *help* a woman. Maybe then the nightmares would go away."

"I hear you, Chaz. That makes a lot of sense."

"I thought it did, too, until I started building this case. The signs began pointing to a woman. You know—no physical attacks made, phone calls and emails as the form of harassment. But by then I was already in too deep. My feelings for Lacey are so strong, I've never known anything like them and haven't been able to walk away. But it's what I should have done." He groaned. "Now that things are coming together, I'm terrified of where it's leading."

"You're talking about one of her best friends. That's tough, all right," he murmured in compassion.

"Except that since I had breakfast with you and Travis, they're no longer at the top of my list of suspects," he corrected Mitch. "There've been new revelations." Without preamble Chaz brought him up to speed on the conversation he'd had with Ruth and all the lies she'd told.

"You're telling me the stalker is Lacey's *sister?*"

"I'm ninety-nine percent positive. Lacey said her sister changed after their father died." One thing Chaz had learned about the father/daughter relationship: it was usually the first long-term male/female relationship for a woman. To lose him at a crucial age could be devastating.

"She's a loose cannon, Mitch. I mean, for all I know she wears a concealed weapon. If she thought I was onto her and drew a gun on me… I simply can't take that chance. I feel like I'm back in South America confronting a situation that's eating me alive. That's why I got out before. Now here I am again, but this time it's double jeopardy."

"What do you mean?"

Chaz had reached the office and pulled into his parking spot. "You think Lacey will ever look at me the same way again when she learns I suspect her sister? That I've suspected Ruth for the last few days and haven't told her? Lacey deserves the right to know I think her sister's the stalker. But I could be wrong. Until I get the results of the DNA, that's the hell of it."

"You're never wrong. By getting her to go along with the pretend engagement, look what's happened! You've solved her case with lightning speed. Moving in with her changed the whole dynamic for her sister. Ruth wasn't careful and that phone Abby found is a dead giveaway."

"I agree, but—"

"But you're worried that when you tell Lacey, she'll shoot the messenger."

"Yes," he muttered. "I couldn't bear it if she accused me of jeopardizing her life and Abby's because I didn't yet have the DNA proof. I have to tell her what I know. But maybe I should let someone else handle the case from now on."

"Why? Tell Lacey the truth today when you're not around her sister. Whatever follows will be dealt with by the arresting officer when Ruth is apprehended. In that regard you will have been honest with Lacey, and you'll still be keeping the promise you made to yourself when you got out of the SEALs. The police will take care of the suspect. You won't have to do battle with a woman."

What Mitch said made sense, but Chaz was afraid Lacey would turn on him when he told her his suspicions about Ruth. His prime suspect was her sister! How would anyone handle news like that? He'd be walking on shaky ground with her, but he knew in his gut he had no other choice.

He took a long, deep breath. "I owe you big-time for listening to me, Mitch."

"Then we're even because I've unloaded on you

more times than I dare admit. Hang in there. It sounds like it's almost over. You know we're in your corner all the way."

"I know. Thanks." He clicked off.

Roman had just driven in. Chaz got out of the car to approach him.

Chapter Ten

"In the midfield I see another familiar face. Will Johnson makes his anticipated return in the middle of a firestorm. His shot was blocked by Rimando. A good ball to Noyes. And the foul by Gonzalez. We may have a charge coming. It's a bad foul, but he got away with it before. Yes, it's a foul. A red card is coming. Yes. Gonzalez is gone and done!

"There goes the sign for three minutes. Ten men apiece now. Jory is looking for Findley. Cooper just laid a beautiful ball at his feet. Findley scores and Real Salt Lake has taken the lead! The crowd has gone wild. Alvarez goes inside, but there's no space. Cooper almost gets there. Rasha is active tonight. Feeds to Jory. What do you know, Jeff Cunningham is now at the top of the box. There's a scramble and the shot and goal for Jeff Cunningham! That's two goals for him! Rimando didn't see it coming. Dallas ties it up 2–2."

Lacey listened to the announcer, but the play went back and forth so fast, she couldn't keep up. Chaz had brought his binoculars. They would have helped a lot if Abby hadn't wanted to look through them every few minutes. She also moved to the seat below them periodically to sit next to her new friend Cindy.

The noisy crowd was too excited to mind the heat. Between snacks and drinks, and the hugs Abby gave Chaz on impulse, it was clear her daughter was having the time of her life. So was Lacey. She enjoyed his friends, who were fun and friendly.

He leaned close enough to Lacey's ear that she could feel the side of his jaw. The contact sent trickles of delight through her body. "Look at those two little heads of blond and red curls gleaming in the sun like that. What a sight!"

She'd just been thinking the same thing. "Aren't they cute together? But I'm afraid Abby is already turning out to be a social butterfly and she's driving everyone crazy, especially you."

"This is what family life is all about. As you said on your show last night, there's no place I'd rather be than right here, right now."

Maybe she was mistaken, but she thought she heard a throb in his deep voice. It found an echoing chord inside her. While she was immersed in thoughts of him, enjoying the feel of their bodies touching, a huge roar went up from the crowd signaling the end of the soccer match. Some fans started leaving the stands.

"Don't look now, but Real Salt Lake just defeated Dallas. A lot you guys care."

At the sound of Travis's dejected voice directly behind them, Chaz stood up with Lacey and they both turned around. Though Travis's attractive features looked pained by the loss, his eyes were lit up in a smile. "Do you two even know the score?"

"Three to two?" Lacey ventured a lame guess. That was the last she'd heard, but with Chaz sitting next to her, she'd been too distracted to pay much attention.

"Wrong," Travis responded with a devilish grin. "For a brilliant astronomer studying one of Jupiter's moons at my old stomping grounds, I have to admit I'm shocked over your answer, Lacey Pomeroy."

Laughter bubbled out of her. "Blame it on the summer solstice. It's still having its effect on us earthlings."

"I can see that it is," he murmured, eyeing Chaz pointedly. "Maybe that's the reason this old SEAL decided to get himself engaged."

Mitch had been sitting next to Travis, but was now on his feet. "You know what that means? More women for us, even if they are disappointed."

Lacey could well imagine how many women had hoped Chaz would be interested in them. A picture of Ruth's deflated expression over Chaz's disinterest flashed into her mind. As for his friends, he'd warned her about their teasing. "What *are* you guys? The Three Musketeers?"

All three men burst into laughter.

"Sorry I missed out on your show last night," Mitch said after it subsided. "I'd planned to listen, but business interfered. Tonight I'm going to be all ears."

"Tonight would be a good night to tune in. I'll tell Stewart to get you in the lineup if you call in. We're going to have a NASA expert on during the first segment to tell us about UFO reports the government has covered up forever. It ought to be interesting."

"You're right." He was trying hard not to smile, but she could tell he was having a difficult time holding it back.

"It's okay to laugh, Mitch. Chaz doesn't believe in any of it, either, but my feelings aren't hurt. I've studied galaxies trillions and trillions of light-years away.

Earth isn't the only inhabited speck of dust. It couldn't be…" she mused aloud, warming to her favorite topic.

Mitch's appealing face sobered. "I got gooseflesh just then."

"She'll make a believer out of you," Chaz warned as he reached down for Abby and pulled her into his arms. She immediately began patting his cheeks and tried to open the binoculars case.

Lacey took one look and said, "I think it's time my little girl was home in bed." She turned back to Chaz's friends. "This has been loads of fun. I'm so glad I could meet you."

"It's been our pleasure."

The others clustered round. She said goodbye to everyone before they started to make their way to the exit. Over Chaz's shoulder Abby called out, "Bye, Cindy."

"Bye, Abby."

They'd chosen to bring Lacey's car because it had the car seat for Abby. Once she was strapped in, Chaz offered to drive them back to the condo. Lacey liked not having to do the driving all the time. She turned to look at him. "Thank you for a wonderful outing. Abby and I had a marvelous time."

He shot her a glance. "I did, too. That's why it makes what I have to tell you so much harder, but the time has come for you to know the facts on your case. You need to hear them before we get back to your condo." Chaz looked back at Abby. "Don't worry about your daughter hearing us. She's fallen sound asleep."

Lacey's happy smile abruptly vanished.

"I wouldn't be a good P.I. if I didn't do a thorough investigation of every suspect, and that includes your sister."

She clutched her purse. "What about Ruth?"

This was it. "She's been lying to you and your mother."

"How do you know that?"

Naturally her defenses had gone up. "I flew to Idaho Falls and learned she never had a pilot's job with any air cargo company in that region of the state."

"What?"

"She's been living with a pilot by the name of Bruce Larson who works for Landis Air Cargo. They cover routes in all of the western states where your death threats and phone calls could have come from. He lives in an eightplex in Idaho Falls.

"It's the same address she wrote down on the registration form at last year's UFO seminar in Albuquerque. When she left your condo two mornings ago, one of my crew followed her to Salt Lake International airport and she flew in a small plane with him to St. George and back. It's possible she flew there job hunting."

"Oh, Ruth—" Her moan squeezed his heart. By now, Lacey had buried her face in her hands. Though it was killing him, she needed to hear it all.

"She said Shelley Marlow introduced herself at Ted's funeral. But I spoke with your husband's best man, Rob Sharp, and he told me Shelley died from a probable drug overdose two years ago, so she couldn't have been at the funeral."

Lacey was quiet for a long time, then finally lifted her tear-drenched face. "How much more is there?" she asked in a wooden voice.

"I need you to tell me." He pulled a small photograph from his shirt pocket and handed it to her. "That's a picture I took when I was helping Abby try to find her teeny baby in her big-girl bag. Do you recognize the GoPhone among her small toys?"

The silence was palpable while she studied it. "No."

"Abby told me she found it in Auntie Ruth's closet. I'd give you the phone, but it's still with Roman. He had it traced to the person who bought it. The name that came up was Bruce Larson."

A terrible tension held them both in a vise before she said, "You think *Ruth* is my stalker? *My own sister?*" she cried out.

"Yes."

"I don't believe it. You *can't* think it!"

"Believe me, I don't want to, Lacey. You have no idea how much I don't. Remember there are other suspects who have motive and opportunity. I'm waiting on positive proof."

"What proof?" The question came out more like a hiss.

"I took the note and envelope you were sent from the Albuquerque UFO Seminar Committee to the police forensics lab. They couldn't find a fingerprint, but they found two blond-hair samples. I had an expert come to your condo while you weren't home and he went over Ruth's room to get some hair."

Her gasp resounded in the car. "The police came to my home and you didn't tell me?"

"Would you have allowed it?"

Lacey's face closed up, shutting him out.

"By Monday I'll know if your sister's DNA is a match."

Tears gushed down her face as she broke down sobbing. He felt her pain in his gut.

"If it isn't a match, then she's off the suspect list.

Nevertheless she does have serious issues you and your mother should know about for your own peace of mind."

She shook her head. "This just can't be happening. It's going to kill my mother."

"Keep in mind I haven't ruled out Jenny and the other blonds from your group. I still need to keep going with the investigation. That means we'll fly to Albuquerque the way we've planned."

"You expect me to go after what you've just told me?" She looked like a victim of shell shock.

"Yes, because no matter what, you want Abby to be safe. The stalker has to be caught so you don't ever have to be afraid again. You're the strongest woman I've ever met, Lacey Pomeroy. For a little while longer I know you can pretend in front of Ruth and your colleagues that nothing's wrong. I'll be there to protect you and Abby every step of the way."

Lacey remained mute for the rest of the drive to the condo. He parked in her space and shut off the engine. When he looked at her, an expressionless mask had replaced her tears. "I'm sorrier than you will ever know to have been forced to tell you all this, Lacey."

"That's your job," she said in a voice he didn't recognize. "It's why you were hired." He knew she was living a new nightmare. But he was glad that before another minute had gone by, he'd told her what he knew, even if she hated him for it. Oh, yes, she hated him.

"One thing is certain." She climbed out of the car, refusing his help. "Guilty or innocent, I don't want Ruth tending Abby."

Thank heaven Chaz had followed his instincts. "Since she's not here yet, let's hurry inside while you get ready for work. When she arrives, tell her that since we're leaving so early in the morning, we're taking Abby to your mom's on the way to the radio station tonight. That leaves her free to do what she wants. She won't suspect anything's wrong."

Her features hardened. "I hate doing this to Mom, but I have no other choice."

Chaz climbed out and pulled his little butterfly princess from her car seat. She slumped over his shoulder as he carried her up the steps. By the time he unlocked the door, she awakened, wanting some juice.

After a snack it came time for her bath. It turned out to be a quick affair. Jammies followed. Lacey packed a small suitcase for her along with her big-girl bag. Chaz offered to play with her while her mommy got ready for work.

LACEY STEPPED INTO THE shower suffering a pain like she'd never known in her life. Chaz hadn't said Ruth was her stalker, but he'd said he *thought* she was. Much as Lacey didn't want to believe it, her instincts told her he was the best at his job and didn't make mistakes.

Last week he'd suggested that a stalker often had a personality disorder. Was that the reason why Ruth had always been different? In order for her to have written those gruesome thoughts or said them through some voice-distortion device, they had to have sprung from a swirling cauldron in her brain Lacey couldn't comprehend. It saddened and sickened her to think that if it were true, her sister's dark side had manifested itself in a manner that was beyond horrific.

Assuming Ruth was the culprit, how many more threats would her sister make before she took action?

Chaz had said that most female stalkers didn't make physical attacks on their victims. But what if Ruth didn't fit the norm? To think that all this month Lacey had left Abby in her sister's care…

Forewarned was forearmed. She'd heard that saying all her life.

You want Abby to be safe. The stalker has to be caught so you don't ever have to be afraid again. You're the strongest woman I've ever met, Lacey Pomeroy. For a little while longer I know you can pretend in front of Ruth and your colleagues that nothing's wrong.

To keep Abby safe, Lacey *would* do anything.

She slipped into a fresh pair of jeans and a short-sleeved knit top in a light blue. While she was brushing her hair, she glanced in the mirror and realized she'd picked up a lot of color sitting in the sun. Her lips felt dry. She applied two coats of peach-bronze lipstick.

Before leaving her room, she phoned her mother and asked her if she would be willing to tend Abby tonight to save them time in the morning. Her mom was wonderful, as always, and told her to bring Abby right over. Lacey kept the call short. The conversation she needed to have with her mother would have to wait a little longer.

She walked through to the family room with Abby's suitcase and big-girl bag. "How come you didn't wear a hat?" That was the first thing to come out of Ruth's mouth. Her sister had arrived while she'd been in the shower. Abby was over on the couch with Chaz, playing with her nesting dolls. "You look like a lobster."

Lacey had put up with her sister's taunts for years. This was nothing new. "I forgot to take one to the game."

Chaz shot her a level glance. "It wouldn't have stayed on your head anyway," he commented. "Abby would have stolen it for herself, wouldn't you, sweetheart?" Chaz had been learning fast about being around a three-year-old.

"How come Abby's still up?"

"Since we're leaving early for Albuquerque in the morning, I'm dropping her off at Mom's tonight. I'm sorry I couldn't have told you any sooner, but it was a last-minute decision. Feel free to do what you want."

Ruth flashed her a strange look. "This works out perfect for me. I was going to tell you my news after you got home from the radio station, but now I won't have to wait. I'm not going to be able to tend Abby for you any longer."

That *was* news. In light of Chaz's revelations, Lacey froze in place. "What do you mean? Did you get a job?"

"No. I'm going to look for one in Denver."

"Denver?"

"Why not? I haven't had any luck here. Don't worry. As long as you don't need me, I'll clean my room and bathroom and leave tonight."

"You mean you're going to drive all night?"

"Sure. I prefer it in order to avoid the summer traffic during the day. Mom will tend Abby until you find another sitter." She disappeared down the hall to her bedroom and shut the door.

Lacey didn't dare comment or look at Chaz, but she knew what he was thinking because the same thoughts flooded her mind. Ruth had no qualms about walking out on Lacey and dumping Abby on their mother without warning. The idea that Lacey's family needed her during this time of crisis didn't even register with

Ruth. Lacey's sister had always been impulsive, but not flighty.

Ruth was on the run. There was something fundamentally off in her brain. It added credibility to Chaz's theory. The fragile thread of hope Lacey had been clinging to, not wanting to believe the truth about her sister, was stretched so thin it was close to nonexistent. Ice filled her veins.

Chaz held the front door for her and they walked out to her car in silence. Once they were on their way to her mom's, he glanced at her. "Whether she's been the one terrifying you or not, it's beginning to make sense why Ruth has held so many jobs in her life. But I know this is tearing you apart."

"For a lot of reasons," she whispered in pain. "There's something wrong with her. She hasn't been the same since Daddy died."

"In what way?"

"She was the baby. I think after he was gone, she lost her security and is still trying to find it, but this behavior isn't normal, even for her."

"I'm sorry, Lacey. Do you think you'll be able to get the same girl to tend who helped you before?"

"No. She's not available, but she has friends. One of them might be willing to fill in short-term."

"What do you mean, short-term?"

"Because I've made the decision to get out of broadcasting. I'm going to call Barry when we get back from Albuquerque and give him my notice."

Lacey heard his sharp intake of breath. "Then you'd be letting the stalker win."

"No, Chaz. That's not my reason. When I first moved back to Salt Lake, Barry talked me into doing

the show here. He was very convincing at the time
and told me it could be lucrative. I *was* worried about
money, but I'm doing fine now."

"There'll never be another Lacey Pomeroy." His
voice sounded husky.

"Someone else always comes along. Alicia, the journalist you're going to meet at the seminar, could do a
good job. Or Stewart, who wants to be a paranormal
radio host badly and would be great at it. In fact, he's
going to fill in for me as host tomorrow night. But of
course the final decision is up to Barry."

The producer had been incredibly good to her and
had gone out on a limb for her by hiring the P.I. agency.
Because the stalker hadn't been caught yet, she hoped
he'd understand the horrible strain she'd been under
and would find a replacement as soon as he could so
she could be let out of her contract.

"I'm afraid Mr. Winslow will be beside himself."

"I hope not, but I can't worry about that. Abby's getting older and to be honest, I don't like being so regi-
mented. She'll be grown up before I know it. Already
she's asking questions about why I have to leave every
night. You don't see her cry while I'm getting ready to
go to work, but she does. That's a worry for a little girl.
If she had any idea there was a stalker after me, possibly her *aunt*…

"Today at the game I was watching Cindy, and
thinking that when she went home tonight, her mother
wouldn't be leaving her. She would go to sleep without
a care. I wish I could say the same thing for my Abby.
I suspect her terror of bees is all part of *her* insecurity.

"Ruth and I lost our father and there was nothing we
could do about that. Abby's already lost one parent, but

she doesn't have to lose me every weeknight. All I have to do is quit my job. What you've told me about Ruth has clarified my priorities."

They'd arrived at her mother's house. He shut off the engine. "Let me help you."

"Thank you, but no. I'll take her in and be right back."

It had begun. Chaz felt her putting distance between them. By telling her the facts as they had lined up, he'd made his fear of losing her a lot less far-fetched. After she got back into the car, they drove to the radio station in silence.

While she began her broadcast, he planted himself in her office and listened to his phone messages. Chaz figured Ruth would be gone by the time he and Lacey got back to the condo. Anticipating as much, he phoned Lon and Jim on a conference call because he needed Ruth followed wherever she went.

"The situation has changed, guys. Lacey's sister won't be staying nights at the condo any longer. Don't let her out of your sight." He left it to the two of them to coordinate with each other. "If you need more help, call Lyle."

Ruth's sudden decision to look for work in Denver didn't ring true with Chaz any more than it had with Lacey. She was in too big a hurry to leave Salt Lake. He didn't trust her. That Bruce Larson had bought the phone Ruth had used underscored the fact that she and the pilot had some kind of secret relationship going on.

Any way you looked at it, the situation was ugly and getting uglier by the second. Somewhere in all this lay the truth, with Ruth and her boyfriend in the mix. Chaz was so close he could taste it.

Having done all the business he could for the moment, he joined Stewart to listen to and watch Lacey through the glass. Her ability to carry on in such a courageous manner impressed him beyond words. Chaz could only do so much to make her feel safe. He couldn't get inside her mind and ease her pain over her sister.

When she introduced her NASA guest Richard Fulquist on the last segment of the show, she said, "Richard, there are always those in the audience who take a cynical view of what you'll be talking about tonight. One of them could be listening, so I'll say hello to Mitch, who missed out on last night's program, but said he'd arrange to be 'all ears' tonight."

Chaz hoped Mitch had tuned in to her program. He'd noticed her visual impact on his friends, but he knew hearing her in action on a subject she loved made the fascination with her grow to a whole new dimension.

To his amusement, her last caller before she went off the air was Mitch. "Tell your producer thanks for letting me get in a final word. The conversation with your NASA guest has caused me to rethink certain opinions, and that doesn't happen very often.

"If I may quote what was said at the beginning of your show, you managed to open my mind to all the possibilities in an unending number of universes. For those who would love to see me eat crow, and you know who you are, you've gotten your wish."

Mitch couldn't have made it any plainer he was talking to Chaz, who smiled to himself before Lacey came out of the booth. But she wasn't the same woman who'd kissed him with passion the other night. This woman was the professional who said good-night to everyone and walked out to the car without waiting for him to help her.

After they got into the car he started the engine, then turned to her. "Thanks for making Mitch's night."

"I'm glad he called in." With that comment, she remained quiet for the drive home. When they reached the complex, there was no sign of Ruth's car. They went inside, and without looking at him Lacey said, "Let's grab what sleep we can."

He nodded. "Five-thirty is going to come fast. Good night, Lacey."

"Good night."

Everything about the situation was tearing him up. Much as he wanted to comfort her, he couldn't do that. Not until he could prove the stalker's identity, so the harassment would stop.

He turned on his heel and headed for the deck. A man could take only so much. He got ready for bed and lay down. As his mind went over everything he knew about Ruth, he found himself breaking out in a cold sweat. There'd be no sleep for him tonight.

When he brought his bag and mattress into the kitchen the next morning, he discovered Lacey at the sink. She'd dressed in a soft yellow two-piece suit with a silky white blouse. On her feet she wore white heels that added two inches to her height.

He locked the sliding door. She heard the noise and turned to him, causing her red hair to settle like a cloud at her shoulders. Her beauty disarmed him, but she was in tears and looked as if she hadn't slept, either.

"What is it?"

"I called my mom and told her we would drop by before we left for the airport. I need to see Abby."

"Of course."

He carried their bags out to her car and made their way to her mother's house. En route his phone rang. It was Lon reporting in.

"What's happening, Lon?"

"Ms. Garvey didn't head for Denver. She's about a half hour away from Idaho Falls. I'm a few car lengths behind her."

That didn't surprise Chaz. She was getting back to her boyfriend as fast as possible. "Stay on it and keep me posted."

He pulled into the driveway and helped Lacey from the car. The minute they went inside the house, Lacey's mother noticed the difference in her. "What's wrong, honey?"

"Everything." She hugged her mother for a long time. Chaz felt a swelling in his throat.

"Let's talk in the living room while Abby's still asleep."

Chaz sat in an easy chair while Lacey sat on the couch with Virginia. "Mom? Have you heard from Ruth or seen her since yesterday?"

"No. Why?"

Lacey's face blanched. "Because last night she quit her job with me and said she was driving to Denver to look for work."

The older woman looked shocked. "Denver?"

"Oh, Mom…there's something terribly, terribly wrong with her. Chaz has found things out about her while he's been doing his investigation. She's been living with that guy Bruce she sometimes talks to on the phone. Chaz found out she never did get a pilot's job while she was in Idaho Falls. Whatever has been going on, it's not good. I'm sick to my stomach over her."

"So am I, darling." Her mother jumped up from the couch. "She's been distant and secretive since your father passed away. Since Ted died, she's been even worse. I haven't known what to do, but I can't let this go on any longer. No matter how much she doesn't want me interfering, if I knew where to find her in Denver, I'd go after her."

"I know where to find her, Virginia." Chaz couldn't keep quiet any longer. "She's in Idaho."

Both women stared at him in surprise. The hurt look in Lacey's eyes gutted him all over again.

"As you know, I've been keeping all of you under surveillance for your protection and one of my men tracked her there. You're welcome to talk to Lon. He'll help you in any way you want." Chaz wrote down Lon's cell phone number and gave it to her.

"If you decide you'd like to drive or fly to Idaho, he'll be happy to meet you and drive you to her. He'll stay with you the entire time. Lacey and I would go with you, but I'm still working Lacey's case and it's critical we show up to that seminar. We'll take Abby with us."

The silence was palpable. "Why don't you two talk for a minute," he suggested. "Lacey? I'm going out to the car and making another seat reservation for Abby. We only need to stay at the seminar long enough for me to conduct my investigation, then we'll fly back tonight instead of Sunday."

Her lovely features had hardened. She nodded before turning to her mother. "I think you ought to go to Idaho,

Mom. I've never been able to get through to Ruth, but I know *you* can. Chaz has promised you full protection. I'll get Abby ready."

Chapter Eleven

During the hour-and-a-half flight to Albuquerque, Lacey's whole attention was focused on Abby. Chaz had to sit farther down the aisle. Brenda sat in the opposite direction from Chaz. Lacey was thankful she didn't have to talk to either of them. She couldn't.

"Oh, Abby," she whispered in torment, rocking her daughter back and forth. Her mother shouldn't have to face Ruth alone, but Lacey knew there was a side of her sister that hated Lacey in a way that knew no boundaries. Her mother would have better luck confronting her on her own.

What if Ruth really was the stalker?

Lacey must have asked herself that question a dozen times in the limo on the way to the hotel. Brenda kept up a running commentary with Chaz, unaware she was doing Lacey a favor. If she talked to him right now, she might have hysterics.

Thankfully she and Abby were swarmed by convention-goers the moment she approached the hall table to get her name tag. Jenny hadn't arrived yet. Brenda created an explosion of excitement when she announced to the UFO committee that Lacey was engaged, and the gorgeous guy with the black hair she had in tow was none other than her fiancé, Chaz Roylance.

Every female attendee within viewing distance zeroed in on him. Why not. Having been blessed with a tall, rip cord–strong physique and rugged features arranged to stop a woman in her tracks, he looked exceptionally fantastic in a tan suit and white open-necked sport shirt.

She watched him charm her core group of friends, who'd assembled around her. He'd studied the background on each one and knew what to say to draw them out. Ken was conspicuously absent, something Chaz would have noticed immediately. When the announcement came over the loudspeaker that the seminar was about to begin, he moved closer.

His eyes played over her in a way that said he liked what he was seeing. But maybe all this was for show. She didn't know what was real anymore. "If you'll let me take Abby, I'm going to walk her around and get her something to eat in the restaurant. We'll come in and out to see you, but this is your day to enjoy yourself, so take advantage of me."

After having gone to the extent of pretending to be engaged, Lacey couldn't very well say no to him in front of her friends who were listening. With Abby in his arms, he had the legitimate right to circulate and study the crowd. Her stomach clenched to realize he was here to meet Jenny, the second suspect on his list.

"That would be wonderful. I'll just take her to the little girls' room, then we'll be right back."

When she returned, Chaz plucked Abby from her arms. "Come on, sweetheart. Let's go look around."

Her cute little red head peered over his broad shoulder. "Okay. Bye, Mommy. Don't go away."

"I'll be right here."

Lacey purposely chose an aisle seat near the back of the conference room. She saved the two seats next to her for Chaz to have easy access. But from the moment the key speaker started the program, her brain was trying to fathom Ruth's troubled mind instead of concentrating on the latest UFO sightings throughout the world in the past month.

With her body in a fight-or-flight mode, she sat rigidly in her seat studying the faces of her friends. By the time lunch was announced and the divider removed for them to take their places at the tables, her nerves were shot. She was grateful for a glass of water to take a painkiller for her full-on headache.

"Lacey!" Jenny cried and rushed around the table to hug her. "My flight got in late. Where's your fiancé? I'm dying to meet him."

Her blonde friend wouldn't be so eager if she knew Chaz had suspected her from the very first. "He's taken Abby for a walk."

"You brought Abby?"

"Yes. I didn't want to leave her."

By now the chicken-and-rice entrée was being brought to the tables. "I don't blame you. Oh, I can't wait to see her." She sat down next to her. "When are you getting married?"

"That's what *I* want to know." Brenda had just joined them.

"I-it's too soon to make plans," Lacey stammered. "Abby needs time to get used to him being around for a while. I have to be sure." Though the lie was still necessary, Lacey hated this subterfuge with every fiber of her being.

"That's what engagements are for," Jenny whispered. "You can always break them and there'll be no harm done. My husband didn't want us to get engaged. Like a fool, I thought *how romantic* and dived into the deep end of marriage headfirst." Her eyes watered. "If I'd had your smarts, I would have insisted on an engagement. It would have saved me a lot of grief."

"Mommy."

Lacey swung her head around. In that brief instant she glanced up at Chaz, who held Abby in his arms. But his attention was focused on Jenny. The sheer intensity of his stare sent a chill down Lacey's spine.

"Come here, honey." She reached for her daughter, needing the comfort of her little body close to stop the tremors. "Chaz? I'd like you to meet Jennifer West, my other closest friend in the world. Jenny? This is Chaz Roylance."

He flashed that bone-melting smile he wasn't aware of. "At last we meet."

Jenny's gaze had leveled on Chaz. Like every woman, she was struck by his dark good looks. It was there in her eyes, still guarded by a layer of distrust of men in general. "I understand congratulations are in order. Lacey's one in a million."

"You don't have to tell me that. I knew the moment I started reading her Stargrazer novel." Chaz sat down on the other side of Jenny—it was the only empty chair.

Lacey hadn't meant for them to get separated. Jenny hugged Abby and didn't seem to notice or jump up to change places. Lacey was glad. Sitting next to him wouldn't be a good idea. Her pain and fear over what was happening in Idaho made it impossible to talk to him, so it was better they couldn't.

"I've been curious about something. When did you girls first learn she'd had a book published?" Chaz had thrown the question out there. He could have asked them anything. Why he'd brought up that subject baffled her.

"Mrs. Garvey told us. But we knew about everything from Rita."

"Rita?" Chaz questioned.

"The school librarian. We were all friends with her and she told us Lacey was looking for a publisher."

Brenda nodded. "We knew she'd been writing a novel about Percy."

"*How* did you know that?" Lacey couldn't believe it and stared at them in total astonishment.

They both burst into laughter before Jenny said, "We always saw you working on it in class while you were supposed to be studying. At the slumber party for your birthday, you fell asleep. We found your looseleaf and took turns reading it. If you hadn't sent it in to get published, we would have done it for you. It was that good!"

"The only thing I didn't like was the ending," Brenda blurted.

"Neither did I," Chaz interjected. "Why didn't *you* like it?"

Brenda winked at him. "Why do you think? She'd written it for young adults, so the part we adult girls were all waiting for never came."

That got to Chaz. He let go with his rich laughter, and a laughing Chaz rocked Lacey to her foundation. It caught Abby's attention. She wiggled away and ran to him. He pulled her onto his lap. "Help me finish my lunch. What does my butterfly princess want?"

"Cake!"

While everyone at the table laughed, Brenda eyed Lacey. "Butterfly princess?" she mouthed the words.

Lacey smiled. She had to admit it was pretty cute. More than cute. He was so wonderful with Abby, she had to look away while she choked down the little sob that rose in her throat. She'd been so blindsided by Chaz that first night, she hadn't seen he was first and foremost a professional P.I. just doing his job.

Her little offshoot, Abby, was no different. Chaz had gotten to her, too. But Lacey could feel things were coming to an end. In a few hours they'd be flying back to Salt Lake. She hadn't heard from her mother yet, but feared the news about Ruth couldn't be good.

Chaz had been the one who'd uncovered everything and was waiting for the results of the DNA match.

Her breath was trapped painfully in her chest. Her mother shouldn't have had to go to Idaho alone, she thought again. If there were no stalker... But there was, and Chaz had been working her case nonstop. She should be feeling nothing but gratitude, but human nature was more complicated than that. Her deepest emotions were confused and complicated.

More anxious by the moment, she excused herself from the table and took Abby to the ladies' room. From there she walked her outside for a minute and phoned her mom. When there was no response, she left a message for her to call.

As she turned to go back inside, she almost ran into Chaz, who'd come out the doors. He took one look at her and demanded to know what was wrong.

"I haven't been able to reach my mother yet."

He grimaced before examining her upturned features. "Are you getting anything out of this conference?"

"No," she answered woodenly. "I came because you said we should come."

His mouth tautened. "I've seen what I needed to see. Let's head to the airport. We might be able to get on an earlier flight back to Salt Lake. I'll arrange it."

"I—I need to say goodbye to my friends," her voice faltered.

"I'll run inside and tell them Abby's too restless and we need to go. They'll all understand. You find us a cab."

She nodded.

"Chaz!" Abby called to him. "Stay here."

"I'll be right back, sweetheart."

Stay here.

Lacey wondered how long her daughter would ask for Chaz after he'd gone out of their lives. In her heart she knew he'd be going soon.

Just now he'd told her he'd seen what he needed to see. At his office last week he'd said the next step would be to bring in the police so an arrest could be made.

Chaz had promised to keep her and Abby safe. So far he'd kept his word. He'd asked her to trust him. He'd said the pseudo engagement would produce results sooner.

When she thought back to the day Barry had first hired a P.I. from the Lufka firm, she couldn't imagine anything coming of it. Yet nine days later, it appeared Chaz had accomplished the impossible.

But not without collateral damage.

Her heart thudded painfully. Her mom hadn't called yet. Lacey was growing more and more anxious over Ruth's lies. So many of them. Such serious ones. Had she really sent that fax and left those evil phone messages?

AFTER TOUCHING DOWN AT Salt Lake International at six-thirty, they drove to Mrs. Garvey's house. Chaz had called Lon to find out about Mrs. Garvey, but their call had been dropped driving through a non-service area. As they pulled up in the driveway, he saw Lacey's mother appear on the front porch.

"Oh, I'm so glad you're back." She came hurrying to Lacey's side of the car.

"Did you talk to her, Mom?"

"No. After discussing everything with Lon, I decided to wait. They're keeping a close eye on Ruth." She looked inside the car at Chaz. "He felt you should be the one to discuss everything with me and Lacey after you got back."

He nodded. "We'll do it as soon as I check in at my office. It won't take long. Is that all right with you, Lacey?"

"Yes," she said without looking at him. "Take my car. Mom can drive me home in hers. She has a car seat for Abby. I have to get her ready for bed."

"I'll hurry," he murmured.

Abby started crying. "Stay here, Chaz."

"I'll be back, sweetheart."

He had to harden himself against her tears. After backing Lacey's car down the driveway to the street, he headed for work. It wasn't far away.

The place was as quiet as a tomb. He guessed everyone was either out working on their cases, or done for the evening. Someone had put a fax from the crime lab on his desk. He picked it up.

Mr. Roylance. Because this is a stalking case, I knew you wanted this info ASAP. Won't send complete printout now, but there was a match on the hair samples from the envelope and the DNA found in the bedroom. Hope this helps your case. S. Evans

For a brief moment Chaz felt exultation that Ruth had been conclusively identified. Lacey and Abby were no longer in danger. But his emotion was short-lived because of what he had to do now.

Do you like your job?

Ruth had asked him that question several days ago. He squeezed his eyes tightly for a minute. After pulling himself together, he checked in with Lon. "What's the status on Ruth?"

"Except to go out for a hamburger, she's been in Larson's apartment since she got here. He hasn't shown up yet. Jim drove up and we're spelling each other off. Where are you?"

"Back in Salt Lake. I just got the proof I've been waiting for. Ruth Garvey is Lacey's stalker."

"Oh, boy," Lon muttered.

"If her boyfriend has been in on it, the police will learn soon enough. I'm phoning Roman now to get hold of the authorities in Idaho Falls to make the arrest. Then I'll be on my way over to Lacey's condo to give her and her mother the bad news. Once I know how they want to proceed, you'll hear from me. Thanks for the great work, Lon. I'll let the guys on surveillance know it's over."

"I don't envy you for what you have to do."

Chaz didn't even want to think about it.

THE NEXT AFTERNOON CHAZ met Lacey and her mother at police headquarters in Salt Lake. Virginia did all the talking as he ushered them into the detective's office. He learned that Julie Howard, the girl across the street from the Garveys, had agreed to tend Abby for the day. Lacey said nothing to him. She wouldn't even look at him.

Ruth and Bruce had both been arrested. He was being held in Idaho Falls while a full investigation was carried out. Ruth had been transferred to Salt Lake. At the moment, she was being held in jail prior to arraignment before a judge.

Roman had given Chaz the name of an excellent defense attorney, Art Walker. Virginia had already talked to Mr. Walker and he'd been willing to take Ruth's case. This would be Lacey and her mother's first chance to talk to Ruth. Their haunted expressions as they left the room with the detective devastated Chaz.

After they'd gone, he pulled out his cell and phoned the office. Lisa answered. "Roman told me you did an amazing job of investigative work," she said.

"So amazing Lacey can't even look at me right now."

"She's working through a living death, but it will pass."

"I need to do the same thing. Will you put Roman on? I'd like to get out of town for a while to clear my head."

"I'll let him know you're on the phone. Hold on."

Ruth sat in a chair behind a desk wearing jail garb. When she saw Lacey and their mother, she smiled. The two of them sat down. Once the guard closed the door she said, "I'll admit Chaz knows his stuff, Lacey. You do manage to pick the studs."

Her mother leaned forward. "We've hired an attorney for you, honey. His name is Art Walker. He's going to help you."

"Nobody can help me. If Dad were here…but he isn't. No one else ever loved me."

"From what I've learned, Bruce Larson loves you and has been taking care of you for a long time."

"Until he found out I was using him. Then he broke up with me. I drove back to Idaho to tell him I wouldn't play those tricks on Lacey anymore, but he doesn't believe me. He's not Dad. No one is. You lucked out, too, Mom. You and Lacey…you always land on your feet."

Lacey's pain for her sister cut deep.

"I never would have hurt you or Abby, Lacey. I was only playing a joke because your world has always been so perfect. Then your navy SEAL moved in and ruined everything. I tried to put the moves on him like I did with Ted, but neither of them took the bait."

She'd been attracted to Ted, too? Lacey tried to absorb it all, but it was too heartbreaking.

"I'm not like either one of you, but Dad thought I was beautiful and wonderful. I wish he hadn't died." After saying that, she just sat there staring at the table, as if she were in another world.

"Do you want us to stay with you?" their mother asked, but Ruth didn't answer. The minutes ticked by before Virginia patted Lacey's arm. "Let's go," she whispered.

They got up. Her mother knocked on the door and the guard let them out. When they were alone in the hall she looked at Lacey through pain-filled eyes. "She needs psychiatric care."

Lacey nodded. "I had no idea the damage Dad's death did to her."

"Neither of us realized. Maybe a good doctor can tell us why. Let's go to Mr. Walker's office and find out what happens next."

They left the police station. Lacey looked everywhere, but Chaz had disappeared. She shouldn't have been surprised. His job was done and he'd probably gone back to the office to get started on his next case. Lacey felt as if she'd just fallen into a black void.

Chapter Twelve

By the time Lacey pulled up in front of the Lufka P.I. firm a week later, her whole body was trembling. She walked inside on unsteady legs. Lisa, the woman she'd met at the soccer game, was sitting at the front desk. When she looked up and saw who it was, she got to her feet and came around to give Lacey a hug. "I'm so sorry about your sister."

"So am I. She's finally getting the therapy she needs, so that's something anyway."

"Of course it is. What can I do for you?"

"Is Chaz going to be coming in? I didn't see his car out in back."

"I'm sorry, but he's on vacation."

The news sent her heart plummeting. "Do you know how much longer he'll be gone?"

"I don't, but when he calls in, I'll let him know you were asking for him."

"No…that's okay. Thanks, Lisa." As she started to leave, she heard her name called and turned around. "Mitch…"

He hurried toward her. "The second I saw a flash of red hair, I knew it couldn't belong to anyone else." His eyes looked at her with compassion. "I'm sorry to hear about your sister."

"Me, too, but she's in custody under psychiatric care now and with time I know she's going to get a lot better. I was hoping to talk to Chaz. It's been a week since I last saw him at police headquarters. I need to thank him."

"I'm sure he'll appreciate that."

It was impossible to swallow when her mouth had gone dry. "Do you know when he'll be back?"

"No, but if it's any help, he told us where he could be reached if an emergency came up." He stared hard at her. "Is this an emergency?"

She knew what he was asking. It was a time for honesty. "Yes. My daughter asks for him constantly."

Mitch's eyes softened. "He's staying at the Old Miner bed-and-breakfast in Deer Valley for a little R & R."

Lacey hadn't heard of it, but there were a lot of new places being built up there. She'd find it. "Thank you, Mitch." She gave him a hug before hurrying out to her car.

A half hour's drive in the mountains and she came to the charming Swiss chalet–type retreat. The man at the front desk nodded to her. "I can save you the trouble of asking for a room. We're a small establishment and are filled up until the middle of August. I'm sorry."

"Actually, I'm here to see a guest. His name is Chaz Roylance."

"He went out after breakfast and hasn't returned. If you'd like to leave a message on the phone…"

"I'll write him a note instead." She sat down on one

of the armchairs in the small lounge off the foyer and pulled pen and paper from her purse.

> *Olivia got separated from Percy after they reached Algol. She's going to die in the rarified atmosphere if he doesn't find her quick and revive her. He has the only antidote.*

Lacey got up and handed the paper to the desk manager. "Will you put this in his box?"

He nodded.

"Is it all right if I wait here?"

"Of course. Help yourself to coffee or tea."

"Thank you."

She had no idea how long Chaz would be out, but it didn't matter. Jenny was still in Salt Lake and had begged to tend Abby today. She'd insisted it would help get her mind off her father, who was going through a hard time with his chemo treatment.

Twenty minutes later Lacey sucked in her breath when she saw Chaz's dark head. He strode swiftly through the foyer dressed in jeans and a black polo.

"Mr. Roylance," the concierge called to him. "I have a message for you."

His expression fierce, he backtracked long enough to take the note before disappearing down the hall without a word.

Wondering what he would do after he read it, Lacey's heart pounded so hard she had to get to her feet. Thankfully she didn't have to wait long to find out. He was back at the desk in a flash. "Where's the redheaded woman who delivered this message?"

"I'm right here."

He spun around, out of breath. There were brackets around his mouth. She could tell he'd been suffering, but his fabulous eyes flew over her, taking on that green-and-yellow glow. It was like that night at the radio station when they'd first seen each other. She couldn't breathe then, either.

"Lacey…" He groaned her name.

She shook her head. "I don't know why you've stayed away, but I couldn't take it any longer. Mitch told me where to find you. Do you mind?"

Chaz let out a frustrated laugh. "Mind? Just now I came back here to check out and come find you. We have to talk."

"I agree." She closed the distance between them. "You think Mom and I don't know how hard this was for you? You're my hero, Chaz. We're both so grateful to you, and now it's over. My sister is finally getting the help she's needed for years. Bruce was innocent in all this, and he's standing by her. Now it's time for us. Let's go somewhere private."

He rubbed the back of his neck, as if he needed to do something with his hands. "Where's Abby?"

"With Jenny. Since you've been gone, she's been the unhappiest little butterfly I've ever seen. 'Where's Chaz?' she keeps asking me. I've been asking the same thing. Whatever has put you in this dark place, I'm here for you."

She felt his hand reach for hers and squeeze it so hard, she realized he didn't know his own strength. "My room's at the end of the hall. If you come in, I won't let you out."

"Why do you think Olivia went to Algol with Percy?"

"You'll have to tell me," his voice grated. "You cheated this adult out of the end of the story I was waiting for, remember?"

"Let's get away from prying eyes first," she whispered.

He pulled her along with him. The second they were inside the room, he pressed her against the closed door with his body. Both their hearts were racing. "You're still wearing the ring," he said against her lips.

"Since I got to Algol, it won't come off. It's grown onto my finger."

"That's good because those diamonds are real."

"*That's* why they dazzle my eyes. But real or fake, I'm in love with you, Chaz. Why have you stayed away?"

"Because I should have given your case to one of the other guys the second I suspected your sister. I was afraid I'd ruined my chances with you. To hear about Ruth from me must have been so traumatic, I wouldn't have blamed you if you despised me forever."

"How could I do that? I admit it was horrible to learn the truth, but it wasn't your fault, darling. Why would you think that?"

"In the SEALs we had orders to kill the enemy, but there was a time when I came face-to-face with women brandishing automatic weapons. It made me ill to do my job. So ill I had to get out. I promised I'd never put myself in a position of facing a female enemy again.

"I thought I was safe being a P.I. When I asked to take your case, it was because I thought it was a man stalking you. I wanted to protect you and Abby. It made me feel good for the first time since leaving the service. But the signs kept pointing to a woman. Your sister—

I didn't know if she carried a weapon. I didn't want to find out. I couldn't bear the thought that I might have to shoot her to protect you."

"Oh, darling…" She wrapped her arms around his neck and clung to him. "You *did* protect me. You made me feel safe from the moment we met at the radio station. If it weren't for you, Ruth might have gotten much worse with time. Hearing what you've just told me, I love you more for having taken that risk for me."

She covered his face with kisses. "I love you, Chaz. No other man will ever measure up to you. I need you. Abby needs you."

"Talk about needing…" He devoured her mouth until she was gasping for breath. "How long are you going to keep me waiting to marry you?"

"I don't want to wait. Everyone thinks we've known each other for a year anyway and they won't question it. In case you didn't know, I'm off the radio and a free woman. Barry's giving Stewart a try." She tasted his mouth over and over again.

"I need to do something spectacular for that man. When he went to your firm for help, he had no idea it would produce the real Percy who'd been living in my heart for years."

Chaz crushed her in his arms. "I adore you, Lacey, and couldn't love Abby more if she were my own child."

"I know you mean that, but just wait till you have one of your own, hopefully with black hair. Abby needs a sibling. What do you think?"

He cupped her face in his hands. "I think the gates of paradise just opened."

"Now you know the end of my story. But it's really

only the beginning of a new one, unfolding in a universe expanding with new possibilities. That is, if we ever stop talking."

As he picked her up and swung her around, the last sound she heard was Chaz's laughter, the most beautiful sound in the world.

* * * * *

"I don't know how to thank you."

Mitch cocked his head. "Do you have any idea how much fun I've had all day? If you want to know the truth, I felt just like your son. When you said it was time to go home, I didn't want it to end, either."

That makes three, Heidi thought.

Mitch was getting to her in ways she was scared to examine. He was a PI whose firm had been hired to find out what was going on at her company. But already he was coming to mean much more.

"What can I do to help you tomorrow?"

"Anything you'd like. Just don't go near your office or the plant. After I've gone in the facility to install the devices, I'll phone you and we'll go from there. Expect a call around two."

He turned to leave, then looked back over his broad shoulder. His eyes appeared black in the fading light. "For what it's worth, I think your ex-husband had to have been out of his mind to let you and Zack get away from him."

Mitch shouldn't have told her that. Particularly since she knew he'd be leaving Salt Lake soon.

Dear Reader,

Up by the University of Utah where I lived and went to college, there was a wonderful place to get a snack and drinks. It was called The Spudnut Shop. Everyone used to go there. The place was terribly popular because of the unique recipe of the doughnuts.

For a while I dated the son of the man who owned the franchise. Of course when he first asked me out (we were in a college class together), I had no idea of his relationship to the owner. For one thing, he was from California, not a local guy.

You can't imagine how surprised (and delighted) I was when, after going to a movie, he took me there. It was closed, but with a mysterious smile, he used a key to let us in. It was so much fun to be waited on by him. He turned on the radio and served us those famous spudnuts and root beer. Talk about exciting, with just the two of us in the shop where I'd been many times with my high school and college friends.

Sadly the shop eventually closed. Years later I was watching a documentary on the highlights of old Salt Lake and was reminded of it again. I got thinking about what a romantic date that had been, and suddenly the idea for a new novel came to mind, *The Marshal's Prize*.

Enjoy!

Rebecca Winters

THE MARSHAL'S PRIZE

BY
REBECCA WINTERS

First published in Great Britain 2012
by Mills & Boon, an imprint of Harlequin (UK) Limited,
Eton House, 18-24 Paradise Road, Richmond, Surrey TW9 1SR

© Rebecca Winters 2012

ISBN: 978 0 263 89439 4
ebook ISBN: 978 1 408 97115 4

23-0612

Harlequin (UK) policy is to use papers that are natural, renewable and recyclable products and made from wood grown in sustainable forests. The logging and manufacturing processes conform to the legal environmental regulations of the country of origin.

Printed and bound in Spain
by Blackprint CPI, Barcelona

Rebecca Winters, whose family of four children has now swelled to include five beautiful grandchildren, lives in Salt Lake City, Utah, in the land of the Rocky Mountains. With canyons and high alpine meadows full of wildflowers, she never runs out of places to explore. They, plus her favorite vacation spots in Europe, often end up as backgrounds for her romance novels, because writing is her passion, along with her family and church. Rebecca loves to hear from readers. If you wish to e-mail her, please visit her website at www.cleanromances.com.

To my terrific editor, Kathleen Scheibling,
who believes in me and my ideas. I'm very lucky.
Every author should have the privilege.

Chapter One

"Your rotary cuff has healed, Mitch. You have one hundred percent mobility and are cleared to return to work full-time. Today I'll have the office fax the information to your superior, Lew Davies, in Florida. After being away from your job almost a year, I'm sure he'll be happy to get you back on active duty."

No doubt about it. Lew Davies, more like a father figure to Mitch in the past year, would be ecstatic at the news. He needed Mitch on the job yesterday. That was a given.

"Thank you, Dr. Samuels," he said. "I appreciate all that you and the staff have done for me."

"You worked hard on your physical therapy and it really shows. Remember, you can get some plastic surgery done on the scars if you feel it's necessary. I guess you know how lucky you are to still have a great future ahead of you."

"I do."

"Take care."

After they shook hands, Federal Marshal Mitchell Garrett walked out of the Orthopedic Specialty Hospital, better known as TOSH, in Salt Lake City, Utah. TOSH was one of the finest facilities for his type of injury in the world, which was why Lew had arranged for him to be flown from Florida to Utah eleven months ago for surgery.

You know how lucky you are to still have a great future ahead of you. As he climbed into his used Audi, Mitch knew how fortunate he was to have fully recovered. Having the full use of his right arm again was his "get out of jail free" card. For during that nightmarish week after his surgery when he went crazy from total inactivity, he'd felt as though he'd been thrown in jail. Lew knew how Mitch had felt. To make certain he didn't climb the walls during the long recuperation period, he'd arranged temporary work for Mitch at the Roman Lufka Private Investigators firm in Salt Lake.

Lew had maintained that a P.I. job would be a less hostile work environment for Mitch, yet still keep his brain revved. It was a feasible solution for the off time while he trained the muscles in his arm and shoulder to function properly again.

Mitch had liked Roman Lufka from the start. The man was a total professional. It didn't take long to understand why Lufka's firm was recognized as the best P.I. firm in the Intermountain West. To his surprise Mitch found he enjoyed the work there, too. The cases were varied and challenging. Better yet, he didn't have to watch his back every second, the way he did as a marshal.

As a result he found more time to make friends with the office staff, especially a couple of the P.I.s, Chaz and Travis. Like Mitch, they'd both come from military and law-enforcement backgrounds. Chaz, who'd lost his wife to cancer, had recently married again and was now a stepfather to a cute little girl. Travis had been with the Texas Rangers until his wife was murdered in a revenge killing. He'd resigned and brought his son to Salt Lake, where he could have the support of his sister's family.

Mitch had come close to marriage several times, but he had a tendency to be somewhat of a loner and liked his own space. Because he didn't crave doing things as a couple all the time, the women he'd gotten close to felt it reflected on them and the relationships fizzled out. Though Lew argued with him to the contrary, Mitch was getting to the point where he didn't believe marriage was for him. He'd dated several women lately, but felt no spark.

Now that eleven months had passed and he was fit to resume his duties as a federal marshal, he felt conflicted.

To be conflicted was a state of mind he'd never experienced and didn't understand, because until this point in his life he'd always known exactly what he wanted to do and had felt good about his decisions. He should be excited and happy to know he could get back to his career in Florida. But he wasn't and it disturbed him.

After he turned on the Audi's ignition, he drove to his apartment, near the University of Utah. Though he should phone Lew and tell him the news, he wasn't ready to do that yet. What he needed right now was coffee. It wouldn't help his nerves, but he craved the caffeine.

When he wheeled into the double carport he shared with a pair of female college students in the next apartment, he saw the mailman chatting with them. They loved to party and were probably hitting on the guy.

Not wanting to have to turn down their dozenth invitation to hook up, Mitch remained in the car, put his cell phone to his ear and pretended he was deep in conversation. To his relief the girls finally went back into their apartment.

He got out of the car, then grabbed the mail out of the box and hurriedly unlocked the door into his kitchen. He was looking for a letter from the Florida Bureau of Vital Statistics. He wanted any information he could get in the course of his ongoing search for his birth parents.

Over the years, he'd sent the bureau numerous inquiries. Each time he'd hoped the bureau would find a new name to add to the list they'd compiled and sent to him. When he saw the envelope, he felt a rush of adrenaline and tossed the rest of the mail on the counter so he could open it.

Dear Mr. Garrett, in regard to your letter of June 30—the following birth records on those individuals with the last name Garrett, taken from the dates you specified, appear below. If this doesn't help, we suggest you search out every church in the Tallahassee area. They'll have baptismal and christening records. Don't forget the local hospitals, which keep thorough records.

Mitch had already made an attempt to do all the things suggested, but because the nature of his work left him little leisure time, his attempts were sporadic and he couldn't provide the follow-through. An in-depth investigation required months of work without interruption, a luxury he didn't have.

As a last resort, you might hire a genealogist. This can be expensive, but some of the professionals have done years of work on certain lines and can be of significant help. The best of luck to you.

Mitch appreciated the information. That was one angle he hadn't pursued. While it was on his mind, he sat down at his kitchen table and looked up genealogists in Florida on his laptop. He came across a website for the Florida chapter of the Association of Professional Genealogists. That would be a good place to start, but not right now. He was too restless and had other things to do.

Once he'd rifled through the bills and ads on the counter, he walked into the living room and turned on the TV to see who'd won the most recent stage of the Tour de France. Mitch had done a lot of cycling before his injury. He'd found it relaxing. Right now he was rooting for the American team, but it was the Belgian who won the yellow jersey today. He turned the TV off and went back to the kitchen to make some instant coffee.

While he waited for water to heat in the microwave, he checked his watch. It was 10:00 a.m. He ought to be hungry, but his appetite had deserted him. Once he'd made the coffee, he sweetened it and wandered out onto the veranda. He never tired of the view.

The small apartment for college students he rented was simply a place to sleep while he'd been recuperating. Lew had arranged for him to stay here where he could keep a low profile. Mitch preferred lots of space and the miniscule rooms provided little, but the sight of Salt Lake from this spot made up for it.

Before he'd come to Utah, he'd heard about the Valley of the Great Salt Lake. It was flanked by the Wasatch Mountains on the east and the Oquirrhs on the west, names that came from the Goshute and Paiute Indians respectively. The sight of both ranges rising close to eleven thousand feet in the dry air took his breath every time.

A unique part of the country, Salt Lake. When storms did roll in, they grew into cloudbursts at colossal heights with lightning and thunder that rocked the whole region. Right now there wasn't a cloud in the sky. It was hot already. By this afternoon the temperature would reach one hundred again, typical for mid-July.

Being a Florida native, he was used to the heat. In Florida, in fact, the heat was made more intense by the humidity. If he had to choose between both places to live and work in the U.S., the West and Salt Lake would probably win out. *Except...* Whether rational or not, Mitch didn't know if he could leave Florida for good. The sooner he contacted a genealogist in the area, the better.

He swallowed the last of his coffee. Tomorrow he'd phone Lew, who would have received the fax from Dr. Samuels. In the meantime Mitch needed to get to the P.I. office. He'd finally nabbed the culprits in the mail-fraud case he'd been working on, and there was paperwork to finish up. Anything would be better than staying here and dwelling on this new freedom, which had brought him to a crossroads he wasn't ready for. Mitch would wait until the end of the day to tell Roman his sick leave was up.

THE SECOND HEIDI BAUER NORRIS walked into her office at Bauer's Incorporated after her lunch break, the phone rang. She was the director of human resources for the company that made SweetSpud Donuts, and Mondays were always like this for her. You didn't have time to catch your breath before everything over the weekend that could go wrong came to light. She dashed to her desk and picked up the receiver on her extension. "This is Heidi."

"I'm glad you answered. It's Phyllis from No. 2."

Bauer's had twenty donut shops in the Salt Lake Valley. Heidi knew them by number. "Yes, Phyllis. How's your daughter?"

"She still has a lot of morning sickness."

"I'm sorry to hear that. I went through those days while I was carrying Zack. Tell her to hang in there and eat soda crackers before she gets out of bed. It works. What can I do for you?"

"Jim didn't come in this morning. His wife just phoned and said he was sick on Saturday so he went to the doctor. It seems he has to go into the hospital for a series of tests to find out what's wrong with his stomach. He'll be out until Thursday. I can handle today without him, but somebody needs to be here for Tuesday and Wednesday."

"I'll take care of it right away and be in touch with you."

She'd barely hung up when her great-uncle Bruno Bauer, the CEO of the family-owned company, rolled

into her office. He still had his brains and the energy
of ten people, but since the stroke that had left him
unable to walk, he'd had to rely on a wheelchair to get
around.

Last week he'd started coming into the office in
the afternoons. She'd visited him a lot during his recuperation period and knew how much he'd hated the
restrictions. At least now he was back at the work he
loved.

To her surprise, he closed and locked the door
behind him. Intrigued by his action, she crossed the
room to hug him. "This is a surprise. Why didn't you
ask me to come upstairs?"

He patted her hand. "Because since I've been back,
my office is like Grand Central Station. Too many
busybodies. Too many ears. I didn't want anyone walking in on us, but no one's going to question my wanting to talk to my favorite Adelheide first."

"So what's up?" she asked. Besides the father she
adored, she loved Bruno. He and her grandfather
were brothers who'd also been best friends. When
her grandfather had died, she'd claimed Bruno as another grandfather. He'd always gone out of his way to
be kind to her. After her divorce two years ago, he'd
brought her into the home office.

The action had miffed some of the family, who'd
questioned his action for their own selfish reasons.
She'd been only twenty-seven at the time; they were
older and more qualified. But none of them had any
idea how he'd helped her restore a little self-worth.

"I phoned your father last night and then spent hours
talking to him. Sit down and I'll tell you about it."

Heidi took her place behind the desk while he drew around the side to be close to her. There had to be major trouble for him to call her father, who'd gone on a trip to Nebraska with her mom. They were visiting Heidi's older sister, Evy, who'd just had her third baby.

"What's wrong?"

His eyes, light blue like hers, suggested their Austrian roots, but today the blue seemed to have a grayish tinge. He looked troubled. "I have reason to believe Jonas and Lucas are stealing from the company."

"Oh, no!" Jonas and Lucas were the son and grandson respectively of Bruno's sister Rosaline.

Bruno nodded solemnly and told her what he'd discovered. "In all the years this company has been in business, we've had small thefts here and there, but we've never had anything major like this." He went on to give her the details. "Your father agrees with me we need immediate expert help from an outside source."

"You mean the police."

"No. They'll bungle it." He waved his hand. "I want answers fast in an environment of absolute secrecy. This is where you come in. I've done some checking and want you to go to this P.I. firm today. They're reputed to be the best. I've called them and they'll be expecting you. Talk to the owner. Tell him the problem and find out what he suggests."

He pulled a paper from his suit pocket with a name and address on it and handed it to her. She was surprised to discover it read "Roman Lufka Private Investigators," located on Wasatch Boulevard. She must have passed it thousands of times, but she'd never known anything about it.

Bewildered, she stared at Bruno. "You trust me to take care of something this critical?"

He eyed her steadily. "No one knows the ins and outs of this company better than you do, and your father agrees with me. You're as brainy and savvy as my grandmother Saska, who started the whole thing. One day you'll be the CEO, mark my words."

Not if some of the family had anything to do with it, Heidi thought. Besides, she didn't have aspirations in that regard. But she loved him for saying it. Tears pricked her eyes before she got up from the chair and hugged him again.

Bruno could have asked anyone on the twelve-member board—all family—to do this. They'd had years more experience and wisdom. Yet the fact that he and her father had so much faith in her gave Heidi a much needed morale boost. Her bad choice of husband and ugly divorce had badly undermined her confidence.

"I want you free to work with this firm, so I'm going to ask your aunt Marcia to take over your duties temporarily. I'll tell her you'll be busy for the rest of this week visiting our outlets around the valley. That way no one will suspect anything. I trust you to handle this any way you see fit. This has to be between you and me and your father, no one else."

Though Bruno had bestowed a distinct honor on her, she couldn't help but be troubled. "Do you think Rosaline is behind this?"

He looked agonized. "My sister and I have always been at odds, but I don't think she put Jonas and Lucas up to this. Unfortunately I can't rule it out as a possibility."

She nodded. The Bauers were a huge family with many internal problems. Bruno had put out little fires for years on a regular basis, but Jonas and Lucas stealing from the company was a totally different level of concern.

"Go ahead and leave now," Bruno said. "Phone me tonight and tell me how it went." He patted her hand before wheeling out of the room.

Heidi took care of some emails, then grabbed her purse and headed out to her white Nissan, parked at the side of the building. After dropping her six-year-old son, Zack, off at school earlier in the day, she'd driven to work wondering what new problems she might face. She'd never have entertained the thought of their family being on the brink of an internal war, let alone that Bruno would have put her in charge of working with a P.I. to handle it.

The Bauer building was located just below Wasatch Boulevard on Thirty-third South. She got in her car and headed for the Lufka firm farther north. After she'd done business there, she would find a substitute for Jim. By then it would be time to pick up Zack.

When she entered the P.I. building, the receptionist said they'd been expecting her. She was shown into Roman Lufka's private office. The attractive, dark-haired owner listened and asked questions, then excused himself. "I need to see if the P.I. I want to work with you has arrived at the office yet. Can I get you a coffee while you wait?"

"No, thank you."

MITCH HAD LEFT HIS OFFICE door open. To his surprise Roman walked in and put a cup of coffee on his desk. "Do you have a minute?"

"Sure. Thanks for this." He took a sip. What harm was there in one more dose of caffeine? "I was planning to have a talk with you at the end of the day, but as long as you're here, maybe I should get this over with now."

Roman's brows furrowed. "You saw the doctor this morning. What's the verdict?"

His boss was a straight talker. It was one of the reasons Mitch liked him so much. He deserved straight talk back. Letting out a deep sigh he said, "I'm free to return to Florida."

"That's what I was afraid of. I guess I don't have to tell you no one in this office—and I mean no one—wants to see you go, least of all me. Since your arrival, you've become an invaluable asset to the firm. But much as I'd like to twist your arm and beg you to make this your career, I happen to know Lew Davies has been counting the days until your return. I can only imagine you must be anxious to leave, too."

Mitch shot to his feet. "Hell, Roman—I don't know what I'm feeling right now. I've been in a fog since I left TOSH this morning."

"That doesn't surprise me. You may be a crack federal marshal, but you're also a natural-born P.I. I don't want to lose you. Would you like some advice from a man who's been in your shoes?"

"Of course." Mitch had immense respect for Roman, a man in his midforties who'd done and seen a lot in his life.

"Now that your body has healed, give yourself a

little more time to let the news sink in before you make any decision. In the meantime, I have a new case that might appeal to you. It requires your bloodhound instincts." Roman cocked his head. "I hope you're interested, because if you are, I'll talk to Lew Davies and tell him I need you for a little longer. When you've solved this case, maybe by then you'll know if the federal marshal in you won't let go."

"Bless you for the reprieve, Roman." Mitch felt that an enormous weight had been lifted from his shoulders. "Who's the client?"

His boss's face broke out in a broad smile. "You're going to love it."

Mitch chuckled in spite of the seriousness of the situation. His boss was the best and also one of the biggest teases he knew. "I know you're dying for me to ask why."

Roman nodded. "You're not going to believe it. Every guy in the firm would give his eyeteeth to work on it."

"That good, huh?"

"'Good' doesn't begin to describe it. I'll give you a hint. What could none of us around here live without?"

"Coffee."

"Think what goes with it."

Mitch didn't have to think. "SweetSpuds."

"This is your lucky day. I'll bring her in to meet you."

"Her?"

"Heidi Bauer Norris, twenty-nine and divorced with a six-year-old son." He paused at the door. "She's the great-great-granddaughter of Saska Bauer, who emigrated from Austria to Salt Lake in 1892 and founded the Bauer Donut company. Her family has been making SweetSpuds ever since. They're the premier-selling donut in the western half of the U.S. Our firm has helped keep them in business."

Mitch could vouch for that.

"I've already discussed the fee with her. But you might tell her we'd be happy to negotiate part of it. I'm sure you can think of a way that will please everyone."

Laughter rolled out of Mitch, a much needed re-lease. But it quickly subsided when Roman escorted the woman in question into his office seconds later. She was probably five six. Her tailored blue summer suit with the short-sleeved jacket revealed a trim figure.

When Roman introduced them, he found himself looking into impossibly light blue eyes. Her tiny ear-rings were crystals of the same, which sparkled from beneath a mop of pale gold curls that he bet had looked that way from childhood.

She was in a word, beautiful.

"It's a pleasure to meet you, Ms. Norris. Please sit down."

"Thank you, Mr. Garrett. I appreciate your being available so quickly."

Roman's narrowed eyes sent him a private message. "I'll leave you two alone to discuss the case."

"Being available goes with this business," he said after his boss departed. "It's the nature of the job. Every client's needs are immediate."

She nodded. "My great-uncle Bruno couldn't get me out of the office fast enough this afternoon to talk to someone from your firm."

"We'll do all we can to help you." He smiled, and

in an effort to make her feel comfortable, said, "I understand you have a six-year-old son. Lucky you."

"Yes. His name is Zack and he's the light of my life."

"I can imagine."

He sat down opposite her. "I'm going to record our conversation. Is that all right with you?"

"Of course, but does anyone ever say no?"

"You'd be surprised."

"Then what do you do?"

"Take handwritten notes, but I have difficulty reading my own writing."

"So do I."

When her heart-shaped mouth curved into a smile, Mitch realized he would have to figure out a way not to stare at her. An attraction like this hadn't happened to him for so long, he felt out of his depth.

His boss had been up to his old tricks when he'd teased him about this being his lucky day. He hadn't just been talking about the donuts.

Before he got started, he drank some of his coffee. "I'm going to ask you a lot of questions. Try to be as explicit and detailed as possible. It will help me get the picture I need."

"I'll try."

"Good. Let's start with your great-uncle Bruno. What's his position in the company?"

"He's been the CEO of Bauer's for forty years."

"That's a long time. What's the reason he suddenly needs a P.I., and why didn't he come himself?"

"Bruno is eighty-seven now and confined to a wheelchair because of a stroke he had six months ago. It's hard for him to go many places, but his mind is still razor-sharp, and his wife, my great-aunt Bernice, still fusses over him. His grandson, Karl Bauer—he's thirty-five—works in lower management and drives him to work and back. On his lunch hour Karl picks up Bruno—Bruno puts in half days at the office—then they both go home together."

Despite recording, Mitch took notes just to keep his eyes averted as much as possible. "I assume you're talking about the Bauer building on Thirty-third South? I've passed it many times."

"Yes. It's our headquarters. When I got back from lunch today, Bruno came to my office and told me in private he fears someone within the company is stealing from us. As I've learned over the years, most businesses can expect a certain amount of theft, but we've never had anything this big or alarming until now."

"Does he always confide in you over a serious matter like this?"

"Well, we've always been close. I think of him as my grandfather now that my real grandfather has passed away. They were brothers and best friends. I spent a lot of time with him while he was recovering from his stroke. He says I remind him of his grandmother Saska, who started the company. There's an old family picture of her at the age of twenty-five. I do look like her and he loved her a lot."

"Obviously he loves and trusts you. Who else has he told?"

"My father, Ernst Bauer. He's sixty-three and the general manager of operations for the company. Right now he's in Nebraska with my mother, Marva. They're visiting my older sister, Evy. She's thirty-two and just had her third child. They won't be back for about five more days."

"What's your position in the company?"

"I'm the director of human resources."

"How long have you worked in that position?"

"Two years."

"So if I wanted a job with your company, I would apply to you."

"Right. I don't have the power to hire, but I make recommendations. So far every prospective employee I've vetted has been hired."

"I'm sure your great-uncle finds that impressive. Do you have any siblings besides Evy?"

"Yes. My brother, Rich. He's thirty-six and has been head of the accounting department for five years. He's married to Sharon and they have four children."

Mitch sat back in his chair. "Explain to me what exactly is being stolen."

"The mix for our donuts. It's manufactured and bagged at our plant in Woods Cross. We ship it all over the western states in our own fleet of trucks. The bags are loaded from the warehouse onto the trucks and they're delivered to our various outlets and franchises."

"How did Bruno discover the theft?"

"Through his closest friend, Victor Tolman. Vic's son Don owns a Bauer donut franchise in Phoenix. Bruno and Vic talk all the time. When he found out Bruno was well enough to get back to work, Vic confided something he'd been holding back.

"It seems that over the last five months, one bag of mix in every shipment arriving in Phoenix was missing. In its place was a bag of potato flour."

Mitch eyed her in puzzlement. "Potato flour?"

"Yes. Our SweetSpuds are made with potato flour rather than wheat. It's from an old recipe Saska brought with her from Austria. When there was no wheat available there, they cooked potatoes, then dried them and crushed them into powder to make their bread. It's the reason our donuts outsell other kinds. Potato flour makes a much lighter donut."

"I had no idea. That's fascinating. I can eat a dozen at one sitting."

She laughed softly. "Bruno would love to hear you say that."

"Do you grow your own potatoes?"

"No. We buy a special kind in Idaho and have them shipped down to our plant. Through a unique process we turn them into flour and put it in bags. They're stored in the Woods Cross facility before being taken to the other part of the plant where the mix is made up and put into bags to be shipped."

"Are all the bags the same?"

"Yes, but they have a different tag. The flour-only tag is red, the mix tag is blue—they're sewn into the bottom seam of each bag and the expiration date for the contents is stamped beneath them. The men loading and unloading the bags on dollies wouldn't notice the color of the tags unless they're looking for it. But they wouldn't be looking because the bags are kept in separate areas and depend on the quality-control person to catch mistakes like that."

"How many locations receive deliveries?"

"Four hundred and thirty. When the mistake happened the first time, Don dismissed it. But it happened again in each of the three subsequent shipments. By the fifth shipment he talked to his father who advised him to email the plant office. Don received an email back telling him his next shipment would contain five extra bags of mix and sorry for the inconvenience.

"When Bruno tried to pull up the emails, they weren't there. Suspecting something was wrong, he phoned the manager of our outlet in Albuquerque and learned the same thing had been happening. The manager had reported the errors by email, and the plant had shipped him an extra bag each time. Again Bruno couldn't find those emails. After another call to one of the franchises in San Bernardino, Bruno heard the same story and came to the conclusion it was happening everywhere."

"What's the shipping frequency?"

"Shipments go out every weekday to all the western states, including Utah. Bruno figures that over the last five months, hundreds of bags of mix have been stolen."

Mitch let out a low whistle. "That's quite a few bags pilfered while Bruno was ill. If unstopped it wouldn't take long to stockpile a nice stash that could be used to sell donuts under another name."

"Exactly," she said. "When Bruno first had his stroke, there was talk that he would never be able to come back to work. But he's a fighter and went to therapy. He put in his first half days last week, yet since his return, neither Jonas—he's the plant manager—nor his son, Lucas, who runs the warehouse, has mentioned there's a problem. He believes one or both of them are covering up."

"Not necessarily. It might be some underlings deleting the emails and pulling this off under their noses."

"You're right. Could be anyone in the warehouse."

"Tell me about Jonas and Lucas."

"Jonas is the son of Bruno's oldest sister, Rosaline Martin. He's sixty-one and the head of the plant. He could be masterminding the thefts through his son, Lucas, who runs the warehouse and is the quality-control person."

"How old's Lucas?"

"Thirty-seven. He has a wife and three children."

"Aside from assuming that greed and/or jealousy could be the motive, plus the fact that these two hold key positions in the company—which give them the means to carry out this crime—is there any other reason Bruno has suspected them particularly?"

"Rosaline has always wanted to expand Bauer's to the Midwest and East Coast. We know she has indoctrinated her children with that idea. Some of the other family members agree with her, but Bruno has never seen the need to grow the company because of the headaches involved. So far there haven't been enough votes for her wishes to prevail at the family board meetings."

"So it's very possible either Jonas or his son, or both, have decided to take things into their own hands," Mitch surmised. She nodded. "Run me through the quality-control process."

"During the workday, the mix is made up and put into bags. A crew of warehouse workers loads them on motorized carts and they're taken to the warehouse bay where they're left overnight, ready to load on trucks the next day. Jonas's job is to count them and put all the information in the computer.

"The next day the bags are loaded on trucks. When

they're filled, the crew boss, Randy Pierson—he's another Bauer—checks off the shipments and stores the information in the computer. Lucas prints out what has been stored in the computer and makes a hard copy, which he leaves in Jonas's in-basket.

"One of the employees working at the outlet or franchise on the receiving end of the delivery helps take the shipment off the truck and sends an email receipt back to Lucas. It shows the itemized list that includes the date, actual hour of delivery and amount of goods delivered.

"But again, the people receiving the goods wouldn't think to look at the tags. All they're concerned about is the correct number of bags arriving. It might be a week or two before the bakers opening a new bag discovered the flour and realized a mistake had been made. Obviously that's what happened in Don's case. It's all very random, so that—"

"So that it looks innocent enough," Mitch broke in. "What's done with the flour?"

"It's disposed of."

"Why not returned?"

"Because the flour we use must be freshly bagged. That's company policy. It can't be used outside the plant and we can't take it back once it has left the plant."

"That means you're not only losing money on all the stolen mix, you're losing revenue from the wasted flour, the cost of the bags, money paid the warehouse workers loading the trucks and flour, money paid the drivers, etc."

"Precisely. If there's anything Bruno hates more than laziness, it's waste."

Mitch's brows lifted. "Guess that's why he's been in charge all these years. No doubt his stroke caused the culprits to believe they were home free. By disposing of the emails, there's no 'paper' trail."

She let out a troubled sigh. "Bruno talked to my father. They want to catch them in the act, whoever it is. That's why Bruno decided to hire a P.I. firm—he wants definite proof before confronting them."

"Your great-uncle sounds like a shrewd man."

"He's brilliant, but he's torn up inside to think members of our own family are doing this. Still, he refuses to see the company suffer under his watch."

"How many are on the board?"

"Twelve."

"Give me the names of the family members who would like to see the company grow."

"Besides Rosaline, my great-aunt Frieda and uncle Ray Owens have been outspoken about it for a long time. Frieda's my grandfather's next oldest sister. When I'm around them, she grumbles about Bruno being too steeped in archaic ideas to run the company any longer. She was upset when I was put in the human resources position instead of her grandson Anthony. But she has two other grandchildren who hold responsible positions—Randy's the crew boss and Nadine runs the operation for the mix."

Mitch steepled his fingers. "Considering the foment going on, I'm impressed your great-uncle has managed to run such a successful enterprise. Tell me—who's the keeper of the flame?"

"You must be talking about the recipe. It's locked in a safe-deposit box at the bank. No one has access to it but the CEO, currently Bruno. It can't be opened without him, the head of the bank and the attorney for the company being present. The various workers only know one part of the recipe. No one knows the whole thing.

"When Bruno retires or dies—" Mitch could see the thought upset her "—a new CEO would have to be chosen before he or she had the right to go to the bank and look at it in the presence of the other two witnesses."

Mitch nodded. "That's the best way to safeguard a secret recipe for famous wine or chocolate these days. But as your great-uncle has found out, no measures are foolproof. Since no one in your family but him can get to the actual recipe, it appears certain members are determined to do it the old-fashioned way. I wouldn't put it past them to hire a chemist to analyze the ingredients and try to duplicate your recipe, but that's a very difficult thing to do."

She shivered. "It's so cold-blooded."

"That's the nature of crime. Clearly it's happening at the warehouse. Do you hire trucks?"

"No. We own a fleet of twenty-two located on the Woods Cross property."

"How many workers total are employed there?"

"Including the drivers, one hundred and ten people. Fourteen are family members who oversee the various divisions within the facility."

"That was going to be my next question. There may be more than two family members involved in the thefts out there."

A pained expression crossed her face before she nodded.

"It's evident they're the total opposite of your ancestor Saska."

"What do you mean?"

"From what you've just told me, she was one of those exceptional pioneers I've heard about who helped forge the West into greatness."

The light blue eyes grew shimmery. "That's exactly what she did."

For a brief moment he felt a tug on his emotions that surprised him. He finished the rest of his coffee while he gathered his thoughts.

"Large families who work together are notorious for having inside problems. I'm sure yours is no different, with its mix of angels and less than angels who, because of ego, greed or dreams of power, want to take shortcuts to success."

A sadness crept over her face. "That describes some of our family members."

"And possibly some nonfamily employees who are being paid off because they want or need the extra cash and feel no particular loyalty to the company or your great-uncle. It happens every day. I'm sorry it's happened to your family's company."

"So am I." Her voice caught. "No one has worked harder than Bruno to keep the company profitable and provide every benefit for the employees."

"Some people are never satisfied. They'll always want more."

"That's true," she whispered. Mitch heard a haunted note in her voice, wondering if she was thinking about something that had nothing to do with her family's business.

"In order to find out what exactly is going on, it'll

be necessary for me to infiltrate. But first I'll need a little hands-on experience in the shortest amount of time before you move me out to the plant. What kind of a job can you give me right now to familiarize myself with the product?"

She was so quiet for a minute, he thought she'd been too deep in thought to hear him.

"Ms. Norris?"

Her eyes finally lifted to his. "The baker at our No. 2 shop will be in the hospital undergoing some tests for a few days. Phyllis, the manager, called me earlier today to ask me to find a replacement. I'll tell her no one was available because they're away on summer vacation. Therefore I was forced to hire a new applicant and will train you myself. We'll start first thing tomorrow morning."

The idea of working with her appealed to Mitch like crazy. "What time?"

"Six? Does that sound awful?"

"No. I'm an early bird. But what about your job at headquarters?"

"Bruno has asked my aunt Marcia, who oversees the insurance department, to cover my position at the office for the rest of the week. She had my job before she was moved to that department and can fill in without problem. He's instructed me to assist you so you can resolve this problem ASAP."

He felt a sudden rush of excitement he couldn't explain. All the time they'd been talking, he'd been wondering how he could get to know her better without seeming too obvious.

"Where's the shop located?"

"At SweetSpuds on Foothill, not far from here."

This was getting better and better. "That's our home away from home during working hours around here. My apartment's near the entrance to Emigration Canyon, maybe two minutes away. The situation couldn't suit me better."

"It suits me, too. My house is in the St. Mary's area near the Foothill shopping center. Zack's school is only two blocks from there. Which reminds me, I have to leave now or I'll be late to pick him up."

"Let me walk you to your car." He got up from his desk and followed her out the door, enjoying the trail of her subtle lemony fragrance. "Is he in a summer school camp?"

"No. It's year-round school. He'll be off track in two weeks. That's when I'll take my vacation to be home with him."

"I see." They went down the hall past Roman's office. His door was closed. Everyone in the office looked busy, but he noticed them casting glances at her. You couldn't help it. He wouldn't be surprised if she stopped traffic when she stepped outside. Lisa Gordon, Roman's married assistant, gave him a secret smile before they went out the front door. She was always trying to interest him and Travis in some terrific single woman she knew.

In a minute he was helping Heidi into her Nissan. "I'm going to need more information from you, but there's no time now. Will you be free to talk on the phone later?"

"I can after I put Zack to bed."

"Will eight-thirty be all right?"

"Yes. He'll be asleep by then."

"If you'll give me your cell phone number, I'll program it in mine right now."

They exchanged phone numbers before she started her car and drove out of the parking area.

Mitch walked back inside the building unable to relate to the man who six hours ago didn't know which foot to put in front of the other. Now would be the time to email Lew and set up a time to discuss his clean bill of health, but he was in the middle of a case. After it was solved, he would call him to discuss future plans.

Chapter Two

Heidi got out of her car and waited by the passenger door for Zack. Her dark-blond first-grader came running over in his shorts and Shrek T-shirt, carrying his backpack. He used to have a head of curls, but when he told her how much he was teased at school, she took him to the barber and he now sported a buzz. In an instant her little boy had disappeared.

While they were still on the school grounds, she couldn't expect a hug and a kiss. The big guys didn't do that. He wanted to be a big guy so badly, he climbed in the backseat and strapped himself in his car seat.

"How was school?"

"Good. Can we get a grape slushie?"

"Sure. It's hot out." She pulled in at a convenience store. Once they were on their way again she said, "What was the favorite thing you did today?"

"Recess." He rarely gave her a different answer. From what she'd learned at the last parent-teacher conference, he was doing well in all his subjects, but needed work on making better letters. "When will Grandma and Grandpa be home?"

"This weekend." But she knew better than to give him an exact time. Heidi realized he was missing them. Though he didn't see them every day, it was the idea that they'd gone far away. They'd always fussed over him. "I thought we'd see if Tim wants to come over for a while."

Her brother, Rich, and his family lived a few blocks away. Though Tim was a year older, Zack liked him a lot and they'd played well together, until recently.

"Can we just go home instead?"

"What's wrong? Are you feeling sick?"

"No. I just want to watch SpongeBob."

He'd been watching quite a bit of TV alone after school lately while Heidi got their dinner ready. "Tim likes that cartoon, too."

Through the rearview mirror she saw Zack shake his head. "All he wants to do is ride his bike."

Ah. Heidi got the picture. Rich had taught Tim how to ride, but Zack still had to rely on training wheels for his bike and he felt stupid around his cousin. She'd tried to help her son, but he cried and got frustrated. He probably didn't want to look like a baby who needed his mother to help him. When Rich tried to offer a suggestion, he said he wanted to go home.

A problem for another day. After she'd divorced Gary, she'd tried to make up for the lack of a father in the home, but it was hard. And of course Rich wasn't Zack's father. A boy wanted his own father.

Zack didn't remember Gary. At the time of the divorce, he'd only been four. Heidi had put some pictures of him on Zack's dresser and the rest in an album she'd put away. Some day he'd want to see them. Gary, who'd worked for her family's company, had been too eager to get ahead fast. She hadn't realized how power hungry he was. Toward the end of their marriage, her father had fired him for getting into too many struggles with his immediate boss.

Among the many things Gary had found wrong with Heidi during their four years together, he'd been furious that she didn't fight to help him keep his job. After the divorce, he only came around one time. Though he'd said it was to see Zack, he'd really shown up to harass her and tell her she'd ruined his life. It didn't surprise her that the first of the court-ordered child support payments didn't arrive. None did.

Heidi made enough money without them and never reported the failure because she wanted nothing more to do with the angry man he'd become. She'd felt nothing but relief when her attorney found out from his attorney that he'd signed away his parental rights and had left Utah. He'd gone back to Oregon where he'd been raised by his grandparents.

Zack had accepted Heidi's explanation that she and his daddy didn't get along and he now lived somewhere else. But the day was fast coming when her son would want more in-depth answers. Just the other day he'd asked how come his uncle Rich and aunt Sharon weren't divorced. Heidi had said that some couples were more compatible. She'd sat down with him to explain the meaning of compatibility. He'd listened, not saying anything before he went to sleep.

While Zack watched cartoons in the family room, Heidi phoned her sister-in-law and made arrangements to drop Zack off at their house early in the morning so she could be at the shop by six. Sharon was the best, and said she would drive him and her children to school later.

With that settled, she fixed dinner. Afterward she

helped Zack with his homework, then he took a bath. Once he'd put on his Transformer pajamas and had said his prayers, she let him pick out a couple of his favorite books and they read together until he fell asleep.

It was quarter to nine and her cell phone hadn't rung yet. To her irritation she'd been anticipating talking to the P.I. since she'd left his office. Maybe he'd had something else come up and couldn't call. Impatient with herself, she walked into the living room and sat down on the couch to phone Bruno. Her great-uncle usually went to bed early, so she thought she'd better make contact now.

He liked what she had to tell him about Mitch and approved of the infiltration idea. Halfway through her conversation with him, she discovered someone was trying to reach her. She told Bruno she'd talk to him tomorrow and clicked off to take the other call.

"Hello?"

"Ms. Norris, it's Mitch Garrett." The male voice she remembered sounded deeper over the phone, curling her toes. "Sorry I'm calling a little late, but it couldn't be helped. If this isn't a convenient time—"

"It's fine. I just got Zack to sleep."

"Then I'm glad I didn't interrupt. Since we need to talk, how would you feel if I dropped by your house? I can be there in a few minutes."

An unexpected feeling of excitement swept through her. "That's fine. I'll watch for you."

After they hung up, she hurried into the bathroom to brush her hair and put on lipstick. She hadn't been out on a date since before she'd met Gary. Not that this was a date or anything like it. Still, Mitch Garrett was a very attractive man. Something about him made her aware of herself as a woman. He probably had that effect on every female he met.

When she saw lights in the driveway, she felt another quickening inside of her. What on earth? He'd come over to discuss this terrible thing happening in the company and here she was waiting for him with this fluttery feeling in her chest.

She opened the door for him. "Come in."

"Thank you." The minute he stepped into the living room of her house, he noticed the stand-up framed photo of Zack and paused to look at it.

"Your son looks amazingly like you, but he's darker blond and his eyes are a deeper blue." Mitch managed to notice everything. "He even has your curly hair."

"He did until recently when I took him for a haircut. Zack told the barber to make him look like a Marine."

Mitch chuckled. "Every boy his age wants to look like a man. With a tough name like Zack, he's got to fit the part. Did you cry when he was sheared?"

Heidi laughed. For that kind of understanding she supposed he was married with a family, even if he didn't wear a wedding band. "Yes, I shed a few tears while he wasn't looking."

"Just remember he's cooler this way."

"I'm sure that's true."

Mitch walked around, studying the rest of the family pictures, nodding when she told him who he was looking at. "You have a beautiful home," he murmured before turning to her. "And thanks for helping me put names and faces together. It's good for an investigation like this."

"Of course."

His glance went to the painting over the piano.

"I covet that oil of Mt. Timpanogos. The first time I drove south of Salt Lake, I saw it as I rounded a curve in the road. It's spectacular with snow on it."

"I think so, too. It's a painting my grandfather did years ago. He hiked that mountain many times when he was younger."

"I've meant to do it myself. One of these days I will."

"Won't you sit down?" She'd motioned to one of her striped Italian provincial chairs, noticing details about him as he took a seat. He wore his dark-blond hair fairly short. In the lamp light she glimpsed gold highlights on the tips, and the slight cleft in his chin. The rest of his features were hard, rugged male.

"I have a couple of questions," he began. "First, what should I wear to work in the morning?"

"Anything casual. Everyone who works there wears jeans. You'll be supplied an apron that goes around the neck."

"That sounds fine as long as my colleagues don't see me in it."

Mitch Garrett didn't need to worry. With his masculine features and tall, strong physique, he couldn't have been more manly. When Bruno had asked her to report to the Lufka P.I. firm, she'd pictured working with some overweight, middle-aged television-attorney type.

The midthirties man with brown eyes almost piercing in their intensity had come as a total surprise. Coupled with his dangerous, unconscious air of power, his image had refused to leave her mind and was now indelibly inscribed.

She flashed him a smile. "We make the donuts at

the back of the shop, so if any of your coworkers pop in when it opens, they won't see you."

"That relieves my mind more than you know. Now for the next question. What would be the best way for me to access your company's personnel files without going to your office? I need to see everything."

"If you'd like, after we've finished work tomorrow, we'll drive to your office and I'll download the files to your computer from my phone."

"Excellent. When will we be finished work?"

"By 9:00 a.m."

"Good. That means we'll have enough time to go over the names and backgrounds of the employees until you have to pick up your son. I'm going to need other kinds of information, too." He pulled a folded sheet of paper from his pocket and handed it to her. "If you can be prepared to answer these questions I've written here, our work will go faster."

"I'll go over them before I get in bed."

"You've been more than helpful already," he said, and before she was ready to see him go, he got to his feet. "I know six o'clock will come early, so I'll say good-night and we'll discuss everything else tomorrow."

Heidi walked him to the door. After he'd driven away, she sank down on the couch to read over his checklist. He wanted to know where every stop was along every route. He was so thorough, it was positively scary. Finally she got ready for bed, but it took her a long time to fall asleep. Today had turned into such a challenging day. A threat to the company from within the family ranks had prompted Bruno to hire a private investigator.

Of all the P.I.s out there, the man she'd been thrown into the middle of an investigation with was cast from a different mold than most men. If Jonas and Lucas were behind the thefts, they had no idea of the kind of force they were up against.

AFTER A SHOWER AND SHAVE, Mitch dressed in jeans and a T-shirt before leaving for the donut shop. When he pulled up in front of SweetSpuds, the sun had just peeked over Mount Olympus.

So many times he'd dropped by here on his way to work, never dreaming that one day he'd be making donuts with the most appealing woman he'd ever met. She seemed to have an inner beauty that made her whole being light up. By the end of the day today, he hoped he hadn't been imagining it. Too many times he'd been disappointed by some feeling he'd thought was real, only to discover otherwise. Over the past few years these letdowns had taken their toll, making him feel older than his years.

He got out of his car, noticing the sign on the glass door. Open eight to six, Monday through Saturday. Closed Sunday.

"Good morning, Mr. Garrett." She'd pulled in and parked next to him. When she climbed out of her Nissan, the sun gilded her mass of curls. His shuttered gaze took in the rest of her down to her sneakers. Yesterday she'd worn a suit. Today she was in jeans and a loose-fitting navy T-shirt. No matter what she wore, nothing could hide her gorgeous figure.

"Call me Mitch, please. Mind if I call you Heidi?"

"Not at all," she said, looking for the right key to open the shop door. He followed her inside. It was a small facility. Behind the counter he saw a door that led to the back room. Next to it were the tall racks of shelving that held the donuts. The place served coffee and soft drinks from the side counter. In the front were four small round tables and enough chairs to serve sixteen people at a time.

"Come through this door and we'll get started. The restroom for employees is back here, too."

The modern kitchen was outfitted with a massive fridge and all the necessary equipment, including a washer and dryer. Built-in shelves held the fifty-pound bags of mix with the blue tags. More shelves on wheels contained the donut trays. A half-dozen donuts remained in one of them. When she saw where his eyes had wandered, she said, "Help yourself, Mitch."

"Don't mind if I do." He reached for one with chocolate icing. "My boss told me I was going to love this job."

She chuckled. "Working here has ruined many a figure. I can't tell you the number of diets I've had to go on over the years." She handed him an apron from the cupboard, then grabbed one for herself.

As they put them on, Mitch flicked her another glance. He decided not to comment that her efforts obviously hadn't been in vain. There wasn't an ounce of surplus flesh he could see on her anywhere. "Did you always work for the company?"

"Yes," she replied. "My parents' home isn't far from here. Dad started me off in this shop when I was old enough to sweep floors and help do cleanup. I was probably nine. Slowly I graduated to more duties.

"By high school I was making donuts and selling them after school and on Saturdays. I put myself through college in this shop. Later on I worked in the plant learning every job, then I was transferred to headquarters where I've been in charge of payroll and now personnel."

"Sounds like you've done it all. Will you start Zack out here when he's nine?"

"I don't know yet. He's got a mind of his own."

"Meaning you didn't?" he teased.

"My dad was my idol and still is. I'd do anything for him." Her gaze met his. "Do you feel that way about yours?"

"I never knew my parents," he said. "I was a baby abandoned in a church in Tallahassee, Florida. Someone found me lying inside an orange crate with the words Garrett Fruit Company stamped on it. I was always called the Garrett boy."

Heidi let out a quiet cry.

"When I got old enough I called myself Mitch. I don't know why. It's one of those stories you read about on occasion and can't believe. I went from foster home to foster home. At eighteen I joined the Marines. Don't get me wrong. It's been a good life, but a different one. It wasn't my destiny to have a family of my own."

She didn't move a muscle, but her eyes darkened with emotion. "I'm sorry to have asked you that question. My home life was pretty idyllic. For a minute I forgot that not everyone starts out the same way."

"There's no need to apologize, Heidi. Most people know their parents, or know of them. I'd have given anything to know either parent. I don't have a clue about my heritage on either side. If I have siblings or relatives, I'm not aware of them. No connections of any kind make me think your Zack is the luckiest of boys to have come from a family like yours you can date back to the nineteenth century."

"I…I think he is, too." Her voice caught, then she cleared her throat. "If you'll wash your hands, I'll give you some gloves to put on and we'll get started." He watched her put on a hairnet before joining him at the sink. Her little blue earrings glinted through the netting. No matter what she did, she exuded a sensuality she doubted she was even aware of. But Mitch was feeling it and had to fight hard to concentrate on the task at hand.

Once the vat of oil was heating, she measured the mix from the bag and put it in the hopper, adding the precise amount of liquid ingredients. After the batter was power-mixed, she checked the oil to be sure it was the right temperature. Then she turned the switch and the dough dropped down through nozzles into the fat. He watched in fascination as rotors turned the donuts over at proper intervals and then moved them onto a conveyor belt for a sugar glaze. Soon they were guided onto trays.

"This goes fast because we use baking powder rather than yeast," she explained. Before he knew it, she'd done another batch. This time it went through a chocolate-glazing process. Another batch received a white glaze with multicolored sprinkles, another with nuts. Already an hour had gone by. "Our general rule of thumb is to make sixteen hundred donuts a day."

"That's a lot of donuts."

"I know, but the high school and college students will eat up a thousand of them by two in the afternoon. Would you believe we usually run out ten minutes before closing?"

"Yup. I've come here at the last minute and had to go away hungry."

Her laugh delighted him. "Okay, we've already made eight hundred. Now let's see you mix the next batch of dough in the hopper."

He did all right, but she had to caution him to check the heat on the oil again. "The frying oil is the most expensive ingredient in the production process, and if the donuts absorb too much oil, it reduces the profit margin."

You learned something new every day, Mitch thought. Somehow he managed to cook the second eight hundred without the place going up in flames.

She grinned when he let out a sigh of relief. "I know how you feel. Good job! Now comes the part we all hate."

"The cleanup," he muttered as he put the last of the loaded trays on the shelves.

"You catch on fast. I'll wheel out this stack of trays to the front. It's eight o'clock. Phyllis should be here by now setting up."

They worked like a team washing the equipment, making everything so spick and span the kitchen gleamed. The vat of oil was cooled and discarded in metal containers she placed outside the rear door. After she removed her hairnet, they took off their gloves and aprons and did a wash that included towels and cloths. While they waited for everything to dry, he mopped the floor.

She eyed him over her shoulder. "You don't have

to do that. We have a janitorial service that comes in every night."

"After doing KP duty, I'm afraid it's a habit. Tell me something. How many of these shops do you own around the Valley?"

"Twenty."

"I imagine their inventory is all sold out by the end of the day, too."

"Always."

"I've noticed that donuts get a bad rap by the media."

"Our company is a great target for the people screaming about obesity, but the sales don't change. Self-control is everyone's problem, not the fault of the free enterprise system."

He smiled at her. "My sentiments exactly." Mitch liked the way she thought. In fact, there wasn't anything about her he didn't like, and that feeling was growing stronger by the second.

As he put the mop away in the utility closet she asked, "How long have you been a P.I.?"

Mitch had been waiting for that question to come up. He shut the door and turned to her. "Ten months or so."

Judging by the silence, his answer had surprised her. "Then you're barely out of the Marines."

"Not exactly." He took a steadying breath. "Tell you what. Before we go to my office, let's head to the Cowboy Grub for breakfast and I'll answer your questions. Have you ever eaten there?"

She finished folding everything from the dryer and put things away. "Many times. It's close to the office and one of my favorite places."

"And mine. I'm glad we're in agreement because I'm starving. Sugar does that to me. I should never have eaten a donut on an empty stomach."

"I'm afraid I learned the same lesson a long time ago." She started out the self-locking rear door ahead of him.

It was ten after nine and already there were half a dozen cars, not counting theirs and Phyllis's, in the parking area. He got a sense of satisfaction from realizing those people would be eating the donuts he and Heidi had cooked from scratch. They weren't just any donuts. That recipe had come from the Old World, guarded and unchanged to this day.

As he helped her into her car, their glances met briefly. He felt the strangest sensation lift the hairs on the back of his neck. The culprits had been emboldened enough to have stolen hundreds of bags of mix, maybe more by now. If they suspected someone was on to them, they could present a physical danger to those around them. He didn't like the idea of her being anywhere near.

Chapter Three

Heidi sat in a booth across from Mitch. He'd ordered cinnamon rolls with his eggs and bacon. She'd decided on a ham omelet and corn bread. As she munched on the last of it, she said, "I won't need to eat another thing until tomorrow. If you want to know a secret, I've tried to figure out this restaurant's recipe for their bread since the first time I tasted it."

He eyed her steadily over the rim of his coffee cup. "You still don't have it down pat and refined?"

"Afraid not."

"Are you as big a whiz in the kitchen as you are making donuts at the shop?"

"I love to cook, but when you have a little boy who doesn't eat a lot and prefers a peanut butter and honey sandwich to anything else, there's not much point. What about you? Do you turn into a master chef when you go home to your family at night?" Since they were working together, she would at least like to know his marital status. If he had a wife, the knowledge might help her to stop the fantasizing.

After draining his coffee, he put the cup down, submitting her to a frank regard. "I never married and am better at warming up a frozen TV dinner."

Never married? It went to show that she really didn't have a clue about men. Furthermore, a whole history of unknowns lay behind his smile, but there was one thing she did know for certain. He was the most exciting man she'd ever met.

"I'm surprised," she responded and wiped the corner of her mouth with a napkin. "When we were talking about my son's haircut, you sounded so knowledgeable, I got the impression you must have children."

"No, but I do know a lot about little orphan boys who need to act tough and are counting the hours until they're free to make their own choices."

Heidi couldn't comprehend his life, but it wasn't difficult to imagine how hard it would have been trying to fit into a foster family. He'd said he'd had more than one. "Did you always want to go into the military?"

"No, but after high school it seemed to be one of the fastest ways to get an education funded. I put the time into pay back Uncle Sam's loan, then got out and went to work as a federal marshal. I've been one for six years."

Federal marshal.

They live dangerous lives.

"Meaning you still are?" Everything he told her came as a surprise, intriguing her. She realized he'd had a harder fight from the beginning than most people. And it had turned him into the kind of man she and her great-uncle wanted on their side.

"I'm on medical leave. I was shot in the shoulder and flown out here to TOSH for the surgery and rehab."

She winced. "Shot?"

"To make a long story short, an escaped felon who wanted revenge tried to kill the judge who'd sent him to prison. I was on duty to protect him. In the process of saving the Honorable Judge Wilken, I had to kill the felon. But I hadn't counted on him having another prison escapee for a partner named Whitey Filmore. We exchanged gunfire and I got the worst of it."

"What happened to him?"

"He's still on the loose."

Her stomach clenched. "That's terrifying."

"It's the nature of the business I'm in. Recently there's been a dramatic increase in the number of threats against members of the judiciary. Our department assesses the level of danger. On average, about a hundred threats are logged each year. We develop a plan to determine the appropriate preventive response for each one."

"In other words you always have to watch your back," she said, tight-lipped.

"Yes, but I didn't do such a good job that time. During the recovery period after the surgery, my boss contacted Roman Lufka, the owner you met at the P.I. firm, and he put me to work so I wouldn't go crazy with nothing to do."

"You mean your boss got you out of the way to preserve your life."

"That, too." His smile didn't make her feel relieved or reassured. "I've received expert medical care and I'm now fully recovered."

She didn't realize she'd been holding her breath. "That's a great blessing. Your health is everything."

"Agreed. Once I've solved your case, in all likelihood I'll be going back to Tallahassee."

The news that he'd be returning to Florida shouldn't matter to her, but to know what awaited him made her sick inside. She bit her lip. "If you go back, he'll be lying in wait for you."

"That's a chance I'll have to take. Somebody has to do the job. We can't allow our judges to be killed off because there's no protection for them. Where would our country be if we didn't have men and women fighting for our freedoms?"

"You're right, of course." But she didn't have to like it. "Do you miss Tallahassee?"

"Not particularly, but it's where I was found and grew up. When I was in the group home, I used to think my birth mother might come looking for me if I stayed put."

His words pained Heidi. She averted her eyes. "Did you try looking for her?"

"I went through that stage, but as I grew older, I realized she might not have been Floridian and was only looking for the nearest church to leave her baby on her way to somewhere else. I went through every conceivable Garrett name asking questions, but received no satisfactory answers. It seemed a hopeless quest.

"By then I'd decided to go into the military. Occasionally I still write to the Bureau of Vital Statistics in Tallahassee to search for any new Garrett names that I can check out. In fact, just yesterday I received a letter suggesting I contact a genealogist."

"Bruno's the big genealogist in our family. If you asked him, I'm sure he'd have contacts who could help you."

"I might do that."

"What other sources have you investigated?"

"I've left my name and phone number with the church where I was found and the group home, even with my foster parents, in case someone inquires about me."

Heidi feared she was going to break down and have a huge cry. "Don't ever give up, Mitch. One day maybe a miracle will happen."

"Maybe." He didn't sound hopeful. "Even if I did find either of my parents, they obviously don't want to be found. I'm not sure it would change anything except to satisfy my curiosity over what kind of people they are or what they look like. It's probably better I don't find them."

But he wants to. Heidi took a quick breath. "You've led an extraordinary life. We have a Marine in my great-aunt Barbara's family. Rob says it was an experience he wouldn't have missed for the world."

"He's right."

Their conversation had left her drained. She was ready to leave. "Thank you for breakfast, Mitch. It was delicious."

"You're welcome."

"I'm ready to leave for your office and download the files whenever you're ready," she said. "I know my great-uncle Bruno is anxious to put an end to the stealing and is grateful for your firm's help."

"I'm grateful for the work."

Mitch sounded sincere, but being a P.I. couldn't compare to his chosen career as a federal marshal. He pulled out his wallet and put enough money on the table to cover their bill. "Let's go."

They both got to their feet and headed for the door of the restaurant. One of the waitresses smiled at him. She'd probably waited on him before. Throughout their meal Heidi had noticed several females staring at him in unabashed admiration. She'd struggled not to do the same.

Once in their cars, she followed him to his office and parked alongside him. After she got out, he called to her. He was leaning across the seat and had opened the passenger door.

"Before we get started on those files, I've decided I'd like to drive out to Woods Cross with you in order to get a visual of the plant facility. We can go in my car and return within the hour. Do you have sunglasses?"

"Yes."

"Good. To be sure no one recognizes you, I'll run inside our shop and find something to cover those curls. Be right back."

Heidi climbed into his Audi and drew her glasses case from her bag. Pretty soon he'd returned with a straw gardening hat that tied under the chin. She put it on with her sunglasses.

"I can't believe you found anything so perfect."

"The P.I. business often calls for a disguise. We keep all kinds of things on hand for emergencies. This early in the investigation we can't afford for you to be recognized while I'm looking around."

"I'm so covered up, no one will know who I am." Heidi loved the idea.

He started up his car and they headed north. "I've only driven past Woods Cross on my way to Ogden on business. Tell me about it."

She peered at his arresting profile through her sunglasses. "Do you want the family reunion version that goes on and on? We have one every year and the tales get longer." He chuckled. "Or, I can give you information on a need-to-know basis."

He maneuvered expertly through the morning traffic. "I want to hear what Heidi Bauer Norris would like me to know if I were a tourist out here visiting for the first time."

"Once I get started, you might be sorry—tell me if you get bored. Okay, let's see. Woods Cross lies near the bottom of the Great Salt Lake Basin and is located eight miles north of Salt Lake.

"The town of nine thousand was officially chartered in 1935, but was originally a big unincorporated area with the Great Salt Lake on one side and the mountains on the other. Saska's family of ten emigrated here in 1892. Her parents and grandmother were ailing and she had six siblings to feed. With the little money they'd pooled, she rented a shack and immediately planted potatoes. With the sales from her sweet buns, she bought up land bit by bit, and their first plant was erected on it.

"It was hard work because they had to build wooden troughs and ditches along the watersheds of the foothills to channel the water where they wanted it to go. Saska herself helped install drains to carry the excess to the Great Salt Lake. Her family also built holding ponds and an underground cistern to save the runoff.

"Today I'll show you the place in the foothills where we have a ranch house and horses. On the site is the original shack and plant. Below it is the modern facility. You'll notice the fleet of trucks and garage for the mechanics farther on.

"My relatives Sylvia and her husband Daniel Bauer live on the ranch year round with their five children to maintain it. Zack and I come out here riding every chance we get. My dad joins us when he can. Right now they're building a float for the Days of '47 parade coming up on the twenty-fourth."

"I've heard about it, but I wasn't flown here until last August and missed it."

"It's our state holiday commemorating the arrival of the pioneers in the Salt Lake Valley in 1847. The parade is next Monday. Maybe you'll have time to see it."

"I'll *make* time for it."

He was getting to her more and more. She took a deep breath and went on, "This year the children will be wearing pioneer clothes and riding on the float. Zack can't wait. Daniel will be driving the float behind my father, who'll be riding his horse. He's the grand marshal. The parade committee asked him to open the parade this year."

Mitch turned his head toward her. "A marshal, you say?"

"Yeah. How about that. In a cowboy hat, no less."

This time he flashed her a broad smile. You wouldn't think it could affect her so, but what else would have made her heart suddenly double thump in reaction?

The man was a quick study. Inside of twenty minutes he'd seen what was needed by driving around the plant while she answered his questions. On their way back to Salt Lake, he pulled into a popular Mexican restaurant. "I'm hungry," he declared. "If you're not, please humor me. I've been dreaming of their fish tacos wrapped in blue tortillas since early morning."

A soft laugh escaped her lips. "I love them, too. For your information, I'm starving." She removed the gardening hat he'd given her.

"You're a woman after my own heart." For a second she had the feeling he wanted to kiss her. For much longer than that, she'd wanted him to. It was insane. Crazy.

After they'd gone inside and ordered, the waitress brought them virgin margaritas. "Have you always loved Mexican food?" She couldn't learn enough about him.

"If it's good, yeah."

"My thoughts exactly."

He flashed her a sly look. "How come you always agree with me?"

An imp got into her. "You're the P.I. Let me know when you've figured it out."

His deep laughter resonated inside her.

BEFORE LONG THEY RETURNED to Mitch's office. "That was well worth the time," he said as she sat down in the chair opposite his desk. "I can now picture the single-story layout from one end of the plant to the other." But the picture he preferred was the one of Heidi seated across his desk.

She'd brought the gardening hat in from the car and laid it on his desk. Her hair was a golden mass he wanted to plunder. "Better yet, no one knew I was there."

Except for Mitch, who would have kidnapped her

if he'd thought he could get away with it. "The ranch in those green foothills is a wonderful spread."

"As I think I told you, Zack and I love to go riding there." She pulled out her iPhone to start the download.

"I can understand why. Saska chose the perfect spot to settle. When you see the growth of the communities north of Salt Lake, it makes you appreciate your ancestor's vision in buying the land before others discovered the value of the area."

"In her diary she mentioned how many times someone came along trying to get her to sell, but they didn't know her." Heidi's voice rang with pride. "Saska had a dream."

"One that your great-uncle Bruno is determined to keep alive. More than ever I'm anxious to catch the persons responsible," he asserted. "To get started, why don't you draw me an organizational chart showing the heads of the different divisions and who reports to whom. I'll read over the pertinent information from their files and you can fill me in on anything else you know that might be significant."

They worked for several hours. Mitch found her an unending source of knowledge. Between that and her sunny disposition, he enjoyed every minute with her. After studying the files complete with ID photos, he said, "While we've been going over the information on everyone who works there now, I've made a list of the names of those people who've left the company in the last five years.

"I need to know why they left. Was it for maternity leave? A higher-paying job? Or maybe a move out of the city or state? Are they still friendly with any of the workers who are there now? Do any of them have a grudge you're aware of? Maybe some who are disgruntled? Anything you can tell me will help."

She nodded and they dug into working through that list. Eventually he made up another list consisting of ten nonfamily workers let go by the company. According to Heidi, they'd been fired for every reason—from being habitually late to calling in sick too many times to being sloppy on the job. One of the truck drivers had complained that they didn't pay him enough money for the work he did and he didn't finish a delivery to Arizona.

"What about this last name, Gary Norris? Any connection?" He flicked his gaze to her.

"He's my ex-husband."

Mitch had assumed as much and studied the picture in the file. Nice-looking guy with brown hair and blue eyes. Born in Salem, Oregon. Attended University of Utah two semesters. Started out working at the counter part-time at the No. 2 shop at Bauer's seven years ago. Graduated to full-time as a baker and assistant manager. Two years later transferred to plant. Worked in the warehouse until terminated two years ago at the age of twenty-nine.

Already Mitch didn't like him. "Being that he was your spouse, it couldn't have been an easy decision to fire him. Who actually let him go?"

Heidi held his gaze. "My father. If you were to ask Dad why, he'd tell you it was Gary's attitude. Basically he wanted an upper-management position, but it's company policy to have obtained an MBA first in order to rise to the top. Bruno and Dad are adamant about that. They believe it shows a person has stuck to something long enough to understand the persistence it takes to run a company."

"College does that for you," he concurred. "When I was reading their backgrounds, I noticed that of those of your family still living, your aunt Marcia, you and your brother, Rich, are the only Bauers besides your father and great-uncle who obtained an MBA."

"Yes. I attended the U of U at night and worked during the day, but Gary didn't like school. He's not the only one. Four of my cousins work at the plant, yet none of them wants to study that hard even though the company has set up a fund to pay half tuition for anyone wanting to go to college."

"Lucky people who decide to take advantage of it. What does your ex-husband do now?"

"I have no idea. After he was fired, I divorced him for personal reasons. He's gone back to Oregon where he was born and raised."

"Then how do the two of you work out visitation with your son?"

She looked away. "We don't. He couldn't get out of the marriage and fatherhood fast enough."

Mitch couldn't comprehend a man doing that. To have a wife and son, then turn his back on both of them, especially on a woman like Heidi…. It was anathema to him.

Your birth father apparently did the same to you, Garrett.

Odd how the two situations didn't seem comparable.

"Forgive me for asking that question, Heidi. It's none of my business."

"There's nothing to forgive," she murmured. "The

truth is, while we were dating, Gary told me how much he looked forward to being a father one day, but once Zack was born, he showed virtually no interest in him. After we divorced, he never paid child support."

"You didn't take him back to court?"

She shook her head. "You have to understand something. I make a good enough income on my own and always have. He was counting on that. Throughout our marriage and more so by the end of it, he accused me of being born with a silver spoon in my mouth.

"I simply didn't know how to fight his flawed logic. Everyone in our family works hard. There are no shortcuts to success. Before he packed his bags, Gary told me that living around us was like wearing a straitjacket." She paused. "Have I shocked you?"

Mitch sat forward. "How could I be shocked when I grew up not even knowing who my father was? But I'll admit I'm saddened for your son's sake by what you've told me."

"Toward the end of our failed marriage, I cried my eyes out for Zack's sake. But I got over it when my attorney informed me Gary had given up his parental rights and had signed papers to that effect. By that time nothing really surprised me, because by then I realized what my dad had said was true. Every man can make a baby, but that doesn't necessarily make him a parent."

"Amen," Mitch said. "Evidently my parents came to that realization the moment I was born. Does your son know his father gave up all claims to him?"

"Not yet. I'm waiting for the proper time to tell him, but I'm not sure when that will be."

Before they traveled down that path any further, he

quickly changed the subject and turned to the computer once more. "I see here that Jonas Bauer attended Westminster College in Salt Lake for two years, but didn't finish."

She nodded. "If you study the applications carefully, you'll find that forty percent of the employees, family or not, have some credits beyond high school, but not enough to move higher. The rest either started with the company after graduation from high school, or worked at different jobs before coming to Bauer's."

The more he learned, the more Mitch imagined this highly successful, family-owned company was like one of those old pressure cookers that built up steam. Without a release valve, you could count on some kind of explosion. Mitch was eager to get inside the plant and find out who was doing what.

He saw her glance at her watch, reminding him it was getting late. "We've accomplished a lot today, Heidi, but I can see it's time to let you go so you can pick up Zack. Thanks for working with me all day. This is a great beginning."

Much as he didn't want her to leave, he had no choice but to get up from his chair and walk her out to her car. "I'll see you at six tomorrow morning."

After she slid in behind the wheel, she flicked him a wicked glance. In full sunlight, her eyes and hair gleamed, dazzling him. "Thanks for the delicious lunch. For a reward, tomorrow I'll let you make all the donuts." He chuckled. "If you pass the test, then you'll be ready to move on to greater things."

Greater things meant no more just the two of them.

Mitch could wish this part of the training period lasted longer. Heidi was growing on him in quantum leaps. Instead of needing his own space, he found he wanted her to share it with him. He was disappointed, in fact, that he had to wait until tomorrow to see her again.

Their conversation had touched as much on the personal as on the thefts that had brought her to the P.I. firm. He rarely opened up to anyone, but to her he had, and she'd put her finger on the truth about one thing— Lew had two motives for sending Mitch to Utah; the first that he would receive the best medical care, the second that he'd be kept out of harm's way for a time.

Long enough for him to have met Heidi Norris.

After seeing her off, he went back to work, checking backgrounds on the ten nonfamily members let go from the company in the past five years. Each would have worked with Jonas and his son.

Of the ten on the list, only one had been a woman. Her job had been to work in the mix division. Of the nine men, eight of them had worked in the warehouse. The other one was the truck driver Heidi had told him about. Only two of the men, Dennis Blake and Gary Norris, had been fired within three weeks of each other and might have become friends in their mutual dissatisfaction with the rules.

Mitch found he couldn't get his mind off Heidi's ex-husband. His leaving her and their son without any concern for their welfare was incredibly selfish. Mitch had known a few guys in the military who'd abandoned their wives and children, but now that he'd met Heidi, he couldn't fathom how any man could give her up.

With a grimace, he purposely returned his mind to the task at hand. The employees on the list who'd left the Bauer company needed to be investigated. He was curious to see what they were doing with their lives now. It was a painstaking process, but once Mitch was working inside the plant, he'd pick up information fast.

"ZACK? BREAKFAST IS READY." Heidi had made scrambled eggs and toast.

Her son came in the kitchen dragging his backpack. "I don't want to go to Aunt Sharon's."

She finished pouring his orange juice. "How come?"

"Cuz I want to be with you."

"You can't, honey. I'm training a pri—a new employee this morning." She'd almost let it slip. Zack knew about private investigators after watching all the super-sleuth shows on the cartoon network. If her boy caught wind of who Mitch really was, he'd tell his cousin, and soon Sharon and Rich would know about it. Then the questions would start and word could leak out to the company, destroying Bruno's plan to catch whoever was stealing unawares.

"But I don't want them to drive me to school."

Heidi sat down to eat with him, but so far he hadn't touched his food. "Why not?"

"Because Uncle Rich is going to take us. He wants to talk to Jenny's teacher."

Something was wrong here. "Why do you care?"

"He's not my dad."

"He loves you, Zack."

His blue eyes filled with tears. "I don't want to go to school with them." He took off for his bedroom. Heidi raced after him and nearly collided with the door he was trying to shut.

"Honey…" She picked him up and held him close while he cried. "I've never seen you act like this before. Did your uncle hurt your feelings?"

"No."

"Did Tim?"

"No."

"Then help me understand." She lowered him to the floor, then sat on the end of his twin bed so they could talk.

He refused to look at her. "The other kids know he's not my dad."

She was trying hard to figure this out. "Why does that matter?"

More tears rolled down his flushed cheeks. "They'll ask me where my dad is."

A pain stabbed her heart. "Oh. I see." She *did* see and this situation wasn't going to be resolved with one conversation. Heidi wondered how long Zack had been actively dealing with this burden. Weeks? Months? The problem was, she'd run out of time. Mitch was probably at the shop right now waiting to be let in. The conversation they needed would have to wait.

"Tell you what, honey. Come to work with me, and I'll drive you to school at eight, but you'll have to sit at one of the tables and read while I'm training this person."

His face brightened. "Okay."

"Come on. Let's hurry out to the car. Grab the toast I made for you."

While he did her bidding, she reached for his backpack and they dashed through the connecting door to the garage. En route to the shop, Heidi phoned her brother. She thanked him and Sharon for being willing to help out, then told him there'd been a change in plans.

Sure enough, Mitch's Audi sat in the empty parking lot. When she pulled up next to him, he levered himself from the driver's seat, looking incredibly attractive in a yellow polo shirt and jeans that molded to his powerful thighs.

After Zack got out of the backseat, he was all eyes.

She reached for the backpack on the front seat. "Zack, I'd like you to meet Mitch Garrett, who's in training for our company. Mitch, this is my son, Zack."

"Hi, Zack." Mitch got down on his haunches in front of him, giving him his full attention.

"Hi." Zack spoke right up.

"I like your haircut. When I was in the Marines, we all had to wear one like yours. It feels good on a hot day."

"Yeah." Her boy grinned. "How long were you in the Marines?"

"Ten years."

"Wow." Zack paused for a moment, then said, "Did you have to do a lot of...well, you know...scary stuff?"

Mitch nodded.

"Do you ever get nightmares?" Zack's question astonished Heidi.

"Sometimes. How about you?"

"Sometimes after I've played a zombie video game at my cousin's house. My aunt doesn't know Tim traded one of his Indiana Jones Lego games for it." Heidi didn't know that. No wonder he sometimes cried out in the night and got into her bed.

"I've played that game before, but those zombies are harmless."

"I know," Zack said, "but they're different in my dreams."

Mitch smiled. "Next time they're in your dreams, knock them over with one of those golf carts or the lawn mower."

"Yeah."

"The thing is, they're not real. That's why they're pathetic. Do you notice how they walk slow and wobble?"

"Especially that old man," Zack pointed out.

"Yeah. The one with the hat pulled over one eye."

While both of them were laughing about the game, relating perfectly, Heidi stood there in mild shock. Zack was normally a boy of few words except with family. Hearing him now, she saw a different child from the one she'd been raising for six years. Mitch was wonderful with him, trying to help him not be afraid.

"Do you live around here?" Zack asked him.

"Let me ask *you* a question. Do you ever go to the Hogle Zoo?"

"Yeah. I go with my mom a lot."

"Well, I live in an apartment near the street that takes you up there."

She could hear her son's mind working. "Hey, Mom—"

"Zack—" she broke in, having a hunch where this conversation could be headed "—Mitch and I have work to do making donuts." Heidi opened the door of the shop and they filed in. "I want you to find a table and get out your homework. You're falling behind on your summer reading program."

"Okay. Can I come and watch in a few minutes?"

"Yes, but you'll have to be quiet. Mitch has to concentrate."

"Yeah," the P.I. agreed, regarding Heidi with a devilish gleam in his eye. "It's a lot harder than peeling potatoes."

He would have been good at that, she thought. She realized he was good at everything, including talking to children.

"Hey, Mitch," Zack said, "did you know our donuts are made from potatoes?"

"That's what your mother told me. You know what I think?"

"What?" Her son was mesmerized by this man.

"There ought to be a cartoon like SpongeBob called SweetSpud."

"Yeah!" Zack exclaimed. "That would be so cool!"

"Okay, Zack, no more talking." Heidi undid his backpack and pulled out two of the books he was supposed to read. "I'll come and check on you in a little while."

"I want some of Mitch's donuts when they're done."

"I'll bring one home for you after school. No donuts without a good lunch first."

Chapter Four

Mitch washed his hands and got into his garb before he started mixing the dough. "That's quite a little guy you've got there. Smart and funny."

"I've never seen him that open with a stranger before."

"Video games are the universal language with kids, young or old."

She laughed. "Being a Marine didn't hurt, either."

"It's a credit to you that he's an all-American boy. Now that I've met him, I have to tell you again you're a lucky mom." Mitch warmed up the oil and started cooking while she watched his movements. He was a fast learner. She didn't have to remind him of anything.

"You're right. I love him to death, but I need to apologize for bringing him to work with me this morning. He wanted to be with me and wouldn't let my brother drive him to school. I'll have to leave here at eight to take him. But I won't be gone more than ten minutes. You can enjoy a break."

"If I'd had a mom, I would have wanted to be with her, too."

Halfway through the second batch of eight hundred

her son walked in the kitchen. He moved over by Heidi and watched Mitch making donuts.

"Hi, sport."

Zack beamed. "Hi! Is that fun?"

Those midnight-brown eyes glanced at him with affection. "It sure is. When you're a little older, you'll be able to make them, too."

"I know."

"Have you finished your homework?"

"No." He sighed. "I needed a break."

Laughter rumbled out of Mitch. "What are you reading for school?"

"Dumb stories."

"That's no fun. What do you like to read?"

"Spy stories."

"So do I. What are your favorites?"

"*The Black Paw* and *Spectacular Spy Capers.*"

Heidi heard the surprise in Mitch's voice as he said, "You're talking the Spy Mice?"

"Yeah!"

"Now *those* are fun!"

"Mom—" Zack looked up at Heidi "—Mitch likes them, too."

"Isn't that amazing?" She exchanged amused glances with Mitch before the last of the dough dropped from the nozzles into the oil. The donuts cooked for the exact amount of time before he put them through the glaze. "Your performance was excellent, Mr. Garrett. You get A plus."

"That's a gross exaggeration, but I'm glad it met with your approval."

"You're on track to be moved to the plant."

While she tried without success to tear her gaze

from his, Zack said, "I'm going to be a spy when I grow up."

Mitch's warm smile settled on her son. "Guess what? I have a friend who owns a spy shop with all kinds of stuff."

His blue eyes rounded. "Could I see it?"

"I guess that depends on your mom. Maybe both of you would like to come."

"Mom!" This time Zack's cry of delight reverberated off the kitchen walls. "Can we go after school? Please?"

Mitch's invitation was perfectly natural, considering the direction of the conversation with Zack. But if she accepted, it put their relationship on a different footing. She'd be crossing that line from the professional to the personal. After her disastrous marriage, she'd been guarding herself against making another bad decision where a man was concerned. Besides, Mitch would be going back to Florida after he'd discovered who was stealing their donut mix.

"Honey, we don't even know if Mitch will be available this afternoon."

Mitch had removed his apron. "I'll be free to meet you there, but you might have other plans. Why don't you two talk about it on the way to school and let me know?"

School— That's right. It was eight o'clock. Heidi was supposed to be driving him right now. Instead, her head had been somewhere else…concentrating on someone else.

She quickly took off her apron and gloves. "Come on, Zack. We'll be late if we don't leave now."

"Okay," he said in a grumpy voice. "But I wish I didn't have to go to school. See you later, Mitch."

"See you, sport."

Heidi hustled him out of the kitchen. He pulled his backpack off the table. They met the shop manager coming in the front door.

"Hi, Phyllis," said Heidi. "Mr. Garrett's in back starting to clean up. I won't be long. I've got to run Zack to school."

As Zack headed for the car, Phyllis said, "I caught a glimpse of Mr. Gorgeous yesterday. What a hunk!" Phyllis was happily married with three older children, but she still had eyes to see.

"He didn't make a mistake with the donuts, either. Will Jim be here tomorrow?"

"That's what his wife told me last night."

"Let me know if there's a problem."

"Will do."

Heidi hurried out to the car. During the drive, all Zack talked about was Mitch. By the time they reached the school, where the children were lined up to go inside, she couldn't take any more of his pleading.

"If it's still all right with Mitch, we'll stop by his friend's shop for a few minutes after school, but you have to remember he's a busy man."

"I will." To her shock, he undid the strap of his car seat and leaned forward to give her a kiss on the cheek before climbing out of the car. He was so excited, he forgot to act like a big guy.

When she got back to the shop and helped with the rest of the cleanup, she told Mitch he'd made her son's day.

"Do you want to know something?" He'd just pulled

the items out of the dryer to fold and put away. His gaze darted to hers. "You've just made mine by telling me you'll bring him to the office after school."

The way he was looking at her produced a fluttery sensation in her chest. "Just keep in mind he's at a very impressionable age and will drive you crazy with questions."

"He's wonderful. What time do you think you'll be there?"

"Around twenty to four."

"I'm headed there now to keep working on background checks. That's going to take hours. I'll meet you in the parking lot and we'll go into the shop directly. He'll never know the attached office is my place of business."

She nodded. "I'm interested in seeing it myself."

"Roman's brother manufactures spy equipment back east and ships it to him. When Zack gets in there, he's never going to want to leave, so be warned." The warning bells were already going off for Heidi, but already she'd ignored them by agreeing to meet him over something that had nothing to do with the case.

A minute later they walked through to the front of the donut shop. As they went out the door to the parking lot, Phyllis winked at Heidi. This was how gossip got started. Thankfully today was Mitch's last day making donuts.

Before they parted company she said, "I'm going to run by Bruno's house and tell him what's going on. Now that you've had your crash course, it's time to move you to the warehouse where the bags are loaded onto the trucks. He'll arrange it with Randy, who's responsible for working out the shifts."

"I'd like to start work there on Friday because I have other plans for tomorrow. What's the schedule for the employees at the plant in terms of lunch?"

"Everyone takes the same one-hour break at twelve."

"Is there a lunchroom?"

"Yes. Some bring their food and eat in there. Others leave and go out for a bite."

"Ask your great-uncle to arrange for the fire department to have an evacuation of the building during the lunch hour tomorrow. That way the employees will be prepared. An evacuation means everyone out—no exceptions—while the fire department does a safety inspection to see if everything is in compliance since the last inspection. It'll give me time to plant some surveillance cameras and listening devices."

How incredibly clever.

"While I'm in there, I'll get a good look at the interior layout, including the offices for Jonas and Lucas. I want to see what they have on file and on the computer."

"What if they have a password Bruno doesn't know?"

"No problem. If it becomes necessary, our firm has the technology to get into the hard drive."

Obviously nothing was impossible for Mitch. She'd heard the FBI had the means to crack millions of passwords per second.

"Today while we're in Roman's shop, I'll pick out the equipment I need. Zack can help me without knowing what I'm doing."

Mitch's brilliant mind never stopped working. "He'll be in heaven."

"What do you say we go for a pizza afterward? We should all be hungry by then. The Pizza Oven is practically next door. We can walk to it."

Her toe was already in the water. Why not go all the way and plunge in, just this once? "We'd love it. Now I don't have to worry about what to fix for dinner."

"And it saves me from having to eat frozen fish sticks."

She smiled before they parted company. Heidi took off for Bruno's two-story Cape Cod house on upper Yalecrest, not that far from the apartment where Mitch lived. To think he'd been in Salt Lake for the past year, but she'd had no knowledge of him until Monday afternoon….

Bruno's eyes gleamed when she told him Mitch's plan. He got right on his part of it and gave her the go-ahead for the P.I. to do whatever he wanted. Heidi drove back to her house and did some laundry before it was time to pick up Zack.

He came flying out of the school to her car. It didn't take long to reach the Lufka firm.

"There's Mitch!"

Heidi had already spotted the hard-muscled man in the yellow polo and her heart began to thud without mercy. He was so handsome, she could croak. That's what her sister, Evy, would say if she ever saw him.

Zack scrambled out of the car. Mitch seemed to look at her with male pleasure before he greeted her son and walked them around the back of the private shop not open to the public. He unlocked the door and ushered them inside.

When he turned on the lights, she found herself looking at a treasure trove of gadgets and equipment.

Zack walked around inspecting everything, his eyes big as saucers. "Oh, man!" he blurted several times, obviously having picked up the expression from some kids at school. She heard Mitch's deep chuckle in the background.

"Oh, man" was right.

MITCH SAT IN THE BOOTH across from Heidi and Zack, enjoying the view. "More pizza anyone?"

Her blue eyes widened. "You're joking."

He chuckled. "I was just making sure."

"Zack never eats two whole pieces. I don't think he could find room for another bite."

"This pizza's good," Zack declared. "What's that meat called?"

"Canadian bacon," Mitch answered.

"Yum. I wish I could live in that spy shop. Then when I get hungry I could walk over here."

His comment was too much. Mitch's laughter merged with Heidi's. Her son was an entertaining, lovable little character with a huge imagination. He surmised Heidi had a full-time job on her hands keeping up with him.

"I'm glad you had fun in there."

"I loved it! Do you think your friend would let me look around again sometime?"

"Zack..."

"Whenever you'd like. Just ask your mom." Mitch reached for the sack at his side. "While we're still on the subject, I wanted you to have this."

Zack took it from him. "What is it?"

"Look inside."

The boy's hands were trembling as he pulled out a box, but it was fastened up tight.

"Here. Let me help you." Mitch undid everything. "These are walkie-talkies that fit on a bike. You can let a friend put one of these on his bike, and then when you go riding, you can talk to each other while you spy."

Mitch didn't know what he expected, but was surprised when Zack lowered his head and didn't say anything. "Hey…if you don't like these, I'll take them back and get you something else you'd rather have."

An anxious expression crossed Heidi's face. "He loves these, don't you, honey?"

Zack nodded.

"Then thank him for the wonderful gift."

"Thanks, Mitch." The boy's shoulders were shaking.

"What's wrong, buddy?"

"Nothing," he said, but it came out muffled.

At this juncture Mitch was racking his brain to figure him out. On impulse he said, "Don't you have a bike?"

"Yes." Zack finally lifted his tearstained face. "But it's got training wheels and I don't know how to ride it without them."

That pretty well explained everything. "You don't need training wheels. I'll show you how to ride your bike."

"You will?"

The hope in his eyes reminded Mitch of himself when he was a boy, always having to wait for someone to show him how to do things when they didn't want to.

"Of course. It'll take about fifteen minutes. After that you'll be cruising around the neighborhood with your friends and using your walkie-talkies."

Zack jumped up. "Will you show me tonight?"

"There's nothing I'd like more, but that's up to your mother." Mitch darted Heidi a glance.

"Mom? Come on! Let's go home."

Heidi looked frantic. "Are you sure you have the time, Mitch?"

That wasn't all she was asking. He sensed she was afraid. That was because their relationship was moving in a direction over which she felt she had no control. Mitch had news for her. He'd been feeling out of control since the moment Roman had introduced them at the office.

"I can spare an hour if we leave now. I'll follow you to your house."

"Th-that's very kind of you," she stammered.

Zack scrambled out of the booth clutching his present tightly. Heidi caught up to him. Mitch put some money on the table and followed them out of the restaurant to their respective cars parked in front of the firm.

En route to her house, they passed a church with a big flat parking area in the back, the perfect place for Zack to practice. When they reached her street, he followed her into the driveway of the charming, white-brick rambler. He'd been over here before, but not in daylight.

It had pale aqua shutters and cut-out window boxes full of orange-and-pink flowers. Their design was reminiscent of those he'd seen in the Swiss and Austrian Tyrol when he'd vacationed in Europe on leave from the military.

Mitch drove up behind them and waited until they'd brought Zack's bike and helmet out of the garage. He retrieved his tool kit from the trunk of his car so he could remove the training wheels. "I'll put your bike in the back of my car and we'll drive around the corner to the church. You'd better go with your mom because she has the car seat for you. Does that sound okay?"

Zack nodded with excitement.

"I'll follow you," Heidi told him. "In case you were wondering, he wouldn't let me or my brother teach him."

"I know how he feels. A guy wants his own father at a time like this. Barring that, I guess an ex-Marine will do."

She studied his features for a moment. "If anyone understands, you do. I can't thank you enough for your generosity to him."

"Let's hope I'm a good teacher."

"The thought never crossed my mind you could be anything else." With a smile he felt permeate his body, she turned away to get in her car.

He backed out and drove to the church. The sun wouldn't be setting for a while. They had enough time for Zack to get the hang of cycling before Heidi took him home to bed.

When Mitch had left TOSH the other morning, he couldn't have imagined what was awaiting him back at the office. Since meeting Heidi and her son, his world had undergone a dramatic shift.

HEIDI STOOD AGAINST THE front of her car to watch. Zack fell off his red bike several times, but Mitch was right there to help him get up and try again. It took exactly twenty minutes before Zack was riding around the parking lot by himself. "Mom! Look at me! I can ride my bike!" Joy burst out of him.

"I'm looking!" she shouted back. "That's terrific, honey!" She couldn't believe how much they looked like father and son from a distance. Zack was a little taller than average for his age and they both had the same dark-blond hair. Anyone seeing them would think they belonged to each other.

Soon Zack rode up to the Nissan with Mitch jogging alongside him to make sure no fall happened at the last second. Both faces were wreathed in smiles. Mitch held on to the bike as Zack got off and ran into her arms. She leaned down to hug and kiss him. "You did it! I'm so proud of you."

Over his shoulder she looked up at the man who'd just made her son's day and mouthed a *thank-you*. *You're welcome,* he mouthed back. He looked like he'd had a good time, too.

"Mitch is going to show me how to attach my walkie-talkie." Her son was so happy he seemed to have grown another inch.

"Not tonight, honey. You've got school in the morning. We need to get you home."

"Your mom's right," Mitch said before the protests could start. He put the bike in the back of his car. "We'll take care of that tomorrow."

Tomorrow? A little thrill passed through her.

"But before we leave here, I'll show you how the

walkie-talkies work. Tonight you can send messages to your mom from your bedroom."

"Yay! They're in the car. I'll get them!"

Quick as a wink Zack reached into the back of the Nissan, grabbed his present and gave it to Mitch. In another couple of minutes he'd set them to the same channel frequency and the two guys walked around talking and saying things like "Roger" and "Over and out." Heidi knew for a fact her son had never had such a marvelous time. Thanks to Mitch, his confidence level was over the top.

Mitch finally wandered up to her and handed her a walkie-talkie. The brush of his fingers was like touching a live wire. Maybe the contact had affected him, too, because his eyes seemed to go an even darker brown as they met hers. "Press this button and hold it down while you talk. If you press this other button, it acts as a loudspeaker."

"It's easy, Mom."

She pressed both buttons and said, "Now hear this. Now hear this." The speaker was powerful. If anyone else had come into the parking lot, they'd have heard it. "This is Special Agent 409."

Mitch's shoulders shook with silent laughter. 409 was a spray cleaner a lot of people used around the house. "An all-points bulletin has gone out for a six-year-old boy who should be home getting his bath. If you see this individual, report in. He has blond hair and blue eyes and answers to the name Zackatron."

Peals of laughter broke from both males. Mitch pressed his own speaker button. "Roger and copy, 409. This is Field Marshal X12." A popular bug spray. "I have Zackatron in my sights."

"Excellent, Field Marshal X12." Heidi wondered if he'd been assigned a real number as a marshal. "Please deliver him immediately. Over and out." With a grin she couldn't prevent, she handed her son the walkie-talkie.

"I don't want to go home yet," he wailed.

"I know you don't. Sometimes I don't like to do things, either, like scrub the bathroom, but certain tasks have to get done and you *have* to go to school. Can you thank Mitch for teaching you how to ride and feeding us pizza and giving you these walkie-talkies? You're the luckiest boy I know."

Zack nodded before looking up at Mitch with all the signs of hero worship. "Thanks for everything, Mitch." In the next instant he did something unprecedented and hugged him.

Heidi's heart melted as she watched Mitch pick up her son and give him a big hug back. "Good job," he said before putting him down again. She knew Zack was hungry for a father's love, but seeing him show it so openly really shook her. "I had more fun than you did." Mitch handed him the other walkie-talkie.

"No, you didn't."

"Yes, I did," Mitch came back, sending her son into a giggle fit. "Go on and get in the car with your mom. I'll follow you home with your bike."

In a few minutes they were back at her house. She pressed the remote to let them in the garage. Mitch carried the bike inside and rested it against the wall next to her mountain bike. "Nice," he said.

"Hurry and get your bath started, Zack. I'll be right in."

"Okay. See ya tomorrow, Mitch."

"See you, sport."

After Zack disappeared into the house, she turned to the incredible man who'd helped her son over a very rocky patch. "I don't know how to thank you."

He cocked his head. "Do you have any idea how much fun I've had *all* day?" She didn't miss the emphasis. "If you want to know the truth, I felt just like Zack. When you said it was time to go home, I didn't want it to end, either."

Make that three people.

Mitch was getting to her in ways she was scared to examine. He was a P.I. whose firm had been hired by Bruno to find out what was going on at Bauer's. But already he was coming to mean much more than that to Heidi. She needed to remember why he was in her life at all. "What can I do to help you tomorrow?"

"Anything you'd like. Just don't go near your office or the plant. After I've entered the facility to install the devices over the lunch hour, I'll phone you and we'll go from there. Expect a call around two."

He turned to leave, then looked back over his broad shoulder. His eyes appeared black in the fading light. "For what it's worth, I think your ex-husband had to have been out of his mind to leave you and Zack."

Mitch shouldn't have told her that. Particularly since she knew he'd be leaving Salt Lake soon.

AT QUARTER TO TWELVE, Mitch put on a firefighter's uniform and climbed onto a truck from the Davis County Fire Department. Roman had arranged for their cooperation. When the truck pulled into the parking area of the Bauer plant in Woods Cross, Mitch jumped down with the three firefighters assigned to this engine and they approached the main entrance.

Earlier that morning Mitch had been on the phone to Bruno, who'd said he would tell his secretary to open the front doors for them before she went to lunch. The minute the building was cleared, the three men got busy doing their official inspection while Mitch started installing cameras in each area.

It was a medium-size facility. Everything looked immaculate. When Mitch found Jonas Bauer's office, he put in a camera, then looked around for a spot to place the listening device. There was a pot of fake flowers on an end table. Perfect!

Since there were no papers in the in-box, he opened the file cabinet with a device and went through the contents. He found some past email printouts of the shipments and studied the contents before heading for Lucas's office two doors down the hall. Once there he installed a camera and put a listening device in another fake plant on top of the file cabinet. Mitch studied the contents of his file cabinet, too.

Within the hour, the fire department had accomplished their work. Mitch walked out to the fire truck with the guys and they drove back to the station. After removing the borrowed uniform, Mitch thanked them for their help and got in his own car.

Lyle and Adam, two of the crew he'd worked with many times before, were handling surveillance of the facility in one of the firm's vans loaded with the latest state-of-the-art electronic equipment. After briefing them on the case, Mitch had asked them to park off the road behind a thick bank of trees on the east side of the plant. As he drew alongside them, he was pleased to see that the van was invisible from the road.

He climbed out of the Audi and into the van. "The deed is done, guys. It's one-thirty. People should be filing back in."

They watched the screens. One of them displayed the view of the parking lot. Like an army of worker bees, the employees converged on the scene and returned to their jobs. Within twenty minutes the place was a hive of activity. "No sign of the queen bee yet," Lyle murmured.

"Jonas could be anywhere. For that matter, so could Lucas. It might be a while before anything of importance happens." Mitch reached for the door handle. "I'm going out to take pictures of every license plate in the parking lot and get Tom to do the background checks. I'm anxious to nail the culprits.

"If anyone else drives in after I've gone, make a note of it. The camera will catch it and we'll blow it up later to get the license plate number. Jeff and Phil will relieve you at midnight. Stay in contact with me."

"Will do."

After Mitch had driven around getting pictures, he sent them through his iPhone to Tom, then headed for Salt Lake and phoned Heidi. His pulse accelerated while he waited for her to answer.

"How did everything go?" she asked as soon as she picked up.

"Without a hitch. My spy gadgets are in place. Too bad Zack isn't older. He could've helped me. What are you doing right now?"

"I'm on my way to pick him up from school. Before

that I was pulling some weeds around the side of the house, but I'll never do it again in this heat."

"It's a scorcher today." He switched lanes. "Why don't I drop by your house and I'll put that walkie-talkie on his bike?"

"My son will be thrilled."

And you? "Then I'll see you in a half hour."

Coming into Salt Lake, he took the Sixth South exit and headed home. On the way he stopped at Emigration Cyclery on Foothill Drive. They had an array of mountain bikes. Seeing Heidi's bike in her garage last evening had given him an idea. He bought a bike and put it in the back of his Audi. Now that he had full use of his arm, he could resume activities he'd enjoyed before the shooting. His old bike was still in storage back in Florida.

One of the college girls from next door saw his new purchase when he pulled into the carport. She and her roommate cycled a lot and she wanted to ride with him, but Mitch had other plans. For one thing, both girls were too young. And even if they weren't, his interest was engaged elsewhere.

As politely as he knew how, he told her he was running late and would have to talk to her another time. On that note he hurried through the apartment to change into shorts and a T-shirt. He had plans to be with the two people who'd changed his world.

Chapter Five

"Mom!" Zack came running into the house. He was already wearing his helmet. "Mitch is here." Heidi's son had been watching for his hero. "He brought his bike!"

She realized Mitch was offering himself as a stand-in because Zack didn't have a friend to ride with right now. Heidi was learning fast that he was a caring, sensitive man. She decided his being raised by a succession of foster and not his biological parents didn't matter. Mitch had been *born* with qualities a lot of people lacked, including her ex-husband.

Without hesitation she hurried through the house to the front porch. What she saw was a modern-day version of a golden god helping Zack attach his walkie-talkie to his bike. Those were her own words this time, not ones her sister, Evy, might have said.

Mitch lifted his head. "Hi," he said as his gaze swept over her. "Is it all right with you if we ride to the church from here and test out our walkie-talkies? Then we'll come back."

"Of course."

With Mitch's help getting started, Zack started down the street. "Bye, Mom," he called over his shoulder. Mitch put on his own helmet before getting on his bike. He caught up to Zack with the agility of a man in amazing shape, considering he'd been recovering from a bullet wound all this time. She longed to go with them.

As soon as they disappeared around the corner, she dashed into the house and pulled on a pair of shorts and a knit top. Once her sneakers were tied, she locked the front door and hurried to the garage for her bike and helmet. In minutes she was flying down the driveway.

She felt like a little kid again, hurrying to meet up with friends. But she was a woman now and none of the boys on her old block had looked like the hardmuscled male racing around the church parking lot with her son. Heidi pedaled hard to catch up with them. When she did, she asked Zack, "Mind if I help hunt for bad guys, Zackatron?"

Her son pressed the speaker button on his device. "We're looking for stolen cars, Agent 409." Zack stepped right into the mood of the moment.

Her gaze darted to Mitch, who was grinning. "No luck yet," he said into his speaker. "Any suggestions?"

"Maybe we'll see some at the convenience store. Zackatron knows where it is."

"Yup. Follow me."

It didn't take long before they were drinking icy slurpees. Mitch finished his off fast. "That tasted good, but I'm getting hungry for dinner. I only live four blocks from here. Would you two spies like to come to my apartment? We'll throw some hot dogs on the grill and roast marshmallows afterward to make s'mores."

Zack's head whipped around toward her. "Could we, Mom? Please?"

This was her fault. If she hadn't joined them, she wouldn't be in the position to play the bad guy by refusing Mitch's invitation. She didn't have a reason to say no. In truth, she didn't want to. But if she accepted, it meant she'd crossed way beyond the line into territory where she was vulnerable and could be hurt again.

Unfortunately the pleading in Zack's eyes overrode her caution. He was very vulnerable right now, too, yet she had to admit this man was boosting her son's belief in himself. You couldn't buy that kind of help.

"I think it sounds like fun. We'd love a barbecue."

"Yay!"

A satisfied gleam entered Mitch's eyes. "You took the words right out of my mouth, sport. Let's go."

Zack was growing proficient at climbing on his bike and taking off by himself. Heidi was secretly delighted with his progress. It was all due to this man whose intention to infiltrate the company had somehow spilled into her private life, as well. *With her permission.*

She and Zack followed Mitch onto a side street that avoided the heavy traffic on Foothill Drive and cut through the residential area to his apartment complex. How many years had she driven past it on her way to the zoo or up the canyon? He'd been living here almost a year without her knowledge. The chances of their homes being this close to each other were probably a million to one.

Mitch headed for the third carport and hopped off. "We can leave our bikes here." They took off their helmets, then he unlocked the door and ushered them into the kitchen. "Welcome to my abode. Normally the management only rents to college students, but an exception was made for me. The bathroom is down the hall on the left."

Mitch had been well hidden. With the killer still on the loose looking for him, the chances of him being tracked down clear across the country weren't that great. Furthermore no one would think to look for him in a housing complex meant for college students. But that didn't ease Heidi's fears. They lurked in the back of her mind and came out of hiding at odd moments.

"Come on, Zack," she said. "Let's go wash our hands."

His apartment was tiny, but thankfully it had good air-conditioning. Only two small bedrooms, a bathroom, a living room and kitchen with a small dinette set. The unoccupied bedroom was filled with fitness equipment. Zack noticed it before they rejoined Mitch on the veranda off the kitchen, where he was heating up the grill.

There were four deck chairs surrounding a round glass table with an umbrella. He'd pulled down an awning to shade them from the sun. It wouldn't fall below the Great Salt Lake for another hour at least.

Mitch's glance took in both of them. "When I'm home and not sleeping, this is my favorite room in the house."

She nodded. "It would be mine, too."

"This porch isn't a room," Zack said.

A chuckle escaped Mitch's lips. "It is for me. Want to help?"

"We both do," Heidi chimed in.

They worked in harmony. Zack set the table with

paper plates, potato chips and condiments. Mitch started the hot dogs and Heidi tossed a green salad with the ingredients he had on hand. She fixed her own version of Thousand Island dressing. By then Mitch had made up a pitcher of lemonade and soon they were ready to eat.

"After dinner can I play with some of the stuff in the second bedroom?"

Mitch was working on his third hot dog. She was pleased to note he'd had several helpings of salad with liberal portions of her dressing. He'd already complimented her on it. "You mean the treadmill and exercise bike?"

"Yeah."

"I have a better idea. If you want to come over on Saturday, we'll do a real workout when we're not starving and hot."

"Okay! That's how come you're so strong, huh?"

"The machines help, especially when I have to work odd hours sometimes. But I much prefer going for a bike ride outside. It keeps you in great shape. Now that you can ride your bike, you'll build lots of muscles and it's good for your heart. You know, you're lucky to live in Salt Lake where you can ride your bike outdoors almost year round."

Zack stop munching on his potato chip. "*You* live here, too."

"I do right now."

Heidi schooled her features not to react, but her son's little face fell on cue. "How come not all the time?"

"Mitch's home is in Florida," she interjected, not wanting to let this discussion go any further. But she decided it was best he knew the truth. "Mitch is only working here temporarily." She switched subjects. "Hey, guys, I don't know about you, but I'm hungry for a s'more."

Their host got up from the table before she could. Whatever was on his mind had put an expression on his face that puzzled her. "I'll bring everything out."

"Come on, Zack," Heidi said. "Let's clear the table."

In a few minutes they were cooking marshmallows over the grill with fondue forks. Heidi put them between graham crackers and chocolate. Soon they'd devoured everything, with Mitch pronounced grand champion for eating the most.

"Speaking of champions, have you ever watched the Tour de France, Zack?"

"What's that?"

His mouth curved upward. "A big bike race in France that lasts three weeks."

His eyebrows lifted. "That long?"

"They don't ride continuously. Every day they cover a certain section of the route, then they go to bed in the town they come to. The next day they get up and eat, and then ride the next section."

"What if it rains?"

"They ride through anything. Rain, wind, snow."

"Snow?"

"That's right. Their route might start in a valley. But when they have to climb to the summit of a mountain, they sometimes end up in a snowstorm."

"Don't they get cold?"

"Yup. They get cold and hot and have to layer their clothes for every eventuality. Just two days ago they biked through snow. But you have to realize these guys are in fabulous shape. A few of them are Americans. The race is going on right now. I've been recording the stages. Want to see a little bit of it?"

"Yeah!"

After a quick cleanup, all three trooped into the living room and sat down on the couch and love seat. For the next half hour they watched the last third of the day's race while Mitch patiently explained the aspects including the significance of the peloton.

"Wow!" Zack exclaimed as he watched the cyclists climb a twisting road. "That road winds up like a snake!"

Mitch nodded. "It does. Look at that one poor rider at the back. He's lost his legs. He's starting to wobble."

"Just like the zombies in the video game."

"Exactly like that. Uh-oh. Someone crashed."

"Why do they get so close?"

"The first guy faces the wind. The guy close behind him doesn't have to work as hard. They plan every move to conserve their energy until they try to make a break and become the leader."

"The scenery is stupendous," Heidi said. "Oh, it makes me want to go back there so badly I can hardly stand it. There's no scenery like it in the world."

"You've been there?" Zack sounded incredulous.

"Yes. With a bunch of friends while I was in college."

"I didn't know that." He jerked his head toward Mitch. "Have *you* been there?"

He nodded. "Several times when I was on leave from the military. A couple of my friends and I rented a car and drove through a part of the French Alps." As he spoke to Zack, his gaze met hers. "I agree there's no place like it. Those cyclists climb the summits like mountain goats."

Heidi expelled a sigh. "I don't know how they manage those climbs day after day. They're *iron* men."

Zack thought that was funny and laughed. Then he suddenly blurted, "Hey, Mom, look at that cool castle!"

"Europe's full of them. When you're a little older, I'm going to take us there. I want you to see Austria and England."

"England?"

"Yes. Your Grandma Bauer was a Taylor before she got married. The Taylor family is from the Isle of Wight. You have an ancestor, Thomas Taylor, who was a pioneer. He lived in a town with a huge castle. When we explore it you'll be able to spy like crazy through dark passages and dungeons and watch towers."

Her son's eyes were still glued on the racers. "Maybe I could ride in that race when I'm older! And at night I could sleep in one of those castles."

"Anything's possible." Her eyes met Mitch's and they both chuckled quietly. Zack had only learned how to ride his bike yesterday.

Once they'd watched the French rider climb today's podium and put on the yellow jersey, Heidi stood up. "Guess what, honey? It's time to go home. You've got school in the morning."

Following that thought, she realized Mitch would be starting work in the warehouse. They wouldn't have this kind of togetherness anymore. And soon he'd find out what was going on inside the plant. Then he'd leave for Florida, taking all the excitement and wonder of this week with him. How was she going to handle that?

She didn't even want to think about Zack's reaction when he learned Mitch was gone.

Their host turned off the TV. "The sun's gone down. Our ride back to your house won't be so hot now."

"I wish we didn't have to go."

Oh, Zack. I'm with you on that, honey.

She put her arm on his shoulder as they walked him out to the carport. "Even spies need their sleep, no matter how old. Isn't that right, Agent X12?"

Mitch shot her a piercing glance. "Right." He adjusted his own helmet strap. The man was so handsome, Heidi forgot not to stare. But she had to remember he would be on a huge spy mission starting tomorrow morning. Just thinking about it made her tremble for whoever was stealing from the company.

They would have no idea Mitch was on to them until it was too late. So far she and Zack had only seen the thrilling part of him, but she knew deep down he had a forbidding side when he went in pursuit.

AT FIVE TO EIGHT THE NEXT morning, Mitch reported for work at the Bauer's plant in Woods Cross. As per Heidi's instructions, he wore a dark blue polo shirt and khaki shorts. He'd already stopped by the surveillance van to pick up all the tapes to study later.

The receptionist in the plant told him to be seated. Over the loudspeaker she called for Randy to come to the front desk. Mitch had memorized the names of the people in charge. Randy Pierson was the Bauer who'd be Mitch's shift boss.

In a few minutes a blond guy in a similar blue polo shirt and khaki shorts appeared and shook Mitch's hand. "Welcome to the company, Mr. Garrett. I can see Ms. Norris prepared you and sent me a copy of your file. I'm Randy. Mind if I call you Mitch? We're not formal around here."

"I'd prefer it."

"Great. I was told we'd be getting a new man today. You'll like it here." Randy, who looked to be around Mitch's age, seemed an affable fellow.

"I'm looking forward to it."

"I'll show you around. When we finish today, you can put in an order for the polos we wear. You should have those shirts by Tuesday of next week. Come with me."

While Randy explained the schedule and the breaks, they toured the premises Mitch had covered by himself yesterday. They ended up in the warehouse and truck-bay area located at the south end of the plant.

"Let me introduce you to the man you'll be working with." They walked out to the loading dock where a truck had backed in.

"Harold? Come here a minute."

A middle-aged man with thinning brown hair and a barrel chest pushed an empty dolly down the ramp and walked toward them. "Where's Jack?" he said. "We've got a lot to load this morning."

"I've been told he wanted to train for a SweetSpuds manager job in one of the shops. This is Mitch Garrett, his replacement."

Harold didn't look too happy, but he shook hands with Mitch, sizing him up. "Ever done any warehouse work before?"

"No."

"Mitch will be working with you, Harold. Show

him the ropes. If you need anything, just come by my office."

"Will do. Thanks, Randy."

As he walked away, Harold squinted at Mitch. "I can't figure out how come you got Jack's job. There are guys in other parts of the plant who've been waiting years to work here. Are you a Bauer?"

Naturally that was the man's first question. "No." *But I'm crazy about a couple of them.*

"What kind of work have you done?"

"I'm just out of the Marines."

"Marines, huh?" He eyed Mitch once more. "Do you know anything about Bauer's?"

"I've been in orientation all week."

He nodded. "Okay. See these motor-driven carts?"

"Yeah?"

"They're piled with bags of donut mix the guys from the mix area loaded yesterday. See this card here?" He pointed to a yellow, eight-by-ten piece of cardboard sticking out beneath one of the bags with the number three hundred on it.

Mitch nodded.

"When we put these bags on the truck and lift the bag off that card, it will have their destination. They've already been counted, but we'll do it again to make sure it's the right amount. Then we'll push the slider against the shipment and fasten the strap. Before you start more loading, you stick the yellow card in the slot on the back of the slider so the destination is clear."

"Got it." So far Mitch couldn't find anything wrong with the unique system that checked the load twice. The problem lay with the culprits who were stealing the merchandise.

"Load as many as you can onto this dolly and push it up the ramp into the truck all the way to the end. Thirty-two bags across from roof to floor make one row. How many are we loading?"

"Three hundred."

"That makes how many rows?"

"Ten."

"Then start counting." Harold had all the makings of a drill sergeant. Mitch got busy while Harold kept an eagle eye on him and followed him inside. When they reached the back of the truck, Mitch could see his partner had already done a row of four stacks. Nine more rows to go.

"Start filling up another row just like it."

"Yes, sir."

Mitch got busy. As he loaded the next row, he checked the ends of the bags that had already been loaded. No red tags. He called out the number of the row every time he finished one. Harold probably didn't like that, either, but Mitch didn't want to give him any reason to tell him he wasn't up to the job.

The rest of the time they worked in silence. During the process Mitch checked the bottom seams of each bag looking for red tags among the blue. He found five before Harold pushed the slider against the row and attached the strap.

Harold finally spoke again, handing Mitch the yellow card. "Okay." It said San Francisco. "Put the card in the pocket on the back of the slider." Mitch did as he was told. "Now we'll keep loading until it's full, then we'll eat lunch. After that we'll load one more truck. Your shift will be over at four-thirty."

Randy had already given Mitch the drill, but Mitch

didn't say anything because it was obvious Harold was the type who liked to feel important. They worked steadily until noon. Mitch had checked every bag. All in all, twenty-five bags of mix had been switched for flour on this truckload headed to San Francisco through Elko and Reno.

Without saying anything to Mitch, Harold made his way to Randy's office and went in. After a moment the two came out. Randy checked off the shipment on his clipboard. "How's it going, Mitch?"

"Good. Everything's straightforward. Harold's an excellent trainer." For now every person in the plant was suspect in Mitch's eyes.

Randy smiled at Harold. "We couldn't get along without him." That comment didn't seem to please Harold at all. Maybe it felt patronizing. Mitch didn't know. "Enjoy your lunch, guys."

After Randy excused himself, Harold took off. That gave Mitch the freedom to go out to his car. In another minute he met up with his crew in the surveillance van. They had a hamburger and fries waiting for him. He washed his hands before eating with them.

"I counted twenty-five bags of flour on that shipment we loaded. If Harold's in on it, I'm convinced that's why he's so upset his partner was replaced. At the moment you could say he doesn't like working with me. If he doesn't know about the thefts, then he's just a bitter man."

Adam grinned. "You kept one step ahead of him. It probably bugged him, but that back of yours is going to be aching by tonight. I groaned every time you bent over. How's your arm?"

"I'm supposed to be a hundred percent. So far, so

good." He gobbled his food while he looked at the various screens. "I'll be loading another truck this afternoon. If Bruno hadn't recovered from his stroke well enough for his friend to tell him what was going on here, this kind of crime could have gone on indefinitely."

"Do you get any vibes from the guy with the clipboard?"

"Randy's nice and friendly, but maybe it's a cover. One thing I've noticed. Only Harold and I were doing the counting of the bags. Randy just checked the load off at the end. There was no sign of Lucas, who's supposed to be in charge of quality control. I understood he does it while the carts are loaded. I'll find out more when I go over the tapes tonight."

"Don't kill yourself out there and ruin that arm, Mitch."

"I'm all right." He downed the rest of his Coke. "Now I've got to go." He thanked the guys and drove back to the plant to start his afternoon shift. The truck they'd loaded had already left the bay and a new one stood parked at the dock ready to load.

Harold joined him as he was putting the last bag on the dolly before starting to fill up the truck. "Who are you trying to impress?"

Just for fun Mitch flashed him a quick smile. "You."

Harold wasn't amused. "Eager beavers can wear out fast."

"Would you like me to slow down? Just say the word."

The other man frowned before turning away and getting to work. For the rest of the afternoon they loaded shipments for San Diego, California, through

Las Vegas and Utah. So far no bags of flour were in the bunch, but he still had a hundred more bags to load before the truck was full.

Suddenly his adrenaline surged. Fifty of the last hundred bags had *red* tags. Something different was going on with this truckload. Maybe because the thieves hadn't been caught yet, they'd grown more daring. While he piled the last of the bags onto the dolly, Harold again made his way to Randy's office.

Mitch worked the slider and shoved it around. According to the yellow card, this last load of two hundred and fifty bags was headed for Beaver, Utah, a small town a couple of hours south of Woods Cross. He attached the strap and put the card in the pocket. With the truck loaded, he set the dolly against the side wall and walked down the ramp.

Once more Randy came out of his office and checked off the shipment. He flicked Mitch and Harold a friendly glance. "Great job today. In case you've forgotten, we're closed for the twenty-fourth on Monday because of Pioneer Day. See you on Tuesday morning."

"Thanks for the reminder, Randy. Good night," he said to both of them.

Mitch hurried out of the plant to his car and drove it to the surveillance van. Once inside, he changed into a T-shirt and jeans. "I made a fascinating new discovery, guys." He put his New York Yankees baseball cap on backward. "The truck you'll see leaving in a few minutes is headed for Beaver, ostensibly with an order of two hundred and fifty bags of mix. But fifty of the bags are flour."

Lyle let out a whistle. "Why are they stealing the flour?"

"Who knows? I'm going to follow it and see what happens. I might need backup."

"Phil's available."

"Good. Tell him to get down to I-15 on Thirty-third South and wait to hear from me."

"We're on it."

"Keep your eyes on the storage rooms. The switches will be happening pretty soon. Lucas is supposed to count the bags loaded on the carts. You've been given pictures of the main players and will be able to spot him if he's there doing his job. Let me know."

"Will do."

He got back in his car and called Roman to give him a progress report. Just as he disconnected, he saw the Bauer truck head for the entrance to the freeway headed south. He switched on the ignition and followed.

"MOM? CAN WE DRIVE TO Tim's with my bike? I want to cycle with him."

Now that school was over for the week, Heidi was glad he had someone else on his mind besides Mitch. She couldn't say the same for herself. Mitch had been working at the plant all day. She was anxious to know what he'd found out. More than that, she was eager to hear his voice.

"Sure, but before we go, we need to have a little talk."

His blue eyes fastened on her. "Am I in trouble?"

She chuckled. "No, honey. But if anyone should ask, just tell them a guy in our neighborhood helped you learn to ride without your training wheels. Don't mention that Mitch has been training with the company."

"How come?"

"Because it's temporary and pretty soon he'll be going back to Florida."

A frown appeared. "How come?"

"It's his home, remember?"

"Oh, yeah." He looked downcast. "Do you like Mitch?"

"Of course."

"Me, too." No kidding. "I wish he didn't have to leave."

Heidi gave him a kiss on the forehead to cover her feelings, then phoned Sharon to make the arrangements. Before long Zack and Tim were cruising around his neighborhood using the walkie-talkies. While her sister-in-law was getting dinner ready for her family, Heidi volunteered to watch the kids from the front porch.

Later Sharon came outside. "When did the training wheels come off?"

"A couple of days ag— Uh-oh, that's my phone. I'd better get it." Saved by the bell. Heidi reached into her purse for her cell and clicked on. "Hello?"

"I'm glad you picked up." Mitch's voice.

Since Sharon was within earshot, Heidi had to improvise. "Hi! What's the verdict on Jim?"

"Obviously you can't talk. Call me when you can." He disconnected. Mitch was all business, letting her know something serious was going on.

She gripped her phone tighter. "That's good news, Phyllis. Thanks for letting me know. Bye." Heidi clicked off.

"What was that about?"

"Work. Jim's the baker at the Foothill Shop. He

doesn't have to go in for surgery, after all. Now I won't have to find a substitute."

"One less headache for you."

"You're right."

"Are you sure you won't stay for dinner?"

"You're sweet, but tonight Zack wants me to watch the *Clone Wars* with him on TV. The show will be starting in a half hour. Thanks, anyway."

After hugging Sharon, she called to Zack, who came speeding up the driveway. Once they put his bike in the trunk, they were ready to go.

"See ya, Tim."

"See ya, Zack." He handed him the walkie-talkie.

On their way home, she darted her son a glance. "I bet Tim was surprised."

"He couldn't believe it. I told him Mitch gave me the walkie-talkies, too. He wants to go to that spy shop."

Oh, dear. "Who wouldn't? Did you guys have a good time?"

"Yes, but he's not as fun as Mitch."

Nope. Heidi was fast discovering there was no one like Mitch.

"Do you think he could come over to our house to-night and watch the bike race with us?"

"Not tonight."

"Why not?"

"He's still at work."

Once they were back home, she told him to wash his hands while she fixed fruit salad and homemade corn dogs for their dinner. While he was occupied, she called Mitch, but all she got was his voice mail. What-ever he was doing, he'd sounded intense earlier.

While she was fixing dinner, the phone rang again. She grabbed it. "Mitch?"

"No," sounded another familiar voice. "It's your mom. I've got the speaker on so your father can hear us, too."

"Oh, hi!" she exclaimed, hardly able to think. "I thought it was someone else. Are you two already home? I assumed you wouldn't get back before tomorrow."

"We're just leaving Rock Springs, Wyoming, and ought to be in Salt Lake in about three hours. It'll be too late for you to come over to the house, so we thought we'd call and see how you are."

"Zack and I are fine." That was the understatement of the century. "How are you? How's Evy?"

"Everyone's great and little Stacy is adorable."

"I can't wait to see this new baby."

"They promised to come for Thanksgi—"

"Mom—" Zack came bounding in the kitchen, breaking in on the conversation "—is that Mitch?" Heidi's mother couldn't have failed to hear him.

She turned her head toward him. "It's your grandma. Do you remember we don't talk when we see one of us is on the phone?"

"I forgot. Are they home?"

She gave up. "They will be later tonight."

"Can I talk to her?"

Heidi handed him her cell. She already knew what he was going to tell his grandparents. For the next minute they couldn't get a word in edgewise as he rhapsodized over his experiences with Mitch. Now that he'd been exposed to the world of the Tour de France, he couldn't talk enough about it or the man who'd breathed confidence into him without even trying.

"I love you, too, Grandma. Here's Mom." He handed her the phone. "Hurry. The *Clone Wars* are going to start and then I want to watch and see if any more guys crash their bikes in the race."

"Not until you sit down and eat." She took a deep breath, then said, "Hi, Mom."

"Hi. I can't decide who sounded more excited when they thought it was Mitch."

Heidi felt her face go hot. "Does he have a last name?"

"Yes. It's Garrett. He's the P.I.," she whispered so that Zack wouldn't hear. As far as she knew her parents had never kept secrets from each other, so she had to assume her mother knew about the thefts. If she didn't, then her mom would ask Heidi's father when they hung up. "Tell you what. As soon as I've fed Zack, I'll call you back. I promise."

MITCH WOULD HAVE ANSWERED Heidi's phone call, but the truck driver had suddenly switched lanes and taken the turn off for Draper, one of the communities in South Salt Lake. He'd only been on the road about forty minutes. Heidi said the trucks were gassed up every time they left the bay, so maybe the driver was stopping for dinner and a bathroom break.

Or maybe he wasn't.

The driver turned left and took several roads before coming to a medium-size storage facility. He knew the combination to get in because the gate opened from the side before closing again. The office wasn't closed yet. Mitch parked his car and went in, asking if he could rent a shed. When the paperwork was done, he was given the key and the combination to the gate before going back outside.

Phil, from Lufka, had pulled up next to his car. Mitch walked over to him. "I'm going in with my car. If by any chance I miss the truck, you follow it and I'll catch up." Phil nodded.

Once inside, Mitch drove around the mazelike facility until he spied the Bauer truck at one end of the K section in front of the last shed. Next to it was an older dark blue pickup. Three guys, all in their twenties, were moving bags from the truck into the pickup as fast as they could. Mitch pulled out his binoculars, but didn't recognize any of them from the application photos.

They hadn't opened any of the shed doors. Mitch wondered if the storage sheds were even being used, but he would come back later to find out. This was the perfect spot to transfer the bags where no one would think anything about it. He filmed them for a minute, then drove out to join Phil.

"What's up?"

"Before long you'll see a blue pickup with three guys come through the gate. They've taken a bunch of bags from off the truck. I'll follow them while you wait for the Bauer truck. See where it stops next, then call me. If you need backup, holler."

No sooner had he gotten back in his car when the big truck left the facility first and started down the road for the freeway. He exchanged glances with Phil who took off after it. It was five minutes before the pickup appeared. All three guys rode in front.

First they stopped at a drive-thru. Mitch was right

behind them and ordered a sandwich. He phoned in the license plate number to Lon, a retired police officer who worked for Lufkas. He would find out the information. Next, the pickup drove out to the freeway and headed south. When it took the Alpine turn off five minutes later, Mitch called Phil.

"Are you in Alpine, too?"

"No. The truck's headed due south at a fast clip."

"If it's supposed to be in Beaver by a certain time, I'm not surprised the driver is trying to make up for lost time at the storage place. Don't follow it past its next stop, since we know the rest of the shipments haven't been switched. Stay in touch."

"Ditto."

Mitch checked Alpine's population on his iPhone. 9500 inhabitants. If there was a Bauer outlet here, then this stop hadn't been put on the normal schedule. But the Bauer truck driver knew to stop in Draper at the storage rental to make a delivery. Was the driver acting on his own? Or was he following orders from the mastermind of this scheme?

Full of questions, Mitch followed the pickup to the business center. When they came to a small strip mall with a variety of shops still open, they drove around to the alley behind it and stopped at the center shop so the tailgate faced the door.

Someone from inside the shop opened the door for them. Quickly the driver lowered the tailgate and climbed in the truck bed. He began handing bags to the others, who carried them inside. Mitch had parked near some other cars and got it all on film. Once the load had been delivered, the guy from the shop shut the door and the three guys all got back in the pickup.

The pickup then went to a supermarket a mile away and pulled into the crowded parking lot. Two of the guys got out and walked to their own cars. Mitch took down their license plate numbers, but he stayed with the pickup and followed it for about a mile, to a small, framed house. The driver drove around the back of it.

When the pickup disappeared, Mitch noted the address, then made a U-turn and drove back to the strip mall. The center shop was called Drop In Family Pub, and it featured music, games, homemade pizza and donuts. Mitch decided this was a great time to pay a visit.

The place brought in a good crowd. He wandered inside, paid for a round of pool, then bought two donuts for takeout from the good-looking young woman at the counter. They didn't serve alcohol.

He smiled at her. "This is a great place," he said with a Southern accent. "How long y'all been in business?"

"About six months. The same time the movie complex went in down the street. Why not try our pizza, too? It's new on the menu."

"I don't know. I'm not a big pizza fan."

"This is different. Secret recipe," she confided. "I promise you'll like it."

"All right, sugar. You've talked me into it. I'll take a medium with Canadian bacon."

After she'd boxed one up for him, he winked at her. "If I like it, I'll be back."

"Don't take too long. My name's Georgia. What's yours?" A flirt, too.

"I'll tell you the next time I come in. See y'all around."

As far as he could tell, there were two other employees circulating. Both were guys in their twenties. Much as he wanted to ask more questions—like who was the owner—this wasn't the time to arouse suspicion.

He left the pub and headed back to Salt Lake. On the way he heard from Phil who'd watched the truck drop off the delivery in Beaver at the Bauer outlet. Now he was on his way back home.

Mitch told him about the pub in Alpine. After they'd talked shop, he phoned Heidi. Eight-thirty wasn't too late. Since it was a Friday, she probably hadn't put Zack to bed yet.

"Mitch?" She'd answered before the second ring. He thought he heard a tinge of anxiety in her tone. "Are you all right?"

More than all right now that he heard her voice. "I couldn't be better. What about you?"

"I'm fine." She sounded a trifle impatient. "I'm dying to hear what's been happening. I got a little worried when you didn't answer."

"I couldn't right then. Is it too late to come by your house?"

"Of course not."

"What about Zack?"

"He's in the tub. I'll be putting him to bed in a minute because he's going to see his grandparents in the morning. They'll be home late tonight. Now that you've helped him learn to ride his bike, he can't wait to show them. On the phone he told them that one day he wanted to ride in the Ter da Frants." She mimicked Zack's pronunciation of the Tour de France. "That's *your* doing."

Mitch chuckled in delight. "I'll be there in twenty minutes. I've brought food."

"I was just going to say I'd make you a homemade corn dog. That's what we had for dinner."

"What a coincidence since I'm bringing *you* something homemade. See you in a little while. I'll knock." He hung up because he knew she needed to get Zack to bed.

As his car ate up the miles, he felt as if he hadn't seen her in years. If he felt like this now, how was he going to feel when he put the distance of the country between them? The way this case was going, it would be wrapped up shortly.

When he thought of the condo in Tallahassee he'd been subletting, the idea of returning to its emptiness left him cold. But he knew Lew wanted him back there soon or he'd have to bring in another marshal. Mitch needed to make up his mind. If he wanted to stay with the marshals, he didn't want to work anywhere else in Florida except Tallahassee, otherwise…

Otherwise what, Garrett? Your mother might come looking for you and not be able to find you? Are you still hung up on that childhood dream?

Since meeting Zack, memories of Mitch's own childhood had been surfacing right and left. The boy had a fantastic mother and a strong support system that would see him happily through life. But in Zack's vulnerable moments brought on because his father wasn't around, Mitch saw himself in the boy.

How pathetic that Mitch was now thirty-four and he still hadn't let the dream go. In his gut he knew he didn't want to live in Florida. It had never felt like home. No place had ever called to him. The closest he'd ever come to such a feeling was right now as he turned into Heidi's driveway. Her garden and window boxes were a riot of color. Everywhere he looked was evidence of her handiwork.

Then he saw her standing on the front porch waiting for him.

She fulfilled him.

She thrilled him.

Chapter Six

"I can smell pizza," Heidi said as they walked into the kitchen. She was too happy to see Mitch to focus on food, but she figured he was starving.

"Before you try it, I want you to taste the dessert in this sack." She turned around, smiling up at the most appealing man she'd ever met. "Close your eyes first and keep them closed until I tell you to open them."

Mitch's mysterious behavior had aroused her curiosity. "What's this? Dessert before dinner? I don't do well on sugar before I eat."

"Neither do I, but I'm asking you to make an exception this once. Go on. Just one bite," he urged in a solemn tone.

Heidi decided she'd better close her eyes, sensing he wasn't just playing with her. He put something right against her lips. It was sweet all right. "Why did you bring me donuts?"

"Will you please stop asking questions and obey me?"

"Obey you?" She laughed "That sounds serious. All right. Because you *asked* me so nicely, I'll do it." She bit into it and chewed it before swallowing. "Mitch, I could have brought donuts home from our No. 2 store if you'd asked me. You're a tease, you know that?"

He didn't laugh back. "There's no question in your mind this is a Bauer donut?"

"None." She kept smiling. "If you're trying to trick me, it won't work. I've probably eaten hundreds of them in my lifetime and know what our donuts taste like." He was standing so close she could feel his warmth. A couple of inches more and she'd find his mouth. More than anything she wanted to taste it. She kept waiting for him to kiss her. "Do you still want me to keep my eyes closed?" The suspense was killing her.

"No. You can open them."

Something was wrong. Maybe he hadn't wanted to kiss her, after all. She felt like a fool and did his bidding.

"*This* is what you bit into."

He held up the donut she'd just taken a bite out of, but her head was still reeling from errant thoughts that had nothing to do with donuts and everything to do with taking a delicious bite out of *him*. Or him out of her, whichever came first.

Hadn't he wanted to kiss her? It was all she'd been able to think about. In her confusion she blinked. "I don't understand."

"Have you ever seen a Bauer donut that looked like this?"

He reached into the sack and pulled out another one, holding both up. They were identical. Forcing herself to concentrate, she noticed they were larger than a normal-size donut, and they had a smaller hole at the center.

She frowned. "I didn't know we were trying out a new nozzle. The idea hasn't come up in our board meetings. Whoever has been experimenting is going to be in trouble for this. Which one of our outlets sold this to you?"

"This is where the donuts came from." Mitch held up the donut sack so she could see the advertising on the front. She hadn't paid any attention to it before. He'd been the only thing to fill her vision.

Drop In Family Pub—featuring music, games, homemade pizza and donuts.
Open to all ages seven days a week, 11 to 11
Alpine, Utah

He watched her, obviously waiting for a response. All the time since he'd arrived at the house, she'd thought he'd been setting her up for a kiss because he couldn't hold back from kissing her any longer. Instead he'd been using her as a guinea pig in order to prove that the Drop In Family Pub was serving Bauer products to the public.

Disappointment consumed her for being wrong about him. She fought to recover so he'd never know what was going on inside her. A tiny gasp escaped her throat.

"You know what else I think?" His eyes bored into hers. "I think this pizza has been made with Bauer potato flour. Are you up for one more experiment?" He lifted the lid of the pizza box.

Heidi took a piece and bit into it. The consistency of the dough was lighter than that of ordinary pizza. She took several more bites before putting it down.

"I've never eaten anything like it before, but I'd have to make some pizza from scratch using the potato flour to prove this pizza was made with it."

Mitch put the donut sack on the counter. "I found out from the waitress that the pub opened six months ago. Quite an enterprise someone is running with your company's products."

Her mind was trying to put all this together. "Mitch, our company doesn't have an outlet or franchise in Alpine, Utah."

"I knew that from the information you gave me earlier. From the beginning I've wondered where the stolen mix bags had gone. Today I followed the truck I'd loaded in the afternoon. I called one of my crew to help provide backup. To my surprise, the truck driver turned off at Draper."

"What?"

"It's true. He drove to a storage facility where a pickup truck was waiting to offload the stolen bags of mix and flour. You can bet a load of fifty bags of mix and flour are dropped off at that storage facility every time a Bauer truck heads south. Once the transfer is made, the driver continues on to make official deliveries in Utah and elsewhere. Someone's got a perfect system in place."

"How does anyone dare do something like this?" She was so upset she grasped his arms, acting on impulse. But when she felt a tremor pass through his powerful body, she realized what she'd done and quickly removed her hands.

"Far too easily, I'm afraid," he answered in a husky voice.

Embarrassed by her impulsive gesture, she said,

"Tell me everything that happened today. Don't leave anything out."

"Why don't we sit down?" he murmured. "I have some videos to show you. Perhaps you'll be able to identify some of these people."

For the next half hour she watched the pictures on his iPhone, but didn't recognize anyone except the driver of the Bauer truck, Matt Sayer, who'd been with the company at least three years. She listened while Mitch gave her a blow-by-blow account of his day at the plant, including the clandestine meeting of the two trucks at the storage facility.

"This is the proof Bruno wants, Mitch. You're a genius," she said in awe. He'd uncovered things with such lightning speed, she could hardly take it in. At this rate he'd be gone out of her life in a flash. She sprang to her feet in turmoil. "Excuse me for a moment."

She hurried to the bathroom, not wanting him to see her tears. The realization had just started to sink in. She needed to get a grip. After washing her face and applying fresh lipstick, she started back to the kitchen, praying he wouldn't know all the reasons she was torn up inside.

Since last Monday she'd been living with the knowledge that someone in her family was stealing from the company. That was bad enough, but in a week's time something else had transformed her personal world, shaking her to the roots.

Mitch Garrett had happened to her. She was crazy about him!

Her pulse raced when she saw him at the end of the hall waiting for her. "I know this has come as a blow," he said with compassion, "particularly because we're getting closer to fingering the suspects spearheading this. Naturally it pains you to think anyone in your family could be this treacherous. If you'd prefer that I deal solely with Bruno from here on out, I'll understand."

No-o— Mitch hadn't fully understood why she was so upset. She didn't dare tell him the truth. How could she? She knew he liked her, but she couldn't be positive he was attracted to her romantically. He'd had an opportunity to kiss her in the kitchen, and it killed her that he'd let the moment go.

When she'd grasped his arms a little while ago, she wasn't sure if the tremor she'd felt was because he hadn't liked the contact. Or maybe he *had* liked it, but didn't feel he could act on his feelings while he was doing his job as a P.I.

"I want to see this through," she asserted, trying to present a calm exterior. "What's the next move?"

An unreadable expression crept over his features. "Tonight I'm headed for the office to go through the videos taken at the plant. One of the crew from the surveillance van is going to bring me the tape taken after I left today. Once I've viewed all of them, I'll have a much better idea of who's involved."

"What can I do to help?"

She heard him take a deep breath. "Nothing at the moment. I'll phone you in the morning and tell you what I've learned. We'll go from there." At the front door he paused and turned to her. "What would be the best time to call?"

"Any time," she replied, wishing he didn't have to go. "I'm always up early."

Heidi thought she glimpsed a flash of desire in his eyes, but if she was right, he didn't act on it. The next thing she knew he was out the door. When he'd driven away, she locked up and hurried to the kitchen, needing to do something to get rid of the ache that had attacked her body since his arrival.

The first thing she thought of doing was to place the food in plastic bags and put them in the freezer. Her father and Bruno would want to see the evidence. She flattened the donut sack and slipped it in her purse for safekeeping.

Unable to concentrate on the ten o'clock news, filled as always with terrible things that had happened to people, she turned it off and got ready for bed. She could just imagine the field day the media would have if bad news leaked about the Bauer company.

But even that stayed in the background of her mind because all her thoughts were centered on Mitch. One day soon he'd be gone for good. The pain hit with full force.

Heidi didn't need to put a name to the reason for the pain. She'd fallen in love, totally, gut-wrenchingly in love. She knew it the way you knew the sun was going to come up in the morning.

After a restless night, she showered and washed her hair. Whatever the day brought, she wanted to look her best in case she saw Mitch. No—there was no *in case* about it. She planned on seeing him before the day was out.

Once she was dressed, she fixed breakfast for her and Zack. Together they put his bike and helmet in her car before driving to her parents' home. While she was getting it out of the trunk, she heard her cell phone ring, but she couldn't get to it. She'd left it on the front seat.

"Here you go, honey. Wheel it up to the porch."

She closed the trunk and got back in the car, saw that the call she'd missed was Mitch's and had to phone him. "Mitch?"

"Good morning. You sound out of breath."

She was always out of breath around him. "I couldn't reach my phone in time. Sorry."

"Where are you?"

"In my parents' driveway."

"You haven't seen them yet?"

"No. Why?"

"There's something I want you to look at and help me make sense of."

Her heart thudded. "Where are you?"

"At my apartment."

"I'll ask my folks to watch Zack for a little while and I'll be right over."

"You're sure?"

"Positive. Dad's as anxious as Bruno to stop what's been going on. I should be there in about ten minutes."

"Pull into the carport and park behind my car. I'll leave the door open."

Her body pulsated with excitement. "See you soon." She hung up.

"Are you going to go to Mitch's apartment?" Zack asked. He must've overheard her when he'd come around her side to wait for her.

"Yes," she answered honestly, "but I won't be long."

"I want to come with you."

"You can't, honey. Your grandparents are waiting for you."

"But I want to see Mitch."

Don't we all. "Maybe later."

"How come you're so mean?"

"Zack Norris—" she used her parental tone "—that was not a nice thing to say to me."

"I'm sorry," he muttered. "But can we do something with Mitch later?"

"I don't know what his plans are. Look! There are Grandma and Grandpa on the porch waiting for you. Show them how well you can ride your bike."

MITCH DRANK COFFEE on his veranda while he waited for Heidi. The air was unusually muggy this morning. After a full week of blue skies, fast-moving clouds had started massing. There'd be a thunderstorm before long, the kind he loved.

After coming home from the office late, he'd lain awake afterward tortured by longings for Heidi that were growing stronger by the second. Once she'd touched him, grasped him the way she had, that was it.

Though she'd done it blindly in reaction to the news, his gut told him it was a move totally out of character for her. A watershed moment, as far as he was concerned. If she had any idea how much he'd wanted to devour that gorgeous mouth of hers last night—

"Mitch?"

At the sound of her voice, he turned and went back to the kitchen. His breath caught at the sight of her. She wore a sensational-looking sundress of a rich plum color she filled out to perfection. It had, short pleated sleeves. That color with her golden hair made a miraculous combination. She was bare-legged and wore bone-colored sandals. He groaned inwardly. A man could only take so much.

He set his empty cup on the counter. "You look beautiful." Even that was an understatement.

She came back with "You're nice, but it's the dress."

Mitch saw a pulse throbbing at the base of her throat. Did she really not know how she affected a man? Her bad marriage had done even more damage than he'd thought.

"I get so sick of wearing pants every day," she said next.

"If you wore that at my mostly male office, you'd start a stampede."

She blushed. "Hardly."

Oh, lady. If you only knew.

He reached for a stack of photos he'd printed out at the office. "Let's go out on the veranda. With the cloud cover, the temperature is actually pleasant."

"I noticed that driving over. I noticed something else, too. Your car has Michigan license plates."

"I have my reasons." He followed her out the sliding door, getting the benefit of the subtle lemon scent he associated with her. After they sat down, he put the photos in front of her. Mitch was so on fire for her, he had to force himself not to pick her up and carry her to the bedroom.

"I viewed the tapes last night and enlarged certain segments into eight-by-ten photos for you," he said. "According to the organizational chart you drew for me, Nadine Owens oversees the entire mix process."

"Yes. She's Frieda's granddaughter and runs the show in there. Bruno gave her that job when I was put in as head of human resources."

"That explains why she's the one who inserts the yellow stock cards with the numbers and destinations."

Heidi nodded. "The count is so important, Bruno prefers a family member to be entrusted with that responsibility."

"I need to know more about Nadine. What's she like?"

Heidi averted her eyes. "If you want to know the truth, she intimidates me."

"You?"

"Just a little. She's pretty perfect in everything she does. As long as I can remember, she's worked for the company and still manages to have a happy marriage."

One of the many things Mitch loved about Heidi was her honesty. The divorce had really brought her down. "How old is she?"

"I think she's thirty-nine, maybe forty."

"Does she have a big family?"

"Two children, one in high school, the other in college. She's as dependable as a Swiss clock. That's how Bruno describes her. Hale and hearty. It's the reason he put her in that position. Her work ethic is amazing, a model for everyone else. As far as I know, she's never taken a sick day."

Mitch winced at her comments, hating even more what he had to do. "Take a look at this first picture, caught by the camera in the flour storage room at 2:30 p.m. yesterday afternoon. Isn't that person Nadine who appears to be instructing two of the men to load the motorized cart with flour?"

Heidi studied it for a minute. "Yes. The mix room must be low on inventory, so she's having more flour sent in."

Mitch didn't respond. Instead he put another picture in front of her. "This picture was taken at the same time by the camera in the mix room. If you'll notice, the shelving is full of flour bags and everyone is busy."

He watched her study the picture and noticed how quiet she'd suddenly gone. She didn't move a muscle.

"Here's a third picture. We're back to the flour room. Twenty-five bags of flour have now been loaded. Nadine is inserting the yellow stock cards between the last two bags."

"But those are flour bags…."

"That's right." Mitch handed her another picture. "This is the mix room again. Two men are loading the sealed bags of mix on top of the flour bags already placed on the cart. Now study this series of pictures."

She took them from him.

"You see here? A flour bag has just been put in among the mix bags. Nadine is inserting another yellow card. If you'll notice, all the other employees in the area are doing their own jobs, probably unaware of what's going on. These next two pictures show Lucas arriving ten minutes later to count the load."

Heidi gasped, studying each picture over and over again. "I'm seeing it, but I can't believe it!"

"The next stack of pictures shows the same process starting again at 3:30 p.m. in the flour room with Nadine, and ending with Lucas counting the second load. Here's the final picture." He slid it on top of the others. "It was taken in the warehouse bay at 5:00 p.m. It shows two loaded carts sitting out at the loading dock waiting for Tuesday morning."

"Oh, Mitch…" Her voice sounded desolate. She eventually lifted her head and looked at him through wet blue pools. "To see it happening before your very eyes… Nadine—of all people."

She shot up from the table. "She holds such a position of trust it would never occur to Bruno—to *any* of us. I wonder how many people in the mix room have known what's been going on and turned a blind eye…."

Without hesitation he pulled her into his arms, wanting to comfort her. "Maybe not as many as you think. Maybe none if they trust her so completely," he whispered into her fragrant curls. "We know for certain now Nadine is party to the thefts. Since she arrives at the plant earlier than Jonas or Lucas, she's had access to keys. If they're not to blame, then it's possible she knows their computer passwords and deletes the emails that would give her activities away."

"Don't forget the truck drivers who make the secret drop-off in Draper," Heidi said against his shoulder.

"Let's hold out on blaming them until we know all the facts. I've got to do some more investigating to find out if she's at the center, or if she's carrying out someone else's orders." He also needed to talk to the woman who'd worked under Nadine before she'd been let go by the company.

Heidi's shoulders shook. "When Bruno sees this, I'm afraid he'll have another stroke."

Mitch drew her closer. She fit against his body as if she were made for him. "Your great-uncle comes from tough pioneer stock like his grandmother, otherwise he wouldn't have survived his first stroke, let alone hired Roman's firm to do a thorough job of getting at the truth."

"You're right." Her voice was wobbly.

Her vulnerability was too much for Mitch. He kissed her temple and cheek until he found her mouth. Her immediate response to him was like a miracle. They took small experimental tastes of each other's lips. It was the most delightful moment of his life holding this fabulous woman in his arms, sensing that her desire for him was there pulsating beneath the surface.

But it only lasted a moment. To his frustration she eased away from him before he was ready to let her go and wiped her eyes. "Sorry I got your shirt wet."

"I'm not complaining." He pressed one more kiss to her mouth. "What I'd like to do is finish my investigation and identify the people involved. Then we'll go to Bruno with all the facts and let him deal with it the way he sees fit. If I were to feed him the information in pieces, he'll brood and speculate."

Her gaze searched his. "You're very perceptive."

"You forget I've been in the bloodhound business one way or the other since joining the Marines. You learn to read people fast."

She rubbed her arms with her hands. "Did you notice anything else suspicious while you were working in the plant yesterday?"

"Not really. As for my crew, so far they haven't picked up anything from listening in on the conversations in the offices I bugged. Do you know if Nadine favored company expansion like her grandmother Frieda?"

"I've never heard her express an opinion. Even if she's wanted to work against Bruno's philosophy, I still can't fathom her using her position to steal from the company. How come she feels no loyalty to him or the family? I don't see how that's possible."

"It's my opinion you're not the only one who's felt intimidated by her. Otherwise someone ought to have come forward by now. But her clever scheme of embezzlement is about to come to an end." Mitch gathered up the photos and put them on the counter. He flicked her a glance. "How soon do you need to pick up Zack?"

"Actually I told my parents I'd meet them at the ranch. Mom wants to see how the float for the parade is coming. Dad said he'd take Zack for a short horseback ride."

Mitch cocked his head. "In that case, come snooping with me."

Her face brightened, the sign he was hoping for. "Where?"

"I want to retrace my steps from last evening and check something out. We shouldn't be gone more than a couple of hours."

"I want to see that pub in Alpine."

Mitch thought she might. "So you shall." He reached for her purse and handed it to her. "If you'll back your car out, I'll do the same, then you can park here and we'll go in mine."

She walked out ahead of him. Once in the carport they bumped into his neighbors. He couldn't wait to be alone with Heidi again and only nodded to the girls. When he helped her in the car and they drove down the street, she turned to him with a curious look in her eye. "I believe they were disappointed you left so fast."

He made a turn onto Foothill Drive. "Any disappointment they felt happened when they caught sight of the gorgeous woman coming out of my apartment. In the morning, no less," he drawled.

She chuckled. "You're terrible."

That was another thing he loved about her. She didn't take herself too seriously. "I have news. We males are all terrible when it comes to a good-looking female."

"College girls have the same problem where a hunky Marine is concerned. I wonder how many months they've been waiting for you to come outside and play."

Mitch broke into laughter.

"One thing is certain," she added.

"What's that?" He would never get tired of being with her. Those days of needing his own space had vanished.

"Your parents passed on some attractive genes to you," she said. "If they could see how you've turned out, they'd be overjoyed."

He felt another tug on his emotions. "What brought that on?" By now they were on the freeway.

"I don't know exactly. Since you told me about your past, I've thought a lot about it. I guess it's because I'm a mother. What if you took out an ad in some of the Florida newspapers showing a Garrett Fruit Company crate with a statement like *I'm the baby you put in this crate thirty-four years ago. If you want to meet me, notify the paper at this email address.* Something like that."

Astounded by her interest, he said, "It's a terrific idea, but I'm afraid the paper would receive thousands of emails from people claiming to be that person."

She eyed him speculatively. "If you asked the newspaper to forward them to you, I'd be happy to help you go through them. You never know what might happen, but if you don't like that idea, here's another one. Have you considered taking time off from all your work and doing your own investigation full-time to see if you can trace them? You know—physician, heal thyself?"

What a remarkable woman she was! Mitch gripped the steering wheel tighter. "When I was in the Marines, I used to think that when I'd earned enough money and didn't have to work, I'd do what you suggested. But before I was injured, I watched one of those televised documentaries where a woman who'd been abandoned at birth searched for her mother and finally found her."

"What happened?"

"It was a disaster on both sides and made me realize I'd better be careful what I ask for because I just might get it and not like it."

She studied him compassionately for a minute. "You'd rather they came looking for you?"

"In an ideal world," he admitted. "I'm afraid that's the child in me—just waiting for a dream to come true."

"We all have that child in us," she said in a faintly mournful voice.

The tone of their conversation had turned more serious.

"Were you terribly in love with your husband?"

He heard her sigh. "Whatever that means, at the age of twenty I thought I was. Then the oddest thing happened." She paused. "We got married and he changed, became someone else, someone angry and controlling. By the time Zack was born, my old feelings for him had died. Gary was eventually fired at work and from that point on his anger grew worse. I couldn't do anything right and filed for divorce. Such a relief."

Knowing the kind of principled woman Heidi was, he realized divorce was the very last option she would have considered. Their marriage had to have been unbearable. "How long were you married?"

"Four years."

"Well, I happen to know your son loves his mother with all his heart, so you're doing everything right in his eyes."

She laughed. "You didn't hear him this morning when he found out I was going to be with you. He said I was *mean* not to let him come. I told him I didn't know what your plans would be."

"Zack's a very special boy. When we've finished our business down south, how would you like for us to head north and pick him up? Depending on the weather, we might even drive to that amusement park I've seen from the highway."

"You mean Lagoon?"

"Yes. I've passed it several times, but haven't gone in because it's the kind of place to enjoy as a family."

She went quiet before looking at the sky. "By the time we reach the ranch, we'll probably be wiped out by rain, so it will be better not to mention it."

If she was trying to discourage him, it wasn't working. For days now the chemistry had been building. She wanted this day with him as much as he did—he could feel it. A fire had been licking through the veins of them both back at his apartment. Heat was building. Before long it would turn into a conflagration. His heart thudded at the thought of making love to her.

THE MAN DRIVING THE AUDI was dressed in gray trousers and an expensive-looking silk sport shirt in a charcoal color. When Heidi had been in his arms, she'd smelled the soap he'd used in the shower, and the scent still lingered in the car.

Inside and out, Mitch was close to perfect. She knew no one was perfect, but so far she couldn't find any fault in him. That was a pretty strong conclusion to reach when you'd only known someone six days!

Lost in thought, she didn't realize they'd come to the turnoff for Alpine until she heard a police siren and saw a car being pursued. "Uh-oh. Somebody was speeding."

"That's made the patrolman's day," Mitch said in a dry tone. "It'll help him make his quota to please his boss."

She turned her head toward him. "How many car chases have you been in?"

"A few, but when a felon is fleeing the scene of a crime, more times than not we're both on foot."

Everything he'd done in his life from the Marines to the federal marshals to his P.I. job revealed he preferred to live dangerously. The world needed men like him to keep other people safe, but a woman who cared for him might have a big problem with that. Was it the reason he'd never settled down with a wife? Because he knew she could never handle the risks he took?

Could you handle it, Heidi?

She'd already answered the question several days ago. She would hate watching him walk out the door wondering if it would be the last time she saw him alive. The sooner he left Salt Lake, the better for her and Zack.

While Mitch drove them into the business center, she trembled because the truth stared her in the face.

She was a pathetic mass of contradictions. If she thought it was better he moved back to Florida, then why had she dressed up this morning wanting him to notice?

You know why, Heidi. You want to keep him here for good.

"Here's the strip mall," he said. "The pub is in the center." As they passed slowly by, she was able to see the sign. *Homemade donuts and pizza.* "I'll drive around back. The pub won't be open for an hour, but someone has to be there setting things up. Let's see what we can find out."

There was a flash of lightning in the sky as they pulled into the alley where other cars were parked. Heidi saw a cell phone truck delivering boxes to the store near the other end. When Mitch pulled up to the back door of the pub and got out of the car, she resisted the urge to tell him to be careful. Though he knew what he was doing, he wasn't infallible. He had scars from his gunshot surgery to prove it.

A guy who looked to be in his twenties answered the knock. Wearing a T-shirt and jeans, he'd tied an apron around his waist. Heidi's heart hammered in apprehension while Mitch talked to him. The guy listened, then shook his head before shutting the door.

"What did you say to him?" she asked as he got back in the car. The wind was gusting. She could smell rain in the air.

He started the engine and drove them to the end of the alley. "I told him I was out here from Michigan looking for a friend named Mario. He was supposed to be working at a pub in Alpine with another friend named Eric. The guy said his name was Nick and he'd never heard of either guy. Does the name Nick mean anything to you, Heidi?"

"No."

"He said there was another place in Lehi called Ronny's Pub. Maybe Mario worked there."

She shook her head. "Your creativity blows me away. Did you see anything incriminating?"

His gaze met hers. "A storage room filled with Bauer bags. I could smell donuts cooking from another section. Now that I've seen evidence that the place is in full operation with stolen goods, there's just one more thing I want to check before we drive to the ranch to pick up Zack. We'll have to backtrack to Draper."

"To that storage place where you saw the bags being transferred?"

He nodded. "I want to see if it's just a rendezvous point, or if one of those guys is actually using a storage shed where they were doing the loading. Lon is tracing the license plate on the pickup and the two cars in the supermarket parking lot. I should be hearing from him today. In the meantime, maybe we'll get a break and find something that will give us another lead."

Once they were back on the freeway, he said, "Heidi, I'm not sure you're all right. I shouldn't have brought you with me."

"Bruno asked me to be his eyes and ears. I could cry buckets over what Nadine has done, but I needed to come. It's making everything real."

Mitch reached for her hand. At his touch she felt the contact arc through her. They sped north while the elements treated them to a fabulous display of forked lightning followed by thunder. But another kind of fireworks were going off inside her.

"The wind's so strong, it's buffeting your car."

"We're in for a downpour all right."

By the time they reached the Draper turnoff, the sky was black with clouds. "Ooh—it's getting close," she said.

"Does it make you nervous?"

"No. I love storms."

He gave her hand another squeeze before letting go. "So do I. We're almost there."

Sheet lightning lit up the entrance to the storage facility. She had no idea where they were going, but Mitch had little problem finding what he wanted with his own built-in radar.

"Here we are. Row K." He drove to the end of it and stopped. "This storm has sprung up at the perfect time. No one's here. I'm going to open a couple of these sheds and look around. You stay in the car."

"I want to look with you." She slid out her side and watched him use a tool to open the end shed. Inside were a dozen lawn mowers and snow blowers.

"That shed's no help." Mitch closed and locked it. Jagged lightning flickered overhead followed by a huge thunderclap that shook the ground, but he kept working and opened the next shed. Hail started to bounce everywhere, but she was hardly aware of it because her attention was suddenly focused on the black Mazda Miata parked inside.

More lightning illuminated everything. Before he shut the shed door, she caught sight of the custom-made Bellagio spinner tire rims on the older model sports car.

"Oh, no!"

"Get back in the car, Heidi." By now hail was slamming them hard. Mitch grabbed her around the shoulders and forced her into the passenger seat of the Audi. He shut the car door and ran around to get in behind the wheel, sealing them inside.

The hail was coming down now as if the heavens had emptied, covering the ground like snow. He leaned across and pulled her into him. "Don't be frightened. This'll be over in a few minutes."

A monsoonlike rain followed the hail, enveloping them in the deluge. Shocked senseless by her discovery, she lifted her head. "That's not why I cried out."

"What then?" he demanded anxiously. Heidi felt the warmth of his breath on her mouth.

"That Miata is my ex-husband's sports car!"

Chapter Seven

In the pounding noise of the rain, Mitch's teeth clenched so hard he almost cracked one. With lightning flashing, he could see that her complexion had lost color. He drew in a labored breath. "You couldn't possibly be mistaken?"

"No," she declared with complete conviction. "I'd know his Miata anywhere. It meant more to him than his own family. After we got married, we lived in an apartment. Our goal was to buy a house in two years' time using our savings for a substantial down payment.

"Our problems came about early because he wanted us to have joint savings and checking accounts. But my father advised me not to set things up that way. Gary accused me of being paranoid about money, but as the months went by I realized he was dipping into his savings to work on the car. By the end of our first year of marriage I was expecting Zack, so I asked Gary if he'd given up on the idea of a house.

"That's when he had a major meltdown. He told me point-blank he would never make enough money with his lowly warehouse job at the plant to match my salary. I reminded him he could move up if he finished college and went for his MBA. Or he could go out and look for the kind of job he truly wanted. The next thing I knew, he slammed the door behind him and left to buy those expensive special rims for his car."

Mitch saw her jaw harden. "I should have seen the signs of blind ambition in him, but hormones got in the way. It's clear love didn't motivate him to marry me. He wanted a shortcut to money. It's no wonder he was so upset when he couldn't get into my accounts. What I'm trying to understand is how he and Nadine grew close enough to join forces. All this time I thought he was in Oregon. This is the proof that Zack means absolutely *nothing* to him! I feel doubly savaged."

The hurt in her voice tore him up inside. "So do I," Mitch said, "but remember they've taken wrong paths of their own free will and aren't worthy to breathe the same air you do. I've had to deal with felons for a long time. Most of them have had something happen in their childhoods that a majority of psychiatrists refer to as a brain freeze."

"I've heard that theory, too."

"It's probably because they never bonded with anyone. If certain emotions like empathy and remorse—the kind you and I feel—get cut off, then behavior can grow more immoral over time."

She wiped her eyes. "That describes Gary. He resented having to live with his grandparents after his parents died in a boating accident." Her head jerked around. "But look at you—you never had a family to bond with, yet you're wonderful!"

Heidi, Heidi.

"So are you," he whispered, pulling her across his lap so that she half lay in his arms. "So wonderful and so beautiful, I don't have words. Forgive me, but I have to do this or I won't be able to function."

Her sweet mouth had lured him from day one. At his apartment her lips had teased him. But now that he was covering them with his own, he was lost in sensation after sensation. His heart leaped to realize their hunger was mutual. He found himself kissing her face and hair, her throat where a pulse was madly beating. Her hands on his chest took his breath away, enthralling him in a way he hadn't dared dream about.

"You're more beautiful to me than you can imagine," he whispered against the side of her neck. "Not just physically. I see the way you care for your son, the way you cherish those you love. You're fun and exciting and amazing and so many other things...."

"You're amazing, too, Mitch." She ran kisses along his jaw. "I never expected to meet someone like you when Bruno asked me to drive to the Lufka firm."

As Mitch half moaned her name in longing, a car honked loud and long behind them, causing her to sit up abruptly and move to her side of the Audi. She looked back. "What if that's Gary?" she cried in panic.

"Don't be frightened. It's an older man, but we're probably blocking his shed." The rain had turned to drizzle while they'd been entwined. You could see rivulets of floating hail.

"We'd better move."

Yup. The interruption was ill-timed, but he had no choice except to start the engine and head for the exit.

He knew in his gut Heidi was just as shaken by the passion that had flared between them. It had taken over conscious thought. If that driver hadn't come along...

On their way out to the highway he flicked her a glance. "Before we drive any farther, I want to be clear about something. I have no intention of asking your forgiveness for what happened back there."

"That's good, because I don't expect one," she confessed with her unfailing honesty. That's what he loved about her. That resilient spirit.

"I could blame it on the amazing dress you're wearing, but that wouldn't be the truth. You already know I've been intensely attracted to you from the moment you walked in my office. In all honesty, after we'd finished making our first batch of donuts, I wanted to drag you back to my cave by your incredible hair. Whether you believe me or not, I've never gotten involved with a client before. You're my first.

"Wait—I take that back. Once, when I was a federal marshal guarding a woman who'd been put in the witness protection program, we found ourselves attracted due to the time we'd had to spend together. Fortunately I got out before I jeopardized the case."

He heard her take a swift breath. "Then fortune is still with you."

"What do you mean?"

She stared at him. "Inside of a week you've all but solved this case for my great uncle without jeopardizing it, either. In a few more days you'll have tied up the loose ends and can head back to Florida.

"After watching you in action, I can't imagine this P.I. job holding a man like you for long, not with your skills and instincts." She sighed. "You're overqualified for the work of a private detective, Agent X12."

He grimaced. After getting into each other's arms, those thrilling feelings they'd both experienced had frightened her. *Damn Gary Norris for robbing her of her confidence.* But Mitch wouldn't allow her defenses to thwart him. This called for different tactics. You didn't rush a woman like Heidi.

"Let's not get ahead of ourselves. Those loose ends could take some time. If you feel you've got other things to do and can no longer help me, I understand."

"You know that's not what I said."

"Then you're not frightened of me?"

"Of *you?* No."

It was an answer of sorts. "For your information," he said, "this situation is new to me, too. But none of it matters as long as we have complete trust and are frank with each other." *As long as we stay together and explore what's going on here.*

"You really mean that?"

"Heidi—"

"Let's assume the shoe was on the other foot and after seeing each other for a week, I told you I was headed for my home across the country, still on a quest to locate my mother or father. It wouldn't be a vacation. I planned to return to a job I loved and had held for a long time." Her eyes blazed with fire. "Knowing those facts, how much of an investment would you make in me?"

Once her question had rung out in the car's interior, she reached for her phone and called her parents to find out their plans. When she hung up she said, "Because of the rain, they're already on their way back from the ranch with Zack. If you wouldn't mind, Mitch, I'd like to stop at your place and get my car. I need to talk to my dad about what we've found out and prepare him. He's going to take this hard and will blame himself for firing Gary."

"I don't think so. Your ex-husband took a left turn long before his blowup with your father, and your dad knows it." He reached for her hand. "And you need to stop taking on any more guilt for marrying him."

"Actually, I have stopped," she said before slowly removing her hand from his grasp.

Mitch hoped she meant it. After learning her ex-husband had been close to Salt Lake all along and had played a role in this crime against her family, naturally she would go straight to her dad to talk to him.

Maybe it was selfish of Mitch, but he wanted her to come to him, Mitch. Just the way Mitch wanted his father or mother to come to him?

You're out of your mind, Garrett.

They drove the rest of the way to his apartment in silence. At the entrance to the carport, she was out of his car before he could stop her. He saw the bleakness in her eyes when she leaned in to speak. "In light of what we've just learned, I want to thank you for the drive. But under the circumstances, that doesn't sound quite right, does it?" Her strength after being confronted by such adversity was a revelation to him.

"No," he murmured. "If you and Zack decide you'd like to come over here later, I have calls to make and am not going anyplace. Don't forget I promised him he could work out in my mini-gym."

She nodded. "I haven't forgotten. Neither has he."

On that note he watched her climb into her car, back out and drive off. After her taillights disappeared, he phoned Travis hoping he'd pick up. He needed to talk to one of his buddies or he was going to explode. To his chagrin, he got his voice mail.

"Travis? It's Mitch. When you've got a minute, call me. This is important."

After he let himself into the apartment, he made himself a cup of coffee. While he was draining it, his phone rang. He grabbed for it and checked the caller ID before clicking on. "What's up, Lon?"

"Lots."

"Go ahead."

"I checked the license plate on that pickup. It's registered to a Merrill Warburton, 81, at the home address you asked me to check."

Mitch sat down at the table so he could take notes. "The guy driving the pickup last night had to be in his late twenties, so it could be anyone living at that address with him."

"Right. I made a few phone calls to neighbors and found out Mr. Warburton passed away two and a half years ago. His only son, Cain Warburton, lives in Sacramento, California. His family is grown. He lets his oldest son, Levi Warburton, live there in Alpine and take care of his grandparents' place. This neighbor told me they've been trying to sell it, but no buyers yet. This Levi is single and has a single male living with him."

"You work miracles, Lon. It's all making sense."

"I got lucky and found a next-door neighbor who likes to talk. As for the Honda Accord in that supermarket parking lot, it's registered to a Jeremy Farnsworth, 27. The Ford Taurus is registered to a Noah Eldredge, 29. They both live in Alpine at different addresses."

"Great work. What about the truck driver who works for Bauer's?"

"Yeah, Matt Sayer. If he was on the wrong side of the law before working for them, then he never got caught until you got him on film."

"Things are starting to line up. What have you found on Gary Norris?"

"Well, there's no history of him living anywhere in Oregon in the last nine years. No warrants for his arrest. Zip. He still holds a current Utah driver's license."

Adrenaline charged Mitch's body. "At what address?"

When Lon told him, Mitch let out a low whistle. "That's his ex-wife's address. It means that when he renewed his license, he never changed his place of residence. It'll interest you to know Heidi and I found his sports car parked in one of those storage sheds in Draper this morning. What do you bet he lives at the Warburton house, where he can keep a low profile?"

"I'll drive down there and do some more investigating."

"As long as you're going, buy a meal in that pub in Alpine and see if you can get a visual on Norris. You've got picture ID. Once we can tie him to the pub, I'll have enough evidence to take to Bruno Bauer."

"I'm on my way."

"I owe you, Lon. This case is exceptionally important to me."

"Just doing my job."

"But no one does it like you do."

He'd barely hung up when Travis returned his call. He clicked on. "Thanks for getting back to me so fast."

"You sound upset. What's going on?"

"How long have you got?"

"You want me and Casey to drive in?"

Travis lived in the south end of the valley. "No, no. I just need to talk."

"This wouldn't have anything to do with Heidi Bauer, would it?"

"Who's been spreading rumors?"

"The usual suspects. Lisa noticed you *did* give your client and her son a private showing of the shop. Once she told Roman, that was it."

"Nothing's sacred."

"He comes from fine Russian stock and insists on knowing everything that goes on. He doesn't head a spy ring for nothing."

In spite of Mitch's turmoil, he smiled, but it didn't last. "Here's the problem. This morning Heidi and I found out her ex-husband is involved in this case up to his eyebrows." Mitch brought Travis up to speed.

"So he and this Nadine have been stealing the company blind. They're a real gutsy duo."

"Yup. I'm still reeling from the fact that he abandoned Heidi and Zack a long time ago. He gave up his parental rights after they divorced. Knowing he's indirectly back in her life in such an ugly way has made the case much more complicated for me on an emotional level because—"

"Because you're already emotionally involved with her up to *your* eyebrows," Travis finished the sentence.

"Afraid so. I want to be alone with her. You know what I mean? But I can't do anything about it while I'm in the middle of this case, so I want to offer support from a distance. How would you and Casey like to come to the parade with me on Monday morning? Zack is going to ride on the Bauer float and be dressed up like a pioneer child. I'd like to be there for him and Heidi. After learning of her ex-husband's betrayal, she needs to know I'm there for her."

"Casey and I would love to go to the parade with you. How old is Zack again?"

"Six."

"With Casey being seven, they'll have to meet. Count us in. I'll call Chaz and tell him to bring Lacey and Abby."

"You're reading my mind."

"I'll call him as soon as we get off the phone."

"Thanks, Travis."

"Stealing from her family's company on top of everything else is what I call the ultimate betrayal. I'm sorry for all concerned. Talk to you later, Mitch."

The empathy in Travis's tone stayed with him after they'd hung up. His friend had lived through something much worse after he'd learned his wife had been murdered. Mitch had suffered for him and Casey, too.

HEIDI GLANCED AT HER BOY. "Did you have fun with Grandma and Grandpa?" They'd just driven away from her parents' home.

"Yes, but it rained so we couldn't go riding. I'm glad we came back after lunch. Can we go over to Mitch's now? He said I could play with his gym stuff."

She knew Zack. He wouldn't let it go, so she made a decision. Better deal with this immediately or he'd drive her crazy for the rest of the day. "Tell you what. Here's my phone." She passed it back to him from the front seat. "Press two and Mitch should answer. Find out what his plans are." Heidi was afraid to let Mitch know how eager she was to be with him again.

"Goody." In a few seconds her son was talking to Mitch, who had him laughing. Their conversation went on for as long as it took to reach her house. "Okay. See ya. Hey, Mom? Mitch wants us to come over now. He rented a scary spy movie for us to watch after we work out."

That sounded like Mitch. He *was* pretty perfect. Ask her son. But the haunting thought that he was close to resuming his federal marshal job gripped her like a vise.

"All right. While you put your bike in the garage, I'll change clothes and we'll go." She retrieved her phone and opened the trunk to get out his bike.

"Do you *have* to change? He told me to hurry."

"It won't take me long." The dress she had on was a reminder of the way he'd looked at her before their mouths had fused in raw hunger. That memory would always live with her whether she removed it or not, but she would still feel better showing up at his apartment in jeans and a shirt.

Since seeing Gary's car, she'd had time to put the morning's discovery into perspective. It only underlined the utter deadness of her feelings for her ex. They were so dead that when Mitch had cocooned her in his arms and had driven their kiss deeper, she'd been on fire for him. Forget the world. Forget the case Mitch had been hired to solve. Forget everything except Mitch's way of bringing out her deepest emotions.

Earlier Mitch had asked her if she'd been in love with her husband. Whatever feelings she'd had in those days, Gary had systematically killed them. She didn't know how empty she'd been until Mitch had come along, bringing her back to life.

Ten minutes later she and Zack entered his apartment. "Hi, Mitch! I brought my walkie-talkies."

"So I see." Mitch squeezed him on the shoulder. "I'm glad you remembered." He put them on the counter. "After we finish exercising, we'll have some fun. Go ahead and check out the equipment in the other room. I'll be right in."

"Thanks."

As Zack took off, Mitch's gaze swept over Heidi. She felt a quickening because by the look he was giving her, she might as well have been wearing the sundress. "Did you tell your parents what we've discovered?"

"I told them we have evidence that Nadine is one of the culprits. That came as a huge shock to them. I didn't say anything about Gary, because Zack was right there. We agreed to put off our talk until Monday night. It's going to be a big day and we don't want to ruin it for anyone or act like anything's wrong."

"I think that's the wisest course. It'll give me time tomorrow to check out some more leads."

She nodded. "After the parade, there'll be a big barbecue at the ranch for those in the family who want to go. The kids will play and then I'll take Zack home and put him to bed. My parents will come by then. Dad wants you there. Is that all right with you?"

"Of course. I plan to be at the parade, too, and get pictures of Zack. Where would be the best place to watch it?"

While Heidi waited for her heartbeat to slow down

after hearing that news, Zack called out from the other room. "Hey, Mitch, aren't you coming?"

"I'll be right there!"

"The parade starts at nine and ends at Liberty Park. If you get to the north end of the park early, you'll be able to find a parking spot. I'll be riding in the car with Karl, who's driving the float. Zack told me he's too nervous to ride on it unless I'm there, too. Karl's the one who ferries Bruno to work and back. We'll be the first float behind my father and the horse cavalcade."

Mitch's eyes gleamed. "I'll find you."

Mitch...

"While I'm playing with Zack, do me a favor and see if you can reach that female employee from the mix room who was fired a few months ago. Use my laptop to get into the files and find her phone number. If possible, get her to tell you what led up to her being fired. Use my phone so she won't be thrown off by your name." He put it on the table before striding off to join Zack.

With some trepidation, Heidi sat at the table against the wall to begin her task. They'd gone over that list before. Deena Larson had been let go in April. Since Heidi had been the one to recommend her for the job, it had come as a big surprise to learn she'd been fired after the first day. To Heidi's knowledge, nothing like that had ever happened before, but she supposed there was always a first time.

Deena and her husband had moved from Evanston, Wyoming, to Salt Lake, where her husband was look-ing for work. She'd worked as a pastry chef at a local bakery and came with a high recommendation from her former boss. Heidi had been impressed with her.

The file indicated that Lucas had done the firing, but there was no written explanation for it.

Curious in her own right, Heidi picked up Mitch's phone and called the first number listed. She reached Deena's voice mail, so she tried the second number. After three rings, a female voice answered, probably from her cell phone. "Hello?"

Heidi bit her lip before she said, "Hi. This is Heidi Norris. I'm the person from Human Resources at Bauer Donuts who recommended that you be hired in April. Do you remember me?"

There was a long period of quiet. "Yes. What do you want?"

At least she hadn't hung up on her. "This is an unofficial call. I've been going through some files and came across your name. When you were let go in April, I have to admit I was really surprised because you made a very favorable impression on me during our interview. Have you found another job yet?"

"Yes."

"I'm glad for that. Deena…would you be willing to tell me what happened? You'd only been working in the mix room a day. If you thought you'd been dismissed unfairly, I'd like to know about it."

"I guess from the man's point of view, it wasn't unfair. I *did* challenge him."

"Who? What do you mean?"

"It was the end of the shift. As I was leaving, one of the warehouse men—the name Lewis was on his tag—drove the motorized cart into the room. I saw some bags already on it. That surprised me, so I checked the tags. They were flour bags. I told him to take the bags back to the flour storage area."

"I would have told him the same thing," Heidi interjected.

"Well, he told me those bags were *supposed* to be there. But that didn't seem right since they were supposed to be loaded on the truck. I'm afraid we got in an argument, so I went to Mrs. Owens's office, but she wasn't there. The only thing to do was leave the plant and talk to her about it the next day.

"But I never got the chance. Later that evening, I received a call from Lucas Bauer, the warehouse manager. He told me that Lewis had been with Bauer's for four years and the company didn't tolerate interference or insubordination from its employees. They ran a smooth ship, so I was being let go with a week's pay."

At least they'd given her *some* compensation, but with hindsight Heidi realized Deena had walked into something criminal without knowing it.

"I knew what had happened to me wasn't right, but I didn't have time to fight it. I've learned from experience that if you get off on the wrong foot from the beginning, things don't normally go right. Our family needed money and I needed to find another job quick."

Deena was a nice, decent person. "I'm so sorry, Mrs. Larson. Thank you for being willing to talk to me. I appreciate it more than you know."

Heidi hung up, horrified by what had happened to the woman. She hadn't been wrong about Deena who was intelligent and bright and had tried to prevent what she'd thought had been a mistake. Heidi should have checked into the firing and gone to Bruno, but at the time she hadn't been a witness to the argument, and she'd still been lacking the necessary confidence to go up against Lucas in a "he said, she said" situation.

She jumped up from the table and hurried down the hall. As she peeked around the door her gaze fell on Zack who was lying on a bench doing a bench press with dumbbells. Mitch stood next to him, cheering him on. They both saw her at the same time.

"Look at me, Mom!"

"You're getting a real workout."

"I know."

Mitch chuckled. "We're both worn out. Let's stop for a while."

"Do I have to?"

"Yup. You don't want to strain your muscles."

"Okay."

While he was putting the dumbbells away, Mitch walked over and gave her a searching look. "Any luck?"

She nodded. "I'll tell you later."

"Hey sport," he called over his shoulder, "do you want to watch that spy movie? If your mom will fix the popcorn, I'll make us some wild berry punch. I always drink it after a workout."

"Yum. I'm thirsty."

"So am I."

In a few minutes they'd settled down in the living room with drinks and snacks. Zack got on the floor to watch the film. Once he was involved, she turned to Mitch. In a quiet voice she told him what she'd learned.

He reflected for a moment. "Since you've been in charge of Human Resources, how many people have you interviewed for jobs in the mix room besides Deena?"

"None. That group has been together a long time. Patsy Reardon was forced to give up her job and move to North Dakota to take care of her ailing mother. It was the first job to come available there in several years. Deena's background check was impeccable. When I met her, I thought she'd be a perfect fit."

Mitch's eyebrows lifted. "Too perfect. They had to get rid of her in order to stop her from upsetting a well-laid-out plan of embezzlement that had been functioning brilliantly for several months."

Zack suddenly got up from the floor and came to sit between them. Heidi knew why he'd moved. So did Mitch, whose lips twitched. Her son wanted them to be quiet and pay attention to the movie. As if he couldn't help himself, Mitch put his arm around him and gave him a squeeze. "You like this movie, sport?"

"Yeah. Don't you?"

Mitch burst into laughter. "Yes, but I have an idea. When it's over, let's drive up to the zoo. Since the rain, it's cooler out. We'll buy some hot dogs and walk around. Maybe the orangutans will put on a show."

"Hey—they're my favorite, too! They're funny, huh, Mom?"

"Hilarious."

"Their baby does all kinds of crazy stuff and gets in trouble."

Mitch's face broke out in a grin. "Have you seen him swing that tire around?"

"Yeah. He's strong for a baby."

"Maybe we ought to go to the zoo right now. When we've seen the animals we want, we can come back and finish watching the movie. Your mother and I promise to be quiet."

His blue eyes glowed. "I bet you can't." Her son was a riot.

"Bet we can." Mitch got in the last word.

Two hours later they returned to his apartment, still laughing from the orangutans' antics. The spider monkeys were pretty funny, too.

They freshened up, then went back to the living room, ready to watch the rest of the movie. Before Heidi could sit down, someone was leaving a message on Mitch's answering machine. It was in the kitchen, but loud enough to be heard.

"Now hear this, Mitch Garrett. Remember your old boss Lew Davies? How come I haven't heard from you lately? I hope you're winding up that case you've been working on, because I just received word that has made my day. Whitey Filmore's back in custody. It's time for you to come home. Call me as soon as you get this message."

Zack couldn't have comprehended all of it, but he'd figured out enough to stare at Mitch with haunted eyes. Heidi's heart had already plummeted a thousand feet.

"How soon do you have to go home, Mitch?"

"That's none of our business," Heidi advised her son. "Come on. Let's finish watching the movie."

"I don't want to."

Mitch hunkered down in front of him. "That guy Lew is an old friend of mine who was just clowning around, Zack. I'm not leaving Salt Lake yet. For one thing, you're going to be in the parade on Monday. You think I'd miss that?"

Zack's eyes were suspiciously bright. "You're really coming?"

"Would I lie to you?"

Heidi had to wait to hear her son whisper no.

"Can you say that a little louder please?" Mitch prodded him.

All of a sudden Zack smiled. Miracle of miracles.

"I've already arranged it with your mother."

When Zack looked to her for confirmation, she nodded. "He's going to be at Liberty Park."

"Yup," Mitch said. "I'll be there with my friends taking pictures of you in your pioneer costume. I'll be wearing a cowboy outfit with a white hat because I'm one of the good guys. You won't have any trouble spotting me. Now how about we finish watching the movie. The really good part is coming."

If there was a really good part, it passed by Heidi in a flash. The second the movie was over, she stood up. "We've got to go home now, Zack. Can you thank Mitch for a wonderful day?"

"But we haven't played with the walkie-talkies yet."

"Zack!"

With a penitent look he said, "Thanks for working out with me, Mitch."

"Thank *you*," Mitch answered. "It's a lot more fun when you have a buddy."

"Yeah."

Mitch flicked Heidi a glance. "I'll call you tomorrow evening when I'm through doing my research."

Zack looked up at him. "Do you have to work on Sunday?"

"This Sunday I do."

Heidi opened the front door. "Come on, Zack." She was afraid he was going to ask Mitch to go to Sunday school with them.

"Okay."

She knew how her son felt. Heidi didn't want to leave, either. Their host walked them out to her car and helped Zack inside. "Thanks again, Mitch." Without looking at him, she backed the car to the street.

On the short drive home she made a decision. Once Monday was over and Mitch had met with her father, she'd go back to work at headquarters on Tuesday and make certain there was no more togetherness. The message on Mitch's answering machine had been like a bucket of ice water thrown in her face. Zack had been hit by it, too.

But that was good. It had brought them both to the understanding that Mitch's days out west were numbered. Soon his cowboy hat would be nothing more than a souvenir.

Chapter Eight

"What do you think?" Mitch stood in front of the mirror at the Saddleman's Emporium wearing cowboy boots and a Western shirt with fringe.

"You look like you just walked off a Hollywood Western movie set," Chaz teased.

"Yeah?"

"Yeah. That shirt looks more authentic than the plaid one you tried on." He handed him the cowboy hat. "Now let's see the whole bit."

When Mitch put the hat on and pulled the rim lower, Chaz nodded. "It's an improvement over the marshal hat you left back in Florida. I think this one's a keeper." The subtle hint that Chaz wanted Mitch to stay on at Lufka's wasn't wasted on Mitch. "You'll be impossible for Zack to miss now."

"That's the idea."

Lew's phone message, escaping the way it did throughout his apartment at the worst possible moment yesterday, had caused definite repercussions. Particularly after Heidi had forced him to look at their situation without rose-colored glasses.

Heidi had gone all quiet. As for Zack... To his chagrin, Mitch could do nothing about anything until he'd finished the job for Bruno Bauer.

"Thanks for breaking away from your family to meet me for breakfast, Chaz."

"Lacey was glad to get rid of me for a while."

Mitch flashed him a knowing glance. "Liar. Marriage agrees with you."

"You're right. I'm so happy I go around in a daze."

"I've noticed," Mitch drawled.

He grabbed his T-shirt and shoes from the chair and walked over to the counter. He asked for a bag to put his things in and handed the clerk a credit card. Before he turned away, he said, "You wouldn't happen to have a white cowboy hat like mine to fit a six-year-old, would you?"

"Sure we do." She walked to the end of the store and produced one for him made to order.

"Zack's going to like this." He paid for it and put it in the bag. "Thank you."

He looked at Chaz. "Since I'm driving down to Alpine right now to do some more sniffing around, this outfit ought to fit right in with all the cowboys down there. Maybe I'll get lucky and see Gary Norris on the premises." He squinted. "That'll make my day. Lon didn't have any luck spotting him when he went down there to look around."

They walked out of the store to their cars. "Nevertheless, watch your back," Chaz said.

Mitch nodded. "I'll get to Liberty park early in the morning tomorrow and save us all a place."

"Abby's so excited, she's doing double butterfly loops around the condo because she can't wait."

"Neither can I," Mitch murmured.

After waving each other off, Mitch started his Audi and headed for the freeway. Today there was no sign of a storm. The sky was a hot blue overhead. His thoughts shot ahead. If he couldn't find Norris at the pub, he'd start checking out the three addresses.

Twenty-five minutes later he found parking along the street in front of the Alpine strip mall. It was twelve-thirty and already the place was bustling with moviegoers and shoppers. Sunday was a big day evidently. He got out of his car, noticing people going in and out of the pub. You could hear the music outside.

Mitch checked out a couple of other stores before walking in. He spotted Georgia waiting on a table. Just the person he wanted to talk to. A group of teenagers got up from one of the tables, so he took their place. Pretty soon she came over.

When she saw who it was, she flashed him an inviting smile. "I was hoping I'd see you in here again. You look hot in those duds."

"Thank you, ma'am. You're looking pretty fine yourself. When's your next break?"

"Not until two."

"Can't you take it now?"

"No. My boss would fire me."

"Maybe he'll make an exception if I ask him. Is he in the back?"

"Yes, but please don't bother him. I need this job."

He could see she meant it. "Okay. I don't want to get you in trouble. Then will you bring me a cup of coffee and a donut to go?"

"Sure thing." If a few minutes she was back with his order. "I'm off at six tonight."

"I'm afraid I won't be around then." He handed her a twenty-dollar bill. "Keep the change."

"Thanks. Next time your order is on me."

"I'll keep that in mind, sugar."

He walked back to the restroom area in order to take a look around. This was the second time he'd been in the pub. Three employees had been on duty both times. The strip mall hadn't been there long. In this good a location, the people who owned or leased these properties paid higher rent. Someone with money had to be funding this place.

He tipped his hat to Georgia before leaving the pub. Once back in his car, he drove to the end of the street, made a right, then turned right again into the alley. Most likely the cars he saw here belonged to employees. He spied an empty space near the pub's rear entrance and parked the Audi.

The nearby waste-disposal bin, probably shared by several of the stores, looked full to the brim. On a whim, Mitch got out to take a look. The Dumpster was filled with boxes. He peered inside as many as he could reach and hit the jackpot on the last box, which felt heavier than the others. When he opened it, he found a discarded container of Cramer cooking oil, the same brand Bauer's used in their outlets. If he dug deep, he'd probably find a lot more discards.

Mitch took a picture with his iPhone and hurried back to his car. After removing his hat, he called Lon.

"Hey, Mitch. Got something new for me?"

"Always. I need a couple of things. First, can you find out who either owns or leases the Drop In Family Pub in Alpine?" He gave him the address. "Secondly, the oil used to cook Bauer's donuts comes from a company called Cramer's in Stockton, California. If we could talk to someone there, they might tell you who does the ordering for the Drop In Pub. I know it's a Sunday, and Monday's a holiday, so you might not be able to find out anything until Tuesday."

"Oh, ye of little faith." Mitch smiled. "Where are you?"

"In Alpine doing surveillance."

"If you need backup, holler." They disconnected.

Mitch wanted a look at Georgia's boss and figured whoever it was would leave the pub at some point during the afternoon. Though Mitch was tempted to phone Heidi while he waited, he had nothing new to tell her about the case. Until he'd fingered everyone connected, he couldn't talk to her about future plans. Tomorrow they'd be together. For the moment his job was to sit here and wait for something to happen.

When ten minutes had gone by, he drank his coffee before it grew too cold to tolerate. No sooner had he finished it than he saw a tall man come out of the pub pushing a road bike out the door. He carried his cyclist's helmet. It was Gary Norris!

Mitch had seen his picture at Heidi's house when Zack had showed him his room.

Gotcha.

Mitch took a series of photos, then started up the car to follow him. Sure enough he pedaled to the Warburton home two miles away. When he dropped his bike in the front yard, Mitch got more photos of him hurrying up the porch steps into the house. No sign of the pickup truck.

The guy might be in there for half an hour or all day. It didn't matter to Mitch. He'd found what he'd been looking for and headed to Salt Lake. Norris didn't have enough money for a second car, but he didn't dare drive his Miata, which was too distinctive. Had he always ridden a bike? Had he cycled with Heidi early on in their marriage?

Before he drove himself crazy with questions, he phoned the guys doing surveillance in the van outside the plant in Woods Cross. "What's your day been like?" he asked when Phil picked up.

"Nothing's going on here. We listened in on the conversations until they left the plant last night, but we didn't pick up anything that sounds remotely suspect."

"Maybe Jonas and Lucas aren't involved. Today I got positive ID on Gary Norris. He's the manager at the Drop In Family Pub in Alpine. We have positive ID on Nadine Owens, who handles the switch. We know how the bags are being transferred to the pub. What I'm waiting for is that final piece of evidence to link them on paper. Lon's working on that for me as we speak."

"Anything else we can do?"

"I won't need you on surveillance any longer, but be available in case of an emergency. Thanks for a great job."

"You bet. See you at the office."

After he clicked off, he called Roman and left a voice message, giving him the most recent update on the case. "I'll need your help for a warrant to subpoena the phone records on Nadine Owens and Gary Norris.

"One more thing. Tomorrow morning the guys and I will be watching the parade at the north end of Liberty Park. Zack Norris is riding on the Bauer float. If you're interested, why don't you meet up with us? We're going to have a picnic right there. I'll give Lisa a call to see if she'd like to come, too. See you later."

Maybe Heidi would want to be with her family at the ranch barbecue after the parade. She'd said it was going to be a big affair, but she hadn't shared her actual plans with him. In case she tried to get out of being with him at the park, he would invite her and Zack to join him and the P.I. crowd and see what happened.

The second he got back to his apartment, he sat down on the end of the bed and pulled off his new cowboy boots. He hadn't done much walking in them, yet his feet were already sore. The boots would take some breaking in. That's what the salesclerk had told him and he believed her.

Needing to channel his energy into something physical, he changed into shorts and a T-shirt, then took off up Emigration Canyon on his bike, where he did his best thinking. The exercise was great for releasing tension and Mitch had tension by the bucketloads.

On top of everything else on his mind, he thought about Heidi's suggestion of placing a newspaper ad using the orange crate as a visual reminder. As an idea for locating his mother or father, it was brilliant. But he couldn't imagine anything coming of it.

What he *could* imagine was being with her tomorrow. All day.

And all night? Didn't he wish.

Mitch rode until dusk before returning home to make a certain phone call. Tonight he would have to be content with just hearing her voice.

"DO I HAVE TO WEAR THAT straw hat tomorrow? It looks stupid."

Heidi had put Zack to bed, but he was nowhere near ready to go to sleep. "It's part of your costume. How many pioneer boys do you think walked across the plains with Marine haircuts?"

"Maybe a whole bunch. Mitch says they're cooler."

These days Mitch was the authority on everything. "That's true, but Sylvia planned all the outfits. You don't want to disappoint her, do you?"

"It's itchy."

"Well, you can take it off and on. How's that?"

"I don't like hats."

If Heidi told him how cute he looked in it with those suspenders and plaid shirt, he'd hate it. "Let's not worry about that now. You need sleep so you'll feel good while you're riding on the float. It gets hot when you're standing up there waving."

"What if I get thirsty?"

"Sylvia has water bottles hidden for you."

"I might have to go to the bathroom."

"Just hold it."

"Did you ever have to go to the bathroom when you rode on the float?"

"I don't remember, but I'm sure you'll be too excited to even think about it."

"Do you think Mitch will really come?"

"Has he ever let you down?"

"No."

"There's your answer, then. Good night, honey."

"Hey, the phone's ringing. I bet it's Mitch. He said he'd call."

She'd been waiting to hear from him for hours and

suspected that was why Zack hadn't been able to settle down yet. "Hello?" she said after clicking on, hoping she didn't sound as breathless as she felt.

It was Mitch.

"Hi! Have I phoned too late to speak to Zack?"

"No. He's right here. Just a minute."

Zack had already scrambled out of bed and took the cell phone from her. "Hi, Mitch." They talked for a few minutes. Mostly her son laughed. "Yeah. I have to wear suspenders." More giggles. "Okay. See you in the morning." He handed her the phone. "Mitch wants to talk to you."

"Now will you go to bed?"

Zack nodded and climbed under the covers. She turned off his light and walked down the hall to the living room. "Thanks for remembering to call. I think he'll fall asleep now."

"At his age, I would have been awake all night waiting for the big event. It isn't every day a boy gets to ride on a float in front of thousands of people."

"You're right." She sat down on the couch, tucking one leg underneath her. "Did you learn anything new today?"

"Yes, but I'd prefer we talk about that tomorrow night when we meet with your father. I'm afraid I'm as excited as Zack for morning to come. When I see your float, I'll follow it to the drop-off point. Will it say 'Bauer' on it?"

She smiled secretly. "No, but I promise it will stand out. You won't be able to miss it."

"Especially not with your son stealing the show. It's getting late and I know you have to be up early, so I'll

let you go. I'm looking forward to tomorrow, Heidi."
His voice came across deep and husky.

"Zack and I are, too. Good night."

She hung up, sensing Mitch had learned something
new about Gary he thought would upset her. What he
didn't know was that there was nothing about her ex-
husband's activities that would surprise her now. Gary
had failed to be a father to their son. His relinquish-
ing his God-given fatherly right of his own free will
was the most grievous part of all he'd done in showing
himself to be a miserable human being.

In truth Heidi was glad Mitch hadn't wanted to get
into anything unpleasant tonight. She had no idea what
the future held, but he made her happy beyond com-
prehension. Since time was running out, tomorrow
she would grab hold of that happiness while she still
could.

Sleep came while she was reliving those moments
in his arms during the storm. She'd experienced much
more than a physical rush and wanted desperately to
explore what was going on between them.

When her alarm clock went off the next morning
at seven, she leaped out of bed so excited to see Mitch
that time passed by in a blur before they were on their
way to the city center in Heidi's mom's car.

"There's our float!" Zack called.

Heidi's mom pulled her car to a stop on a side street
feeding into South Temple near the start of the parade.
"I think it's the most beautiful one we've ever had."

"Sylvia's committee really outdid themselves this
year." Her Bauer cousin and her husband, Daniel,
lived on the ranch and took care of the horses. Sylvia
loved the Pioneer Holiday. Heidi got out of the car with

Zack, wearing her jeans and a new blue shirt. "Thanks for the ride, Mom. We'll see you and dad at Liberty Park." Her father had driven into town early.

"Have fun, darling," the older woman said to Zack.

"I will. Bye, Grandma."

Zack was excited to join the other Bauer children, most of whom were already being placed on the float. Sylvia had said there would be sixteen of them from the ages of six to twelve. This was the first year Zack could ride on it. Their costumes looked authentic. From a distance Heidi had a hard time believing they weren't pioneer children from 1847.

Heidi gave her son a kiss. "Remember I'll be right inside the float. Keep waving and smiling. Here's your hat. I love you."

"I love you, too."

Sylvia's husband, Daniel, took Zack in hand and swung him up on the float. While he was being shown where to stand, Heidi slipped through the side of the float into the truck. Karl flashed her a grin from behind the wheel. "I know it's hot in here. The temperature is already ninety degrees and climbing. As soon as Daniel gives us the all clear, I'll turn on the AC."

"You wouldn't think we'd need it with only thirteen city blocks to cover. I'm just thankful we're the first float in the parade." They couldn't get to Liberty Park soon enough for her. When she thought of seeing Mitch, her pulse raced and she felt feverish. Yesterday was the first day they hadn't been together in a week. It had been the longest day of her life.

"Amen to that. I've brought some water bottles if you get thirsty."

"Thanks, Karl. I'll probably need at least one. Is Bruno coming?"

"No. Bernice wouldn't let him. They're going to watch it on TV."

"I think that's a good idea. Oh—I can hear the band. It looks like we're ready to roll. I set the DVR to record so Zack and I can watch the whole thing later."

"Sally didn't want to bring the baby out in this heat, so she's home recording it for me and the kids. Well, here we go." He turned on the engine and before long cool air flowed through the cab. They both looked at each other and said, "Heaven."

WHILE MITCH'S BUDDIES were busy staking out their corner of the park, he sat in one of their camp chairs to watch the beginning of the parade on his iPhone. The television studio producing the broadcast had set up their booth on State Street. He wanted to hear the commentary.

After the welcoming speech and announcement of dignitaries attending the celebration, the parade MC took over. Mitch listened and watched intently.

"Ladies and gentlemen, we are delighted to present the Grand Marshal of this year's Days of '47 Parade. Give a big hand to Erntz J. Bauer, riding his favorite horse, Prince. He's one of our prominent heads of industry in the Beehive State. Bauer Donuts is a name synonymous with the building up of the West. The first Bauer came into the Valley from Austria in 1892 and immediately contributed to the welfare of our community. The Bauer name is renowned throughout the western states."

Heidi had shown Mitch pictures of her father last week. The blue-eyed man was probably six feet tall. He looked trim as he sat astride his chestnut performing maneuvers with great expertise while he carried the Utah flag. He wore a black cowboy hat and fringed Western jacket. Though he was in his sixties, he still had thick, blond curly hair. Heidi had definitely inherited his coloring.

Odd as it was, emotion clogged Mitch's throat. The man being honored was Heidi's father and Zack's grandfather. What a heritage they'd all come from. He watched him lead the sheriff's mounted posse. It was followed by the University of Utah marching band. Then he caught sight of the first float.

"The beautiful float passing in front of the stands with the huge papier-mâché donuts has been made by the Bauer Donuts Company. Their motto is 'Press forward and onward.' Sixteen Bauer children, descendants of Saska Bauer, who started Bauer's, are dressed in pioneer clothing re-created from their family's pioneer photographs. The giant donut dominating the float has a field shaped like the Austrian eidelweiss flower. It's filled with freshly picked Eidelweiss grown on the Bauer ranch. The first thing Saska did after she started growing potatoes was put in a garden to grow eidelweiss in this land of the everlasting hills."

The camera zoomed in on the children. Mitch's eyes smarted when he saw Zack waving to the crowd with a hat in his hand. Heidi's son had gotten to him from the moment they were introduced. Right now that cute little guy was so precious to him he realized that what he felt for the boy was love. Pure love.

After clearing his throat, he got up and walked

around. Chaz flicked him a glance. "Are you all right?" he asked.

"Yes. I'm just anxious for Zack's float to show up here at the park so I can wave to him." Seeing him on his iPhone wasn't the same thing.

"I couldn't tell. Have a drink on me." He handed him a cola from one of the coolers packed with ice. They both drained their cans.

"Thanks. That tasted good. I think I'll walk down a couple of blocks to keep an eye out for them."

"I'll tell the others."

Mitch took off, working his way through the crowds of people lining the street along Ninth South. Many of them had slept along the parade route overnight. The usual clowns and police on motorcycles moved back and forth along the route. Finally he heard the band in the distance. After a few more minutes it passed, followed by Heidi's father, then the posse. But by now Mitch's eyes were focused on the float containing the two people he cared about most in the world. He started taking pictures.

"Hey, Zack, over here!"

Zack's head jerked around. When he saw Mitch, his flushed face broke out in a huge smile. "Mitch!" He waved his hat.

As the float moved toward the park, Mitch wended his way through the crowd to stay in full view of Zack. The procession passed by the area where Mitch and his friends had stationed themselves. It soon entered the park and the float came to a stop.

"Hey, sport!" Mitch crossed to the boy and reached for him. Without hesitation Zack lunged for him. When he felt those arms wind tightly around the neck, he was too moved by emotion to talk for a minute. He finally got the words out. "You were great up there."

"Thanks."

"Was it fun?"

"Yeah, but it's sure hot." Zack leaned back to look at him. "I wish I had a cowboy hat like yours. I could pick you out of everybody."

"That's why I wore it. Let's find your mom."

"She's underneath the float."

Children and parents were clustered around the chaotic scene, but there was only one woman in the world he knew with golden curls like Heidi's. "Mom, over here!" Zack had seen her, too.

Her gaze swung in their direction. Mitch felt a sudden stillness when she emerged from the crowd looking gorgeous in hip-hugging jeans and a summery, pale blue top that matched the color of her eyes. She moved toward them and reached for her son.

"I'm so proud of you, honey." As she hugged him, her eyes lifted to Mitch. They sparkled like precious gems. "Howdy, pardner," she said in a low voice. "Didn't know you'd rolled into Dodge." Zack laughed. "How long do you figure on stayin'?"

Mitch wasn't sure if it was a loaded question or not. He tipped his hat back. "Well, now, ma'am," he said with a smile. "That all depends on how happy you are to see me."

"We're *very* happy to see you, aren't we, Zack?"

"Yeah!"

Her answer would have to do for now. "In that case, stroll on over and meet my friends. I'll rustle you up something to eat and drink."

Though the guys were careful, Mitch saw them

glance at Heidi and give him a silent nod of approval. Once introductions were made and everyone was enjoying the picnic, Abby wanted to play with Zack's straw hat. While she put it on over her bouncy red curls, Mitch produced the hat he'd bought for Zack and plopped it on his head.

"You got me one, too?"

"Yeah. It keeps the sun out of your eyes."

"Thanks!" Buying him a hat was such a small thing, but Mitch was honored with another bone-cracking hug. "I love it!"

Heidi's eyes thanked him.

Travis and his son, Casey, had both come to the parade wearing black cowboy hats. Roman got out his camera. "This calls for a group picture, *Comrades*." He loved to use his Russian jargon on them from time to time. "We need a couple of pictures for posterity."

The wives plied Heidi with questions about her pioneer ancestry. Everyone studiously avoided any mention of the reason she'd come to the Lufka firm in the first place. The guys got up a game of Frisbee, but Mitch failed to catch it several times because his attention wasn't what it should have been.

As perfect and beautiful a picture as all this might appear, it had a lot wrong with it. Today the Bauers had been featured prominently in the pioneer festivities, yet one of their own was stealing from them.

This morning Zack had ridden on the Bauer float. Any parent would be bursting with pride to call him son, yet Zack's father was down in Alpine, getting away with more crimes against the company and his own flesh and blood.

The call from Lew Davies before Mitch had left his

apartment earlier had robbed him of some of the joy in showing off Heidi and Zack to his boss and good friends. *I really need you here, Mitch. We're all missing you and want you back ASAP. How soon can I expect you?*

An hour ago the beauty of this picture-perfect day had been further marred by the question Heidi had posed in a little different way. *How long do you figure on stayin'?*

The answer to that question was still up in the air.

When the Frisbee game had finished, Roman made an announcement. "Brittany and I want everyone to come swimming at our house." His invitation was met with cheers.

Zack walked back to the group with Mitch. "We didn't bring our suits."

"That's no problem. Ask your mother if she wants to go. If she says yes, I'll drive you home in my car and we'll get our stuff."

"Goody!" He ran on ahead to talk to Heidi. She was busy helping with the cleanup. In a second he darted back to Mitch. "She said it sounds like a lot of fun."

It *did* sound like a lot of fun, but he knew she had weightier things on her mind. Today was a case of the sweet. Tonight the bitter would come when they had to sit down with her father and Bruno.

Chapter Nine

"Zack's already asleep, Mom. He passed out early, thank goodness."

"After the day you've had, I'm not surprised."

"Thanks for staying with him."

"I'm glad to do it. Bernice thinks it's better you meet at Bruno's."

"I agree, but I don't know how long we'll be there."

"It doesn't matter. Stop worrying."

Heidi kissed her cheek. "I can hear a car in the driveway. That'll be Mitch."

"One of these days I'd like to meet the man you've fallen in love with."

Her mother's blunt comment caught her off guard. "There's a reason I'd rather you didn't. I may be in love, but he's not in love with me, Mom. It's called lust. The two are different animals."

"Heidi Bauer!" She couldn't remember the last time her mother had been upset with her. But her mother hadn't heard his answer when Heidi had asked him how long he was going to be in town. You don't build dreams on *That all depends on how happy you are to see me.*

What kind of answer was that? She felt certain

he would never pull himself away from Florida—
especially as he had hope of finding his mother there.
Besides, it was clear a job as a P.I. couldn't possibly
compete with the excitement and danger of a job as a
federal marshal. He hadn't even been worried about
Whitey Filmore. The fact that the guy was back behind
bars didn't matter to him one way or the other.

"I learned my lesson with Gary," Heidi said now.
"Facts are facts. Mitch's home is in Florida and he'll
be going back there now that this case is coming to an
end. Gotta run."

She hurried out of the house. "Sorry to keep you
waiting," she said to Mitch, who was just striding up
the walk. Heidi had never seen him in a sport coat and
trousers before. The tan color suited him. Everything
suited him. He looked sensational.

"Was Zack being difficult?" After he helped her
into the car, she gave him the directions to Bruno's
house.

"No. He went right to bed. That cowboy hat is hanging on his bedpost. Thanks for spoiling him. Every
little boy needs special attention once in a while. Since
we're alone, I'd like to tell you how much I enjoyed
your friends today. They're wonderful, all of them."

"They thought you and Zack were pretty terrific,
too."

"That's nice to hear. Brittney and Lacey told stories about how their husbands figured out within a
week who'd been stalking them. I told them you'd only
been on my case a week and had already solved it. You
men are an awesome group. I really can't thank you
enough. You'll hear my family's gratitude when we
meet at Bruno's."

His mouth thinned. "Have you finished?"

She blinked. "What do you mean?"

"I mean it sounds like you're ready to send me off into the wild blue yonder."

"I don't know what you're talking about."

"Oh, yes, you do." He suddenly pulled the car to the side of the road and turned off the engine. "Maybe it's because we haven't had a moment's privacy until this minute." She didn't have time to take another breath before he reached over and pulled her into his arms as he'd done during the storm.

"I don't know about you, but being in that pool with you this afternoon unable to do what I wanted with you has sent me out of my mind. I need this before we do anything else." He covered her mouth with refined ferocity, giving her one deep kiss after another.

At first she clung to him, wanting him with every cell in her body. But as their passion escalated, she feared that if she kept on responding the way she wanted to, she'd surrender her heart and suffer the consequences when he was gone.

"Mitch." She moaned his name, fighting the natural urges of her body.

"Don't pull away from me," he cried softly when he realized she wasn't giving as freely as before. "I've been living for this all day."

"The feeling will pass. It *has* to." Heidi sat up with difficulty and moved to her side of the car. "This isn't going to work, snatching a moment here and another one there. Have you forgotten we're due at my great-uncle's house in five minutes?"

"I've forgotten nothing and am damning the fact that we have to go anywhere or do anything else tonight except be in each other's arms. Do you have any idea how much I want you? Don't make this any harder than it is on us. I can't take it."

"Do you doubt that I want you any less? You think this isn't as hard on me?" Even though they weren't touching, she felt the shudder that passed through his body. "I'm going to be frank with you about something I didn't mention yesterday.

"I haven't been with any man since Gary. My failed marriage has made me nervous to get close to a man again. I was never this on fire for him and it scares me. If I didn't have a child, maybe I'd be willing to give into my desire until it burned itself out, but for Zack's sake I won't act that irresponsibly. Surely you understand!"

"I'm trying."

She threw her head back. "In case you didn't notice, we're now five minutes late."

After a tension-filled silence he started the car and drove them the rest of the way without talking. She'd taken the risk of angering him. He was definitely upset. But it was better than allowing things to get too far out of control.

Her dad's car was parked in front of the two-car garage of Bruno's home. Mitch pulled alongside it and killed the engine. She got out because she didn't want him to come around and help her. There'd be too great a chance of their arms or hips brushing. One look from his dark eyes could set her off and she'd succumb to the needs throbbing inside of her.

Bernice must have seen them drive up and held the door for them.

"Hi, Bernice." Heidi gave her a hug. "I'd like you

to meet Mitchell Garrett of the Roman Lufka Private Investigators firm. The best P.I. firm west of the Mississippi."

"That's what I've heard. How do you do, Mitchell. It's a pleasure." After they shook hands she said, "Your dad's in the study with Bruno. Go on in."

Briefcase in hand, Mitch followed Heidi down the hall to the study. Bruno, in a wheelchair that had been rolled in front of the big oak desk, was dressed in a smart-looking business suit. Her father, also wearing a dark blue suit, was deep in conversation with him, sitting forward with his hands clasped between his knees.

When Heidi walked in, he stood up and hugged her hard. She noticed Mitch shake hands with Bruno and introduce himself.

"You were awesome out there today, Dad."

Mitch joined her and nodded. "Watching you put your horse through the paces was a sight I won't forget." He shook her father's hand. "I'm honored to meet both of you gentlemen."

"Thank you very much. Seeing so many little Bauers on the float was a double thrill for me."

"Can you believe Zack made it through the whole thing?" Heidi interjected. "The children were amazing out in that heat."

"Of course they were," Bruno said. "Bernice and I watched the entire thing on television." He squeezed his wife's hand. She'd pulled up a chair next to him. "I was so proud I could hardly see the screen for the tears."

Heidi hurried over to kiss his cheek.

"Please—" Bernice gestured "—both of you sit down on the love seat."

When they'd done so, Mitch's dark brown eyes took in everyone. "I have to say this family has impressive roots. When Heidi accompanied me out to the plant so I could see the layout, she told me about your ancestor Saska Bauer. She was obviously a superwoman in a literal sense."

Bruno nodded. "Indeed she was and our Adelheide is just like her." Heat swept into Heidi's cheeks. "See that picture on the wall?" Heidi had noticed Mitch looking at it. "They're the spitting image of each other at Heidi's age now and they have the same brains."

"I'm convinced Zack inherited them, too." Mitch smiled. "He's smart as a whip."

"Speaking of intelligence, Heidi tells me you're brilliant at what you do. What about your roots, Mr. Garrett? You have a Germanic/French last name dating back to the seventh century."

Heidi shifted nervously on the seat. Bruno was the genealogist of the family, but this was one problem he couldn't solve and now wasn't the time to discuss it.

"I was abandoned as a baby, Mr. Bauer," Mitch explained, "in a church. I was in an orange crate that said Garrett Fruit Company. I have no idea of my ancestry."

All three of them studied him for a long moment before Bruno said, "Whatever your background, you must have genius in you or Adelheide would have told me we needed to find some other P.I."

Bernice nodded. "That's true."

Mitch darted Heidi a glance. "I'm flattered. Thank you for your faith in me."

Her heart thudded in her chest. "You're welcome."

"We understand you have news for us."

"Yes, Mr. Bauer. I think the best way to start is to let you sift through these pictures while I explain. I made two sets." He reached into his briefcase.

"I'll hand them out," Heidi offered and gave them each a pile. Bernice looked on with Bruno.

"This first set was taken at the plant by the cameras I installed on the day of the fire inspection. As you can see, Nadine Owens is the one setting things up to steal the bags during the afternoon shift."

"Nadine?" Both Bruno and Bernice said her name in a shocked cry.

Heidi exchanged a knowing glance with her father.

"The next set of pictures shows the stolen bags of flour and mix being taken off the truck and loaded into a pickup truck in Draper. More pictures reveal the pickup truck delivering the bags to the Drop In Family Pub in Alpine. If you'll notice the sign, it says homemade pizza and donuts.

"In the last set of pictures you'll see a familiar face coming out of the rear of the pub. It's the manager carrying a cyclist's helmet. You'll recognize Heidi's ex-husband, Gary Norris."

Bruno shook his head. "I don't believe what I'm seeing."

"I believe it about Gary," her normally temperate father declared with undisguised anger. "He was supposed to have gone back to Oregon."

"Mitch found out he never went there," Heidi told her father. "He lives in Alpine and is still driving his Mazda Miata." She reached into her purse and pulled out the plastic bags containing pizza and donuts she'd put in the freezer. "Mitch went into the pub and bought samples of the food, all made with Bauer flour and mix." She handed them around so everyone could examine the goods.

"Pizza?" Bernice sounded incredulous.

Heidi hunched her shoulders. "Who would have dreamed?"

"All this time I've thought it had to be Jonas or Lucas," Bruno muttered.

"Maybe they're involved," Mitch said. "I'm waiting for evidence from one of my crew about the person or persons who either own or lease that property in Alpine. It could be a third party, either family or not, who put up money to get the business started.

"By morning I'll have the pertinent information, but tonight you have enough evidence here to talk over how you want to proceed. Before I report for work in the warehouse tomorrow so no one suspects anything, I'll turn in my notes and film to Roman Lufka. When you're ready, he'll be happy to advise you about contacting the police."

Heidi's dad got up and walked over to shake Mitch's hand. "You've done us an invaluable service for which we can never repay you. The Lufka firm enjoys a stellar reputation. Now we know why." Bruno nodded in agreement.

"Thank you," Mitch said, "but don't forget you asked Heidi to assist me." She felt his burning glance on her. "She was brilliant in laying the groundwork for me in a clear, precise way. Anything I needed to know and she was right there with the answers. This case couldn't have moved as fast without her expertise. She really does know the Bauer Donut Company inside and out."

Bruno, still nodding, said in a voice choked with tears, "I knew it."

Stop, Mitch.

"When my boss told me I was going to love this case," Mitch went on, "it was because our firm can't live without coffee and Bauer SweetSpuds to keep us going. Can you imagine my joy when Heidi trained me how to make the donuts I've been consuming ever since I arrived in Salt Lake? I thought I'd died and gone to heaven."

While the men chuckled, Bernice's teary face broke out in a wobbly smile.

"Though I'm sorry my bloodhound services," Mitch added, "may have brought you untold grief, I have to confess that this case has been a pleasure I'll never forget."

Now Mitch was giving his goodbye speech. Heidi couldn't bear it. "Bruno? Is there any reason I shouldn't go back to work in the morning?"

"None at all."

Good. She turned to her father. "How soon are you leaving?"

"Now. It's late. Bruno and Bernice should be getting to bed and I have to pick up your mother."

"That's right," Bruno said. "We've all had a long day and need our sleep. I'll talk to you first thing in the morning, Ernst."

"Then I'll ride home with you, Dad." She turned to Mitch. "Bruno's right. It has been a long day and work starts early in the morning. Thanks again for driving me over here."

"Thank *you* for making my job not feel like a job."

She could still taste his searing kisses on her mouth and throat. "Good night, everyone. I'll see myself out."

Heidi watched him pick up his briefcase and leave the study on those long, hard-muscled legs. Tonight she was feeling so vulnerable, she needed the buffer her father provided in order not to chase after Mitch and show him what he truly meant to her.

MITCH'S CELL PHONE RANG while he was taking his break in the lunchroom at the plant in Woods Cross. He'd wanted to see if he could pick up any additional information while he ate with the employees. So far no luck.

He checked caller ID, wanting it to be Heidi, but knowing in his gut it wasn't. He'd spent a sleepless night because of her and was feeling like he'd been kicked unconscious and was just coming to.

"Lon?"

"I've got news. Nadine Bauer Owens is the only signer of the year's lease with Thackery Enterprises on the Drop In Family Pub property, dated January 3 of this year."

"The connection is complete, then. I've a hunch she and Gary have kept this between them."

"It appears that way. One more thing. The order for Cramer cooking oil comes from G. Norris, manager of the Drop In Family Pub."

"There's nobody who gets the job done as fast and as thoroughly as you, Lon. Turn in your research to Roman and expect a big bonus in your next paycheck. As of now, you're off the case and deserve a vacation."

"I could use one of those. It's always great working

with you, Mitch. I hope the rumor's not true about you heading back to Florida."

"We'll see. My work isn't quite through here."

"In case you didn't know, you'd really be missed if you left."

A lump lodged in his throat. "The feeling's mutual. Talk to you later."

He rang off before phoning Heidi's father and Bruno with the news about Nadine signing the lease. They'd already talked to Roman and would add this last vital piece of information to the rest. A meeting had been planned at the end of the day in Bruno's office. Mitch and Heidi were requested to meet with them and the police detective assigned to the case.

Gratified to know Heidi would be there, Mitch finished the afternoon shift at the plant. His last one. He was conscious of the fact that tomorrow there wouldn't be any more stolen bags of potato flour going out with the stolen bags of mix. A major shake-up in the Bauer family was about to occur.

But it couldn't be as big as the one happening to Mitch. Tonight after the meeting, he wouldn't let her escape him.

THE SECOND HEIDI GOT OFF the phone with her father, she phoned her sister-in-law. The news that Nadine had signed the lease for Gary put the proverbial final nail in the coffin.

"Sharon? I just found out Bruno has called a meeting in his office in a few minutes and I have to be there. Since it's almost time to pick Zack up from school, would you mind taking him home with your children? I'm sorry to do this to you, but it can't be helped. I promise I'll return the favor."

"I'll be happy to. Tim will be thrilled."

"Thanks. You're the greatest."

Heidi had worn a khaki skirt and a white top to work with her white sandals. She'd wanted to look good for her first day back at work in a week. Now that she would be seeing Mitch in a while, she was doubly grateful she'd taken the trouble. After this meeting, his work would be officially over. She wanted his last impression of her to be a good one before he left for Tallahassee.

She'd cried herself sick during the night and had awakened with puffy, bloodshot eyes. With cold water and concealing makeup, she'd managed to remove some of the sleepless signs. Once she'd made a trip to the ladies' room to brush her hair and add a fresh coat of lipstick, she climbed the stairs to the next floor and entered Bruno's suite.

Her dad met her with a hug, then introduced her to Detective Danvers of the Salt Lake City Police Department. "Honey, Mitch ought to be here any minute. Meanwhile, the detective wants you to tell him about your conversation with Deena Larson, the woman who'd been fired from her job after one day."

While Heidi told him the essence of her phone call with Deena, Mitch entered in the office dressed in a leaf-green polo shirt and khakis. He'd just come from the warehouse. Her body trembled every time she saw him. He flicked her a glance she couldn't read before being introduced to the detective.

Bruno cleared his throat. "If everyone will sit down, we'll let the detective explain what's going to happen."

"Thank you, Mr. Bauer. This evening several officers will arrest Nadine Owens at her home and take her downtown. At the same time, another set of officers who've made arrangements with the Utah County Police Department, will take Gary Norris into custody from his place of residence in Alpine and bring him to Salt Lake. Their pub operation will be closed down.

"Both will be put in jail. They'll be apprised of their rights and a public defender will be provided for them if they don't hire their own. Those of you who wish to talk to them will able to do so in the morning prior to their arraignment. At the time the judge hears their pleas, he'll set bail and name the date for a jury trial. Do any of you have questions?"

Heidi didn't. The reasons for what the criminals had done would come out in the trial. She had no desire to see or talk to Gary. She couldn't feel anything for him. Her heart was too shattered by the knowledge that she would be losing Mitch.

If there were another woman, she could fight for him. At least that's what she told herself. But how could she fight against his need to find his mother or father? It was a need he'd had from childhood. Maybe now he would take advantage of his free time to hunt for—

"Thank you, Detective Danvers," Bruno said, cutting off her thoughts. "This action is harsh, but Ernst and I have talked it over and feel it's necessary. Once we know they've been arrested, we'll phone each family member and tell them what has happened before they hear it on the ten o'clock news."

The old man teared up. "There's no doubt our family will be in mourning for a long time. Nadine is one of our own. Gary was once a part of us. I want to believe each family member will have charity in his heart for two souls who lost their way. We'll have to show increased love to Nadine's family. It's never too late for her or Gary to repent and make a fresh start.

"As for Lucas, he's been at the head of quality control and clearly not doing his job. He'll be reprimanded and put on probation. I'll also be having a talk with Jonas, who's in charge of the warehouse. His love for Lucas has made him less vigilant."

Heidi loved Bruno, who'd carried the mantle for so long. Without conscious thought she got out of her chair and ran over to hug him. "It's the right thing to do." Tears trickled down her cheeks. "I love you for your kindness and your convictions. Never *ever* change."

He wept against her arm. In another second her father joined them. Over his shoulder she saw the pain in Mitch's eyes before he slipped out of the room.

"Excuse me," she whispered.

After grabbing her purse, she ran after him. He moved like the wind. She didn't catch up to him until he'd reached his car in the parking lot. "Mitch!" At the sound of her voice he wheeled around with such a bleak expression on his face, she was shaken. "Why did you leave so fast?"

"My work is done and this is time for family."

Acutely aware he didn't have one, she said, "Agreed. I haven't seen Zack since early morning. I'm just on my way to pick him up at Sharon's. Will you meet us at my house? He'll want to say goodbye to you. I thought we'd order pizza and watch something silly on television that will make my son giggle. I—I need to hear his laughter…." Her voice faltered.

She could hear his mind working. "You're worried what you're going to have to tell him about his father one day."

"No," she answered with conviction. "I'm sure he'll handle it. Tonight I'm craving some happiness with my precious boy. We'd both enjoy your company. You've become a great friend." She stressed the word.

Mitch's mouth thinned to a white line.

"Do you have another commitment?" She remembered the haunted look in his eyes and wished she could take it away. "I don't care how professional you are. Knowing you were catching family and former family of mine in the act, I'm aware you haven't survived the experience completely unscathed."

His chest rose and fell with enough force for her to notice. "A dose of Zack would be a surefire antidote for the downside of my job." He hadn't denied it. "What can I bring?"

Her relief was exquisite. "How about your favorite ice cream?"

"Done."

"I should be home in a half hour. I'll hurry."

By the time she'd reached her car, he'd left the parking lot. She didn't regret inviting him to the house. If she'd had a secret agenda, it was so he could see Zack a final time and part company with him in a way her son would be able to handle. She'd said her farewells last night after wrenching her mouth from his.

When Heidi had been at the park after the parade, Brittany had mentioned how gloomy Roman had become because Mitch was leaving for Florida. The firm was losing a great friend, as well as a P.I. To his consternation, Roman couldn't stop Mitch from reporting back to his federal marshal's job, not now that his arm and shoulder had healed.

"Gloomy" might describe Roman. Heidi had another one for herself. Gutted. But she refused to get any more morose about it and sped home, anticipating their final evening together. When she drew up in front of Sharon's, she saw Zack and Tim playing teams against Rich with some water guns you launched from the shoulder. Her brother was big on anything that got you wet.

"Zack," she called to him. "Put your gun on the porch and come and get in the car. Don't forget your backpack and thank your uncle." She waved to her brother.

On the drive home, she eyed Zack through the rearview mirror. "That looked fun."

"Mitch would make it a lot funner."

She heaved a troubled sigh. "You mean 'more' fun. Zack, I missed you today. Did your friend Jacob go to the parade?"

"No. He said his dad hates them." Heidi tried not to smile. "Can we watch it again on the DVR? I want to see myself."

Her smile turned into a chuckle. "Oh, Zack. What would I do without you?"

"I don't know."

This time she burst into tearful laughter, probably because she was feeling almost hysterical.

"Hey, Mom, there's Mitch! I want to get out."

The blood pounded in her ears. "Not until we've parked the car."

The second she stopped, her son jumped down and hurried over to the handsome man pulling things out of his Audi. A grinning Zack rocked on his heels, a definite sign of joy beyond measure.

"Guess what? Mitch brought bubblegum ice cream and pizza with Canadian bacon from the Pizza Oven!" He was chattering a mile a minute as Heidi let them in the front door. The two males walked through to the kitchen with Mitch making comments here and there.

Heidi got as far as the hallway, then stopped because it came to her that if anyone were looking on, they'd think Zack and Mitch were father and son. Not because of their coloring, but because of the obvious bond between them. Something like the way Tim and Rich were.

Earlier at the office, when she'd seen Mitch standing outside the circle while Bruno wept, she'd sensed his aloneness. When the Bauer children got together with their fathers, how many times had she observed Zack standing off and *alone?* Heidi's was the only divorce in the family. Zack was the only child who showed up without a daddy. All the other children had one and functioned within those special spheres.

Tonight Zack and Mitch were relating within a sphere created by their own enjoyment of each other. Neither was standing outside looking in. This time they were the ones inside the bubble that wasn't visible to the naked eye.

Heidi watched and suffered new agony. Zack would be absolutely crushed when Mitch went away. It would take months for him to get over the feelings of loss. Not every man Heidi might meet in the future would accept Zack or appreciate his wonderful qualities the way Mitch did.

The unique man in her kitchen had grown up without real parents and so showed a special sensitivity around her son. He seemed to know instinctively how to make Zack feel good about himself. Would it bother Mitch to have to say goodbye to the little boy who worshipped the ground he walked on?

Would he miss *her?*

She watched Zack race down the hall to his bedroom. The next thing she knew he'd raced back to the kitchen, oblivious to Heidi. He'd put on the cowboy hat Mitch had given him and was carrying his walkie-talkies. Instead of water guns, they were going to play spy. Zack was in heaven.

Heidi groaned inwardly when she considered the void that would be left when Mitch was gone.

Chapter Ten

"It's past your bedtime, Zack. You've got school in the morning." Heidi gathered the cards to the Apples to Apples junior game the three of them had been playing on the kitchen table and put them in the box.

"Can't we play it again?" She heard the quiver in his voice. The moment she'd been dreading had come. With Mitch making everything exciting, the evening had been magical.

"I'm sorry, honey. Will you say good-night and thank him for dinner?"

Zack fastened soulful blue eyes on their guest. "Will you come to my school program on Friday at two o'clock?"

His question ignored hers and was so unexpected, a quiet gasp escaped Heidi's lips. She saw a flicker in the dark brown depths of Mitch's eyes and knew it had caught him off guard, too.

"You're in a program?"

He nodded. "Cuz it's the end of the year and we always do a big show for the moms and dads."

Adrenaline forced Heidi up from the table. "Honey, Mitch won't be able to come."

Tears filled Zack's eyes. "Are you going to Florida?"

"You know he is," she rushed to remind him. "Come on."

"Don't you like it here?"

A grim expression had crossed over Mitch's features. "Very much."

"Zack, it's his home, just like Salt Lake is ours. He had a job, but he got injured, so he came to Utah to have an operation. Now that he's better, he has to go back. His friends are there." *Family he's searching for.* She picked up her son because it was clear he wasn't about to move from the table.

"Casey said you're a federal marshal and got shot in the shoulder by an escaped prisoner," Zack said. "He said you almost died like his mom."

Oh, no.

When she'd seen the boys playing and talking together at the park, she'd had no idea what their conversation was about. Since yesterday Zack had been carrying this burden around without saying anything. Her gaze flew to Mitch for help. She saw a white ring of pain around his mouth.

"Will you show me?" Zack asked.

"You want to see my scar?" Mitch had asked the question, but he was still looking at Heidi. Though he was prepared to show Zack his scar, he wanted her permission and would do nothing if she didn't give it.

Heidi thought she'd loved Mitch before this moment, but that emotion couldn't touch the love she felt for him now. Since Zack already knew the truth, there was be no point in hiding anything from him. Mitch knew it and she knew it, so she gave him a nod.

"It's not a pretty sight, sport, but you're man enough to take it, right?"

"Right."

Mitch, darling... He always knew the right thing to say.

She watched in wonder as Mitch removed his polo shirt. When they'd gone swimming at Roman's, he'd worn a T-shirt the whole time, claiming he didn't want a sunburn.

In one of her fanciful moments early last week when they were getting ready to ride their bikes, she'd thought he looked godlike in the sun. Being so close she could see the dusting of hair on his well-defined chest, he resembled a Hellenic statue come to life in her kitchen.

But Zack was much more interested in the scar. "Wow! It's big!"

It was. Mitch would have suffered so horribly she couldn't bear it.

"Yup. There's a lot of it."

"Does it still hurt?" His anxious tone was so touching she wanted to cry.

"Nope. There's no feeling in the scar tissue. The great news is, my arm can move just like it did before." He made a circle to prove it.

Heidi managed to hold back her tears. "You really were blessed."

"Don't I know it," he whispered before putting his shirt back on.

"Now that you're better, you can be a federal marshal here," Zack reasoned. "Casey's father said so."

Mitch reached for Zack and carried him into the living room. Heidi followed them. They sat down on the couch with Zack on his lap. "What else did Casey tell you?"

"That you're a P.I. like the rest of them. He told me those walkie-talkies came from the shop at your office. I found out his dad used to be a Texas Ranger, and Chaz was a Navy SEAL."

Mitch's face broke out in a tender smile. "So you've discovered all our secrets. You make a great spy."

"Yup. Just like you. How come you don't stay here? Don't you like your friends?"

Mitch rubbed a hand over the top of Zack's head. "They're the greatest, but there's someone I'm looking for. I have to go back to Florida if I'm going to find them."

Heidi couldn't let this conversation go on without Mitch giving her son one piece of information Casey couldn't have known about or shared.

"Zack," she said, "have you noticed Mitch hasn't talked about his family?"

Her son blinked. "No." She saw alarm creep into his face. "Did something…bad happen to them? You know, like what happened to Casey's mom?"

When she saw lines darken Mitch's face she said, "Will you listen very carefully while he explains and not interrupt?"

Zack looked as surprised as the man holding him, but he nodded.

She stared at Mitch. "You need to tell Zack about the orange crate and go from there. It'll help him understand." Her son was facing a terrible few months ahead of him without Mitch, but Heidi was convinced that if he knew the truth, it might make the parting from his hero more bearable.

For the next few minutes Heidi was treated once again to Mitch's incredible story, only this time he had a captive audience in Zack. True to his word, her son didn't say a word. Even when Mitch had finished, silence filled the room.

Suddenly he slid off Mitch's lap and looked up at him. "My dad didn't want me," he said as one lone tear trickled down his flushed cheek. "But maybe if you find yours, he'll want you."

Mitch leaned forward and kissed Zack's forehead before putting his hands on his shoulders. "When I was your age, I assumed I wasn't wanted. It took years for me to realize that if the people who were my parents didn't have the money or other family members to help take care of me, that didn't necessarily mean they didn't want me. Maybe they were in bad health and couldn't. Do you know what I think?"

"What?" Zack's voice cracked.

"I think they left me at the church because they knew there would be kind people there who would look after me better than they could. Maybe your father felt he couldn't be the kind of dad you needed and he knew your mother would be the greatest mom in the whole world for you. Right?"

Zack nodded.

"I've never met a better mom than yours."

Heidi lowered her head, afraid she was going to break down in a puddle of tears.

"I hope you find yours, Mitch."

She heard Mitch breathe in sharply as Zack walked out of the room. Heartbroken for her son, she started to follow, but Mitch caught her from behind and pulled her against his chest.

"Let him be for a little while," he whispered against the side of her neck. He buried his face in her curls. "As long as everything is out in the open, let it percolate in him for a few minutes. I've been where he is now, both emotionally and physically. He needs time to process what's been going on. So do I."

Mitch spun her around, cupping her face in his hands. His dark eyes penetrated to her soul. "I'm leaving for Florida on the first flight out in the morning, but I couldn't go without kissing you goodbye."

Heidi moaned as he covered her mouth with his own. It wasn't like his other kisses. This one was like a brand, sending scorching heat through her body. When he finally relinquished her mouth and walked out the front door, she wanted to die, but she couldn't do that. She had a little boy to live for and cherish.

Her phone rang. She saw that it was Rich. He would have heard the news about the arrests from their father, but her thoughts were so far removed from anything except her love for Mitch and her son, she only had one need at the moment.

She flew down the hall to Zack's bedroom and wrapped her arms around him so they could comfort each other through the long hours of the night.

A YEAR HAD PASSED SINCE Mitch had entered the church in Tallahassee where he'd been left as a baby. He found out from the secretary that the parish had a new priest. She showed Mitch into his office.

"Father Bouchard?"

The slim, middle-aged priest made a welcoming gesture. "Come in, my son." He spoke with a faint French accent.

"Thank you for seeing me without any notice. My name is Mitchell Garrett. I just flew in from Salt Lake City, Utah, and came straight here."

"Please, sit down. What can I do for you?"

"Thirty-four years ago someone brought me to this church in an orange crate and left me here."

"Oh, yes." He touched his fingers together. "I remember Father Antoine telling me something about that. You're the Garrett boy who's been looking for your parents all these years. Aren't you in law enforcement?"

"Yes. I'm a federal marshal, but I got injured and had to take time off. I've been away, but now I'm back and came here first to see if you have any news for me. The secretary told me to talk to you."

He removed his glasses and rubbed the bridge of his nose. "Obviously if you'd found them, you wouldn't be here."

"No."

The priest sat back in his chair. "I would love to be of assistance."

"I'm sure you would. Everyone who knows my situation has gone out of their way to help me, but after all this time, it seems hopeless. Maybe I've been going about this the wrong way. If you have any suggestions, I'd appreciate them."

"Tell me a little about yourself first. Do you have a wife and children?"

Mitch got a suffocating feeling in his chest. "No."

"Were you ever married?"

"No."

"Why not?"

Mitch took a fortifying breath. "I'm not sure what the answer to that is anymore."

"Shall I tell you? It's because you've been marking time all these years, waiting for your life to happen. What a tragedy! You know how I know this? Because I was abandoned, too, and recognize the signs."

The priest's admission took him by surprise.

"You've allowed yourself to wallow in a land of unanswered questions while there's a whole world outside waiting to embrace you. But you've been afraid. You think you have to know who your people are before you can get onboard."

For the first time in his life, Mitch was hearing someone describe his inner struggle from the inside out.

"You came to this church for help. All I can give you is a piece of advice someone gave me. It changed my life. Do you want to hear it?"

"Yes."

"Leave your parents' whereabouts to God. He knows where they are, but *you* don't need to know. They've done their job. They gave you life. *Your* job is to live it fully. One day in the hereafter you'll meet them. They'll want to hear what you did with your life. Can you imagine how sad they'll be if they thought you spent your entire time looking for them?

"By an extraordinary circumstance, I came to America on the *QE2*. Pure luxury. I remember during the crossing how I thought about all the thousands and thousands of souls who'd come here years earlier by ship under miserable circumstances. Many of them were orphans, or had lost loved ones and were striking out for new shores."

A vision of the words on the Bauer float swam before Mitch's eyes. *Press Forward and Onward.*

"They didn't stay back pitying themselves and their lives," the priest continued. "They arrived here and made new lives. It was during that crossing I had my epiphany and I determined that I would embrace life to the fullest from that point on. I urge you to do the same."

The priest made so much sense, emotion had closed off Mitch's throat. He shot to his feet, breathless with new energy.

Startled, the priest stood up. "Have I been of help?"

"You have no idea," Mitch said in a thick voice. "Bless you."

With time running short—if he were going to get back to Salt Lake in time for Zack's program—he left the church and hailed a taxi. Twenty minutes later he entered the government building that housed the federal marshals' office. Lew Davies almost fell out of his chair when he saw him walk in.

"Mitchell Garrett, as I live and breathe. You look like a totally different man since the last time I saw you." He got out of his chair and came around to give Mitch a hug. "Talk about a sight for sore eyes…."

"It's good to see you, too."

"Damn it, Mitch. I've been waiting for your call. Why didn't you tell me you were coming today? I would have arranged a big bash for you."

Mitch had missed his old boss. "That's why I didn't want you to know."

Lew sensed something was different. He stared at him, trying to read between the lines. "You've changed. Sit down and tell me what's going on."

"So much has happened I hardly know where to start. To put it simply, I'm in love with this fabulous woman, and if she and her son will have me, we're going to get married."

He was rewarded with another hug. "That's the best news I ever heard! When's the wedding, and how soon is she moving out here?"

This was the hard part. "Lew…"

"Uh-oh. Don't tell me. You're going to live there and be a P.I. for the rest of your life."

Mitch nodded. "I don't have a family here. She has a terrific family there and I want to belong to it. I'll be flying back tomorrow night."

"Boy, when you move fast, no one can catch you."

Mitch studied his old friend. "You know I'll never forget my time with the agency. You've been the greatest boss in the world. In fact, I owe you more than you'll ever know. If it weren't for you trying to protect me, I would never have been sent to Salt Lake and I would never have met Heidi."

"Heidi, is it?" Lew smiled.

"Heidi's short for Adelheide. It's Austrian. She's so beautiful, Lew. And she's got a son named Zack any father would pray for."

"I'm going to have to meet them."

"I've got photos. If she says yes, you and Ina will be getting a wedding invitation."

"Is there any doubt your sweetheart will say yes?"

Mitch closed his eyes for a minute. "I haven't told her I love her yet."

A sound of exasperation escaped Lew. "For being the best federal marshal this office has ever seen, it's a different story when it comes to your love life. I've got to meet the woman who's finally brought down the legendary Mitch Garrett."

He patted Mitch on the back, then told him to sit. "You've got a ton of paperwork to fill out before you leave the department forever. I'll tell Nancy to get it ready. Then I want to see those photos."

AT ONE-THIRTY ON FRIDAY afternoon, Heidi went to the school to peek in on Zack. After she checked to see that he was all right, she planned to grab a spot on the front row of the auditorium for her and her parents. But the second he saw her in the doorway of his first-grade classroom, Zack got up from his desk and ran over to her, teary-eyed.

A few mothers were helping the kids put on their costumes. Heidi assumed the white togas and fake laurel-leaf wreaths were meant to convey victory through excellence. His had slipped down over one eyebrow.

"I don't want to be in the program."

She put the wreath back in place. "I know you don't, but you have to." Life had to go on without Mitch, even if they were barely hanging on. Not one word from him, not even for Zack.

Mitch would never be intentionally cruel. It wasn't in him. But it was evident he felt that no more contact was the best way to handle their parting. Her mind recognized he'd done the right thing, but emotionally she was shattered and knew Zack was, too.

"I've got a stomachache."

Heidi believed him. This time she understood the reason. All the other kids had two parents who came to these programs. For the most part Zack had been handling his daddyless world pretty well. Then Mitch had come along. In a week he'd formed an attachment that gave him a taste of how great it would be to have the tough Marine around all the time. But Mitch was no longer available.

She could have told Zack how lucky he was that his grandfather Bauer would be coming. She could point out that there were kids whose grandfathers couldn't or wouldn't be in the audience. But even though he loved her father very much, it wasn't the same.

"I'll be right up front." He didn't like her to kiss him when the other kids were around. All she could do was squeeze his hand. "See you in a minute." As she walked away, the image of a forlorn little Julius Caesar stayed with her all the way to the auditorium.

The gym was filling up fast. She beat another family to the only seats remaining on the front row— at the end. Heidi had no idea where Zack would be sitting on the stage, but at least she'd be close. All of the grades, K-6, would be in the program, so there was a huge crowd. Pretty soon her parents appeared. They sat down next to her just before the principal called everyone to order.

"How's he doing?" her mom whispered.

"I don't know. We'll see if he makes it onstage."

Both her parents knew how crushed Zack was because Mitch had left. She loved them for offering their moral support, not only to him, but to her. There were families in the audience who knew of Gary's involvement in the embezzlement scheme. It had been in the news for several days now. Heidi had done everything to shield Zack.

Besides the fear that he might pick up on it, she

had an even greater worry. For the next three weeks, Zack was going to be out of school. She'd taken time off from work to be with him. A happy Zack would be one thing, but he was depressed. To prevent him from falling into a pattern of not wanting to play with anybody, she'd decided they were going on vacation.

First thing in the morning they were driving to Nebraska to visit Evy and see the new baby. The distraction would be good for him, and he'd be forced to interact with his cousins.

"I want to welcome mommies and daddies and grandparents and great-grandparents and everyone else to our school program," the school principal announced. "We're very proud of our children and their accomplishments. Our first class to come on stage will be the morning and afternoon kindergarten."

The teacher at the piano started playing. Heidi watched the kids with crowns march in, but didn't remember anything else. Her stomach had been upset all day waiting for Zack's part in the program. She was tired of fighting him and exhausted from crying into her pillow half the night.

Her dad nudged her in the ribs. "Zack's class is coming in."

She strained to find him. "I can't see him." Her anxiety increased.

"He's probably the last one," Ernst said.

Or maybe he'd decided to stay in the classroom. In about one second she would slip out and look for him. Being that she was on the end of the row made it easier for her. But someone else had just put a chair next to hers and sat down, blocking her exit.

Surprised, she turned to say excuse me, then almost fainted when she saw who it was. *"Mitch!"*

It couldn't be—

"Sorry I got here at the last second," he whispered. "My flight out of Atlanta was delayed." He grasped her hand, sending shock waves through her body.

She'd never known his dark eyes to be this alive, as if he were the keeper of some marvelous secret. Whatever the reason he was back in Salt Lake, the thrill of seeing the flesh-and-blood man made her giddy.

"Here he comes!" her mother exclaimed.

Heidi tore her eyes from Mitch's in order to find Zack and let him know they were there. He was third from the end on the other side of the stage. He walked with a solemn gait. She knew he was hating every minute of it.

Mitch leaned closer, brushing her ear with his lips. How she was breathing at all was a mystery to her. "He looks as if he's pondering the great speech he has to make before the Senate." It was so true, she had to fight not to burst out laughing. All she could do was squeeze his hand harder.

The children came forward in small groups to say a line. When it was Zack's turn, he and two other children stepped forward. Heidi's heart almost stopped beating when he looked in her direction and saw who was sitting next to her. It caused him to pause for a second before he remembered to say his part. After he got it out, his face lit up like someone had flipped on a switch.

Mitch gave him a thumbs-up.

Pretty soon his class had to file out to make room for the second-graders. Zack waved to the four of them before he disappeared behind the curtain. While the audience clapped, Mitch and her parents acknowledged each other and shook hands across Heidi, who sat there dazed.

When he sat back he felt for her hand again and tucked it under his arm. The proprietorial gesture sent fingers of delight up her arm. She glanced at his profile. "There's going to be a party in his class once this is over."

"You have no idea how much I've been looking forward to this."

Really?

Heidi was filled with questions, but now wasn't the time to ask them. It was enough he'd come to see Zack perform. It was a gesture more important to Zack than possibly even Heidi knew. These children were her son's peers. Now he had Mitch to champion him in front of them.

The rest of the program passed in a blur. She had no desire other than to absorb the reality of him. He'd come dressed in a stone-gray summer suit and tie. With his dark blond hair and rock-hard jaw, Heidi found him outrageously handsome. She rejoiced in being with him.

After the last group had performed, Mitch ushered her out of the gym and down the hall to Zack's room. While her parents went ahead of them, he kept a possessive hand at the small of her back, as if he needed to maintain constant contact. Heidi loved this sense of belonging. She'd never known a feeling like it.

They found Zack in a lineup in front of the room with the other children getting his picture taken in his costume. He was too restless to stand still. The second it was over, her parents were there to hug him. Heidi took her turn next, whether or not he liked her hugging him in front of the other kids.

"You did a great job today, honey. I'm very proud of you."

"Thanks," he said, but his eyes had focused on Mitch.

A lot of the children and parents were staring at the attractive man who let go of Heidi long enough to give him a hug. "You were awesome, sport."

Zack's face beamed. "You *came!* How come?"

"Because you asked me and because I wanted to." He helped him off with his costume. The teacher was gathering them.

"Did you go to Florida?"

That's what Heidi wanted to know.

"Yes, but I had to come back to clear up some unfinished business, and I wouldn't have missed your program."

"Oh."

Heidi's parents sent her a silence message of concern before they gravitated to the table for cookies and punch.

"Do you want to see my collage?" Zack said.

"I want to see everything," Mitch answered. "Lead the way."

It was at the other end of the room on the wall. Heidi noticed Zack's friend Jacob standing there with his parents. The children had made their 10 x 12 masterpieces out of colored paper. Above them was a sign that read *When I grow up I'm going to be...*

Zack pointed to his creation. "My teacher couldn't guess."

"Really?" Mitch's brows lifted in surprise. "Anyone can see you're going to be a master spy. That's a cool-looking walkie-talkie you put in there."

Jacob squinted at Zack's picture, then stared at Mitch. "Who's that?" he whispered.

"I'm Mitch. Who are you?"

"Jacob."

"I've heard about you. You're Zack's friend. He and I ride bikes together and play spy."

"I can ride a bike."

"Maybe you could come with us some time," Mitch said.

"He'll need a walkie-talkie."

Mitch winked at Zack. "That can be arranged."

At this juncture Heidi introduced him to Jacob's mom and dad. Then her parents came over to say they had to leave. "Maybe we'll see you sometime," her mother teased quietly.

"Don't be silly. We'll walk you out. Come on, Zack."

"Okay. See ya, Jacob."

The five of them exited the building. After they'd talked a little longer, her parents got in their car and drove off.

Zack looked up at Mitch. "Where's your car?"

"I don't have one. I came here straight from the air-port in a taxi."

Heidi was still reeling from the fact that he'd come at all, that he was back in Salt Lake. "Where's your luggage?"

"I tipped the driver extra to take it to my apartment and leave it in the carport."

"We'll drive you home, huh, Mom," Zack said matter-of-factly.

Mitch sent her a questioning glance. "Will that be all right with you?"

"Of course," she said, opening her car so she wouldn't launch herself into his arms in front of her son. Everyone got in.

"Do you have plans for the rest of the day?" Mitch asked.

"No," Zack spoke up from the backseat as she drove the car out of the parking lot. "Mom says we've got a lot of stuff to do because we have to go on a trip tomorrow."

Mitch's dark eyes practically impaled her. "For how long?" Maybe she was mistaken, but she thought he sounded disappointed. He'd obviously come back to Salt Lake to see about his apartment and have his things shipped to Tallahassee.

She swallowed hard. "We need a vacation, so we're going to visit Evy in Kimball, Nebraska, for the next three weeks. I think I told you she had a baby recently."

"Are you going to fly?"

"No, drive. I like driving."

"But it's going to take a long time to get there," Zack grumbled.

Mitch looked back at him. "That's half the fun." When her son didn't respond, he said, "I'm thinking of going on a vacation myself."

She gripped the steering wheel tighter. "Do you mean before you go back to Florida?"

"Heidi, there's something you need to know. I resigned my job as a federal marshal. Lew took it a lot better than I thought he would. I'm making Salt Lake my permanent home."

"You are?" Zack cried out in pure joy.

The news was so completely unexpected, she almost ran into the back of his car and had to stomp on the brakes to prevent a collision. "I— I don't understand."

"Come inside and I'll explain."

Zack scrambled out of the car ahead of them, whooping it up. Heidi entered the apartment on legs weak as jelly. Mitch brought up the rear, picking up his suitcase on the way inside. She grabbed onto the kitchen counter while he got a can of lemonade out of the fridge for Zack.

"Can I go in your mini-gym? I promise not to spill this."

"Go ahead. The dumbbells are all yours."

"Yay." He dashed out of the kitchen.

With that taken care of, Mitch turned to her. Their gazes clung. "What about the hope that your mother or father will come looking for you one day?"

He shook his head. "That's no longer my priority. As a very wise man said to me, they did their job by giving me life. Now it's my job to live it fully."

"Oh, Mitch…" She couldn't see him clearly because of the tears.

"I love Salt Lake. I love the friends I've made here. I love my job. Most of all, I love you. I fell totally in love with you the first day we met. I loved everything about you. I remember thinking that if I could ever win the love of a woman like you, I wouldn't ask another thing of life. You're the prize every man dreams of."

"I felt the same about you!" she cried.

"The next day I met Zack. That special feeling happened again. He crawled right into my heart and has been in there ever since. I want to marry you, Heidi. I want you to be my wife. I want Zack to be my son. I want to put roots down with you, the kind Saska Bauer put down when she came here. Would you be willing to risk spending the rest of your life with me?"

She was having trouble believing this was really happening. "Before you came to the program," she said. "I was terrified I would have to try and make it through the rest of my life without you. I couldn't imagine it."

The lines in his handsome face relaxed. "That's all I needed to hear. How would you feel about a wedding while you're on vacation? For convention's sake I'm willing to wait another week, maybe. The truth is, I've been waiting for you to come along for years and I don't want to wait any longer. That is, if you'll have me."

"If I'll have you…"

Mad with joy, she ran into his arms. He let out an exultant cry and carried her into the living room, following her down on the couch while their mouths sought to appease their deep hunger for each other. "I couldn't live without you now, Mitch," she confessed when he let her up for breath.

"You don't have to. I'm all yours."

Heidi was so besotted, she forgot everything until later when she heard Zack's voice. He'd come in the living room and was standing next to the couch. The knowledge that he'd caught them like this brought the blood rushing to her face.

"I've been spying on you. Hey, Mitch? Are you really getting married?"

She felt her husband-to-be's kiss on her neck before he sat up.

"What do you think?" Zack let out a yelp of joy as Mitch pulled him down with them.

Chapter Eleven

Seven weeks later

Mitch was just getting ready to leave the office and drive home when his cell phone rang. He checked the caller ID. It was Morton, Heidi's attorney. She and Mitch had met with him right before their wedding a month ago. He clicked on. "This is Mitch Garrett."

"Hello, Mr. Garrett," a brisk female voice said. "Mr. Morton knows it's late in the day, but he wanted to know if you have time to speak to him for a moment."

"Of course."

"Just a minute, please."

Mitch clutched his phone tighter, wondering if this call had anything to do with Heidi's ex-husband. Gary's jury trial was coming up next week.

"Hello, Mitch. Thanks for taking my call. How's marriage treating you so far?"

Mitch closed his eyes tightly. "If there were words, I would tell you."

"That's wonderful. I'm calling because I have some news that might add to your speechless state. The adoption went through when your marriage documents were filed. Judge Rampton is a close friend of

Heidi's father—that helped speed up the process. Congratulations. You now have a son with the legal name Zackery Bauer Garrett."

"Thank you," he murmured, barely able to contain his joy.

"My secretary tried to reach your wife, but there was no answer and no way to leave a message."

"I'm glad she couldn't. Now I can surprise Heidi myself."

When he disconnected, he was already out the door headed for his car. After he and Heidi had made slow, leisurely love this morning, she'd said she was planning to fix him Wiener schnitzel for dinner. It was a favorite Austrian family recipe she'd promised he was going to love.

Heidi didn't need to promise him anything. He was so in love with her he didn't know a man could be this happy. Lew had flown out for their small church wedding and had taken him aside. "Do you remember the times you told me you weren't cut out for marriage?"

Mitch remembered. In truth he'd been glad he'd almost given up on love ever happening to him. For the prize that awaited him, he had to get shot first. And then he had to get sent to Salt Lake for rehabilitation. And then Roman had to give him one last case to work on. And then Heidi Norris Bauer had to walk through the door of his office.

An adorable, voluptuous, grown-up, intelligent woman with cherublike golden hair and jewel-blue eyes. A tough little blue-eyed Marine as part of the package. His family now, legally and forever.

His pulse hammered in his ears as he pulled into the driveway. "Darling?" he called out, hurrying through the house. A wonderful aroma greeted him from the kitchen, but she wasn't in there. No sounds of Zack, either. He dashed down the hall to their bedroom.

Heidi was just coming out of their bathroom with a towel fastened around her. He'd long since discovered that lemony fragrance came from her shampoo. Finding her fresh from the shower was like finding the pot of gold at the end of the rainbow. She let out a cry of delighted surprise when she saw him.

"What perfect timing." He lifted her and carried her to the bed, then lay her there and followed her down. It was pure heaven to bury his face in her curls; it was like lying in a high sunny meadow of flowers. "Where's our son?"

"He's at Jacob's. They're having hot dogs and his parents will bring him home later."

He gave her a long, hard kiss. "I'm going to take a quick shower. Wait for me."

HE NEVER NEEDED TO ASK. She was his wife, and no wife had ever been more loved or felt more cherished. Marriage to this man had made her feel reborn. Tonight she had a secret she was going to share with him over dinner, but maybe she'd do it now. At least that's what she'd thought until she saw him emerge from the shower. Then every thought was put on hold as she reached out to embrace him.

Phyllis had called him a gorgeous hunk. He was that and so much more. Every time he touched her as a prelude to making love, it was like the first time, filling her with rapture. Her need for him would have been embarrassing if he didn't reveal the same great need for her.

They lost track of time giving each other pleasure. When she came back down to earth, she said, "I'm so deeply in love with you it scares me it might be too much for you."

He covered her face with kisses. "Don't be silly. Would you feel any better if I told you the adoption came through? Zack is now my son *officially*."

"This soon?" she cried in disbelief.

"Mr. Morton tried to get you on the phone. He reached me as I was leaving the office and told me."

"Oh, Mitch—" she sighed "—this is the best news. From now on Zack can call himself Zack Garrett. In case you haven't guessed already, he adores you."

"The feeling's mutual."

She traced the line of his compelling mouth with her finger. "I think only one more piece of news could top this red-letter day."

He blinked.

"Because I know you so well, I can't keep back what I was planning to tell you over dinner."

"What?" His voice shook.

Staring into those dark beautiful eyes of his, she said, "Certain symptoms are showing up that make me pretty sure we're going to have a baby. When we decided we didn't want to wait a long time to have another child, the heavens must have heard us. But I haven't made an appointment with the doctor yet."

She felt the sensation that passed through his body. *"Heidi..."* His elation electrified her. "Have you done a home pregnancy test?"

"No. I thought we'd do it together."

He rubbed his hand over her flat stomach. She knew

how he felt. To think a new life had been formed. A miracle. "I hope my lovemaking didn't hurt you."

Tears of love glazed her eyes. "Of course not."

She could see him swallowing hard. "Have you bought a kit?"

"It's in the bathroom cupboard. Shall we find out now?" He acted like a man who'd gone into shock. She grabbed the towel and slid off the bed. "I'll be right back. Wait for me," she mimicked his earlier words.

"This man's not going anywhere."

A minute later she came out in her bathrobe, saw him sitting on the bed dressed in T-shirt and shorts and showed him the test results. "What does it say?"

He took it from her, but his hand was shaking. "It's positive."

"I knew it. I should have had my period last week."

Mitch looked up at her in wonder. "We're going to have a baby."

"Yes, darling." She sat on his lap and looped her arms around his neck. "Now you've really put down roots. If it's a girl, what do you want to call her?"

"That's easy, but only if you like it, too."

She kissed his hard jaw. "Tell me."

"Saska."

"Really?" His choice thrilled her. "The family will be overjoyed, especially Bruno."

"Do you remember my telling you about the conversation with the priest in Florida?"

"I haven't forgotten anything."

He crushed her to him. "When he was talking about the thousands of people who crossed the Atlantic to come live in America, he was talking about her. I've wanted to claim her for my ancestor ever since."

By now Heidi was beyond happy. "And what if it's a boy?"

"Why don't we discuss it with Zack while we eat that fabulous Wiener schnitzel. I think I just heard the front door open."

"Mom?"

Her husband had the ears of a bloodhound. "In the bedroom, honey."

"Where's Mitch?"

"I don't know any Mitch," she called, teasing.

Zack appeared in the doorway. "Yes, you do. He's right there."

"Oh…you mean this guy?" She kissed Mitch's cheek. "I guess you can keep calling him Mitch if you want to, but he has another name now."

"What?"

"You know how you've kept wishing he were your real dad?"

Zack nodded.

"Well, today you got your wish. The judge granted the adoption. You're now officially *his,* son."

The blue eyes grew huge. "Honest?"

"Cross my heart, honey."

"As of today, your name is Zackery Bauer Garrett. How do you like it?" Mitch asked in a husky voice.

"I can call you Daddy?" Zack's voice came out like a squeak.

"I've been waiting to hear it. Come here, son."

* * * * *

A sneaky peek at next month...

Cherish™

ROMANCE TO MELT THE HEART EVERY TIME

My wish list for next month's titles...

In stores from 15th June 2012:

❏ Valtieri's Bride – Caroline Anderson

& Plain Jane in the Spotlight – Lucy Gordon

❏ Battle for the Soldier's Heart – Cara Colter

& The Navy SEAL's Bride – Soraya Lane

In stores from 6th July 2012:

❏ The Prince's Secret Baby – Christine Rimmer

& Prince Daddy & the Nanny – Brenda Harlen

❏ Falling for Mr Mysterious – Barbara Hannay

& The Man Who Saw Her Beauty – Michelle Douglas

Available at WHSmith, Tesco, Asda, Eason, Amazon and Apple

Just can't wait?

Visit us
Online

You can buy our books online a month before
they hit the shops! **www.millsandboon.co.uk**

0612/23

Special Offers

Every month we put together collections and longer reads written by your favourite authors.

Here are some of next month's highlights— and don't miss our fabulous discount online!

On sale 15th June   On sale 15th June   On sale 6th July

Save 20%
on all Special Releases

The World of Mills & Boon®

There's a Mills & Boon® series that's perfect for you. We publish ten series and with new titles every month, you never have to wait long for your favourite to come along.

Blaze®
Scorching hot, sexy reads

By Request
Relive the romance with the best of the best

Cherish™
Romance to melt the heart every time

Desire™
Passionate and dramatic love stories

Have Your Say

You've just finished your book.
So what did you think?

We'd love to hear your thoughts on our
'Have your say' online panel
www.millsandboon.co.uk/haveyoursay

- 🌹 Easy to use
- 🌹 Short questionnaire
- 🌹 Chance to win Mills & Boon®
  goodies

Visit us Online

Tell us what you thought of this book now at
www.millsandboon.co.uk/haveyoursay